Elizabeth Pewsey was born in Chile and educated in Calcutta, London and at St Hilda's College, Oxford. She has worked as a civil servant and publisher, and now lives in Wells, Somerset, with her husband and two children. VOLCANIC AIRS is the fourth novel in the Mountjoy series, following CHILDREN OF CHANCE, DIVINE COMEDY and UNHOLY HARMONIES. The fifth and latest is UNACCUSTOMED SPIRITS.

SCEPTRE

Volcanic Airs

ELIZABETH PEWSEY

SCEPTRE

First published in the UK in 1996 by Hodder and Stoughton
A division of Hodder Headline PLC
A Sceptre Paperback

British Library Cataloguing in Publication Data

Pewsey, Elizabeth, 1948–
    Volcanic airs. – (Mountjoy series; 4)
    1. English fiction – 20th century
    I. Title
    823.9'14 [F]

    ISBN 0 340 65393 0

Typeset by Palimpsest Book Production Limited,
Polmont, Stirlingshire
Printed and bound in Great Britain by
Clays Limited, St Ives PLC, Bungay, Suffolk

Hodder and Stoughton
A division of Hodder Headline PLC
338 Euston Road
London NW1 3BH

For Eno and Raimonda Koço

'Who?'

A long pause, a rustle of sheets, a soft clunk as the phone cord swung against the crystal glass on the table beside the bed.

'Austin who? Austin Vaulx? I don't know you, so why the hell are you ringing me in the middle of the night?'

A voice quacked down the line. On the other side of the bed Veronica stirred in her abandoned slumbers, yawned, ventured a query.

'God knows,' said Valdemar irritably. 'Some fool going on about planes, a nuisance caller, must be.' He hadn't bothered to cover the mouthpiece and a louder, more indignant quack sounded in his ear. 'And so stupid that he gives me his name. Austin Vaulx indeed!'

He was just about to lean over and thump the phone back in place when Veronica sat up abruptly beside him. 'No!' she said dramatically. 'Stop! I know who Austin Vaulx is.'

'Then it's for you,' said Valdemar, handing the phone over and sliding down beneath the covers.

Veronica gave him a savage prod. 'He's a housemaster at Gryme. Is he Thomas's housemaster? Is it something to do with your boy?'

Valdemar, suddenly wide awake, snatched the phone back. 'Thomas?' he said.

More quacks.

Valdemar's look of impatience gave way to an expression of darker fury. 'And just when did you notice he'd gone? . . . At midnight? By chance? . . . And why was a sixth-former wandering about at that time of night? Happened to go into

Thomas's room, did he? Yes, it may have been a good thing in the circumstances, but nonetheless . . . Oh, never mind. Have you looked in all the other rooms, if your boys are in the habit of wandering about at all hours? Definitely not there . . . two other boys missing but accounted for. Christ, how many thousand a year, and they're missing but accounted for? You didn't put any of this down in all that joining rubbish you sent in September.'

Veronica sat up, pushed a lock of brilliantly blonde hair out of her eye, listened.

'Passport?' Valdemar was saying. 'No, how should I know where his passport is? In Eyotshire, I expect, at Mountjoy Castle, where I keep all the papers like that . . . Plane? Why should he have caught a plane? . . . Yes, I know his mother lives in India, but you aren't seriously suggesting . . . Italy?'

'Italy?' echoed Veronica, surprised.

Valdemar exploded down the phone. 'What is the matter with you people? Have you called the police? . . . Bad publicity? If you're worried about bad publicity, then you'd better get Thomas back very, very quickly . . . Presumably you've asked his friends . . . A poor mixer? Well, that's your bloody job, to make sure he mixes. It's got nothing to do with this. Unless, of course, some of your good mixers have been having a go at him . . . No, I have no reason whatsoever to suppose he's gone to Italy.

'Yes, a member of his family may have property in Italy. Only a distant cousin, however, and Thomas would never go there . . . Why not? Because a particularly ghastly relative is in residence, that's why, whom Thomas happens to dislike intensely. Just as I dislike this cross-examination . . . What do you mean there's no question of your having Thomas back if there's any hint of scandal? If you're a typical example of staff, then he'd be better off in the local comprehensive . . . So what if I did meet you last year? I can't remember a thing about you.'

Veronica was pinching Valdemar's arm.

'Stop that,' he said furiously. 'No, not you. No, you're bloody well not going to ring off, I've got a few questions I want to ask. What *is* it, Veronica? Can't you see I'm talking?'

'Money,' said Veronica firmly. 'Did he have any money? Did he borrow some from another boy? He couldn't get far without money, and you don't give him much. Not enough for plane fares and so forth.'

'And another thing,' said Valdemar, disregarding Veronica's interruption. 'How did you get this number? What? From my wife? You've spoken to my wife? Why the hell did you do that?'

Far away in the northern county of Eyotshire, a light shone out from a narrow, high window in one of the ancient towers of Mountjoy Castle.

Fretting, Magdalena sat at a small table, fingers tapping as she stared at the phone, willing it to ring. She pulled her silk wrap more closely about her; early summer it might be, but summer comes late if at all to Eyotshire, and the chill of centuries was barely kept at bay by a modern heating system which turned itself off in an economical way at bedtime.

The phone rang; Magdalena picked it up before it got to the second brr.

'Ah, Val, you've heard, then.'

'Are you up? Why? You need your sleep and it's three in the morning.'

'Of course I'm up; how could I go back to sleep with Thomas missing?'

'He's not your son.'

'It makes no difference.'

Magdalena's voice was calm, her concern well-hidden. The sound of her soothed Valdemar in the flat in London as he balanced the phone against his shoulder and tugged at the zip of his trousers.

'Has that idiotic man been on to you? Alarming you, it's unforgivable.'

'He was only trying to find you, Val,' Magdalena pointed out in reasonable tones.

'Creep,' Valdemar said furiously, sliding his feet into his shoes. 'Look, ring him back, tell him you're there, at that number, to ring you if he has any further news. If he's gone back to bed, get him up again, I don't care what time it is, it's his job, even if he obviously does it very badly. God knows, they get paid well enough; what a bunch of no-hopers.'

'You insisted that Thomas should go there.'

'My fault, is it? And I suppose it's my fault that he's gone missing.'

'He hasn't gone missing.' Magdalena's voice was crystal sharp. 'He's run away. He was unhappy there. You knew it, and didn't care. I knew it, and did nothing about it. What you need to do is think about where he might have gone.'

'Oh, he'll be wandering round London in a dramatic fashion; the police will pick him up in no time.'

'Thomas isn't stupid.'

'Yes, he bloody well is, or he wouldn't be causing all this trouble.'

'Think back to when you were fourteen; where would you have gone?'

'Me? I didn't run away from school, however ghastly it was.'

'Then Thomas has more courage than you had. Just stop fuming and remember. When you were that age, *if* you had run away, where would you have gone?'

Silence. Valdemar leant forward to do up his shoe-laces. At the other end Magdalena waited, her face showing the worry that she wouldn't allow her voice to reveal.

'All right, I wouldn't have wandered around London. I'd have got away from London, gone to a friend, someone I could trust, someone outside the system.'

'A schoolfriend?'

'Of course not a schoolfriend. You learn pretty quickly not to trust your friends at school; they've all got their own schemes going. Besides, the masters would make life so difficult for them that they'd spit it all out in the end. No, an adult. Not connected with the school, not connected with the family.'

Magdalena thought for a moment. 'I'll ring Sylvester,' she said finally.

Valdemar was about to ask her what bloody use that would be, but stifled his words. Thomas wouldn't have gone to Sylvester, too obvious, too close to home. But Sylvester understood Thomas, he might know where Thomas would be running to.

'Sylvester's away,' he said, remembering. 'In America.'

'I know,' said Magdalena. 'I think I can find out where he is. I'll try, anyway. He won't be in bed, not with the time difference, and he wouldn't mind, in any case. He's very fond of Thomas.'

'Meaning I'm not?'

Magdalena ignored Valdemar's remark. 'I'll get back to Austin, then.'

'Austin?' said Valdemar. '*Austin?* On first name terms with the housemaster, are you? He'll be kissing you on both cheeks soon, what a poseur.'

'He does,' said Magdalena.

'Good God.'

'They all do it,' said Magdalena, her mind elsewhere. 'They teach them to, these days. Good PR.'

'And another thing,' said Valdemar. 'How did you know where I was?'

A pause.

'I didn't,' said Magdalena. 'I gave Austin Vaulx several numbers where I thought he might find you.'

'Including Veronica's.'

'Is that where you are? Well, it was a lucky guess, wasn't it?' And she cut the connection with a quick movement, recollected her thoughts and began to dial the school's number.

Mrs Grobbins carried the news into the village.

'Run away!' she announced with a joyful sigh as she ushered her youngest grandchild into the hall where the twice-weekly playgroup was held.

All eyes turned to Lottie, the Castle nanny, who was unbuttoning her twin charges and pretending not to hear.

'Poor thing,' said Mrs Grobbins, heaving another sigh.

'Who?' ventured a bold spirit, unable to contain her curiosity any longer.

'Why, poor Mrs Mountjoy,' said Mrs Grobbins.

So *she* hadn't run away. Then it must be Valdemar.

Intakes of breath all round.

'He's in London,' objected one young mother. She could see the point of running away from up here, she would herself, given half the chance. But who would run away from London?

'No,' persisted the bold mother. 'I mean, who *with*?'

Lottie felt it was her duty to speak. 'It's Thomas has run away,' she said repressively. 'From school.'

A collective sigh. Not nearly so exciting as Valdemar running off with another woman, a man . . . goodness knows who. Then kindness began to assert itself.

'Young Thomas? From school?'

'They should never have sent him away.'

'They've never treated that boy right.'

'It's his mum's fault, chanting and carrying on with all the darkies in India, that's no help to a growing lad.'

Thomas was known to all the villagers. Why, it wasn't so many years ago that he'd tumbled around on this very floor. 'Always enjoyed himself, Thomas did,' declared a mother of five, whose oldest was a longstanding friend of Thomas's.

'That lovely voice,' said another mother, irrelevantly.

'Broken now,' said Mrs Grobbins with a sigh.

They'd all heard Thomas sing in the church choir before he'd gone to Eyot to become a cathedral chorister. He'd sung for them at weddings and funerals – by special permission of the Dean – and they remembered his beautiful treble voice.

'Made me cry, at Hattie's wedding, when he sang.'

'You're not supposed to cry at weddings; not unless you're the bride's mum.'

'He could be murdered,' said one ghoulish mother, returning to the point. 'If he's alone.'

'Nay, he's a big lad.'

'Could've been snatched by an older woman, they lie in wait for young boys.'

A general hiss of horror passed from mother to mother. Shocking!

Lottie helped one of the twins on to the climbing frame, and settled the other down with a jigsaw puzzle. Then she entered the fray.

'He's like a cat, that boy. He'll always land on his feet.'

Mrs Grobbins regarded her with a cold eye. 'You never liked him, too much of a handful for you.'

'He was never in my charge, I'm employed to look after the twins. If he gets them worked up, then it's my duty to complain; it's not good for children to get over-excited.'

One of the mothers sniffed. 'In a big family, you always get the older ones romping with the little ones. My George is Thomas's age, and he's really good with my toddler.'

Lottie's face expressed the clear view that George and his small sister in Thrang Farm were in no way to be compared with the twins in their castle.

'Run away to his mother, they think, and it's the best place for him.'

'Not necessarily,' said Mrs Grobbins, bristling. 'Magdalena's been as good as any mother to that boy, and why shouldn't he be here where he belongs, with his father?'

'If we were sure who his father was.'

The mothers and grannies all knew perfectly well who Thomas's father was, as did Lottie; but, by tacit agreement, it wasn't spoken about.

'No good will come of it,' added Lottie portentously. 'Now, Hugh, find another piece with bus on it, look, it's a lovely red bus.'

'It should be green,' said Hugh, an obstinate look coming over his firm little face. 'Buses are green, not red.'

'No, sweetheart; in London, buses are red.'

Hugh looked even more mulish. 'I don't live in London. Buses here are green.' He gave the puzzle a contemptuous look. 'It's a stupid puzzle, anyway. It's for babies. I want to go on the frame with Helena.'

'No, Hugh,' said Lottie, in a firm voice. 'You are not going on the frame with Helena, she'll push you off, and then you'll make a scene.'

At these alarming words, the other mothers moved into action. 'Come and play with Angela, Hughie, look, she's got the bricks.'

Hugh advanced on the hapless Angela. 'I will have those bricks.'

'Going to be just like his dad,' said Mrs Grobbins in dark tones.

*   *   *

'Sylvester!'

Three thousand miles away, Sylvester could hear the strain in Magdalena's voice.

'What's up?' he said directly.

'I've been trying to get hold of you for hours,' said Magdalena.

'I know. Messages everywhere. So?'

'Sylvester, it's Thomas. He's gone.'

'Gone?'

'From school. Run away.'

'Thomas?'

Magdalena could hear Sylvester's sharp intake of breath and then some indistinct muttering sounds.

'Sylvester? This line isn't very clear, I can't hear you properly.'

'Gabriel's here, he wanted to know what's happened to Thomas. When did he run away?'

Magdalena, thick-headed with tiredness, tried to get her wits into focus. 'They discovered he was gone last night. At about midnight. But it seems he went missing much earlier, he wasn't there when they do that evening roll-call, apparently another boy fixed it for him.'

Sylvester made a clicking noise. 'So where's he gone?'

'We have no idea.'

'Some boy at the school must know. No one ever ran away without at least one of his chums knowing what he was up to. Thomas must have friends, he's a friendly boy.'

'Yes,' said Magdalena, doubt in her voice. 'He has, I suppose, but no one close, that's been part of the trouble. He says they're mostly boring prats there.'

'They probably are; still, they can't *all* be. And why did he run away? Has he been in trouble?'

Long pause.

'Nothing that we know about. His housemaster says not, although he also says that Thomas is a difficult boy.'

'Difficult! I'll give him difficult. Of course he isn't, he's just unhappy, that's what the problem is. Now, if he's homesick, he'll be on his way back to you.'

'That's what we thought at first. But he would have been here hours ago.'

'True.'

I feel so guilty about him, Magdalena thought wearily. 'I knew he would hate it,' she told Sylvester. 'He should never have gone.'

She held the receiver away from her ear as a rumble of fury came down the line. 'Of course he shouldn't have gone. And once he had gone, and so clearly loathed it, you should have taken him away.'

'Val wouldn't. He said he needed time to settle, he was too home-centred, by the summer term he'd be loving it. And if he wasn't, at least he was getting a decent education.'

'Oh, I can hear him saying all that,' said Sylvester acidly. 'Never mind that now. The question is, if he isn't coming home, where is he?'

'That's why I rang you,' said Magdalena. 'You're very close to him, I thought you might know.'

Sylvester was decisive. 'Not a clue. I would have put my money on him making for home and the hills, that's what he misses. No pointers from the school?'

'Well, there's one boy – not a very reliable boy, though, according to the housemaster – who insists that Thomas was planning to go abroad. And his passport isn't here.'

'Does the school usually keep it? For trips and so forth, they're always gadding off on geography camps in the Urals and choir tours to Peru, these schools.'

'No, it stays here. It was here in the holidays, with mine and the children's; Val's quite sure about that. Now it isn't.'

'When did it go?'

'Oh, Sylvester, I don't know. I don't take any notice of the passports; I never go abroad these days.'

'You should, do you good,' said Sylvester inconsequentially. 'So he had this planned, didn't he. Hmm. India? A long way, and expensive. And you need visas and so on.'

'How could he hope to find Hortense? You know how she wanders about the place. It's such a huge country . . . and he's only fourteen. Sylvester, you don't seriously think he's there?' Her voice betrayed the alarm she felt, imagining Thomas lost among the teeming millions of Delhi or Bombay as he searched in vain for his mother. 'And it's so long since he saw her, he probably wouldn't recognize her.'

'She'd recognize him; pure Mountjoy, that boy,' said Sylvester. 'That's beside the point. You'll have to get flights to India checked, just in case. There won't have been so many of them.'

'Val's doing that. I don't think it's really likely because, as far as we know, Thomas only had about twenty pounds.'

'What about his choir account?'

'Choir account?'

'Yes, wake up, Magdalena. I know you're distraught, but you've got to concentrate. Cathedral choristers earn money. The cathedral puts it away in a building society account for them. Some pittance for the daily services, and then there'd be larger sums for recordings and so on. Most of these boys have a few hundred tucked away by the time they finish. They give them the books when they leave the choir.'

'A few hundred. Oh, no! Can he get at it?'

'It'll be in his name, as far as I know, it's his to do what he likes with.'

'India, then,' said Magdalena, rising panic in her voice.

'Not necessarily. And be grateful; if he's gone off, he'll need some money. Now, I've got a rehearsal this morning – it's morning here, remember – but I'll be back at this number in three or four hours. If I think of anything, I'll give you a ring, and meanwhile you and Val put your heads together, try to think about anything he's ever said about places he likes the sound of. My guess is, he's gone south.'

'South? Why?'

'I would, if I was running away from school and couldn't go back home to the north.'

'Bournemouth, somewhere like that, you mean? Or Italy, do you think? This boy at his school mentioned Italy, so Val told me. Val said it was rubbish.'

'Italy sounds possible. We'll talk later, and don't worry, Magdalena. He'll be all right.'

Click.

Magdalena put the phone down and sat quite still for a moment, looking down at her hands.

The telephone shrilled into action once more. Val? The school? The press? Magdalena sighed and lifted the receiver. 'Hello?'

Some pips, a faint whine, and then a familiar, slightly husky voice.

'Is that Magdalena? It's me, Thomas.'

2

Valdemar did the journey north in less than three hours. Magdalena heard the roar of his engine subside into silence and then the familar bang of the car door. She went down to meet him. He gave her a brief kiss in greeting, his thoughts elsewhere.

'Are you sure about this?'

'It was Thomas, definitely. He said not to worry, he was all right, he had some money, and he was going to stay with a friend. Someone respectable, he said.'

'Respectable! I doubt that very much. No one respectable would take in a boy of Thomas's age without speaking to his family. Anyone respectable would send Thomas back at the first opportunity.'

'A friend wouldn't,' said Magdalena.

Valdemar ignored that. 'And you're sure he was in Italy?'

'He wouldn't tell me where he was, but he was in a railway station, and I could hear the announcements. In Italian.'

'Any names? To give a clue of which station it might be?'

'I think it was Rome.'

'Oh, that's a great help,' he said sarcastically. 'Rome! Does he know anyone in Rome?'

'He might have been at the station because he was catching a train somewhere else. Or because he had just arrived there.'

'Very useful.' Valdemar stood by the window, looking out over the lawns to the looming fells. 'I'll ring the embassy, they'll have to help find him. Who does Thomas know in Italy? Do you know of any Italian friends? Anybody from the school here?'

'Celia?' ventured Magdalena. Celia was the ghastly relative

who lived in Italy. A wraithlike widow, she had been married to Valdemar's uncle. Like so many of the Mountjoys, the uncle had had more than a passing eye for an attractive woman; Celia had removed him to a gloomy palazzo in Italy where she could keep an eye on him.

'Not very likely, is it?' said Valdemar. 'Celia's never taken to Thomas, and she'd have been moaning on the phone straight away if he'd turned up on her doorstep. Ring Justy, though, in case she has any ideas.'

Lucky Justy, thought Magdalena. Living an independent and busy life in London, her mother Celia safely tucked away in Italy, separated from her husband, a delightful lover on tap. How did these Mountjoys manage their lives so well – and so ruthlessly?

'I spoke to Justy yesterday,' said Magdalena. 'Only briefly, because she was on her way out, but she said she wasn't surprised Thomas had run away. She knew he was unhappy at school, and she'd been hearing some iffy things about Gryme recently.'

'Nothing wrong with that school,' said Valdemar instantly. 'It's Thomas's fault for not getting on with it.'

'With what?'

'What are you talking about, with what? You haven't had enough sleep, that's your problem.'

'I don't suppose you had so much either, not with dear Veronica in bed,' said Magdalena under her breath.

'Bloody boy,' said Valdemar, his face darkening. 'Worrying you like this.'

'Worrying you, too.'

'I'm not worried, just bloody fed up. I've got a tremendous load of work on, I don't need all this. Let him wait until I catch up with him, I'll make sure he never tries anything like this again.'

Magdalena spoke calmly. 'I'm sure you'll be very pleased to have him home, safe and sound; we all will.'

'Home? That bloody boy isn't coming home. Straight back to school is where he's going to go.'

'I think not,' said Magdalena.

'I'm not putting up with any nonsense from him. He isn't going to get away with this, no question of it.'

Magdalena got up from her chair.

'And where do you think you're going?'

'To see the twins,' said Magdalena. 'I heard Lottie's car.'

'Oh,' said Valdemar, thwarted of an audience for his spleen.

Magdalena popped her head back round the door. 'Are you staying tonight?'

'Of course I am. What do you think, I've driven all the way up from London to go straight back again?'

'You might want to get back to Veronica.'

On which parting shot, and ignoring the furious remarks being hurled at her through the door, Magdalena headed for the kitchen.

Lottie poured out tea, oozing false sympathy. 'Poor boy, if he's all by himself abroad; he must be very nervous, all those strangers everywhere, foreign ones, too.'

Why do I put up with her? Magdalena wondered, not for the first time. She dunked a biscuit in her tea.

'Now, we mustn't think because Mummy dips her biscuit in her tea that we can all do it,' Lottie told her charges in a bright voice. Helena immediately dropped her half biscuit into her glass of milk. Hugh looked smug. 'I'm eating my biscuit properly, Lottie, look at me.'

'You're a good boy,' said Lottie, taking the rest of Helena's milk away from her.

Magdalena watched the ensuing scene with a sense of detachment. Their all-embracing self-centredness reminds me of Valdemar, she thought with no great pleasure. They were Mountjoy through and through at present, but perhaps they would grow more human as time passed.

Thomas was a Mountjoy, after all, and he had an insight into other people's feelings and motives which was remarkable for his age and astonishing in one of that family.

Magdalena cupped her tea with both hands, gazing dreamily into the brew as though it had a message for her. Thomas, abroad. Alone. Fear and concern swept over her again. He was a big boy for his age, and at fourteen quite able to look after himself, but even so.

'He doesn't speak a word of Italian, even,' she said in despair.

Lottie told Hugh to wash his hands and then to run along. 'If you're talking about Thomas,' she commented, gathering the plates to stack in the dishwasher, 'he's been learning Italian at school this year.'

'What?' said Magdalena. 'He can't have been, there was nothing about Italian on his report.'

'Maybe he was doing it as an extra activity,' said Lottie primly. 'Like they do at these schools.' There was warmth in Lottie's voice; she approved of "these schools", these were the establishments that her girls and, especially, her boys, were destined for.

'Did he tell you he was learning Italian?' That would be surprising, Magdalena said to herself, knowing how much Thomas disliked Lottie.

'He tried to teach Hugh and Helena some words in Italian. *Ciao*, and *buon giorno*, things like that.'

'I see,' said Magdalena in neutral tones.

Valdemar was shouting for her. 'Justy on the phone, wants to speak to you. I don't know why she can't tell me if she's got any information about Thomas.'

'I'll take it in my room,' said Magdalena, running towards the spiral stone staircase which led up to her sitting-room. 'Can you switch it through, please?'

'You're panting,' said Justinia.

'Yes, I ran up here, I don't like talking on the phone downstairs with Val breathing down my neck.'

There was a moment's silence. 'I think he's breathing down the phone right now, if you don't mind my mentioning it,' said Justinia.

'Val, I've picked it up, you can put your phone down now,' said Magdalena sharply.

Bang.

'Cousin Val cross about something?' asked Justinia.

'He's so nosy, wants to know what we're talking about.'

'Best not,' said Justinia. 'I've had a thought, but I may be wrong, and in any case, I'd rather tell you than Val. Now, listen, do you remember Zephania's memorial service?'

'Of course, in the Cathedral,' said Magdalena.

'Ferenc Latterly was there. The pianist. He played.'

'Yes,' said Magdalena, somewhat puzzled. 'What did this have to do with Thomas?'

'I'm coming to that. Thomas got very friendly with him. No, calm down, Ferenc isn't interested in boys, he's married and he now lives with his Italian mistress.'

'Don't talk to me about mistresses,' said Magdalena viciously. 'Did you say *Italian* mistress?'

'Yes, they live on this island somewhere off the coast of Italy. I'm not sure where, but Sylvester would know. He's friend of Ferenc's, and they play in a trio sometimes. With Gabriel.'

'And?'

'Thomas could have gone there. Ferenc invited him to stay, I know that.'

Magdalena was very doubtful. 'Thomas might have got on with him when they met in Eyot, but that's hardly the basis for turning up out of the blue. After all, Thomas is quite a shy boy, not exactly full of confidence; I can't believe he'd do that.'

'He's got even less confidence now than he had before. Gervase and I went one weekend and took him out, did I tell you? He behaved beautifully, like a robot. I must say, I don't think he should be there. That's why I didn't want to talk to Val, I know he's very keen on the place.'

'For the best reasons,' said Magdalena. Why am I defending him? she thought. She returned quickly to the subject of Italian islands. 'Would Thomas really feel he could visit Ferenc? Unannounced?'

Justinia was on firm ground here. 'Definitely. He's very private, Ferenc, but he's a very warm person. He took a great liking to Thomas, he does that, makes his mind up about people instantly, and Thomas would have known it was genuine. Thomas isn't stupid about people, you know.'

'When did you see him?'

'Thomas? About three weeks ago.'

'And he didn't say anything then, about wanting to run away?'

'He wouldn't. I'm a Mountjoy, after all, and I think he's wary about all his Mountjoy family. No, he just said he didn't want to talk about school, he hated every minute. Gervase asked if he was being bullied, and he shut up like a clam, so I expect he is. Was.'

Magdalena's heart sank. 'Poor Thomas. What did you talk about?'

'Music. Opera, Gervase's work. It did him good, I think. He was much more his old self when we took him back, although you could see him stiffening up when we got to the school. He shouldn't be there, you know. Gervase thinks the same, said he'd never let a boy of his get into that kind of state.'

'He hasn't got any boys, has he?' said Magdalena, hitting back. 'It's different when it's your own son, you want the best for him.'

Justinia was having none of that. 'It isn't best for him, and deep down, Val knows it isn't. But he's not going to admit that he made a mistake, forcing Thomas to go there, is he?'

'His headmaster here thought it would do him good,' said Magdalena weakly.

'That man doesn't have the slightest concern for his pupils or what's best for them.'

'I suppose not.'

'Now, have you been in touch with Sylvester?'

'Yes, he's going to be ringing me again this evening.'

'Then talk to him about Ferenc. It's worth a try, and he'll have a number for him. And don't sound so doleful, I know you're worried about Thomas, but if he's with Ferenc it's the best place for him. A long way from Val, for a start.'

'You've become very forceful since you went to London,' said Magdalena.

Justinia laughed. 'I dare say,' she said. 'Tough business, music, you have to keep your wits about you. Let me know as soon as you have any news.'

'Bye,' said Magdalena to the dialling tone which buzzed in her ear.

Warmth.

Thomas thought of himself as a child of the north; he loved cold, invigorating weather, snow and ice and frost. But there was something beguiling about this warmth which made your very bones feel mellow, which took all the tension and stiffness out of your mind and your muscles.

Long way up, he thought as he clambered aboard the train. It was fairly full, but not overcrowded; he was even able to find himself a window seat. True, the priest sitting further along the seat was very garlicky, but Thomas didn't mind that at all. In the other window seat was a stout middle-aged woman with flying knitting needles. She looks more than a match for the Mafia, Thomas told himself as he swung his suitcase up on the rack and took a fat fantasy novel out of his pocket.

He wasn't afraid. In fact, he felt exhilarated. Planning all this with his friend, Sim, he had listened with a dry mouth to his streetwise friend's strictures. 'It's the men you've got to watch, especially the way you look. Don't trust a man and woman together, well, you've seen the films, you'd know better than that.'

'Seen the films? What films?'

Sim didn't enlighten him. 'Motherly women, Italy's stuffed with them, they're the ones to get on your side if there's any trouble. They'll see anyone off.'

'Mafia?' asked Thomas nervously.

Sim pursed his lips knowingly. 'You've got to be careful, there's a lot of kidnapping still. Don't dress too well, don't look rich. And always walk purposefully, look as though you know exactly where you're going, even if you haven't got a clue.'

'Jeans then, look like a student?'

Sim was definite. 'No. Look like a middle-class kid who's going to meet his mother. Casual, yes, but not rough. And tell people that you are meeting your mother, if anyone asks. That'll put them off.'

Thomas had been alarmed by this 'they', by this dangerous world he was venturing into. Reality, as usual, was different. He felt normal, the people around him looked normal. He politely picked up a ball of yarn which his opposite number had let slip to the floor, and returned it with a smile. She burst into a crackle of Italian, of which he understood about one word in three. Never mind, he hadn't gone to all those Italian classes not to have a go at it. He managed a halting sentence or two, and was rewarded by a joyful smile and slower speech.

Thomas settled down to enjoy the journey.

'I'm going to Eyot. Do you need anything?'

Magdalena folded her napkin and rolled it up into her ring. Valdemar had left his napkin scrunched up on his plate, snug among the crumbs and marmalade; unusable. He hovered by the door, impatient to be gone.

'When are you leaving?'

'Now.'

'I'll come with you. I've got a hair appointment.'

'I've got a meeting with the Dean, he's got some bee in his bonnet about the Cathedral. Then I've got one or two other things to do. I'll be coming back before lunch. Will that suit you?'

'Yes,' said Magdalena.

'I won't wait for you. I've got a lot of work to do here before I go back to London.'

'I can always catch the bus.'

Valdemar raised his eyebrows in disbelief; he hadn't been on a bus in years. 'Whatever suits you,' he said. 'Be ready in ten minutes, I don't want to be late.'

'Of course not,' Magdalena said to the door as it closed behind him.

'Did you say something?' asked Mrs Grobbins, heaving herself into the room. 'Are you off to Eyot? Leave all this, I'll clear.'

Magdalena thanked her, and flew to the nursery to give the twins a hug. She was greeted by their usual wild clamour and shrieks of dismay at the news that she was going off without them. 'We'll have a game when I get back,' she promised, making good her escape. As she walked quickly to her room to collect her bag, she could hear their shrill voices arguing about exactly which game they would ask her to play.

'They're all equally loathsome,' Magdalena said to the portrait of the ninth Baron Mountjoy.

'Talking to yourself again,' commented Valdemar, unamused, as they met in the hall. 'You ought to see someone about that.' He opened the passenger door for her. 'Hurry up.'

Magdalena thought about protesting at his brusqueness, but decided she couldn't be bothered. When he was in this kind of mood he wouldn't pay any attention; in fact she couldn't think of any kind of a mood in which he would pay any attention to her.

Perfunctory, that's the word, she thought, remembering his efficient and uninvolved love-making of the previous night. Burnt out by Veronica; should she mention it? To what purpose? If it wasn't Veronica, then it would be someone else. Mind you, Veronica did rankle particularly. Veronica was a friend as well as a mistress. She and Val went back a long way, Magdalena knew that. They had had a brief spell of mutual indifference when Veronica had married her Philip, but it hadn't taken them long to get back together again.

'I rang the police, and the embassy in Rome,' Valdemar informed her as he accelerated on to the main road to Eyot. 'Told them that he might be in Rome, or could have caught a train from there. They aren't very hopeful, but my feeling is that Thomas won't be able to cope on his own, and he'll end up in trouble somewhere. They're looking out for him, I've given them a description. If they spot him, they'll haul him in.'

Magdalena didn't like to think of Thomas being hauled anywhere. 'They'd better treat him properly,' she said sharply. 'He's only a boy.'

'The worse time he has, the less likely he is to do anything so bloody stupid again.'

'What will happen to him?'

'I'll make the necessary arrangements, and they'll put him on the next flight to London. Then it's back to school, and I hope they give him hell.'

'They may not want him back.'

'What, and lose the fees? No, no, it's not as though it's drugs or anything like that. I'll have a word with that fool who runs his house, he'll soon see reason.'

If I were a housemaster, I would sacrifice any amount of fees not to have Val snarling at me, thought Magdalena, looking out of the window with a smile pinned on her lips.

Valdemar shot her a sideways look. 'Why are you pulling faces? Your teeth hurting or something?'

Magdalena gave up the attempt to smile. 'I'm fine, thank you.'

'That's all right, then.'

Unlike many of her friends, Magdalena didn't discuss her personal life with her hairdresser. In fact she shied away from all therapists, whether professional or amateur. Magdalena was a private person.

On the other hand, no one could be private with Delia around, and Delia was in the salon.

'Magdalena! Wonderful, just the person I want to see, this will save me a phone call.'

Clad in a black gown and with her hair done up in tinfoil and smelling powerfully of something in the drainage line, Delia plumped herself down in the seat next to Magdalena.

Magdalena was fond of Delia, but all Delia's friends were wary of her. Delia spoke her mind.

'How's things at the castle? How's Val? I hear he's up to his old tricks again, you mustn't let him get away with it. I wouldn't stand it for a moment with Seton, I can tell you.'

Seton's the dullest man in England, thought Magdalena.

'Now, you have to be firm. Have it out with him, you can clear the air if it's all in the open.'

Open? Valdemar? You didn't marry a dangerous, difficult man and then talk about things being in the open.

'He can't get away with it, he's not living in the olden days.'

Oh, but he is.

'You got the better of him once, now you have to get the upper hand again.'

Magdalena looked back to that summer when she had been pregnant with the twins, her then husband, Hugh Mountjoy, had been alive, and Valdemar had had his nose rubbed in the mud by Prue.

'Prue's having another baby, Delia,' Magdalena said brightly. 'I had a letter from her yesterday. She's still deep in her bones; I expect the child will be born in a museum. She's very happy, and so is Geza.'

'Good,' said Delia, genuinely pleased, for she liked Prue; poor Prue, who might have married sound Seton, and had gone off instead with a Hungarian musician. But Delia wasn't so easily deflected. 'I hear Val's in a terrific temper about Thomas. What's up?'

'Oh, boys that age can be very difficult,' said Magdalena evasively.

Good God, must she sick it all up in here, the whole of Eyot will know about Thomas.

'I can see you don't want to talk about it,' said Delia perceptively. 'Must go back to my girl now, she'd better get a move on, taking these bits out of my hair, I'm in a terrific rush this morning. That's your trouble, you know, Magdalena, you haven't got enough to do. And no one much to talk to; isn't Sylvester still away playing his cello in America?'

'Yes,' said Magdalena.

'And no Lily, either, I hear?'

Lily was the housekeeper at nearby Midwinter Hall and a great source of pithy comfort in difficult times.

'Lily's visiting her sister in New Zealand while Sylvester's away.'

'Who's minding the house? Peter the gardener?'

'Yes.' Magdalena struggled to defend herself. 'I do have the children, you know.'

'No, no,' said Delia heartily, 'don't talk about the children. Only two, and that excellent girl to look after them for you. I've got three, remember, and no help, and I still find time to do masses of things.'

She bent over and gave Magdalena an affectionate if chemical kiss. 'Tomorrow then, I'll come to lunch at the castle; that's what I was going to ring to say. About twelve.'

Magdalena sank back into her chair, letting her mind drift as Preben combed and snipped.

Not enough to do.

She could write a book, *Impossible Husbands I Have Known*. A guaranteed bestseller, surely.

She could sack Lottie, and take over the children herself. Valdemar would approve of that. It presented a pretty picture for a few brief seconds; never having to listen to Lottie's arch tones again, never having to mediate between Lottie and Mrs Grobbins, never having to listen to Lottie's interminable accounts of shopping for bargains . . .

Hours on end of her beloved children's company. Soggy, tasteless meals at least three times a day. Routine. Games. Baths. Walks. Playgroup. Bedtime.

Forget it. She paid for the nanny, not Val, and having twins at forty-five had been no joke; she felt quite exhausted enough as it was.

Was it natural to feel so tired, when one seemed to do so little? Magdalena glanced around the salon. It seemed full of busy, alert women. They didn't look tired, they looked kempt and svelte and up with things. They clearly read Booker shortlist novels, instead of falling asleep over a detective story. They knew about art, you could tell. They probably ran businesses, painted pictures, bought for department stores, designed sanitary ware.

They did not live in a draughty castle with a wild and roaming husband who swooped in from London every now and again, a twee nanny, twins, and, in the holidays, a teenage boy who mooched about the place because he was so unhappy at school.

Preben held a lock of hair up for her, tching softly.

'It's much more grey, look at the colour. It's time to decide. One choice is to go grey, which is not always so very attractive for a woman of your complexion, very aging, you would look like a camel, it seems to me.'

'A camel?'

'Yes, it would make you beige.'

'You mean you want me to dye my hair?'

Magdalena stared at her thick, familiar head of hair. Goodness, how had it happened? How come she hadn't noticed? Surely last time she had looked there had been a single grey hair, quickly removed. Perhaps two. Otherwise it was the glossy black hair she had always had, one of her great assets. And it was vanishing, turning this nasty, pale, lifeless shade before her very eyes.

Preben was shocked. 'We don't think of it as dyeing,' he said, lowering his voice on the dread word. 'Colouring, restoring it to its natural state.'

'Only its natural state is now grey.'

'Yes, if you leave it as it is. Not if you don't want that.'

'I'll think about it.'

'Then soon,' said Preben. 'I think grey hair will make you very displeased with yourself.'

I do wish Sylvester were in England, thought Magdalena. Or at least Lily. We'd laugh about it; Sylvester would be sympathetic, Lily would be severely practical.

Come on, Magdalena told herself. You don't need props like Sylvester and Lily. It's stand-on-your-own-feet time; you've got to cope with the ups and downs for yourself. And it's only hair.

She promised Preben again that she would think about her grey hair, paid the large bill, smiled, looked pleased and said she'd ring about her next appointment. Then she stepped out of the steamy atmosphere of the salon into a chilly morning with a thin sun struggling to come out. I could pop into the Cathedral for a moment or two, she thought, looking up at the great spires which loomed over the shops opposite. An oasis of calm.

Calm?

The place was rackety with tourists. A recorded prayer boomed out over the nave; scurrying vergers loudly scolded unwary visitors. The organ was rumbling away, and she could hear the distant whine of a floor cleaner.

And there was Val, never a calm figure, with the Dean, standing in front of the choir screen. She had met the new Dean once or twice. They had chosen a man of impeccable reputation, no risk of him repeating the appalling behaviour of the last Dean, who had died while carrying out distinctly non-clerical duties. This was a fanatical, pure Dean, whose life was an open book. Magdalena felt sorry for his wife.

And he's annoying Val, she noticed. She knew that coiled look; possibly Val would mind his manners in the precincts of the Cathedral, equally well he might not. I don't think I care very much one way or the other, she thought. Let him get on with it, he wouldn't care what anyone thought of him, whether it was his wife's bad opinion or the Dean and Chapter's that he was earning.

And his hair didn't have a trace of grey.

3

Thomas wouldn't have been surprised to learn that Valdemar had asked the police to look out for him. As the boat edged its way into the famous harbour at Aeolus, he was convinced that the army, police and half the British embassy staff would be lined up on the quay, waiting for him. They would have his description; they would stop him.

But no one gave him a second look as he helped the lady of the knitting down the gangplank, and then forced himself to walk slowly to the sign saying *Uscita*. Thomas wasn't to know that Valdemar had described him as he was at ten or eleven, a little boy with a chorister's haircut, not the taller fourteen-year-old that Thomas was now, with longer, thicker hair, and the assurance that a year at public school had given him. No policeman would have matched Valdemar's description with the teenager heading for the centre of town.

Something to eat, that was the priority. His senses were assailed by the bustle around the quay, the flowers, the fish in baskets, the vigorous, voluble bursts of conversation, the darkly tanned faces, the smell of fresh bread. He felt hungrier than ever, and here was a bar open on to the street, a tray of crusty *panini* and quarters of pizza laid out on the counter.

A moment's confusion, as Thomas struggled to understand that he had to pay first, order afterwards, and then he was supplied with a hot ham and cheese roll and a glass of fresh orange juice. The woman behind the counter had even directed him to the bus, on being shown a scribbled address.

I've made it, Thomas told himself with pride as he climbed on to the bus. Valdemar can rant and rage as much as he likes, I'm not going back until he agrees I can leave that terrible school. And he looked at his watch, and realized that his class would just be going into dreary classroom 14 for French, Set 2.

Without him.

Mrs Grobbins was big with news. 'Your hair looks nice,' she said. 'Young Thomas rang.'

'Damn it,' said Magdalena, putting her bag down with a thump. 'And I wasn't here. I should never have gone out.'

'You can't stay cooped up here for ever just in case.'

'When did he ring? Is he all right?'

'Course he's all right, least, he says he is. Safe, in any case. With friends, he said. We had quite a chat,' she went on with satisfaction. 'I told him he had no business causing all this rumpus; you're a right gummock, I said, running away from that school to foreign parts when you could just have taken the train back home where you belong.'

'And what did he say to that?'

Mrs Grobbins paused. 'Ay, well, that's the nub of the matter. He says it isn't back home and he doesn't belong here. Or anywhere else, was what he said.'

Magdalena winced.

'I put him right on that. Bloody nonsense, I told him, of course it's his home. If it isn't, where is, that's what I'd like to know.

'"And so would I, Mrs G," he says in his saucy way. "That's what I want to find out." Won't find out scarpering off to Italy, I tells him. Then he goes quiet. He's still there, though, I can tell.

'"What makes you think I'm in Italy?" he says. Sounds just like Valdemar, when he's looking down his nose at someone, you know how he is.

'Because we do, I says, and he says he isn't, and I don't believe him, and then he says to give you his love, and the twins. And then ping! he's gone.'

What would he have said to me, if I'd been here? wondered Magdalena. Would he have been polite, affectionate, reproachful, angry? 'Was he ringing to say, come and bring me home?'

'I don't reckon so,' said Mrs Grobbins sympathetically. 'He's in a right muddle, that lad, and he's not happy, for all he's not at that school any longer.'

'How do you know?'

'Well, he was crying, wasn't he?'

Mrs Grobbins sailed off importantly to make a pot of tea. Poor Magdalena, she looked dreadful. She shouldn't blame herself, all the Mountjoys caused nothing but worry to their families; everyone knew they'd been doing it for generations. Of course, it wasn't just that dratted Thomas that'd upset her, she informed Lottie as she bustled about the kitchen. Trouble with Valdemar, too, she knew the signs.

Lottie's eyes grew big and bright with curiosity, and Mrs Grobbins backtracked quickly. Lottie was hardly one of the family, not a local, she didn't understand their ways.

'Going off to London all the time, driving back in the middle of the night, waking everybody up, you never know when he's coming or going. Very unsettling.'

'Is that all?' said Lottie, disappointed. 'I though he might be gambling, or doing something criminal. Or a girlfriend on the side.'

Mrs Grobbins was quick to squash that. 'Him? Girlfriend on the side? Never, that isn't his way at all.'

'Which is the exact truth,' she told Alfred in the Midwinter Arms that evening. 'Valdemar? A girlfriend? Don't make me laugh; that'd be the day, two or three at the very least.'

'He's getting on,' said Alfred, now a family man. 'Time he stopped all that, and spent a bit more time with the missus and the little 'uns. He's lucky to have a wife like that Magdalena, only a born fool would leave her at home and go chasing after floozies.'

Mrs Grobbins protested at that. 'High-class, all his bits on the side.'

'Floozies,' said Alfred firmly. 'There comes a time when a man has to take on responsibilities. It's that time for him, and past it. He should take a good look at himself in his silver shaving mirror and mend his ways.'

'Valdemar? Change his ways? Pigs'll fly,' said Mrs Grobbins

with scorn. 'Another half pint, Alfred, and your wife's a lucky lass to have a man like you at home keeping the bed warm.'

When Magdalena was alone in the castle she took her meals in the kitchen, or had her supper on a tray. When Valdemar was at home, they ate in the dining-room. He wasn't a kitchen and tray man. Magdalena found the dining-room oppressive; it only got the evening light, and on a thinly grey day like today it lacked the sparkle and cheerfulness which makes for a pleasant place to eat.

'There's going to be trouble with the new Dean,' said Valdemar, crumbling a roll in his restless fingers. He took a bite of fish. 'Tasteless, this, what is it?'

'Monkfish.'

'Disgusting.'

'I'm sorry,' said Magdalena. Why am I apologizing? He never cooks anything, he has no right to complain.

'At least the previous Dean had more than cottonwool between his ears.'

I'm not interested in the Dean, thought Magdalena, rolling a mouthful of fish on her tongue. And I'm not at all hungry. Val was right, the fish was very tasteless. Not that she liked fish much in any case, but it was healthy. Val had reached the age when he should be careful about his heart and arteries. She was being a good wife, serving fish for his sake.

Valdemar, glowing with energy and health, his eyes snapping as he recalled his morning's talk with the Dean, looked like the last man to be in need of a healthy diet. They say adrenalin keeps you alive longer, Magdalena recalled, washing her fish down with some mineral water. Getting in a temper and being unpleasant to all your friends and relations prolongs life. In which case, Val will live for ever.

'Trouble is, he has the Heritage Committee in his pocket, he's bamboozled them all into giving him a free hand, what a bunch of idiots.'

'Surely not,' said Magdalena politely, her mind on other matters.

Valdemar exploded. 'Bloody bad manners, you're sitting there not listening to a word I'm saying. You're always on at me to spend less time in London; now I'm here, and talking about a local scheme, you clam up and look as though you're on Mars. What's the matter with you?'

'Thomas rang,' said Magdalena.

'Thomas? When? Why the hell didn't you call me? I'd have given the wretched boy something to think about.'

'Mrs Grobbins took the call. It was while we were out.'

'Then why didn't she tell me the minute I came in? Useless woman. Mrs Grobbins,' he yelled in his very commanding voice. 'Here.'

Mrs Grobbins heard him quite clearly, even though the kitchen was at a very inconvenient distance from the dining-room. She lay low; she knew better than to go in there and be roared at.

'Well?' demanded Valdemar. 'Come on, Magdalena, stop playing games. I suppose she told you what the boy said. Spit it out. I suppose it's too much to hope that he was calling from an Italian police station.'

'He said he was with friends, and all right. He isn't coming home, because this isn't his home.'

'It's the only home he's got.'

'A home is more than a place.'

'He's been nothing but trouble, that boy. First, he drives us all mad saying he didn't want to go to boarding school. Then, when we get him – with a great deal of effort, I would point out – into one of the best schools in the country, he does nothing but moan and whinge. Why the hell can't he just settle down and get on with it? That's what other boys do, what's so special about him? Not his home, indeed. Bloody ungrateful, that's what he is.'

'Val, a home is more than four walls and a plate of food.'

'Oh, spare me the crap about loving environments. That boy's had a perfectly good family life, always been looked after, and you dote on him as if he were your own son. What more could he want?'

'You're his father, you should know.'

'Pity I've never liked wearing a condom,' said Valdemar crudely. 'Would have spared me a pack of trouble one way and another. There's Cleo, always up to something, and . . .'

He realized he had gone too far as he looked at Magdalena's rigid face.

'I won't have you upset. I'm going to find out where that boy is and bring him back, and he's going to stay at that school, work for his exams and shut up. I'm not standing for any more of this nonsense. The trouble with that boy is that he's been spoiled and over-indulged, thinks he can get away with murder. Not any more.'

Bang.

'Spoiled?' said Magdalena. Upset by *Thomas*? A tear splashed on the back of her hand, and she brushed it away with irritation. Ridiculous, a woman of her age crying. What good would crying do? I've got to pull myself together, she thought wearily.

'There she was, burying her face in her napkin, sobbing like a baby,' said Mrs Grobbins with relish. 'Poor woman, she's in a dreadful state. Worried about Thomas, her best friends from Midwinter are away abroad, and then That Man shouting at her. Sooner he takes himself off back to London, the better.'

'Looks as though you're in luck, then,' said Lottie. 'His car just went out of the gates.'

'Good riddance,' said Mrs Grobbins. 'Now, put the kettle on, and just keep those perishing twins out of her way this afternoon. She won't want them morrising about, not feeling like she does. I've told her to have a good lie down, exhausted is what she is. Poor thing.'

Poor thing?

Who was a poor thing? Were they talking about her?

Magdalena stood motionless outside the kitchen door, her hand stretched out to open it. The voices within became indistinct as Mrs Grobbins began noisily to empty the dishwasher.

Poor thing? She could have been called poor thing when her husband had died, and she had had to live through those last weeks of pregnancy without him.

Not so alone, though. Val had been at the castle day after day, amusing her, coaxing her to eat, insisting she get fresh air, driving her to clinic appointments. When the doctors had pulled long faces and called her into hospital, Val had packed her bag for her, driven with astonishing care into Eyot, filled her room full of flowers.

Val had told her friends when the twins were born, so that letters came, and welcome visitors arrived at the hospital to chat and cheer her up and bring her fruit and advice.

He was so kind, then. Now he was, what, indifferent? Careless of her feelings? Busy, occupied with his work and London life, which seemed to leave no space for a wife with young children.

And other people had noticed. Felt sorry for her.

How galling.

In the distance, the phone began to ring.

Magdalena turned and headed for the hall, anxious to answer the phone before Valdemar did. His study door was open; a quick glance inside showed that the room was empty. The phone on his desk rang on, unanswered.

He'd left without a word, angry with her for interfering in his affairs, for daring to have an opinion about Thomas which was different from his.

'Hello?' she said, sinking into Valdemar's deeply comfortable swivel chair.

'Mrs Mountjoy?' asked an unfamiliar man's voice.

A nice voice, she thought vaguely, as she noticed with a tiny part of her mind that Val's briefcase had gone. A voice with a trace of an American accent, a warm voice.

'Mrs Mountjoy?' the voice said again. 'This is Ferenc Latterly. We met last summer, if you remember. In Eyot, on the occasion of Zephania's memorial service. I'm ringing from my home in Italy.'

'Of course,' said Magdalena. 'Mr Latterly, is Thomas with you?'

There was a pause.

'Yes, he is. I am delighted that he came here, because as you know, a young man travelling alone these days . . . However, he arrived safely.'

'Is he all right? Can I speak to him?'

'Nothing has happened to him, he is safe, unharmed. But, I think, very unhappy, quite suddenly, and this is making him ill.'

'Ill? You mean flu, tummy upset?'

'Like a virus,' the voice agreed. 'But I think he's troubled in his mind. He's been under some great stress, is that right? Surely, to make him come such a long way from home, and alone. Perhaps he's given in, quite suddenly, and collapsed.'

'Collapsed?' Magdalena was alarmed, and her voice showed it. 'Unhappy, suddenly, what do you mean?'

'When he arrived, he was fine. Very self-possessed, very charming, very relaxed, liking the sun, pleased to be here. We had lunch, everything was fine. Then I may have been insensitive, I told him he should ring home, let his folks know he was all right. He said he had done so, yesterday. Of course, he was still travelling then; he did quite see that you would want to know that he was safely with friends.'

'That was very thoughtful of you.'

'He rang, spoke to someone at the house, not you.'

'Mrs Grobbins.'

'Just so. He said he'd left a message for you, and then, just like that, he went as white as a sheet, and, well, kind of passed out.'

'Passed out?'

'Now listen, Mrs Mountjoy, Thomas is not suffering from any life-threatening illness, I can assure you of that. We called a doctor, a very good one, who speaks English, and he agrees, there is perhaps some post-viral problem; Thomas said he had had a lot of sore throats and colds recently. Mostly, Dr Fuseli says, the boy is exhausted. He has worried and fretted to a point where he can no longer cope.'

'What am I to do?' said Magdalena. Thank God Val hadn't taken this call.

'You aren't his mother, isn't that so?'

'No, no, I'm not.'

'Then can I get in touch with his father? Is he there?'

'No, no, you mustn't do that.'

Magdalena's reaction was immediate, and quite definite. 'That would be the worst thing you could do. His father . . . how can I put this? He's a man with decided views.'

'Mrs Mountjoy, I remember your husband. No one who had met him could forget him in a hurry. I quite understand that he might not be best pleased with this escapade of Thomas's.'

Magdalena's loyalty fought with her fondness for Thomas. Thomas won. She took a deep breath.

'Val is being singularly beastly about this whole affair. I think for the moment, if you don't mind, that it's preferable to leave it to me to talk to my husband. I'd better warn you that he's alerted our embassy in Rome and the Italian police, who will be on the look-out for Thomas.'

Ferenc Latterly sounded amused. 'I can imagine, yes, that even English diplomats might stir if your husband got hold of them. Don't worry about the police, I can make sure that they'll turn a blind eye if they find out that Thomas is here. At least for the time being.'

Magdalena paused for a moment, making up her mind to do something which would make Val utterly furious. 'You are kind,' she said. 'I can't thank you enough. Look, I'm not sure how to arrange it, but he'll have to come home as soon as possible.'

'Then one of you will have to come and fetch him. Even if he is better after a long night's sleep – the doctor prescribed a sedative – there is no way I'm going to put him on a plane or the ferry or whatever. Nor will I hand him over to the police, or to any official who turns up from the embassy or consulate. I like your Thomas too well to do that to him. No, one of his family will just have to come over and coax him back. I'm sorry if you don't like it, but that's the way it is.'

Magdalena traced in her mind the pathways along Valdemar's fine Persian rug. Best rug in the castle, she thought inconsequentially. 'I understand completely,' she said. 'Apart from anything else, I don't want the papers to get hold of this.'

'Would they be interested?'

Magdalena could see the headlines. *Gryme boy runs away to island idyll* or *Lord Mountjoy's brother on the run*. 'The tabloids would be, yes.'

'That would do Thomas no good at all. He seems a sensitive boy.'

'He is, unfortunately. Look, I'll sort something out and get back to you as soon as I can.'

'You'll need my number' He gave it to her, and she wrote it down, mechanically, on the large pad of white paper which Val always kept beside the phone. ·

'I'll wait to hear from you, then,' said Ferenc politely.

'Thank you again,' said Magdalena. She put the phone down, and reached for the directory and Val's address book. Hortense, now how could she get hold of her?

'I'm sorry, Mrs Mountjoy, but I'm not driving in this fog.'

'Fog?' said Mrs Grobbins with a sniff. 'Bit of mist, that's all.'

Magdalena looked out of the window. 'It is a little misty,' she agreed. 'But why should you need to drive anywhere, Lottie?'

'It's some of the children's food I need. Things I can't get in the village. They need to be got from Eyot.'

'Why didn't you say this morning?'

'You didn't ask,' said Lottie, affronted, 'if there was anything I wanted, like you usually do. You went so quickly, I didn't have time to check on my cupboards.'

Mrs Grobbins snorted. 'Cupboards, indeed. There's no reason why the children's food shouldn't be kept in the same place as everything else. Then other people would notice when we're getting low.'

'If there were a cook here, someone trained,' began Lottie.

Magdalena cut across what was developing into a promising argument. 'I'll go,' she said. 'Give me the list. Mrs Grobbins, I'll drop you off on the way.'

'I've got an hour or so to do yet.'

'Of course, but you often stay longer than you should, and I think it's just me for dinner tonight. Best get home before the mist gets really bad.'

Mrs Grobbins grudgingly accepted the lift. She would be pleased to get home early, but on the other hand, there were one or two things she wanted to say to that Lottie . . .

Anything to pass the time until I can get in touch with Val, thought Magdalena as she guided a troublesome trolley round the supermarket. She felt detached, as though she were watching someone else in a film. It was another woman searching the shelves for 'Scrunchy-pops, medium size please, Mrs Mountjoy, because they go stale so quickly and then Hughie makes a fuss.'

But do I want to get in touch with Val? she asked herself as she cruised down the line of kitchen towels and tissues.

Bananas, apples . . . she should have got those when she came in. Tinned peaches? In June? Wasn't there enough fresh fruit about? 'Helena likes tinned peaches for a treat, Mrs Mountjoy.'

By the time she got to the checkout she knew that she didn't in the least want to phone Val. He would be furious with Thomas, and therefore with her. He would make a scene and then catch a plane and drag Thomas back.

Sorry? Oh, of course. She dug into her wallet while the checkout girl patiently waited. 'Thank you, yes, it is getting foggy, isn't it?'

She went out into the strangely chilly air, and loaded the bags into the car. Now where? She was reluctant to drive back to the castle, it was still at least an hour before she could have any hope of getting through to Val. She had run out of ink cartridges for her pen, that was something she had meant to buy this morning. Was it only this morning? She would go to the stationer's, always a soothing place, and get the cartridges.

The city was quiet in the thickening mist, with few people about on the pavements or the shops. Magdalena found a parking space with little trouble and walked slowly along the narrow streets to the stationer's. The light from the shops was welcome in the grey mist, it was ridiculously gloomy for a June afternoon, surely this mist was unusual for this time of year. A fluorescent poster in a window caught her eye. 'Fly away to the sun!' it screamed. 'Spain, France, Italy . . . seats available on many flights. Immediate departure.'

Magdalena stopped.

Italy.

Lucky people, able to fly off to the sun, away from this greyness, away, too, from all their English problems. Val would be flying away to the sun very shortly, but hardly in a holiday mood.

Funny, that you could just walk into a shop and book a flight, no fuss, no formalities. How different from the organized and complicated journeys of her childhood.

And how long since she had taken such a flight? Trips to America with Val were her flights to the sun. Hotel rooms, endless pleasant people connected with his work, a little shopping, a museum, a gallery, then home. Val never took a holiday; his idea of rest and relaxation was a few weeks thundering around the castle, stirring everything up until the tapestries shook on the walls and the bracketed lamps rattled in their sockets.

Magdalena walked on to the stationer's, bought the cartridges, slipped one into her pen. Then she walked back past the travel agent. There was a telephone number written on the bottom of the poster. Without thinking about it, she scribbled it down on the back of an envelope she found in her bag. Then on, into the mist, fog you would have to call it now.

And a slow, extremely slow, drive back to Mountjoy, to Val's answering machine with its cool message. And the certainty that if she dialled Veronica's number, he would be there.

I'll ring Sylvester, she decided, doodling on Val's pad as she sat at his desk.

'Mr Tate checked out this morning. No, I'm afraid we have no knowledge of Mr Tate's itinerary. Glad to help, thank you for calling.'

Magdalena poured herself a whisky in one of Val's heavy glasses. She sat, pensive, staring into the grate where some dying embers told of the fire lit earlier in the afternoon by Mrs Grobbins. She flicked the switch on the television, caught the local weather forecast.

A haar. That was what had rolled across Eyotshire, covering the landscape with its heavy, salty darkness. A sea fog, which hung still and relentless over Cathedral, city and country.

'Now for the national weather forecast . . .

'. . . And a look at the weather on the Continent. Fine, sunny weather in the Mediterranean, with temperatures in the low eighties.'

Magdalena finished her whisky and went to her solitary bed.

4

Agatha closed the front door behind her. She didn't slam it; she just closed it, firmly and deliberately. Then she picked up her bag, went down the three steps to the pavement and waited for a taxi. She felt certain there would be a taxi, it was that kind of day.

A window was thrown up on the second floor, and her daughter's head emerged. 'Mum! What are you doing? Where are you going?'

Agatha looked up and waved. 'I'm leaving,' she said. 'Going north. To stay with Magdalena, and then who knows?'

'Mum, don't go away. Is it Pa? I know he's being difficult, but surely you can sort it out.'

Agatha tilted her head back to get a better look at her daughter. 'Your father is being impossible, and I've had enough. Take care of yourself, darling; I'll write to you.'

'Mum, you can't leave.'

'Oh, but I can.'

A taxi drew up, clicking and rumbling, and Agatha got in quickly. 'King's Cross,' she said to the driver, and then she pulled the window down and waved at her daughter. The taxi turned the corner, cutting her house from view.

Elation.

She had done it. She had left.

She was still elated when she arrived at King's Cross. There was a train to Eyot in three-quarters of an hour. Time to buy a ticket – a single ticket – have a cup of coffee, browse in Smith's for a mag or a book, and then to board the train and find herself a good seat.

The elation began to fade at Peterborough, was barely evident by Grantham and had disappeared altogether by York. How could she have done it? Walking out on her husband and two children. It wasn't her style, she wasn't a scene-maker or a stance-taker, whatever had come over her?

Sense, that was what.

Two grown-up children, she reminded herself, gazing out at a one-carriage train which was pulling out for Scarborough. And it wasn't as if they had anything to do with it. Not really. She was going to keep in touch with them, it was George she was fed up with.

Stirring anger began to fight her doubts. George had behaved extremely badly. Even Edmund, who always sided with his father, tiresome boy, agreed that George had possibly gone Too Far.

'The whole business is ludicrous, Pa,' he had said in his slightly serious way. That was a mistake. George had nearly had a fit, he hadn't been grumbling and seething for weeks to have Edmund say the business was ludicrous.

'If it seems ludicrous to you, you must have a very deficient sense of humour,' he said in that nasty cold way of his. 'It is a family matter, and an important one. Your mother was aware how much this meant to me, and she was unforgivably careless. I almost think it must have been deliberate carelessness.'

And he had stomped sulkily off to his club.

He'll be spending a good deal of time there, thought Agatha, settling herself back in her seat as the train gave a jolt and began to pull out of the station. He may grumble about the food at the club, but just let him wait until he's had to fend for himself for a few days. I expect he'll bully Thea into cooking, and in a fit of daughterly duty she might oblige; that'll give him a shock.

I'm so fond of Thea, she thought, looking out of the window and thinking how dull the Vale of York was. And yet we're always at cross purposes. We never seem to get time to have a proper conversation, she's always dashing off somewhere, and I'm busy. She thinks I disapprove of her life and her friends, and I don't. Her friends alarm me, that's all; the terrifying self-possession which the young have these days.

Doubt still had the upper hand as the train ambled across the flat Yorkshire landscape; then a sense of defiance came over her as the scenery began to change into the familiar fells and patterned fields of Eyotshire, dimly visible through the thick coating of fog which was making the train so late.

What a muddle it all is, she thought, gathering her belongings as the train slowed down on the long curve into Eyot. I can't wait to see Magdalena; I long to have a sensible conversation about things with someone. Magdalena is always so balanced and clear-minded about things.

'The last train for Mountjoy left ten minutes ago,' said the ticket collector in satisfied tones. 'No train now until tomorrow morning.'

'Oh,' said Agatha. 'Is there a bus?'

'I doubt it, not with the haar the way it is,' said the man, even more pleased.

Agatha handed over her ticket and walked through the almost deserted concourse. Outside, the air was cold and clammy and heavy. The taxi driver shook his head. 'No way to get you to Mountjoy, not tonight, not in this. Put up in a hotel for the night, that's my advice; this may clear by the morning.'

Agatha's spirits sank. She wanted to be with a friend, not alone in some gloomy hotel. Then she pulled herself together. There was no reason why she should stay in a gloomy hotel, no reason at all. She would stay somewhere pleasant, have a good meal, watch television.

All by herself.

Her spirits rose.

Magdalena woke at first light. She drew the curtains; it was still misty, but this was the thin, ghostly mist of early morning, not the dank, clinging haar. She switched on her tea machine and then got back into bed, plumping the pillows up behind her.

Thinking.

She should phone Val, tell him about Thomas. He would be at his office by half past eight, that would be the sensible thing to do. If she didn't want to speak to him, which she didn't, then she could leave a message with his secretary, or on the answerphone.

He would ring back, demand details, criticize her for not contacting him sooner, or not leaving a clear message, or for something else. For anything, or nothing.

She could pretend that Ferenc had never rung. That would give Thomas a few days' grace.

But then, he didn't need a few days' grace, not if he was ill. If he was ill, what he needed was someone who was fond of him; a member of his family.

Val? Oh, very soothing, that would get Thomas back on his feet in no time.

'Land him in hospital, more like,' Magdalena said out loud, reaching out for the teapot and pouring herself a cup of tea.

For a moment she wondered about Thomas's mother. Perhaps she shouldn't have rung her late last night. She had lain in bed worrying, and then had sat up, switched on the light. If it were a child of mine, I'd want to know, she said to herself, dialling one of several numbers where Hortense might or might not be found. She had been in luck; for once Hortense was there.

Magdalena had told her about Thomas's escapade, told her how unhappy he was at school, how angry Val was about the whole affair. If she hadn't rung Hortense, would Val have told her? Probably not, Val never consulted Hortense about Thomas. He simply told her what he had decided, or had done. That was Hortense's fault, really, distancing herself in India, showing no inclination to come back to England.

Val should have allowed Thomas to go out to India to be with his mother last Easter, instead of making him stay to have extra cramming for that ridiculous entrance exam. It would have been better if Thomas had failed it, thought Magdalena, then none of this would have happened.

And then saying he could go out to India in the summer, but it not being convenient for Hortense.

No wonder Thomas was confused. No wonder he felt he'd rather throw himself on the mercy of virtual strangers than trust his own family.

'Oh, hell,' said Magdalena. This tea tasted foul, was the milk off? She clanked the cup irritably on to its saucer and lay back again, her hands folded behind her head.

She thought of the day ahead.

Help get the children up. Not that Lottie wanted help, but they were her children, after all.

Breakfast.

Lunch.

Oh God, Delia was coming to lunch. I don't feel strong enough for Delia, she thought. She'll turn my mind inside out, give me a good spring clean, get things sorted out to her own satisfaction and leave me feeling like a piece of chewed string.

A game of tennis with the vicar's wife. What a treat.

Children's tea. A game. Bath time, and a bedtime story.

Then dinner, while watching TV if there was anything to watch.

And so to bed.

That's ridiculous, she told herself firmly as she swung out of bed, thrust her arms into her silk wrap and made for the bathroom. There's plenty to do. Gardening. Work on the tapestries. Several letters to write.

Or she could go to Italy.

Magdalena resolutely turned the shower to a chilly setting; she needed a bracing awakening, something to drive such a silly thought out of her head.

Words from the poster swam into her head. 'Our phones are manned 24 hours a day. Ring now to book your flight.'

No.

She padded wetly to the bed and gazed at the phone. She put out a hand, snatched it back. No.

Ten minutes later she was downstairs in Val's study. She hesitated for a second and then picked up the receiver.

'Yes, we have a seat available on the twelve noon departure from Manchester. Can you make this flight? Check in forty-five minutes before departure.'

'Yes,' said Magdalena. She could always cancel.

'And the return flight?'

'I'll leave it open for now.' She must be mad.

'Can I have your credit card details, please?'

'Just a minute . . .' She searched in her bag for her wallet. What on earth was she doing, this was irrational behaviour. She could hear Val saying it, Irrational, what the hell does she think she's up to?

'Thank you. I'll just confirm the details . . .

'. . . Your ticket will be ready for collection at the travel desk. I hope you enjoy your journey.'

Magdalena looked up from her desk. 'Lottie, I need you to drive me to the station at Eyot. I've got a train to catch, we'll have to leave in about fifteen minutes. Mrs Grobbins will look after the twins.'

'No, I can't, Mrs Mountjoy, it's playgroup this morning, and . . .' Lottie sounded very put out. What about her routine? Sudden changes of routine were so bad for young children.

'They'll have to miss playgroup for once.'

Lottie had never seen Magdalena in this kind of mood. She wasn't very perceptive, but something warned her that this wasn't the moment to argue.

'I've heard that Thomas isn't well, and I have to . . . um, see someone about him,' said Magdalena, tucking the letter she had been writing into an envelope and writing an address on it in a firm hand.

Lottie was big with news. 'It was addressed to Valdemar,' she said.

'Mr Mountjoy to you,' said Mrs Grobbins grandly. She was longing to hear every detail, but any pretensions on Lottie's part had to be crushed before she got ideas in her head. 'In London?'

'Yes.'

'He hasn't rung since he left,' said Mrs Grobbins, mulling it over in her mind.

'Perhaps she's leaving him,' said Lottie hopefully. 'Perhaps this letter is Ending It All.'

'Perhaps it isn't,' said Mrs Grobbins getting up to refill the pot. 'You dropped her at the station, didn't hang about to see which train she got on, I suppose?'

'Of course not,' said Lottie self-righteously. 'It was the York train, though. That's the only one at that time, I know.'

'Mmm. But where after that?'

'Could be anywhere, from York. London, or Scotland.'

There was a pause as they considered the geography of England.

'What do I say if he rings?' asked Lottie. 'I mean, I'll have to answer the phone, won't I? If it rings when you've gone?'

'Say nothing. Except the truth, of course. That you took Mrs Mountjoy to the station and she didn't say where she was going or when she was coming back.'

'And that it was to do with Thomas?'

Mrs Grobbins gave her tea an extra stir to invigorate her thoughts. 'You could mention that. Nothing else, mind. If he starts getting demanding, you know, shirty, just put the phone down quickly.'

'Won't that make him angry?'

'Too bad, he's a long way away, and he'll be angry about something else by the time he gets back here.'

'Mrs Grobbins,' asked Lottie after a biscuity silence, 'who owns the castle?'

'And why do you want to know?'

'I just wondered. I mean, Mrs Mountjoy's first husband, he was Lord Mountjoy, wasn't he?'

'Her first husband,' said Mrs Grobbins repressively, 'was a no-good young man who drove into a wall while under the influence.'

Lottie's eyes grew round. 'Under the influence of what?'

'Drink, of course.'

'Oh, I thought perhaps you meant something from Another World.' Lottie lowered her voice to a whisper. 'Spirits. You know.'

'No, I don't, and I don't hold with any of that witchy nonsense, that's what they get up to in Lancashire. The only spirit her first hubby knew about was whisky.'

'So then she married Lord Mountjoy and got the castle.'

'Then she married Lord Mountjoy. Not exactly then, because it was a good few years on. Very fond of her, he was, and so happy when he knew there was a baby coming.'

'Then he died.'

'Yes. Heart.'

'So then she married Valdemar Mountjoy.'

'Yes, Lord Mountjoy's nephew.' Mrs Grobbins gave a warning sniff, they'd had enough raised eyebrows about that at the time without this Lottie putting in her two penn'orth.

'So she had the same name, but wasn't a lady any more.'

'She didn't use the title any more, that's right.'

'So Hugh is Lord Mountjoy, not Valdemar.' A thoughtful expression came over Lottie's face. 'But if it hadn't been twins, just Helena, would he be a lord?'

'Maybe. But he wouldn't have owned the castle. That's in trust for the children, and would have been Helena's if she'd been the only one. Now, that's enough of that, we haven't got time to sit around gossiping, not with this great place to look after. You run along and see what those twins are up to, and I'll just get things straight here.'

Lottie ran along, and Mrs Grobbins switched the radio on before settling back in her chair to finish her tea.

Delia's car bumped its way into the courtyard and Delia flew out, adjuring two large dogs in the back to stay. They settled down in a disgruntled way, and Delia bounced up the stone staircase to the back door.

'Hello, Mrs Grobbins, it's me. I've left the dogs in the car, otherwise they'll be after the castle cats, and that would never do, would it?' She gave a hearty laugh and plumped a jar of jam down on the kitchen table. 'Made it yesterday,' she said. 'Is Magdalena in her room?'

Mrs Grobbins was wary of Delia, who could be fairly forceful. Best to mind what you say to that one, she had warned Lottie on a previous visit.

'Magdalena isn't here,' she said. 'Expecting you, was she?'

'Not here? Rubbish. I saw her in Eyot yesterday, we fixed lunch. Oh, you mean she's popped down to the village. Don't worry, I'll go and have a look at the garden, see how your roses are coming on.'

'No, she isn't in the village,' said Mrs Grobbins. 'She went away, on the train.'

'Train?' Delia's attention was really caught now.

'On the train.'

'Well, where's she gone?'

'That's it, we know nowt about it, except that she's gone. Took a bag with her.'

Delia reflected for a moment. Magdalena had her little ways, but it wasn't like her to take off and forget a lunch engagement.

'Has she got anything on her mind?' she asked Mrs Grobbins. 'Ah, of course, it'll be to do with Thomas, won't it? Aren't they having a spot of bother with him at that school of his? Great mistake to send him to a southern school, too far away, and you get nicer boys in the northern schools.'

'Nowt wrong with schools in Eyot,' said Mrs Grobbins, but under her breath. 'I wouldn't know why she's gone, and I don't know anything about Thomas.'

Delia's eyes narrowed. 'Bet you do,' she said. 'Still, if you aren't saying, I'm not going to press you. Gone up to be with Val, has she? Bet he's ranting and raging if Thomas has been up to mischief. She didn't leave a note for me, did she?'

'Not that I know of.'

'I'll be off, then,' said Delia. 'Pity, I was looking forward to lunch and a chat with Magdalena. I've been thinking about her a lot, you know, got some good ideas about things she could do.'

Lottie put her head round the door. 'There's a car just come up the drive.'

'Yes, it's Mrs Sandman's, who's here, as you can see, Lottie.'

'No, it's a taxi. I thought it might be Mrs Mountjoy back.'

Mrs Grobbins and Delia took the short cut across the lower walkway. They could look out over the main entrance from the ruined tower at the end.

'Isn't it that friend of Magdalena's from London?' said Delia as she and Mrs Grobbins hung over the ramparts. 'I remember her because she reminds me of Olive Oyl in the old Popeye films.'

It was true, Agatha's neat, round face, bright, birdlike eyes and button of a nose did give her a look of Olive Oyl. However, such a comparison did no justice to her slim but shapely physique or her tremendous air of chic.

'Ay, that's the one,' said Mrs Grobbins, smoothing her apron over her stout thighs as she lowered her feet to the ground. 'Agatha, she's called.'

'Yes, I met her in London once. Made me feel like a country

cousin. Which is what I am, when you think about it,' she added, booming with laughter.

'She's got a suitcase with her,' said Mrs Grobbins ominously.

'I'll go and see what she wants,' offered Delia. 'Looks as though Magdalena's invited a household and forgotten about it.'

'Nobody told me guests were expected,' grumbled Mrs Grobbins as she went back to the kitchen.

Delia took Agatha off to the pub for lunch, feeling that it was better not to try Mrs Grobbins' patience too far. 'The dogs can do with a run in any case,' she said with her loud laugh. Agatha, who wasn't too keen on large and boisterous dogs, gave them an unfriendly look, but said nothing.

All traces of the haar had vanished, and it was warm enough to sit outside. Alfred brought them out plates of bread and cheese. 'Country food,' said Agatha, looking doubtfully at a sad piece of lettuce.

'Bound to be delicious,' said Delia, who wasn't what she called a fussy eater. 'So, now, what about Magdalena, who seems to have done a bunk.'

Agatha was so surprised that she dropped a large piece of cheese to the ground, where the dogs pounced on it.

'Magdalena? A bunk? Are you sure? How very surprising.'

'Is it? Yes, Magdalena always seems quite a calm and organized person.'

'Had she and Valdemar quarrelled?'

'No more than usual, I don't think,' said Delia with a merry laugh. 'But they have been having a few problems with Thomas.'

'Thomas? Val's boy?'

'Yes.'

'What kind of problems? Girls?'

'No, he's too young for that. Unhappy at school, I think, hasn't seemed to settle.'

'They don't, sometimes,' said Agatha with a sigh, remembering difficult times with her own Edmund. 'And their fathers get so het up about it.'

George had been impossible, refusing to believe that Edmund wasn't going to enjoy school the way he claimed he had. Which I don't believe for a moment, Agatha had confided to Thea, because he wouldn't go on about it so much if it had really been that good.

'Has Magdalena gone to get him?' she asked Delia.

'Don't ask me, I don't know the details. I had heard – it's only rumour, mind – that Thomas had run away.'

'Oh, poor boy,' said Agatha.

'And poor Magdalena, she'd be worried stiff. She adores that boy.'

'No wonder she's rushed off without a word.'

'Was she expecting you today?' Delia asked, tossing one of the dogs a pickled onion.

'She wasn't expecting me at all,' said Agatha frankly. 'I've done a bunk, too. Only, in my case, from my husband. I thought I'd come up here for a few days, a long way from London, you know. Have a think, talk to Magdalena, decide what to do next.'

'Husband, eh?' said Delia, interested.

Agatha nodded.

'Beasts, the lot of them,' said Delia cheerfully. 'You have to keep them under the tightest possible control, like I do Seton, otherwise they're up to mischief before you can sneeze.'

Alfred brought them out some coffee. 'There's a message from the castle,' he said. 'Mrs Mountjoy has rung, Mrs G said to tell you. Apologizing for not being here, and missing your lunch date, Mrs Sandman, and she'll get in touch when she's back. And she didn't say when that would be, so Mrs G tells me. And you're to make yourself at home, if you're Mrs Fimbul,' he told Agatha, with the air of one bestowing a favour.

Delia and Agatha looked at each other.

'Well!' said Delia. 'I wonder if Valdemar knows about this.'

5

Valdemar didn't.

The first he knew about it was when he rang home.

'What?' His voice was raised. 'I want to speak to Magdalena, go and get her. Not there? Don't be ridiculous. Why are you answering the phone, anyway?'

Lottie stood her ground; the twins were doing destructive things at her feet, and she knew that the first rule of good nanny behaviour was never to show fear or panic or anger in front of your charges. She tried to make her voice calm and soothing. 'Magdalena left on a train.'

'What? This is a terrible line, I don't understand a word of what you're saying. Look, get me Mrs Grobbins, will you? And be quick; I can't hang about here on the phone for hours while you waffle on.'

'Mrs Grobbins has gone home.'

'So you're alone there, with the twins?'

'That is my job, Mr Mountjoy. And I'm not alone, because Mrs Fimbul is here.'

'Mrs Fim—Oh, Agatha. What the hell's she doing there? Oh, put her on, then, put her on. Right away, I haven't got all day.'

Lottie walked slowly to the door, no easy task with a twin clasped to each leg. She stood on the landing and called out. 'I'm sorry to shout, Mrs Fimbul, but it's Mr Mountjoy on the phone, and he'd like to speak to you. There's a phone in the study,' she added, as Agatha came swiftly into the hall. 'That door over there.'

She shuffled back into the bedroom which she was trying to

get ready for Agatha. She wasn't tempted to listen in, listeners heard no good of themselves.

She was wise.

'That girl's distinctly lacking,' Valdemar was saying.

'Hello, Val,' said Agatha. 'How are you?'

'Agatha? Ha, that's where you are, is it? George is ranting and grumbling all over the club about you. What are you doing at Mountjoy?'

'Visiting Magdalena.'

'George doesn't like your being away. You'd better come back.'

'George can lump it,' said Agatha sweetly. 'If you want Magdalena, she isn't here.'

'That's what that gormless girl said. Where is she?'

'Nobody knows. She went off in a train, towards York. The impression she left was that she was going to rescue Thomas.'

'Thomas? As far as anybody knows he's gone to Italy.'

'Then maybe that's where Magdalena's gone.'

'Have you taken leave of your senses? Magdalena couldn't manage a day out in Boulogne on her own, and besides, she never goes to the Continent. Doesn't like it. Why didn't you ask her where she was off to?'

'Val, do not shout at me. I'm not your wife, nor a minion at your office. I'm a friend, if you know what such a thing is. I didn't ask Magdalena because she had gone by the time I arrived.'

'Bloody rude, inviting people and then careering off. I suppose she's gone to look up some useless Italian crony in London, just the sort of stupid thing she would do. Quite unnecessary, too. I've got the Italian police on the job, it's only a matter of time before they pick the boy up and ship him home, why does she have to interfere?'

You must have a different experience of Italian police from me, Agatha said to herself, fiddling with a sharp silver paper knife she had found on the desk.

'In any case, we don't know exactly where the boy's gone, so how could she be any use? Unless,' he said, his voice deepening with suspicion and irritation, 'unless she's heard something and hasn't told me.'

'Now why do you think she might do that, Val?' asked Agatha, all innocence.

'Because she's been in a mood for days, no, weeks; can't have a civil conversation with her, probably needs HRT or whatever it is you women take to make you human.'

'I hope Virginia isn't there listening to you. She'd have a fit.'

Virginia was a formidable senior partner in Valdemar's firm of structural engineers. She was probably the only person of whom Valdemar was even remotely afraid.

'Why should Virginia be listening? She's in her office.'

'Lucky for you, then.'

'Virginia's working. Which is what I should be doing instead of wasting my time with all this.'

'Now Val, I've had enough of you. I'll stay here at the castle until we know what's happening with Magdalena.'

She held the receiver away from her ear as a series of crackles and growls came down the line. 'Are you prepared to drop everything and come up here? No? I thought not. In that case someone has to stay here with your nanny and children . . . Yes, I know you pay her a salary – no, I don't suppose for a moment it's an exorbitant one – for her to look after the children, but the castle is another matter. She won't stay, in any case, because of the ghosts . . . There aren't any ghosts? How do you know, Val? You're hardly the sensitive type, are you? . . . Anyway, it's irrelevant whether there are any ghosts or not. Lottie thinks there are, and the effect is the same either way. Now, go and have a nice long rage, Val, and we'll speak again in the morning. Goodbye!'

Valdemar would have been astonished if he could have seen Magdalena, who was at that very moment sitting in a restaurant in Palermo in the company of an elegant and handsome Italian in his sixties, enjoying an ambrosial wine and savouring every mouthful of the exquisite food.

Far from being unable to manage a day trip to France, Magdalena had got herself to Italy with no trouble at all. The train from York to Manchester had been on time, the connection to the airport straightforward, and her ticket was waiting for her as promised.

Magdalena passed the first stage of her journey in a complete sense of unreality. This isn't me, she thought as she watched the early summer landscape flash by, sodden from weeks of rain. Sad-looking sheep tugged resentfully at thin grass, cows steamed as a pale sun brought a touch of heat to their soaked hides. This is England; no, not just England, this is the north of England, Magdalena told herself. This is where I live, where I belong. But I'm travelling through it, on my way to somewhere quite else. I'm abandoning my children and husband and home, going off on a whim.

Not a whim, though, she told herself.

Thomas needs me. The twins don't. They need food and routine and lots of attention and affection, all of which Lottie is far better able to supply than I am.

And Val?

Magdalena bit nervously at the inside of her lip.

Val doesn't need me. If he needs anyone, which I doubt, he needs his colleagues at work; his friends in London. And perhaps Veronica. Me? No, a housekeeper would look after the castle better than I do, and as for companionship or friendliness or lust or comfort . . . let alone love . . . Forget it.

It was strange to be travelling economy class, but perfectly comfortable. It was also very restful, travelling on one's own.

It was particularly restful to be flying without Val. It wasn't that he shouted at her or was embarrassing; by and large he was briskly helpful, ushering her at speed on and off planes, through customs and immigration, in and out of taxis. Like an efficient if rather lupine sheepdog with a woolly charge, thought Magdalena as she waited for the plane to take off. No, the trouble with Val was his boundless energy. He was so vibrant that you felt worn out just being with him.

If I were younger . . . Magdalena watched the houses and roads below, getting further and further away . . . And then, it's as though I'd left all my life down there, she thought dreamily, and that this was another me, flying away, unencumbered, unbothered.

It was a very strange and extremely pleasant feeling.

'Would you like anything to drink, madam?'

'Yes, please,' said Magdalena. 'A large gin and tonic, with plenty of ice and lemon.'

Val never let her drink while flying. 'Dehydrates you.'

'It soothes me, Val. I don't like flying.'

'Gin won't make it any less dangerous; not that it is. Your drink won't keep the plane in the air. Have some mineral water or an orange juice.'

Whether it was the gin or the absence of Val, Magdalena felt perfectly relaxed. The plane was only half full, so there was no one in the seat next to her, no one she had to talk to. She opened the guidebook she had just had time to buy at the airport, ready to take an intelligent interest in Roman remains, hundreds of thousands of lire for the simplest things, thermal and volcanic springs . . . Her eyelids drooped. She slept.

Back at the castle, Agatha felt that she, too, could do with a nap. She had forgotten how exhausting small children were, what a mistake, offering to entertain the twins while Lottie did some vital shopping.

I don't remember mine being so awful, she said to herself as she handed them over to Lottie before going into hiding in Val's study. 'That's the one place they never go,' Lottie had confided to her. 'He can be quite nasty, you know, when roused, and he doesn't seem to take any notice of the fact that they're so little.'

'I wouldn't have thought he'd have any time at all for them,' Agatha said bluntly.

'He can be very sweet with them,' said Lottie earnestly. 'When he's in the mood.'

What a perfect room, thought Agatha, taking in her surroundings. Comfortable, elegant, not too new-looking; old surfaces, polished; lighting just so. The room of a man who knew his own mind and his senses. Wonder if he had planned this himself, or if Magdalena's had been the guiding hand. It was a personal room, either way.

Doodles on his pad.

Agatha paid attention. Doodles always told you a lot about the doodler. This doodler was Magdalena, she recognized the writing. She'd written the name Thomas several times, in a tight hand. Then the word Italy in a more relaxed and flowing script. There was a stylized sun, looking rather severe, and a wavy palm tree. She had drawn the outline of an island, and had printed underneath it the name Aeolus. Beneath that was the inscription, 2 hours by hydrofoil from Messina, 4 flights daily.

Ho, thought Agatha. So that's where you've gone. Aeolus . . . Aeolus. Off the coast of Italy, near Sicily. A defunct volcano, wine, fruit, obsidian . . . That was the one. Just becoming fashionable, if she remembered rightly. Certainly not a package holiday destination. Yet.

She hummed a little tune and thought.

Why should Magdalena go there? To be with Thomas. Okay, but why should Thomas be there? She shrugged her shoulders, no point in trying to work that one out. None of those Mountjoys ever did what you expected.

Would Magdalena do a flit like this, because flit was what it looked liked, on Thomas's behalf? Possibly.

Agatha tore off the sheet with Magdalena's doodles and took up the heavy fountain pen which lay on the table. Lovely pen, she said to herself, trying a few flourishes as she did some more thinking.

She'd last seen Sylvester a few weeks before, and, she remembered, he'd been worried about Magdalena. He was unwinding after a recital, on edge, but he had carried her and George off for a meal. George, in awe of Agatha's arty friends as he called them, had simply eaten and gazed into space, Agatha recalled with irritation. Flush with wine and a meal unsupervised by his waistline-watching housekeeper, Sylvester had confided to her that Magdalena was looking peaky, and, he suspected, was very unhappy.

'Won't say much, she doesn't like to burden other people with her woes, you must know that.'

Agatha nodded as she ate a fragrant morsel of duck. 'She's always been like that, going to a lot of trouble to hide her own feelings, but always putting herself out for other people who've got troubles.'

Sylvester snorted. 'And when you consider what she's been through . . .'

'So what's making her unhappy? Or is it who?'

Sylvester nodded, finishing a tasty mouthful and taking a gulp of wine before he spoke. 'Who,' he said, lowering his voice slightly and giving George a swift look.

'Don't worry about him,' said Agatha. 'He's practically deaf although he won't admit it; can't hear a word anyone says to him in restaurants and at parties unless they shout in his ear. So it's Val, is it?'

'I'm afraid so,' said Sylvester gloomily.

'Women?'

'I have heard that he's taken up with one or two of his old flames, and isn't averse to collecting the odd new one.'

'Oh, it's too bad,' Agatha burst out. George looked up, surprised, and she gave him a quick pat on his hand before carrying on in a quieter voice. 'He's so lucky to have Magdalena, why does he have to carry on like this? She knows, I suppose.'

'I'm sure of it. She has plenty of friends in London who'd be delighted to fill her in.'

'Not me,' said Agatha. 'And who's so bitchy that they'd pass that sort of thing on?'

'Friends who feel she ought to know. Friends who dislike her for being the kind of person she is.'

'Yes, kind and funny and generous and a good friend; oh, it makes me furious. What about the children? Are they okay? I mean, it was four years ago, but she had a rotten time with them, and then Hugo dying just weeks before. She went through hell, didn't she?'

'She did,' agreed Sylvester. 'But they're fine; wicked as can be, and very Mountjoy.'

'Ah,' said Agatha.

'Valdemar adores them.'

'Does he now?' Agatha found that very unexpected.

'Yup,' said Sylvester, inspecting the plate of beautifully arranged vegetables and sweeping the broccoli on to his plate. 'Dotes. When he's there. Which isn't very often.'

'I thought he was up there every possible moment, hasn't he got what almost amounts to an obsession with that castle?'

'Yes, I think he has, and in theory he's up at weekends. That wouldn't be too bad, lots of marriages work quite well with the two of you being apart during the week and together at weekends. But he's been up less and less. Very busy at the office, Magdalena says, and I dare say it's true. But even so . . .'

'If Thomas is away, she must be lonely.'

'It's desperate for her,' said Sylvester frankly. 'There's Mrs Grobbins, well, a little of her goes a long way at the best of times. Then there's a particularly dense and uninspiring nanny, and the two infants. And that's it.'

'While Val has his work, his club, his friends, his mistresses, concerts, opera, theatre and all that goes to make a thoroughly enjoyable life.'

'Exactly,' said Sylvester, signalling for coffee.

'Poor Magdalena,' said Agatha.

What a bind she's in, thought Agatha, gazing down at her doodle of a dark-haired Giacometti figure bound from head to foot in trailing string. She jumped as the phone rang, and looked at it without enthusiasm. That'll be George, I know it will.

It was.

'FarFlung Travel? Yes, I want a flight to Sicily . . . No, not the Scilly Isles, thank you all the same. Sicily. Off Italy, you know. No, it needn't be a charter, although I don't want to pay more than I have to. . . Thank you, yes, I'll hold.' She dug the broad gold nib into the paper. 'Bloody George. No, I wasn't speaking to you. Is George a dog? Why should he be a dog? . . . You thought you heard barking? It's the line crackling. No, George isn't a dog, I wish he were, much less trouble. George is my husband.'

'Funny, that,' said the voice at the other end, quite chatty now that a sale was in sight. 'About Sicily. We had another lady wanting to go there, just a couple of days ago. She wanted a flight quickly, like you do.'

'What a coincidence.'

'Nice to get away somewhere warm, though – sea, beaches; it's ages till my holiday, and it's horrible here, isn't it? How would you like to pay? Cash? Oh, that's unusual. Hold on, I'll have to ask the manager if we can accept cash.'

Agatha stared down at the pad and did some more doodles, wondering at the strangeness of life.

The voice came back. 'Yes, that'll be all right, but you'll have to collect and pay for the ticket right away.'

'In about an hour.'

'Oh, that's fine. Bye for now.'

Cash, thought Agatha bitterly. I hope George is having a huge lunch somewhere and gets the most terrible indigestion. Cancelling my credit cards and telling the bank to cut off funds, how dare he. She grumbled to herself as she wrestled with the gears of Magdalena's car. I hope it's insured, how on earth does she manage it? Four-wheel drive for the snow and ice in winter, I suppose, God, how horrible.

And how clever of me to have my little building society account with all that money in case of a rainy day, she thought with triumph, as she drew out enough money for the plane ticket and for travelling expenses. The smug little man behind the window was reluctant to give her traveller's cheques as well as the cash, although he had finally to agree that she still had a substantial balance in her account. He ought to work for George, she thought crossly, as she sailed out of the building society holding firmly on to her bulging wallet and headed for the travel agents.

'I won't stay here alone, and that's flat,' said Lottie tearfully. 'This is a creepy place, it makes noises all night long, there's things wandering about and I won't get a wink of sleep.'

'Things?' said Agatha impatiently. 'What things? The only thing that ever wanders around in the middle of the night is Valdemar, and he's in London. Now, pull yourself together.'

'You promised you'd stay. You told Mr Mountjoy you would.'

'What I said I'd do was stay until we found out what had happened to Magdalena, which I have. And you're used to being here without Magdalena now, so I'm sure you'll manage splendidly.'

'It's no good,' said Lottie. 'I'll give in my notice, I can't stay.'

'You can't just walk out on the children while their mother's away. I bet it says something about that in your contract; you'd be struck off the nanny register.'

'I don't care,' she wailed.

Mrs Grobbins put her head round the door. 'What's going on?

What are you making all this fuss about, Lottie? Blow your nose and dry your eyes, what a sight!'

'Mrs Fimbul says she's going, and I'm not staying here alone.'

'No, I don't suppose you are, no gumption, you young folk. I'll stay overnight until Mrs Mountjoy comes back, now give over with that hiccuping.'

'Will you, Mrs Grobbins?' said Agatha. 'Magdalena will be very grateful.'

'I expect that Valdemar will be back soon, and then it's up to him to get things sorted out. But I'm not one to let folks down,' said Mrs Grobbins, thinking how nice it would be to settle down in the drawing-room with a roaring fire, a huge telly, no perishing children or husband to annoy her, and a little of what she fancied in a glass to pass the time.

'Oh, thank you,' said Lottie, sniffing gratefully. 'I'm ever so sorry, Mrs Fimbul, but I can't face the ghosts alone.'

'And I can't be doing with gorms that go imagining things round every corner,' declared Mrs Grobbins as Lottie went off to find her charges.

Magdalena had met Ettore while she was buying a ticket for the hydrofoil.

'I've just missed it?' That's because the plane was late, she thought. What a nuisance. 'And the next one is in four hours? Are you sure there isn't one sooner than that?'

'There will be next week,' a voice said in English. Magdalena turned and saw a silver-haired, very good-looking Italian standing behind. He smiled and bowed his head in a courteous greeting.

'The new timetable begins on Sunday,' he informed her. 'It is early in the season still, so this is now the spring timetable. With fewer sailings.'

'Oh,' said Magdalena. 'Thank you for explaining.' She was keyed up, anxious to get to Thomas, and this four-hour wait suddenly seemed intolerable. 'So we won't get there until quite late.'

'Unfortunately not. You have booked a hotel? They will know when the hydrofoil arrives, and will expect you then.'

'No, no, I'm not staying at a hotel.'

His eyebrows rose in a polite question.

'Do you know the island well?' Magdalena asked.

'I live there.'

'I have to get to the Villa Saraceno.'

'Then,' he said, with an even more charming smile, 'you must be Lady Mountjoy.'

Magdalena looked at him blankly. 'Mrs Mountjoy, actually,' she said. 'How did you know?'

'My daughter lives in the Villa Saraceno. I live nearby, I shall take you there.'

'Ah,' said Magdalena. 'So that's how you know my name.'

'Not only that,' he said. 'I knew Hugo Mountjoy, many years ago. Before you became his wife, I think. I was sorry to hear of his death.'

'Who are you?' said Magdalena. A memory stirred in her mind; surely among the endless letters at that terrible time, there had been one expressing a real sense of affection for Hugo . . . from an Italian.

'Did you write to me then?'

'I did. And you wrote back, a charming note.'

'I don't remember my reply, I'm afraid,' said Magdalena frankly. 'It was a . . . well, things were difficult then.'

'To answer my letter at all was a kindness,' he said. 'I lost my wife, many years ago now; I would not wish to put any extra task on a wife or husband at such a time. Now, to talk of more cheerful matters, we are finished here. Please allow me to give you dinner while we wait for the hydrofoil, there are several excellent restaurants near here.'

'Thank you,' said Magdalena. 'But . . .' Her voice tailed off. She didn't want to seem churlish, but she wasn't hungry. She was worried, she was longing to see Thomas.

'If you are concerned about the boy staying at the villa, the young Mountjoy, then I can set your mind at rest. Dr Fuseli reports himself very pleased with his young patient; he has slept a lot and he is easier in his mind. He is happy that you are coming. This I heard just now when I telephoned my daughter.'

He ushered her towards the door. 'So the best you can do for him is to arrive refreshed. Is he your son?'

'My stepson,' said Magdalena, not sure if she liked being taken charge of. 'I married another member of the family after Hugo died. Another Mountjoy. This is his son.'

'A complicated family, I believe,' he said with a twinkle in his eye. 'Now, this restaurant is run by an old friend, and I am sure you will enjoy the excellent food.'

Suave, that's what you are, thought Magdalena. Just as used to getting your own way as Val, but with infinitely more finesse. Her mouth watered as the delicious medley of cooking smells floated under her nose.

I've done it, she said to herself. I've escaped, I'm here, in Italy, on my own – well, almost.

Free.

6

Thea sat in a corner seat and watched the fields go by; listened to the clackety-clack of the train swaying over the points.

'The weather will change as you cross the Trent,' her father had warned her. 'Take a mac and some warm underwear, you'll need them.'

Silly old Pa, thought Thea. And what a state he's in over Mum. It's entirely his own fault, he shouldn't have been so beastly to her. Although maybe it's a bit her fault as well, letting him get away with it. He's been beastly to her in a gentle way for ages, come to think of it. Ever since they got married?

Possibly not, possibly it was all right in those days, she thought, flicking over the pages of the magazine she'd bought at King's Cross.

'How to cope when your lover leaves you.' Huh, thought Thea. I'm not reading that; what do they know about it?

'Can you trust your boyfriend?' Stupid question, no, of course not. Where were these people living?

'Is work more important to you than love?' Got it in one, thought Thea.

Wonder if Mum will still be at the castle, or have I come on a wild goose chase? Where else could she have gone? Further and further north, perhaps until she could go no further. Then she'd have to set sail for the island of Ultima Thule, Thea told herself, yawning ferociously.

She turned to the evening paper and read a vitriolic exposé of the doings of the director of the London Opera Group. Poor Timmy, he didn't deserve that. Written by D. Quarles. Clearly you didn't mess with Quarles. Thea tried to imagine what a

Quarles might look like. In his fifties, she decided. Not very tall, small feet, needed glasses but too vain to wear them. Suits, to show he was a worker and not an arty shirker. Chain-smoked, probably, and lived in Kent.

That was him settled.

A week off. How would they manage without her? They wouldn't; it would be chaos, she'd come back to find piles of music everywhere, a week of unpaid overtime getting everything in order again. Lucy? What a joke. She'd just sit there, buffing her nails, completely uninterested. 'Oh, I thought you said Rachmaninov, not Rimsky-Korsakov, does it matter?' And gesturing to any wandering player who came in to 'just dump the music down there, anywhere, it doesn't matter.' And back to her earphones, jigging her head from side to side with the beat in that incredibly irritating manner.

At least, a week off would be seven days without having to see Lucy. That was a week down on the plus side of life. On the other hand, a week spent trying to act as go-between for her parents was quite likely to go down on the minus side. She took a bite of the sandwich she'd bought before she got on the train.

Pity I didn't ring to let Mum know I was coming, she thought, as the train drew into Eyot. She heaved her bag out from between the seats. She could have come to meet me.

'Thea Fimbul?' said Mrs Grobbins suspiciously. 'Your mum isn't here, if she's the one you want. I don't know what's going on here, like Clapham Junction this place is with people coming and going.'

She noticed the tiredness round Thea's eyes and took pity on her. 'Come in, leave your bag there, it looks right heavy. You come along to the kitchen and have a cup of tea, that'll set you on your feet again.'

Lottie was delighted to see some young company at the castle, although this one didn't seem on her wavelength really. She was kind of vague and as though her mind was somewhere else. A bit lacking, perhaps; still, one had to take people as one found them.

'So you've come looking for your mum, have you?' she said with a bright effort at conversation. 'And she's gone.'

'You mean she's in Eyot? Out for the day?'

'Oh no, Mrs Grobbins says she's gone to Italy.'

'Italy?' Thea was thunderstruck. 'Oh, no, you must be mistaken.' She just stopped herself from saying, she can't have gone to Italy, she hasn't any money; no need to air her mother's problems in public. 'I mean, she wasn't planning to go to Italy.'

'Who says she was?' said Mrs Grobbins. 'Who says she was? Same as Mrs Mountjoy; ups in the morning, hops on the train to the airport and that's it. Gone. Left the country.'

Thea blinked.

Pinpricks of light shone in little groups in the darkness; hills, thought Magdalena. Lights from the cafés and bars around the landing stage were reflected in glassily calm water; further along there was a great bustle as a fleet of fishing boats was readied for a night's sailing. Magdalena could see the gay paint on the boats in the wavering light of the lanterns. And the eyes: each boat had a bright single eye painted on its prow.

She took a deep breath, glad to be out of the hydrofoil and on firm land, her senses delighting in the velvety darkness with its scents of flowers and cypresses and the sound of cicadas. It was so warm, the warmth was almost tangible. And it was so quiet, just the odd sound of a car and otherwise only voices, people talking and laughing as they chatted in the bars or strolled along the front.

She was grateful to Ettore for not talking much as they drove through the little port and along a steep, narrow street, up a winding road to the Villa Saraceno. Here the night smells were even more concentrated, more beguiling.

Then there were welcoming voices, and the sturdy figure of Thomas flinging himself into her arms; hugging her and hugging her and not wanting to let her go.

Then, finally, a bedroom with shuttered windows and a warm marble floor; a high, wide bed with carved wooden ends, white linen smelling of the sun and the scents of the island, and then the bliss of a deep and seemingly dreamless sleep.

*   *   *

Magdalena was woken in the morning by the rattle of shutters being opened, and the sound of voices.

'No, Thomas, ssh, it isn't good for people to wake up suddenly.'

'But she's been asleep for hours, she'll want to be awake, she hasn't seen anything properly yet, only in the dark. How can she wait?'

Magdalena blinked and sat up in bed, sleepily taking the glass of fruit juice which Carla was offering her. It was Carla who had greeted her last night and had made her welcome. And it was Carla who had been so kind to Thomas. You would have known her for Ettore's daughter, she had all his charm. In her case it was mixed with a merry eye and a great propensity to laughter. Magdalena could see that she had Thomas eating out of her hand; well, that would do him good.

'You are a bad boy,' Carla said to Thomas in mock severity as he sat on the end of Magdalena's bed and bounced on it. 'Quite hard, these beds,' he said, 'but very comfortable. Magdalena, you must get up quickly, there's so much to see.'

Magdalena drank her juice all in one go; it was freshly made and sweet and delicious. 'Peaches?' she asked, putting the glass down on the table beside the bed.

'Peaches everywhere, here,' said Thomas. 'Shall I run your bath?'

If he had a tail, he'd thump it, thought Magdalena, looking at him with great affection. Of course she adored her twins, but however much she loved them, she would always have a specially soft spot for this gangly boy, who was looking at her so intently now, with bright and confident eyes.

Val's eyes, she thought with a horrid lurch of her stomach. Such beckoning eyes, such a deep blue. So attractive. So deceitful in Val's case, she thought bitterly, and so innocent in Thomas.

And he trusts me. He's quite happy now that I'm here, he feels sure that I'll make everything all right as I did when he was a little boy. He doesn't really understand that Val is more than a match for me, and it'll be Val who will decide what's to become of him, not me.

Anger crept up her spine, making her skin prickle. To hell with that. Val had bullied and thwarted her long enough. If she didn't have the energy or spirit to fight for herself, she could at least take him on for Thomas's sake.

'Let's see who wins this time,' she said fiercely.

'What?' said Thomas, startled.

'I'll have a shower,' said Magdalena.

'Shoo, Thomas,' said Carla. 'Leave Magdalena to get up in peace. Tell Giulietta that we'll need coffee and breakfast in about twenty minutes.' She turned to Magdalena. 'Is that enough time for you?'

'More than enough,' said Magdalena. 'Thank you.'

'Be careful with the shower, it isn't always reliable, sometimes it is hot when it should be lukewarm and then the other way about.'

'It won't bother me,' said Magdalena. 'I don't think anything here could bother me.'

'I hope not,' said Carla, chasing Thomas out of the room and closing the heavy wooden door behind them with a soft clunk.

'Ferenc is working,' said Carla, pouring coffee for Magdalena, who was so dazzled by the view that she could do nothing but sit and stare.

'Goodness, how lovely it is,' she said, taking the cup of coffee.

'It is very beautiful here, I never get tired of looking out to the sea.'

The two women sat overlooking a hillside of terraced vines which marched almost to the water's edge. Below them were rocks and a glimpse of ivory beach, and then the dazzling water, a rippling azure which stretched away to a darker turquoise. Crystalline, unblemished. A fishing boat made its unhurried way across the bay; otherwise everything was perfectly still.

'Oleanders,' said Magdalena. 'Pink oleanders.'

'And many other flowers,' said Carla.

'I could sit here all day, and just gaze and gaze at the sea.'

'Why not? Although I would like to show you the rest of the villa, and then, later on, there will be another visitor arriving.'

Thomas, who was sitting at the corner of the terrace keeping a watchful eye on Magdalena, looked up at these words. 'A visitor? Who?'

His voice is nervous, thought Magdalena. He's afraid that Carla is talking about Val.

Carla had heard the unease in Thomas's voice. 'A friend, an old friend of ours and yours.'

'Who?' said Thomas suspiciously. 'I don't have many friends who'd be coming here.'

'This one is very special. It's Sylvester.'

Thomas jumped to his feet. 'Sylvester? Sylvester Tate?'

Carla nodded.

'Yes!' yelled Thomas, punching the air. 'Great. Is he on holiday?'

'No, although we shall see to it that he rests and has some relaxation. He has had a punishing schedule this summer, too much work for an artist who needs time to reflect. He is coming to work with Ferenc, for some recordings they are making, and also to begin on a new work. And, later on, Gabriel will join us as well, because they play as a trio, you know, and will be doing some concerts in the autumn and again the recordings.'

'Gabriel, too,' said Thomas ecstatically. 'I like Gabriel, although I like it best when it's just Sylvester. I don't know Gabriel so well.'

Carla laughed. 'Then it's time for you to know him a little better. Here at the Villa Saraceno everybody gets to know their friends a little better, and also themselves.'

'I can believe it,' said Magdalena.

Thomas was beside her, the old Thomas. 'Magdalena, do you know why it's called the Villa Saraceno? It's because the Saracens once had a castle near here, we can go and see the ruins, Carla says. This was part of a farm then, it was in the countryside, there weren't so many other houses in those days, of course. Do you know who the Saracens were?'

'Arabs,' said Magdalena, knowing she was was going to learn a lot more about them in the very near future.

Thomas pulled out a chair and perched himself on the edge of it.

'Yes, but not the ones who went to Spain. Listen, this is really interesting. They came from Africa, the Moorish bits, and they were pirates.'

'Like your ancestors, then,' said Magdalena.

Thomas stared at her. 'My ancestors weren't Saracens.'

'No, but the Mountjoys originally came from Spain, centuries ago, of course. They were pirates. You want to ask Val, he'll tell you all about them.'

She could have bitten her tongue off the minute she had said the words. At the mention of Val's name all Thomas's eager, confiding happiness vanished, and it was a wary, polite boy who stood up, offered to take the tray in for Carla, and went.

'Oh, how silly of me,' said Magdalena, furious with herself.

'Val? You are talking about Valdemar?'

'Yes. My husband. Thomas's father. The man who has alerted the Italian police about Thomas, as well as a posse of diplomats. I'm sorry to say that he will regard it as a point of honour to transport Thomas back to England as swiftly as possible and return him to his English school forthwith.'

'Ah, your famous boarding schools,' said Carla thoughtfully. 'So barbaric, so out of date.'

'Try telling Val that.'

'It may be more difficult for him to take Thomas back to his school than you think,' said Carla. 'We always take an English paper here, and Ferenc said you should see this one.'

She handed over a familiar-looking tabloid with screaming black headlines. Magdalena gazed at it, appalled.

'Oh, no!' she said.

As Magdalena sipped her coffee on a sun-drenched terrace, Valdemar was driving at speed along rain-soaked roads, the skies as grey as the tarmac, his mood as grim as the relentless, driving rain. Beside him on the seat was a copy of the same paper that Magdalena had seen, face down, so that he didn't have to look at the headline.

Valdemar was still fuming from his conversation with Thomas's housemaster.

'I hardly think it's for you to say whether you will or won't take him back. That's my decision.'

'I'm afraid there's no question of it. It seems that your son has run away from this school to go abroad and stay with a man.'

'And?'

'Mr Mountjoy, we have our reputation to consider. It may be

acceptable to you that the boy should keep this kind of company, but . . .'

'What kind of company? Just what are you suggesting?'

'I'm not suggesting anything. The school's position is that we cannot under any circumstances take back a boy who has been involved in this kind of sexual escapade, and so publicly.'

'What?'

'Please don't shout, Mr Mountjoy. The headmaster is completely unequivocal on this point. Any hint of impropriety of this kind is a gift to the press, as you can see. It does irreparable harm to the good name of our school.'

'What about Thomas's good name? What about your complete lack of care, so that he was able to be off and out of the country before any of you noticed he wasn't around? And do you actually believe this garbage in the press? How can you take any notice of such crap?'

'Mr Mountjoy, put yourself in my position. All over Britain people are reading that one of our boys, with aristocratic connections . . .'

'Oh, what a lot of bloody nonsense.'

'. . . is hiding out in a gay love nest in an Italian paradise.'

'You must have had experience of the press. You must know that not one word in ten bears any resemblance to the truth.'

Austin Vaulx's voice moved from PR smarmy to the grave. 'Unfortunately, this report is confirmed by one of our boys.'

'Yes? Perhaps the one wandering around the junior boys' corridor at midnight? Did he tell you the name of this monster that Thomas is supposed to be shacked up with?'

'No, and I don't want to know.'

'Thomas is presently staying in Italy, with family friends,' said Valdemar, his nose stretching across the room. 'Heterosexual friends, since your mind seems to run on sordid lines. Married people with grown-up children, all of impeccable reputations, all of whom would be amazed to know that anyone could take this nonsense in the press seriously.'

'Ah,' said Austin Vaulx.

'And my wife has flown out to join Thomas and make sure he is all right; she will be making a stay of some days there with our friends.'

Silence.

'That does put a very different perspective on matters,' said Austin Vaulx, now sounding a trifle nervous. 'Of course, if this were true . . .'

'It is true,' said Valdemar. 'And when the papers get through to me, which they will in the end, I shall tell them something else which is true, that Thomas ran away from Gryme because he was deeply unhappy and had been severely bullied. Goodbye, Mr Vaulx.'

Valdemar slammed the phone down and looked up to see Virginia Luthier at the door. She regarded him thoughtfully. 'You're in a mess, Val,' she remarked dispassionately. 'Again.' She nodded towards the telephone. 'Was any of that true, by the way?'

'No,' he said frankly. 'I don't know where Thomas is. He's apparently all right, according to the brief telephone messages he left at the castle. I did wonder if he might have joined up with Sylvester; I do vaguely remember something about him going to Italy after America. I'd be glad if Thomas were with Sylvester, but I wouldn't want the world's press to find out about it. I don't think he is, though, because he would have come clean about it; nothing underhand about Sylvester.'

'Unlike some other people,' said Virginia caustically. 'What a naughty world we live in. And Magdalena? *Is* she in Italy with Thomas?'

'I haven't a clue,' said Valdemar shortly. 'She could have run off with the postman for all I know, why the hell doesn't she get in touch? I had a polite letter from her this morning, posted before she buggered off, I suppose, saying that she felt Thomas needed support. Support! If she knows where Thomas is, why doesn't she tell me? It's all bloody annoying.'

'Has Thomas been bullied?'

Valdemar gave a careless shrug. 'How do I know? One usually is at school, you have to put up with it, learn to cope, that's what life's all about.'

'You were bullied at school, so why shouldn't Thomas be?' said Virginia.

'Not after I grew, I wasn't,' said Valdemar with a short laugh. 'Thomas is quite tall for his age, but hardly full-grown. Of course, it was when you were at school that your mother ran off to South America, wasn't it? Because of your father's philandering?'

'Mind your own business, Virginia,' said Valdemar in warning tones.

'No good threatening me, Val,' said Virginia imperturbably. 'So what are you going to do about it? Your family seems to be dribbling away fast. Of course, you've always got Veronica to comfort you, haven't you? And then there's that pretty little thing, what's her name? Oh, yes, Belle. How sweet.'

'Damn you, Virginia.'

Valdemar jostled some pieces of paper about on his desk. 'I'm going north,' he said abruptly. 'I'm worried about those twins, that girl of Magdalena's is pretty hopeless.'

'I thought Thea was there as well.'

'God knows, apparently *her* mother's done a flit now; she's probably in Italy as well by now; everybody else seems to be there. I don't suppose Thea will stay long, and anyway, she's only a child herself.'

'Twenty-three, if I'm not mistaken.'

'Really? I thought she was just out of school. It makes no difference, it isn't her problem. No, I'll have to go and get something sorted out, what a bore it all is. Still, I can go and have a word with the Dean while I'm there, I don't trust that man.'

'You do that,' said Virginia. 'Nasty fogs up there, I gather. Don't lose your way in a sea-fret, Val, will you?'

'It's so peaceful,' said Magdalena, leaning against the stone balustrade which ran round the courtyard garden. A fountain splashed at the centre of the garden. White walls rose to a second storey and the sun bounced off them, dappling through the palm trees on to the dry ground.

'Is Thomas right? Was this a Saracen house?'

'Oh, yes. Hence the rather Arab style to this inner garden. You can see traces in the shape of some of the doors and windows, too. Later occupants obviously kept the style, and when Ferenc bought the house from my father, years and years ago, he carried on the tradition.'

'He likes it here?'

'Loves it. It's so peaceful.'

In the distance a door slammed, and a voice echoed round the walls. 'God-damned madman, how the heck does he think anybody could play this?'

'Ferenc,' said Carla in resigned tones.

'Feeling peaceful,' commented Magdalena.

'One lives in hope,' said Carla, looking round enquiringly at the enraged pianist as he stormed into the garden. He waved his music furiously at them.

'Look at this. Look at it! Pages of garbage, no sense to it at all. Unplayable, and if you could play it, no one in their senses would want to listen.'

'Marcus's new work?' asked Carla.

'And how.'

Thomas slid through a doorway and joined them, eyes full of interest. 'Why are you shouting?'

'Do you understand it?' said Ferenc. 'Only a musician could appreciate what I have to go through.'

Thomas took the manuscript pages from Ferenc's hand and flipped over a few pages. 'Wow,' he said. 'We used to sing some pretty weird things at the Cathedral, but this is seriously peculiar.'

Ferenc frowned. 'Of course, you are a musician. Mind you, I bet you never had to sing anything like this.'

'No way. Sprain your tonsils, this would. And if that's a cello line, I don't think Sylvester's going to be very keen. How do you know when to come in?' he asked, fascinated by a violin part which involved improvising on three unconnected notes with the instruction 'At any speed'. 'I mean, does the violinist wink at you, or what?'

'God knows,' said Ferenc resentfully. 'I can't think why I agreed to this. The last work we did of his was a horror, and I can see he's refined his style.'

'Then why do it?' said Thomas with interest. 'I mean, you don't have to, do you?'

Ferenc gave a dramatic sigh. 'One needs to work with contemporary composers. We must play the music of our time, it's our duty. I just wish that the particular music of our time wasn't written by Marcus Mordaunt. He isn't what you'd call an accessible composer.'

'He's a perfectly charming man,' Carla told Magdalena. 'He's on a crusade to get all nursery rhymes abolished. Reckons that if children don't listen to those tunes when they are little, their ears won't be familiar with tonality, and so they'll like atonal music.'

Magdalena found that very amusing. 'Such as his.'

'Exactly. He wants tunes banned. By law. But he's all right once he's had a glass or two of wine.'

'He sounds a character.'

'Stay for a while, and you'll be able to meet him. He's coming to work with Ferenc and the others on his new piece.'

'Huh,' said Ferenc. 'I hope Sylvester's bringing a cello he doesn't need any more, because by the time he's banged and honked his way through this, his cello won't be fit for anything.'

'Sounds fun,' said Thomas buoyantly.

7

Lost.

This is completely ridiculous, thought Valdemar, peering through the windscreen into a wall of clammy fog. Perfectly clear, and then suddenly this blows up. He shivered and rubbed his hands to warm them. Where was he? For God's sake, this was summer, it should be light until all hours, and here he was, unable to see a yard in front of his nose.

He must have missed the crossroads where he should have turned right to go up the hill to Mountjoy and the castle. So if he turned round and went back, he would come to the crossroads again. He let the window down and peered out, feeling the fog creeping over him, fingering him with its clammy nastiness. There was a strong smell of sea in the air, he couldn't remember a haar like this since his childhood. This was the second one this week, too; what the hell was wrong with the weather?

And here he was, stuck in this evil fog, while Magdalena had swanned off to God knows where. Italy? Rome? Of course he, personally, had no desire to go to any such place, such cities were too hot, too full of revolting tourists and noisy locals and you had to stay in someone else's house, or in a hotel. Complete waste of time and money, when you could be spending the time sensibly in a northern castle.

Nonetheless, he felt resentful. Magdalena was probably warm and comfortable, he was not. And, he reminded himself, working up to a temper, she wouldn't be at the castle when he finally got there. No kind welcome, probably no fires, and if Mrs Grobbins had been at work in the kitchen, nothing fit to eat, either. That girl who looked after the twins, whatshername, she couldn't cook except horried messes for the children. Perhaps George's girl was a whizz in the kitchen; judging by the way George had been stoking up in the club, it seemed unlikely.

It was so cold, and so quiet. If Valdemar had been affected by such things, the eeriness of the silence would have got to him. As it was, it simply added to his annoyance. Lost! Two miles from the castle, in country he knew like the back of his own hand. It was too bad.

Valdemar had excellent hearing, and in the middle of his growing if impotent rage, he could hear a distinct chug chug.

Tractor, he thought. And then, hell, it will probably run into me. He groped for the controls to make sure the fog lights were on, not that they cast much light in this kind of weather. It was enough to be visible, though, and the chugs became slower as they got louder.

'You all right, there?' enquired a familiar face.

'No, I'm not, don't be so bloody stupid,' said Valdemar.

'Ah, hello, Mr Mountjoy. Wasn't expecting you to be out here. You're on the wrong road if you're heading for the castle.'

It was Jack. Well, at least he must know where he was. 'I missed the turning,' he said shortly.

'Ay, that you did. No point in going back, you'll miss it again, mortal thick it is down there. You follow me, and I'll take you along to the road by Gossiby. That's your best way from here. Take a bit longer, like, but you'll know where you are.'

He rumbled past Valdemar's car. Valdemar, giving in with a bad grace, started his engine and began the slowest journey he had made in years.

By the time he finally reached the castle he was in one of his more thunderous moods. He pushed open the door, threw his bag down and shouted for attention.

In centuries past, minions would have hurled themselves out of doors and come running from kitchens, stables, bedchambers, at such a roar. In these decadent times he was rewarded by Lottie's anxious face peering down from the landing.

'I can't come down,' she said. 'Helena's on the toilet, and she'll need a hand, she's a terror with the paper.'

'What?'

'I think Mrs Grobbins is in the kitchen,' she added helpfully.

The kitchen? Mrs Grobbins? He'd known this was what would happen. It was all Magdalena's fault.

Mrs Grobbins was indeed in the kitchen.

'Why didn't you answer when I called?' said Valdemar, glowering. Mrs Grobbins took no notice, she never took any notice of Valdemar's little moods, as she called them.

'Because I was minding my beans.'

'Beans! Where's that girl, the Fimbul one, George's daughter? Is she still here, or has she flounced off to Italy as well?'

'She hasn't,' said a voice behind him. 'Although the temptation is great.'

Valdemar swung round and saw a slim girl with a lot of coppery hair, who was coolly extending her hand.

'I'm Thea, and you must be Valdemar. We have met, although some time ago, so I don't suppose you remember me very well.'

Valdemar looked her over with critical eyes. 'Hmm, you were a scrubby schoolgirl then, I seem to remember.'

'No more,' said Thea.

'No,' said Valdemar. Far from scrubby, this was a very appealing young woman. Fancy George engendering anything like this, what a surprise. And Agatha was no beauty, although he knew a lot of people found her very attractive. His grim look vanished, and a smile transformed his features.

'I'm delighted to meet you again, and I'm very grateful to you for holding the fort here. I'll just go upstairs and change, and then I'll be fit for company, and I can offer you a drink. Ten minutes in the drawing-room, shall we say?'

'Coo,' said Thea, as he banged the door shut behind him. She relaxed and abandoned her gracious look. 'Some man.'

Mrs Grobbins shook her head as she reached for the Bisto. 'Not to be trusted, that one, not an inch. And I can see he likes the look of you, you just be careful. Gobble you up before you know where you are.'

'No way,' said Thea. 'I can see his charm, but I don't go for older men.' Besides, she thought, I've heard all about you from Mum, and I'm not going to be chewed up and spat out by you. Still, it explains why Magdalena stays with him. 'No, Mrs Grobbins, let's slop some wine in, I'm sure that'll taste better than gravy powder.'

'There's someone on the phone for you, Magdalena,' said Carla. 'A woman,' she added quickly, seeing both Magdalena and Thomas stiffen.

Magdalena perched herself on the beautiful but uncomfortable seventeenth-century chair by the phone, relishing the feel of marble under her bare feet. 'Hello?'

'Magdalena? It's Agatha.'

'Agatha! However did you find me? Why are you calling? Where are you?'

'My dear, I'm here.'

'Where's here?'

'On this wonderful island, such bliss, such warmth, such colour, such good-looking men, I'd forgotten how wonderful they are, with those sparkling white vests.'

'What? Here?'

'Just off the hydrofoil, I've run away from George. I'll explain when I see you, can you come down? I need to find a hotel.'

'Of course, hold on, have you enough coins?'

'Gettoni, darling, yes, masses, I'm in a wonderful bar.'

Magdalena left the phone hanging and ran back to where Carla was chatting to Thomas. 'Carla, a hotel, which one? An old friend is ringing, she's here, on the island.'

'An old friend? Then she must come here.'

Magdalena protested, Carla insisted, and, in order to save Agatha's gettoni, Magdalena gave in.

'If she's just come off the hydrofoil, then Sylvester may be there, tell her to look out for him.'

'Agatha, is Sylvester there?'

'Sylvester? Are you mad? Why should . . . ?' Her voice rose to a delighted shriek. 'Good gracious, yes, he is, he's just come out on to the street at this exact moment. How amazing.'

'No, it's not amazing,' said Magdalena. 'He's come to work with Ferenc. Share a taxi, if you can both fit in.'

'I'll try,' said Agatha. 'He's got a mountain of luggage though, and his cello, of course. What fun, I'll see you very soon, then. Bye!'

'What I want to know is,' said George crossly, 'how she got the money to go to Italy.'

Thea was surprised at this. 'Pa, it's hardly a world cruise with all the extras, just a flight to Italy.'

'Your mother shouldn't have been able to afford the bus fare to Eyot, let alone planes to the continent. And where's she proposing to stay when she gets there? What will happen when they discover her credit card is no longer valid?'

An awful suspicion was dawning in Thea's head. 'Pa, you didn't.'

'Didn't what?'

'Stop all her cards, cut off her funds.'

'Indeed I did.'

Pause.

'You, Pa, are a scumbag,' said Thea in her clearest and chilliest tones. 'You are unbelievable, a primitive, you belong in the ark. How could you do such a thing?'

'It makes a lot of sense,' said George huffily. 'If she hasn't got any money, then she'll have to come back home where she belongs.'

'Pa!'

'Oh, I dare say you have all kinds of modern views on wives and freedom and I don't know what. But I'm not putting up with it.'

'I think it was a completely stupid thing to do, apart from being extremely mean. And not very effective, either.'

'Why not?'

'Well, she must have had some money tucked away, or borrowed it or something. Because she's gone, and that's that. I expect she hocked some jewels.'

George gave a howl of anguish. 'Jewels! Don't mention that word.'

Thea sighed. 'Pa, you are behaving incredibly badly. I offered to come to Mountjoy and try and coax her back, because I miss her, too. But now I'm glad she's gone, and I wouldn't advise her to go back home under any circs.'

'Now listen, Thea.'

'No, and I'm not coming back, either, at least not for some time. And don't you for one moment think that you can blackmail me by cutting off my allowance. I have a perfectly good salary, and I don't need anything from you. And don't try to ring me again. Goodbye.'

Sylvester made his way to the terrace, wonderfully attired in baggy shorts and a gigantic and colourful shirt. 'You are so big,' Carla said as he manoeuvred his way round some little tables.

'Yes, and look, it isn't flab,' said Thomas helpfully, pinching Sylvester's forearm. 'Feel those muscles.'

'Impudent boy,' said Sylvester amiably. He was indeed a very big man; tall and muscular as well as comfortably covered.

'Are you tired, Sylvester?' asked Magdalena, shading her eyes from the sun as she looked at him with affection.

'Not at all,' said Sylvester expansively. He was possessed of huge energy and stamina, and was quite unfazed by a journey which would have left a lesser man exhausted.

'Did you fly from New York?' asked Carla.

'Yes. I had a few hours to spare in Rome; useful, because there was a man I wanted to see at the Vatican. Then I took a plane across to Sicily, hopped on the hydrofoil and here I am. If that's Perroni you've got there, Carla, I will have one. Thank you,' he said, downing the chilled light beer in a few swift gulps. 'Wonderful.' He gave a sigh and stretched his legs out. 'Delighted to see you here, Magdalena, come after Thomas, I suppose.'

'Yes.'

'So when are you going back?'

A worried look came over Magdalena's face. 'Goodness knows. I can't be away for more than a day or two. I've left the twins at the castle and Val's busy in London; I shouldn't be here at all. And Sylvester, he doesn't know where I am.'

'Good for you,' said Sylvester. 'Time you jolted Val out of his complacent ways. If you aren't there, he'll realize how much he misses you.'

'If he notices,' said Magdalena.

Agatha, refreshed after a shower, came on light feet to join them. 'I feel one hundred per cent better,' she said. 'Carla, thank you for your hospitality, nothing like having unexpected guests rolling up, but I'm so glad to be here. This place is heaven. You can't possibly go back yet, Magdalena. Such a waste, to come all this way and then not take the time to enjoy it.'

'You're looking peaky, Magdalena,' said Sylvester. 'Some time in the sun, a spot of bathing, plenty of rest and relaxation, that's what you need. Put a bit of zip back in you.'

Thomas spoke up. 'You can go back if you like, Magdalena, but I'm not coming. If you try to make me, I'll run away again.'

'None of that,' said Sylvester, his voice kind enough, but quite definite. 'Don't threaten Magdalena, she's got enough to cope with.'

'I know,' said Thomas. 'But I'm not going back to that school.'

'Doubt if they'll have you,' said Sylvester comfortably. 'All over the papers; they won't like that, not if I know those schoolmasters, pack of old women.'

'In the papers?' said Thomas with interest. 'Did you bring one with you?'

'I did not,' said Sylvester. 'Suffice it to say, I think Gryme is going to have to rub along without you.'

'Then we can stay,' said Thomas. 'Great.'

'Thomas, you still have to have an education,' said Magdalena.

'Education can wait,' said Thomas with certainty. 'This is life. And I can learn lots of Italian, think how useful.'

Agatha was sitting upright and alert on a folding chair. 'Now, Magdalena, I have a plan. I'm going to find a house to rent near here. A good-sized one, don't ask me how I'm going to pay for it, probably sell my engagement ring. But then there'll be room for you and Thomas.'

'Sell your ring?' said Magdalena, startled. Agatha and George had never been short of money.

'Magdalena can stay here as long as she wants,' said Carla. 'And you, too, Agatha, we have so much room.'

Magdalena shook her head. 'I can't leave the children for long.'

'Why not? You've got a perfectly good nanny, haven't you? Or has Val offended her?'

'He has not, Sylvester, he hardly knows she's there. Lottie's very good, but she needs an eye kept on her.'

'If she can't do the job, you should employ someone who can.'

'I'm worried about Helena, she's got a horrid cough she can't throw off, imagine how I'd feel if it gets worse.'

'Why should it?'

'And besides, I miss them.'

'Now, that's a perfectly sensible reason for wanting to be with them,' said Sylvester. 'Forget the rest of it, it's just fuss. Understandable, but unnecessary.'

Thomas crouched down beside Magdalena. 'I miss the twins, too,' he said. 'So why don't you get Lottie to bring them out here? The warmth would put Helena's hacks right in no time. And I'd teach them to swim in the sea, it'd be awfully good for them.'

'Impossible,' said Magdalena. But wouldn't it be a pleasure? she thought, briefly closing her eyes. Such an enchanted island, what a perfect place for children, so good for them. And no Val, she remembered, her eyes flying open as she realized that that was what she chiefly wanted, not to have to see Val.

Valdemar wasn't worried about Magdalena, of course he wasn't. It was inconvenient, her being away, that was all. Certainly, she had no business charging off like that, it was dramatic and pointless. She was over-reacting, in his opinion, but she'd come to her senses pretty soon. She won't be able to manage on her own, wherever she's gone, he told himself with some satisfaction.

He wasn't going to waste time thinking about it, he had plenty to occupy him. It wasn't even as though Thomas were her son, he told himself again as he shaved. The whole business was over the top.

Meanwhile, here was this pretty young thing, he would take her out to dinner, Ghercombes, perhaps. Valdemar never minded who saw him dining out with whom; give them something to gossip about if it makes them happy, was his attitude. And she lived and worked in London, how useful, how pleasant, plenty of opportunity to see more of her.

'No,' said Thea. 'The fog's far too thick, we'd get lost, and I hate the cold. There are plenty of things in the freezer, and Mrs Grobbins has made a stew, she'd be offended if we didn't eat it. Besides, Lottie hates being here on her own.'

Valdemar was speechless. He had experience of Mrs Grobbins's stews. She added what she called a 'tunnip, for a nice bit of flavour', if he remembered rightly. What she thought of as a turnip any normal human being would know as a mangel-wurzel. Sheep food, thought Val furiously.

He flung himself bad-temperedly into a chair by the fire. 'Oh, very well,' he said. 'Granted, this bloody haar is a problem . . . but never mind. I've got to get to Eyot tomorrow, though, I'm seeing the Dean.'

'Are you religious?' enquired Thea. It seemed unlikely, but you never knew with his generation.

'He is consulting me professionally. He wants to remove the choir screen.'

Thea was hazy on cathedrals, but even she could smell trouble in that. 'The choir screen? Isn't that very old and so on?'

'Bits of it are, but it was heavily restored. The Dean says it should go, and he's got the Church Heritage people eating out of his hand, so he'll probably get his way. Wants to open up the nave, right through to the high altar. Says it shouldn't be blocked from the congregation.'

'Ah,' said Thea. She thought for a moment. 'Doesn't the organ in Eyot sit up near the choir screen?'

'The organ loft,' said Valdemar grimly, 'is situated over the choir screen. It also is Victorian, as is the organ. Out with the lot of them, says the good Dean.'

'You have to have an organ in a cathedral, surely,' said Thea.

'Yes, but the Dean is a travelled Dean, and on his travels in the Far East he has come across an electronic organ. You can put it where you like, fix up a few speakers and there you are.'

'Not the same,' said Thea in a decided voice.

'You try and tell the Dean that. There's also the slight problem that if you take away the choir screen, which in Eyot acts as a brace, the whole central tower will probably collapse.'

'Coo. Does he want that?'

'Doesn't believe a word I say,' said Valdemar, shaking out the *Financial Times*. 'What do I know? I'm just the structural engineer.

Doubtless God is going to suspend the laws of gravity in order to keep this particular sacred edifice standing.'

'I should think God's got better things to do.'

'I'm sure he has. How's your drink?'

Carla was talking to Agatha with great enthusiasm. 'Little domed houses,' she said. 'Very characteristic of this island, it's the Arabs again, you see, and they still build them like that. Now, come with me, and I'll show you. We use them as guest houses, no, please, we are putting Sylvester and Gabriel in one, and Marcus Mordaunt – do you know him, the composer? – is the only other guest we are expecting until much later in the summer. If you can persuade Magdalena to stay, it would be good for her, I believe. She doesn't look well.'

'She looks awful,' said Agatha. 'Much better here, with a couple of seas between her and her husband. Have you ever met him?'

'No. My father knew her last husband, he says.'

'Hugo. Yes. Well, Val's his nephew, and he's giving Magdalena a hard time. He's a bit younger than she is, and what with one thing and another . . . Anyway, a bit of time to herself wouldn't do Magdalena any harm. She needs to think, get her life back on course.'

Magdalena wandered out of the gate at the far end of the villa's grounds, up the steep street and past the high, narrow painted doorways, each with a pot or urn of dazzling flowers balanced above it. The white painted street ended and turned into a sandy track, still climbing. Magdalena went on steadily, catching breathtaking views of the sea as the path turned and twisted. She was heading for a little bosky of pines she had seen from the house. There, the sun was dispersed and its heat diminished, the ground was soft and silent, the air still and heavy with resin.

On course, she thought bitterly. What is on course? The dutiful life of wife left to mind home and hearth, bring up her babies, while her husband lived exactly the life he liked, the same life he had lived before he had married.

Why had he got married? Magdalena often wondered about

that. Had he been in love with her at all? Was it the longing to hold on to the castle that he would no longer inherit because of her children? Did he have vague paternal feelings, a desire to play a part in the lives of the children he had so casually fathered, children that in the eyes of the world were the offspring of her second husband, not Val's?

Guilt, never far from the surface these days, crept over Magdalena, tensing her muscles, making her throat dry. Had Hugo realized that the children she was expecting weren't his? Had he ever suspected it, knowing that the chances of his fathering children were so small, and he had never managed it before, neither with his first wife nor in his second and seemingly happy marriage.

Why had she had that fling in London with Valdemar? Face it, she told herself honestly. It was because she had been reaching her mid-forties and wanted the reassurance of a dashing lover. And because she had always found Val attractive, for so many of the same reasons that she had fallen for his uncle. How could she regret an affair that had brought her the children she longed for, and had given up hoping for? And to have had two, a boy and a girl, at the age of forty-five. It still seemed like a miracle.

I do miss them, she thought, idly tracing a pattern in the little heap of pine needles beside her. How they would love it here, they could come up to this wood and have a picnic. They could bathe.

Why not? She could stay, and she longed to do so; perhaps here, away from all the daily ties, she could achieve some kind of equilibrium. And Thomas could come to terms with life, they could decide what he was going to do once his shattered confidence was built up a little.

Sylvester had taken her aside, told her she mustn't take him back to England yet. 'The boy's a bundle of nerves,' he had said, sounding almost angry. It was a rarity for Sylvester to sound angry. 'What have you done to him, Val and the school and all of you?'

She owed it to Thomas. He had trusted her, she couldn't let him down.

Her mind drifted to practicalities. Lottie could fly out with the twins. They'd have grown out of their summer things, and the summer in England hadn't been warm enough for them to need any light clothes so far this year. Lottie could take them shopping in Eyot, she'd enjoy that. Hats, they'd need hats. And sun cream, the sort that kept everything out. And sandals.

Come to think of it, she needed some clothes. Clothes for hot weather; she had come out with a single bag and little more than a change of clothes. She could wander down into the town this afternoon, with Agatha. It was a long time since she had done anything like that, to please herself.

I wonder how Val is managing, she thought inconsequentially. I wonder where he is now. What he's doing.

The twins shot through the door, splashes of green in their matching pyjamas, and hurled themselves on to Valdemar. The *Financial Times* fell to the floor in a scrumpled heap, the immaculate hair was ruffled, eager little fingers tugged at the expensive pullover.

'Get off,' said Valdemar, winded.

'Daddy,' shrieked Helena, who had the pole position close to his ear. 'Daddy, look at me.'

Valdemar's face was remorselessly tugged round so that he could observe the tiger on her pyjama top. 'It roars and it bites and it's stripy and strong, and I chose it because it's just like you.'

Hugh tugged with less science but equal determination. 'I got an E-phant,' he announced. 'Bigger than everything else, he's the boss of the jungle.'

'Um,' said Valdemar, half-throttled by the fist clenching his shirt collar.

Lottie came into the room, trying to look efficient. 'Give over now,' she said half-heartedly. 'They're very pleased to see you, Mr Mountjoy.'

Valdemar was blowing raspberries on Hugh's fat little tummy at the same time as tickling Helena's bare feet; the squeals and bellows were deafening.

'Time for bed,' said Lottie, in the tradition of her type of nanny, with an instinctive distrust of children letting rip with their parents.

Hot, flushed faces stared at her in indignation. 'No way,' said Helena pertly, burying her head in Valdemar's shoulder.

'Me neither,' said Hugh, holding tightly on to the nearest knee.

'Daddy's going to read us our bedtime story, aren't you, Daddy?' declared Helena in a cajoling voice. Her dark eyes looked intently and reproachfully at him, so like Magdalena, thought Valdemar. His throat tightened. Bloody woman, he thought, how can she just go off like that? Leaving her children, it isn't natural.

Thea was watching him, interested to see a different man now that the controlled mask had slipped for a moment. She wouldn't have put him down as one to tolerate children; yet they clearly adored him, and there was more than a tinge of besottedness about him, if she wasn't mistaken. Pity he could love children so easily and naturally and yet seemed determined to walk all over his wife with complete insensitivity.

Valdemar stood up, balancing one child on his hip and flopping the other over his shoulder.

'I will read them their bedtime story, if you'll excuse me,' said Valdemar. 'I have learned from bitter experience that it's best just to do what they want and get it over with quickly. Their capacity for persisting with a request and arguing about anything and everything is far more than I can deal with. Pour yourself another drink. Come along, brats, let's make it *The Jungle Book.*'

'Great,' said Hugh, casting a wicked and triumphant look at Lottie, who stood stiffly at the door.

'Night night, Lottie,' said Helena as she swept past.

'No good will come of this,' said Lottie darkly. 'I feel it in my bones.'

8

'So what I'd like you to do, Lottie,' went on Magdalena, 'is to buy them each some summer clothes, use some of the money I left with you. I'm ringing the travel agent, and they'll see to the tickets. You'll fly direct to Palermo, in Sicily, and . . .'

There was a wail at the northern end of the line. 'I can't.'

'Can't what?'

'Bring them. On a plane.'

'Pull yourself together, Lottie. It's hardly difficult. I'll come across on the hydrofoil and meet you at the airport in Palermo, what could be simpler? Now, their passports are in the bureau in my room.'

'No, you don't understand.' The wail grew louder. 'I don't do abroad.'

Magdalena held the receiver away from her ear and looked at it in disbelief. She shook it, and spoke again. 'I can't hear you very clearly.'

'I don't do abroad. I did mention it when you interviewed me for the job, and you said that was okay, you didn't believe in carting children off here, there and everywhere; they were better off in their own home.'

'Well, yes, perhaps I did say that, but this is different. I'm planning to spend some time out here, and I think it would be very good for Helena's chest, after such a cold winter. And with the terrible summer in England this year, I'm sure it would do you good as well, Lottie. Think of it, warm sea, lovely beaches, and it seems quite a lively place,' she added cunningly.

'I'm not that sort of girl,' said Lottie with an outraged sniff. 'And it's no good, I'm not going to foreign parts. I went to France once, on a school trip, and that was quite enough for me, thank you very much.'

'What do you suppose happened on her school trip?' asked Sylvester with interest when he heard about Lottie's strange reaction. 'Mind you, doesn't surprise me, I always thought that girl was a bit lacking.'

'She's very highly qualified,' said Magdalena defensively.

'Yes, and great with the twins, I grant you, but a bit lacking in get-up-and-go.'

'Sylvester, dear,' said Agatha, 'get-up-and-go is just what you don't want in a nanny. Think about it. You want plenty of sit-down-and-stay. We never had a nanny, fortunately, because when mine were little we didn't have two pennies to rub together, that was before George got rich. So I brought them up myself, and it does make me laugh when I see people's lives revolving around creatures like this Lottie.'

Magdalena had forgotten Agatha's days of early motherhood. Although they were of an age, Agatha had had her children when she was in her early twenties, and Magdalena had marvelled at her haphazard but seemingly successful way of raising her offspring.

'That's all very well,' said Sylvester, 'and of course you did a splendid job, look at Edmund.'

'Sylvester,' said Magdalena warningly.

'Edmund will grow out of his pomposity in due course,' said Agatha airily. 'It's just a phase.'

'Magdalena's old to have twins, and she'd be on her knees if she tried to bring them up the way you did. Maybe when they go off to school she can do it all herself, but not at the moment.'

'Why aren't they at school, by the way, darling?' Agatha asked. 'They're huge.'

'They aren't five yet,' said Magdalena. 'They'll start in September, at the village school, and yes, then things will be easier. Of course, I can look after them myself, but it means going back to England to get them, if Lottie won't come. And they do take an awful lot of entertaining.'

'Listen, if those children are coming,' said Sylvester, 'and I'm all for it, then they're coming with expert help. I'd as soon have a herd of wild pigs about the place as those two running free. Nothing personal, Magdalena, you understand, but they're little savages, like all children.'

Magdalena opened her mouth to protest, thought about her precious babies, and shut it again. It was true, they were noisy and difficult, and they could be a great nuisance if you weren't used to them. 'Although I suppose I shouldn't think about my own children like that.'

'Not at all,' said Agatha. 'Realism is necessary, otherwise they've got you where they want you, and that's the one place you never want to be. Now, we must have a good think, there has to be an answer.'

Carla joined them. 'Phone for you, Agatha; your daughter who, I must say, sounds so charming.'

'Darling! Where are you? Is everything all right?'

'Mum, I'm at Mountjoy Castle.'

Agatha was so surprised she nearly let the phone drop. 'No! But why?'

'I came looking for you, and stayed on a bit.'

'Darling, how did you find my number?'

'Actually, I thought Magdalena might know where you were, and there's this Italian number which was on a pad here. I rang, and that nice person who answered said you were there, too. Bingo!'

'Thea, tear that page out of the pad. I'd forgotten all about it, but Val mustn't see it.'

'He would have seen it by now if I hadn't already torn it off, Mum. No flies on me.'

'Who's there with you?' said Agatha suspiciously.

'Mrs Grobbins, who says she does, but seems to run the place. A girl called Lottie, who looks after the twins.'

'I know Lottie. Go on.'

'And Valdemar.'

'Valdemar! Thea, that's most unwise. Besides, what about work?'

'Week off, Mum, don't fret.'

'I've known Val for years, and I don't trust him an inch.'

'No, nor do I, but he's quite something, isn't he?'

'Hmm. Charming, is he? Be very careful, darling, I can't tell you how wickedly clever and dangerous that man is.'

'Never mind, he's far too old for me. Now, listen, the aforesaid Valdemar's in rather a pet just now.'

Agatha blinked. She had known Val in many moods, but she couldn't visualize him in a pet. 'Darling, are you sure?'

'Oh, yes. Shouting and fuming, generally fairly upset. With Magdalena. Lottie says Magdalena's asked her to take the twins to a Place Abroad, but she won't go. Mum, what does she think happens in other countries?'

'Never mind that. Why is Val cross with Magdalena? Why not with Lottie for disobeying orders?'

'He's furious with Magdalena for not being here, for a start. He clearly feels abandoned and neglected.'

'Val? With his harem? No, I didn't say that.'

'And now he says there's no way he's going to let her take the twins out of the country, especially since she won't say where Magdalena is.'

'Ah.'

'He seems to get away with far too much, that man. Anyway, while he was carrying on, Lottie was wailing and keening, and she let slip that Magdalena had asked her to find the children's passports. So, clever me, I nipped into Magdalena's sitting-room and removed them. You should see the photos in them, Mum, they're so sweet.'

'Yes, yes, but does Val know what you've done?'

'No, in fact it's calmed him down, the passports not being there when he went hurtling in to get them. He reckons that that's fixed Magdalena. No passports, no travel.'

'I suppose he does have some say in whether his children should go abroad or not,' said Agatha doubtfully.

'That's just it, Mum, he doesn't. He isn't their father, is he?'

'Oh, but he . . . Ah. No, I see what you mean.'

'He's married to their mother, but he can't legally have anything to do with them. Only Magdalena does.'

'Do you know, you must be right. I've never thought about it, things being as they are.'

'As they are? What do you mean?'

'Oh, Val being quite fatherly towards them, that's all,' said Agatha hastily.

'He is, isn't he? In fact, he's quite a sweetie when he's with them.'

'Don't start having any warm feelings of any kind towards that man,' said Agatha. 'Well done, purloining the passports, but if that silly Lottie is going to dig her rather large feet in, I don't see what can be done.'

'Listen, Mum, I've got a plan.'

Dido was in bed with Fritz. Usually she quite liked being in bed with Fritz, but today she found him tiresome. 'Get off,' she said, pushing at him with her elbows.

'Dido,' he said, smothering her with kisses.

'Oh, do get off,' she said, this time rolling herself away.

Frustrated and cross, he sat up, his hands folded under his armpits, staring at her.

'Why did you do that?'

'I'd had enough,' said Dido, who was on the other side of the room, tugging on her skintight jeans. She pulled her polo neck over her head in a quick masculine movement; Fritz watched regretfully as her breasts vanished from sight.

'Tomorrow then?'

'Nope. I'm busy.' She swept up the ten-pound notes from the table. 'Ta.'

'When then?'

'I'll ring. When I get back. Some time.'

'Dido! Where are you going?'

Bang, and then clatter clatter down the stairs, a pause, a thump as Dido jumped down the last three steps. Another bang as she went out of the front door.

'Bugger,' said Fritz, rolling on to his stomach. 'So near and yet so far.'

'Sorry,' said Dido. She had all but pushed a tall man, who was waiting to cross, under the wheels of a bus as she walked at speed along Marylebone High Street.

He looked down at her through half-moon spectacles. 'Why, hello, Dido.'

'Oh, Christ,' said Dido in her uncouth way. 'Hi, Quarles.'

'I was going to ring you,' he said, falling into step beside her.

'I'm busy, Quarles. Off on me holidays.'

'Oh, hell, where are you going?'

'None of your business, nosey-parker.'

'Listen, Dido, I'm going to an island. An idyllic one, off Italy. Hotel, all expenses paid.'

'Good for you.'

'Good expenses. Enough for two.'

'I told you, I'm booked.'

'Who are you going with.'

Dido stopped and looked up at him, her mouth split in a wide grin. 'Threesome, Quarley-boy. Me, a bloke and girl.'

'That's disgusting,' said Quarles uneasily.

'Only because you've got a nasty mind. I'm going to Italy, too, maybe I'll see you there.'

'Italy's a big place,' said Quarles gloomily.

'Yeah, I'd heard.'

'When are you going?'

'Flying out tomorrow. I'm just on me way to get some new summer kit, got to be smart, see?'

'Come and have a coffee first. Or a peppermint tea. Whatever you want. Please.'

'At your flat? Not likely, mate, I'm in a hurry.' Then, quite suddenly, she took pity on Quarles; what a dejected face. She gave her throaty laugh. 'Come on, then, you silly sod. There's a caff over there, let's go.'

Val wasn't aware he was entertaining a snake in the grass, so he obligingly gave Thea a lift into Eyot.

'You'll have to make your own way back, though,' he said. 'I'm going straight on to London after I've seen the Dean.'

Good, thought Thea. Then he won't wonder why I've got bags marked Tots' World and Rainbow. I hope I get the sizes right. New territory, this.

'I hope the Dean comes to heel,' said Thea politely, blenching slightly as Valdemar roared past two tractors and the bus.

'Never know what a clergyman's going to do next,' grumbled

Valdemar. 'Minds all over the place, no training, no concentration; just a lot of woolly ideas.'

'I thought they were all very sharp these days.'

'Wouldn't last thirty seconds out in the big, cold world, most of them. These senior clergy haven't got anything like enough to do, so they start plotting and planning and getting up to mischief. Usually there's plenty of intrigue and skulduggery in the Chapter to keep them all busy, but now and again you get a loose cannon like this Dean.'

'Sounds fun,' said Thea.

Valdemar screeched to a halt at some traffic lights. 'How long are you going to stay here?'

'I have to be back at work next week,' said Thea evasively.

'I'll give you a ring,' said Valdemar. 'I owe you a dinner, I think we can do better than Mrs G's stew.'

'Thank you,' said Thea. 'I'll look forward to that.'

Liar, she said to herself, glancing at her list and wondering what muslins were, and what Magdalena wanted them for.

'Muslins? Of course. They come in packs of ten.'

'She said four packs,' said Thea doubtfully. 'It seems a lot, whatever are they for?'

'Oh, no children yourself, then? Wiping everything, mouths, work surfaces, bums . . . And then, we sell a lot in the summer for people travelling. Invaluable for spillages, car-sickness, even impromptu mosquito nets.'

'I see,' said Thea. What an arcane world childhood was. Thank goodness Dido's on for this, she thought. Clearly, you needed to be an expert. No way would I take these children anywhere; not even as far as the sweet shop.

'Tell me about this commission,' said Dido, biting into a hot doughnut and licking the warm jam from round her mouth.

Quarles sipped his black coffee in an austere fashion. 'Lots of money,' he said. 'It's for a Swiss mag, but I've sold the idea to America and the UK as well. Interview for a profile of a composer. It's going to be a big feature in one of the Sundays here.'

'Which composer?'

'You won't have heard of him,' said Quarles. 'He's very modern, not a popular composer at all. Marcus Mordaunt.'

'Oh, him,' said Dido, now licking her fingers; the sugary remains had left white patches on her dark purple nails. 'Discordant Mordaunt, as he's known in the trade.'

'You have heard of him, then.'

'Heard him, too,' said Dido.

'Why?' asked Quarles.

'Wanted to,' said Dido. 'Someone took me.'

'Who?' asked Quarles, bristling.

'No one you know,' said Dido matter of factly. 'Horrible!'

'The person who took you was horrible?'

'No,' said Dido. 'The music. Blooming awful, couldn't get my ears round that at all.'

'I thought you didn't like music.'

'I don't want to listen to all the same kind of music that you do, no. You can keep all that. I like music a lot, just not the kind you're interested in.'

'I have very wide tastes in music,' said Quarles, hurt.

'Yeah, but some of what you listen to is a bit outré for me. As for that Mordaunt bloke, what a joke. They pay him good money for that, do they?'

'Well, some money I suppose.'

Dido shook her head and stirred some more sugar into her milky coffee. 'So, you got to interview him? Bet he's a creep.'

'He's all right, actually,' said Quarles. 'A bit fanatical, but I've met worse.'

'So what's he doing in Italy? Why the island?'

'I'm flying to Rome, where he's been giving some lectures and classes. Then I'm driving him down to Sicily and he's going across to this island. He's staying with friends, I get my hotel paid for, and as much time as I need with him to do this piece.'

'Sicily, eh?' said Dido thoughtfully. 'Funny, that's where I'm going. To start with, anyhow. Might see you around, Quarles. Got to go now, don't get up to anything, will you? Here's for my coffee.'

Quarles knew better than to protest; Dido always paid her way. She paused by the door. 'What's he look like, this jingle-jangle bloke?'

'Not your type,' said Quarles quickly. 'Chunky, neck like a bull, slightly reddish hair. Looks like a bouncer.'

'Oh, great. Very artistic and aesthetic. How old is he?'

'About my age, I should think. Late twenties?'

'Is he straight?'

'I have no idea.'

''Spect you'll find out on your little drive if he isn't,' said Dido. *'Ciao.'*

'A friend of Thea's?' Magdalena wasn't sure she liked the sound of this.

'Yes, they shared a flat when Thea was at college. She's some kind of an artist now, but she trained as a nanny, children's nurse, whatever you call it. So that she could always earn some cash in vacs and so on.' Agatha blew on her nails and added an extra dab of varnish. 'Thea says she doesn't do much of it these days, she has other ways of earning money, apparently. No, she isn't a drug dealer or anything like that, what do you think Thea is?'

'No, I know Thea's all right, but a perfect stranger . . . The children might not take to her.'

'Not take to Dido? Fat chance, Magdalena, darling, children adore her, you won't get a look in. They think she's magic, and if she seems a bit weird, well, four-year-olds are pretty weird when you think about it. No, don't worry, she just clinks her dangly earrings at them; terrific, they eat out of her hand. Now, calm down. She's done temp work for several of my friends, and they all end up total converts. Dido's okay, you take it from me.'

'She doesn't sound a Lottie type.'

'So much the better, very dreary your Lottie. Dido's fun, she'll cope wonderfully with the children, give you a chance to have a holiday which you badly need, and there's nothing Val can say or do about it. Thea will take Dido to the airport, you can meet them at this end.' She reflected for a moment. 'You'd better get a message to Val, though, saying they're with you. In case he starts a hue and cry about kidnappers. Now, borrow a hat from Carla, darling; this sun's baking. We'll wander down to the harbour.'

Valdemar was wrapped in black thoughts as he waited to cross the road. If he was any judge of character, that blasted Dean was up to more than mere mischief. He shrugged his shoulders. What could he do? Bring half the Cathedral down, unfortunately. And then blame the Mountjoy Partnership for bad advice. Never mind that their report told him quite clearly it would be dangerous to do any such thing . . .

'Our architect advises us that there is no reason why the screen shouldn't come down.'

'What does an architect know about it?'

The Dean's foxy eyes narrowed. 'Are you impugning the professionalism of a distinguished colleague?'

'If he says it's safe to take that lot down, he's wrong.' Valdemar tried a spot of persuasion. 'Now, let's think about this clearly, Canon Higgs-Boson. Have you considered the outcry there's going to be when this plan becomes generally known? You really will be stirring up a hornet's nest.'

The Dean pursed his thin lips together. 'I am not afraid of opposition. I have been opposed much in my life of service, and I have to say, my opponents have usually got the worst of it. I have the authority to do what I want to do, and I am confident that it is feasible. I think an architect who has worked all his life with old churches and in cathedrals may be supposed to know as much as anyone.'

'No,' said Valdemar bluntly. 'It isn't a matter of architecture, it's a matter of stresses . . .'

He looked at the Dean's set face and gave up. 'On your head be it.'

'Thank you for coming to see me, Mr Mountjoy,' said the Dean with a lean smile. 'The chaplain is outside, he will show you out.'

Valdemar was more worried than he liked to admit. He wanted to get back to London, talk to the others, see what Virginia thought. Hell, they had given good advice, it was all in writing, young Hobhouse had done an impeccable piece of work. Take the screen out, and the tower would be in grave danger of falling down. A senior partner had checked the work, they were covered.

But if the damn thing collapsed, the firm would be held responsible to some extent. Valdemar was a realist and knew the way of the world. His firm had been the structural engineers on Eyot Cathedral works for many years; some of the blame for any disaster would certainly come their way. People would say they should have made their findings public, to prevent the Dean doing something so potentially destructive.

The Dean was far too astute for that. 'Your report is, of course, a confidential one, paid for by us, and it remains our property. You understand the consequences of breaching that confidentiality in any way, I feel quite sure.'

Meaning, don't bleat to the press. He wouldn't anyway. Bloody reporters, you couldn't trust them an inch, he thought, remembering what they had written about Thomas and the Mountjoy family. God, how he hated having that sprawled all over the papers.

No, it would have to be a word or two in the right places, what a bloody waste of time, what a nuisance. And Canon Higgs-Boson would cancel the contract for the cathedral business; Valdemar would mind that, he felt he had a personal stake in the Cathedral. He had been a chorister there as a boy, got married in a chapel there, Thomas had been in the choir there as well . . . What a bugger everything was.

'Hello, Val,' said a woman who had joined him at the kerb. She was pushing a youngster in a pushchair.

'Good God. Um, Heather, isn't it?'

Hers was a voice from the past; she had been Thomas's nanny, employed by Hortense to look after the boy while she went on the first of her ever more frequent trips to India.

Heather had left her job very suddenly; not surprising in the circumstances. Valdemar felt no trace of guilt, it had hardly been his fault. She'd been more than keen, if he remembered rightly.

'Yes, it's me. I've changed my hair colour, that's why you didn't recognize me. Come on, we can cross. How's Thomas? Oh, I was ever so sorry to read all that in the papers. Is it true?'

'No, of course not,' said Valdemar crossly.

'He was such a lovely boy. My Harry looks just like him, of course,' she added with a smile.

'Harry, yes, how is he?'

'He's doing great at school, into everything, real live wire,' she said with pride. 'My Neil's ever so proud of him, even though . . .'

She left the words unspoken.

'He must be, let me see, eight now?'

'Yes, that's right. Just gone up into the juniors. He's a clever boy, doing well at his school work.'

'I'm sure he is,' said Valdemar mechanically.

'Well, I must love you and leave you,' she said cheerfully. 'I hope all's well with you and Lady Mountjoy, Mrs Mountjoy, I should say. Poor lady, she's had a hard time, but lovely to have twins. Ta ra, Val.'

She bustled off, leaving an unbidden question about her Harry floating in Valdemar's mind. He had never set eyes on the boy, yet there he was, part of a family, probably out playing football with his putative father every Saturday.

Valdemar was furious with himself. Your wits are going, he thought. Bloody sentimentality, at your age. What a waste of time, being a father and a family man. Poor Neil, think what he might do if he weren't tied down like that.

Men were fools.

9

'Is the volcano extinct?'

'Slumbering. It's not done anything for some time.'

'No sparks and eruptions, then?'

'Rarely. It has a middle-aged calm about it.'

'Just as well,' said Sylvester, stretching vigorously before returning to his chair and taking up his cello again. 'I wish this piece had a middle-aged calm about it.'

'We'll give it another hour,' said Ferenc. 'And then we'll slope off and have a mud bath.'

'Why slope?' asked Sylvester.

'Because Carla will be on the lookout, making sure I keep my hours up.'

'Surely not,' said Sylvester, looking at his fingers with surprise as they twisted themselves into the strange pattern demanded by the music. 'I wish Marcus had learned to play a stringed instrument.'

'He did,' said Ferenc, resting his hands on his knees. 'That's what's behind all this, so rumour has it. Marcus was an early Suzuki whizzkid. On the fiddle. You know, a year of "Twinkle, Twinkle, Little Star" followed by various other masterpieces. Learn it by heart, get it perfect, you're given the next piece. Often with words to help you along.'

'I know,' said Sylvester. 'I've heard them, tots playing Schumann's "Merry Peasant" while intoning "There was a farmer in his socks", and suchlike. Thousands of children do it. On the cello, as well. Nauseating, but I'm told it works a treat. Why should it have had this effect on Marcus?'

'Clearly one tune too much for him. So at ten years old,

while playing the Bach double violin concerto, he flung his little violin across the room and gave up tunes forever.'

'Nonsense,' said Sylvester. 'Can't have got to college without playing the odd tune. However much he hated them.'

'He never studied music,' said Ferenc. 'Majored in math. Did his music on his own, got Reisburg to take him on as a pupil, Reisburg introduced him in the right circles, and Marcus was made. And once established, he could write what he wanted, and make life as difficult as possible for string players, thus getting his own back on Dr Suzuki.'

'Ah,' said Sylvester. 'That explains a lot. Never mind, Ferenc, we have to plough on. We're getting paid for this.'

'Well, I damn well wouldn't be doing it for fun,' said Ferenc bitterly.

'Tell me about your father,' said Agatha nosily.

'Like what?' asked Carla, who had just joined Agatha and Magdalena in a shady spot in the courtyard.

'Does he come from the island?'

'No, from Rome. His mother came from here, but she left and went to live in Rome.' She shrugged expressively. 'There's very little on the island for anyone with ambition or talent. Farming, fishing . . . it's a hard life. Now, of course, with tourists coming, they give up the land and are getting richer.'

'So he bought a house here?' Agatha liked to get the details right.

'My mother inherited some property when her parents died. They sold these farm buildings to Ferenc, and some land to another family, and it left them enough to modernize a house for themselves.'

'For weekends and holidays?'

'My father is a writer, you know. So when he was working on a book, he came here. When my mother died a few years ago, he decided he didn't want to live in Rome, gave up his apartment there, and settled here, on the island.'

'What kind of books does he write?' asked Magdalena.

'Gangster books,' said Carla. She laughed as she saw their faces. 'Very celebrated, he is like an Italian Maigret. Gritty, psychological thrillers.'

Magdalena blinked. She would have put Ettore down as an industrialist or lawyer or, if a writer, a journalist.

'That's what I've been doing this morning,' said Carla. 'I have two jobs. One is to keep Ferenc working and being where he should be at the right time. And I do a lot of editing work for a publishing house, including my father's books.'

She got up and adjusted the shade over the table. 'This sun is too strong, it will be bad for your skins.'

'Not mine,' said Agatha with confidence. 'My naked face hasn't seen the light of day for years; no sun's rays are going to get anywhere near.'

'My hair is going grey before my eyes, what does a wrinkle or two matter?' said Magdalena.

Agatha sat bolt upright. 'Defeatist talk; how dreadful to hear you say that, Magdalena. You must get your hair done, and take care of your skin, or are you planning to become some kind of appalling natural earth person?'

'Earth person?'

'You know, nothing artificial. No creams, no hormones, no help. Fatal, darling, especially with a husband like Val.'

Magdalena closed her eyes.

'Is he a rake?' asked Carla, interested. 'Your husband?'

A rake, thought Magdalena. Such a dashing, theatrical word. It conjured up ruffled shirts and the hiss of locked blades, of boots and breeches. And chiefly of men who were long dead and gone. Unfortunately, a living rake, and one that you shared your life and castle with, wasn't so attractive. Not at close quarters, at any rate.

Attractive to others, of course. That was what it meant, presumably, to be a rake. And I, Magdalena told herself, would be considered old-fashioned if not unsporting if I showed how much I minded the way he carries on. Flirting, finding women appealing, that was one thing. Bedding them, old flames and new fancies alike, that was another.

'He's a sod,' said Agatha.

Carla flicked an eyebrow. 'A homosexual?'

'Good gracious, no,' said Magdalena.

'Would a Nigel or a Malcolm be worse than a Veronica or an Angela?' Agatha asked rhetorically.

'Angela? Who's Angela?'

'Just a name, darling, plucked out of the air. I know of no Angela in Val's life.'

Carla poured herself a glass of mineral water. 'My father likes women,' she observed. 'Very much. He has had many mistresses, brief affairs, all kinds of encounters.'

'Didn't your mother mind?' Magdalena asked, interested.

'No, because she didn't know,' said Carla. 'Not for twenty years. She had thought him completely faithful. Then, when she found out, she was furious.'

'Ah, with him, I suppose,' said Agatha, nodding her head. 'All that time, being made a fool of.'

'No, not with him. With herself, for not knowing. "I could have married someone else," she said. "And been happy."'

'That's very sad,' said Magdalena. At least I have no illusions, she thought, as she rubbed her itching ankle where a mosquito had attacked in the night. At least I know what Val is like. I knew before I married him, I can't think why I supposed he'd ever be any different.

'You expect people to change when they marry,' said Agatha. 'There needs to be trust, and some shared feelings. Not wanting to hurt your partner and so on.'

'Life isn't like that,' said Carla. 'This is why I stay with Ferenc, but we don't marry.'

'I thought you couldn't, hasn't he a wife in America?' said Agatha.

'They are divorced,' said Carla. 'He has three children, all grown up now and leading their own lives. We could marry, but I feel that marriage is a dangerous state.'

'Yes,' said Agatha, thinking of George.

'It is,' said Magdalena, thinking of Val.

Contrary to Magdalena's gloomy belief that in her absence Valdemar would be like a pig in clover, he was finding life hard and perplexing. With no familial obligations to disturb his merry round, life should have been a bed of roses.

It wasn't.

George was sitting morosely in the club, and Valdemar joined him. 'Whisky, is that, George?'

George shook his head. 'No. Ginger ale.'

'Ginger ale?' Valdemar looked at it with horror. 'Why, George, why?'

'Don't feel like my usual,' said George waspishly. 'That's all. My liver's all to pieces, best to lay off.'

'Too much club food.'

'I'll tell you what it is, Val, I'm lonely. Not a word from Agatha, not a word. And Thea went off to find her, and now she's back home and all wrought up about something. Keeps to her room, won't talk to me . . .'

'Does she live at home?' asked Val with interest, flinging aside a lurking *Times* and sliding into the chair across from George. 'I thought she'd have a flat of her own.'

'She used to, when she was at college, but she's home now. Handy for work. Cheap, too, I expect. Edmund's there, as well, can't get rid of them these days, youngsters.'

'It's company for you.'

'I don't want company, I want Agatha.' George's voice rose to a near howl, and on the other side of the large, dark room, members rustled their papers and snuffled disapprovingly.

'If it's that you're cold in bed, George, the solution is easy,' said Valdemar. 'You're a rich man, plenty of delightful creatures more than willing to keep you warm.'

George regarded him with distaste. 'That may be your way, Val; of course, you've never cared tuppence for one woman more than another. As long as they've got a warm pussy, that's all you care about. All I care about is Agatha. She's my wife, and I want her home.'

Valdemar didn't like the note of criticism in George's remarks. 'You shouldn't have done whatever it was that sent her off like that.'

George lapsed back into the sulks. 'She hasn't got any money. Don't know how she's managing. Got an earful from Thea about that, these young people have no idea.'

Valdemar rose.

'Going into dinner?' asked George.

'No,' said Valdemar. 'Other plans.'

'That's what's driven your Magdalena off,' said George snappishly. 'Other plans. Other women. Serve you right,' he added under his breath as the door swung to behind Valdemar. 'Waiter! Another of these foul drinks. And put some ice in it.'

Valdemar paused in the hall. 'Get me George Fimbul's number, would you,' he said to the porter on duty.

'Mr Fimbul's in the club tonight.'

'I know that. Just tell me his number.'

'There you are, sir.'

Valdemar dialled the number and waited. A strange male voice answered.

'Is Thea there?' said Valdemar.

'Who's calling?'

Valdemar made an impatient noise. 'Is she there?'

'Not at home,' said the voice. 'Shall I take a message? I'm her brother.'

'When are you expecting her back?'

'Thea? God knows. She's off on a toot with some friends. Not too late, probably, she's due back at work tomorrow. Try about eleven.'

Too late for dinner.

Belle? No, he didn't feel like Belle this evening. Veronica was at the opera with Philip . . . To hell with it, he'd pick up a quick meal and go back to the office. Plenty of work. And he'd phone Lottie, make sure the children were all right.

'Gone? What are you talking about?'

There were some scuffling sounds at the other end of the line and Mrs Grobbins came on. 'It's me, Mr Mountjoy, no point you talking to that gummock, you'll get no sense out of her. And if you're wanting to know where the twins are, it's no good asking me. Nor Lottie, neither.'

In distant Eyotshire, Mrs Grobbins held the phone away from her ear. Lottie heard the anger booming from the earpiece and burst into loud and uncontrolled tears. Mrs Grobbins took no notice, and waited for Valdemar to subside.

'It's no good you a-carrying on at me. That Thea Fimbul had a friend come up as what she said had been employed by Mrs Mountjoy to take the children to be with her. Abroad. Where Lottie won't go. Off they went in a hired car . . . No, I did not stop them. Why not? Because Mrs Mountjoy herself has been on the line. She says, it's all right, Mrs Grobbins. All in order. No, I did not think to ring you, seeing as how Mrs Mountjoy said not to bother you. You were busy, she says, and not wanting to be troubled with anything to do with the twins.'

'Now, now . . .'

With a triumphant thunk Mrs Grobbins cut the connection, and then laid the receiver down beside the phone.

'You can't do that, Mrs Grobbins,' said Lottie. 'It'll just be an engaged tone if anyone tries to ring.'

'And it's an enraged tone that Mr Mountjoy's got, and who'll be ringing except him? Shouting at me, which I won't have. Now, come along, Lottie, give over that squealing and keening, I can't be doing with it. You just pull yourself together, and I'll make you a nice cup of tea.'

'What is your castle like?' asked Carla. They had dined on the terrace, and were lingering over coffee, watching the flickers of light of passing boats at sea, and listening to the evening sounds of a hot Mediterranean night.

Sylvester wiped his mouth with a white linen napkin and sat back with a sigh of pleasure. 'Delicious, Carla. Go on, Magdalena, tell Carla and Ferenc about the castle.'

'You must stay with us if you're coming over for the festival this year,' Magdalena said. 'Then you can see it for yourselves. It's best in summer, because it can get very cold later on.'

'It's freezing most of the year,' said Sylvester. 'Much better stay with me, I've got a civilized house. Mountjoy Castle is all thick walls and echoing stone passages. Plenty of history and virtually no comforts.'

'It isn't a very grand castle,' Magdalena said. 'It's more of a fortified house now, at least the bit we live in. The rest is mostly ruin.'

'Nonsense,' said Sylvester. 'There's a twelfth-century long drop.'

'Long drop?' said Carla.

'Lavatory,' said Sylvester. 'Above a stream. Long way up, about sixty feet, isn't it, Magdalena?'

'Yes, it is.'

'And do you still use it?' asked Ferenc, lazily puffing at a cigarette and blowing elegant circles of smoke into the still air.

'Not often,' said Magdalena.

'What are you talking about?' said Thomas, joining them with a noisy scrape of his chair. 'The twins are fine, Magdalena, fast asleep. I say, that Dido is pretty ferocious, isn't she?'

'What a find,' said Sylvester. 'I can see we're going to have some fun around here.'

'The young men will flock to that particular honey-pot,' predicted Ferenc. 'That astonishing silver blonde hair. Is it real?'

'It's very becoming,' said Carla. 'And the purple nails and the tattoo on her face, are these fashionable in England now?'

'Amongst the arty young,' said Sylvester tolerantly. 'She's already looked me in the eye and told me she doesn't like gay men. Splendid.'

Magdalena was horrified. 'Sylvester, I had no idea. I'm so sorry; she'll have to go.'

'She will not,' said Sylvester with great good humour. 'It's up to her who she likes and doesn't like. That's fine, I told her, don't like most of them myself. And I don't like skinny young ladies with swastika bangles. So she laughed, and I laughed and that's okay. She says the swastika goes the right way, incidentally. Not sure that the people on the island will approve, warned her to take it off while she's here. She said she'd ask the other side. She's a channeller, I gather.'

There was a moment's complete silence. Then Agatha spoke.

'Sylvester, my love, are you making this up?'

'Cross my heart,' said Sylvester. 'Fact. She gets messages.'

'Messages? What kind of messages?'

'You're alarming Magdalena,' said Agatha.

Ferenc stubbed out his cigarette in the obsidian ashtray beside his plate. 'Spiritualist, eh? Oh, this could be kind of fun. I haven't met a good one for years.'

'I don't know what you're talking about,' said Carla. 'Channelling? Spiritualism? Is this something to do with masons?'

'Certainly not,' said Sylvester, shocked. 'Don't worry about it, Carla. Best not to enquire, no doubt you're a good Catholic.'

'I'm not, and I'm very curious to know more.'

Thomas crammed the remains of his third peach into his mouth and joined the conversation.

'She's weird. Seriously weird. But the twins think she's great, and she's awfully good with them. You can see she's an expert, got them eating out of her hand.'

'Have a brandy, Magdalena,' said Ferenc. 'You look as though you need it.'

Far away, in Rome, on another terrace, Marcus Mordaunt had dined alone. He'd have company tomorrow, when he joined up with that Quarles man, but tonight he had himself to himself, which was what Marcus liked best. That was when his ideas came buzzing into his mind. A lesser man would have said humming into his mind, but Marcus was relentless in his crusade against anything tonal, so hums were out.

He poured himself more wine and pondered what the Villa Saraceno might be like. It was a tough name, he decided. Rough stone walls, looking out over a barren landscape. Marcus liked barren landscapes.

And perhaps there would be twisted wreckage from the war, entangled with barbed wire on the beach, a monument to the folly of men and their fighting. Marcus lived in hope.

Ferenc was intelligent; that helped.

Sylvester Tate, well . . . Marcus pursed his lips. Too much associated with the great romantics for his taste, and he always had that uneasy feeling that Sylvester didn't take him seriously. Marcus took himself very seriously, and he liked others to do the same.

Carla, now there was a civilized woman. And they had no children. Good. Marcus felt very uneasy with children, and then they were inclined to sing. Marcus winced. No, his time at the Villa Saraceno boded well. This Quarles man would be staying elsewhere, and it was a compliment that a London paper had sent out a key critic and journalist to do an in-depth piece. He remembered Quarles as an unobjectionable man, not one likely to disturb the delicate equilibrium of a leading modern composer.

A waiter watched him from the shadows. He was intrigued

by this guest. Giorgio on the desk had said the man was English, but there was something more American about him. 'A famous musician,' Giorgio had said. You couldn't rely on that. Giorgio always exaggerated the fame or celebrity of the hotel's guests, and it wasn't as though they were one of the really big smart international hotels, with film stars and other grandees washing through. Theirs was well-known in certain circles, had a good reputation, and yes, a lot of visiting musicians. What kind of musician then, was this burly man? No elegance to him at all, the waiter decided. Not a violinist, or any kind of string player.

Marcus turned his head, saw the waiter lurking in the shadows and waved at him. The waiter left his place and slid over to the table. 'Signore?' he said, whisking away a few crumbs with a napkin.

Not a singer, either. The waiter was a keen opera-goer, and knew a singer's voice when he heard one. He could be a director, or a conductor, he had a forceful air about him. Not good-looking, with that reddish, wiry hair and pale skin, but definitely dynamic. A brass player? Of a loud instrument, such as the trumpet? No, he had a resolute mouth, without the over-used look to his lips of the professional brass player. He would ask Giorgio to find out more; his girlfriend Cecilia would be interested, she loved to hear about the more interesting of the hotel's guests.

'Another bottle of this wine,' said Marcus. Make the most of it while you can, he said to himself. He didn't think that Ferenc and Sylvester were abstemious or cranky types, but one could never tell.

Carpe diem, who was the old rogue who said that? Wasn't it a Roman, Horace? Quite right, said Marcus, raising his glass in a toast to the memory of a long dead poet.

Valdemar stormed into Virginia's office.

'Go away, Val,' she said, without looking up from her work table. 'I'm busy.'

'Too bad,' said Valdemar. 'Virginia, the twins have gone.'

Virginia swung round on her stool. 'Gone?' she repeated.

'Yes. Left the castle. Can you believe it? Magdalena's let

them go off with a total stranger. What kind of a mother is she?'

What kind of a father are you? thought Virginia. 'Calm down, Val,' she said. 'Where have you got this nonsense from?'

'Mrs Grobbins,' said Valdemar. 'I rang home, well, to see if Magdalena had come back, if you must know. She hasn't, not a sign of her. And the twins have gone.'

'Gone? What do you mean by gone?'

'This creature turned up, saying Magdalena had asked her to take the children abroad to join their mother. Thea, who is not what she seems, must have been in cahoots with her, because she drives this person, with the children, off in a hired car, and that's the last anyone's seen of them. Just wait until I get my hands on Thea. Double-crossing little . . .'

'Have you spoken to Thea?'

'I have not, she was out making whoopee last night, obviously doesn't give a bugger about what's happened to my children. Not there this morning, gone to work. Can't get hold of George to find out where she works . . . I shall have to call the police, and it's going to be more bloody scandal. Just one damned thing after another.'

'Calm down,' said Virginia. 'You've heard nothing from Magdalena, I take it.'

'No,' said Valdemar sulkily. 'Unless she's left a message on the answerphone.'

'Have you checked it?'

'No, I have not, I've been far too busy to listen to it.'

'That's very stupid of you,' said Virginia in her forthright way. 'Check it now.'

'My children,' said Val furiously, heading for his office. 'They're my children, and that woman has no right to take them off like this.'

Virginia followed him into his office and clicked the playback button on his answering machine. Highly uninteresting messages burbled past, then a pithy one from Canon Higgs-Boson – 'That bloody Dean, we've got to have a talk about this cathedral business, Virginia' – more messages and clicks.

'Ah,' said Valdemar.

Magdalena's voice, sounding very neutral and composed, Virginia thought; cold and unfeeling in Valdemar's opinion, came out from the speaker.

'Just to let you know, Val, that the twins have arrived safely and are with me. They're well and happy. I expect you're in a frenzy because they were taken by a stranger, but don't worry. I employed her to bring them, and she is a fully qualified and experienced nanny who came highly recommended by a friend.'

There was a pause; Virginia flashed a look at Valdemar, who was white with temper, his knuckles clenched in anger.

'I don't know when I'll be back, Val, possibly not for some time. Don't bother to try and find me, I'm actually feeling very relaxed and happy and I'd like to go on feeling like that. I've left Mrs Grobbins in charge of the castle, and Peter will call in to give a hand as necessary. And I'm sure you're full of concern about Thomas. He's here, with us, and is very well. He doesn't send his love, because he'd be desperate if he knew I was talking to you. Ignorance is bliss, you know. I won't ring again. Goodbye.'

Valdemar was speechless. He thumped the machine into silence and slammed the drawer of his desk shut and kicked his chair out of his way.

Virginia watched, coolly amused by his antics.

'I don't believe it,' he finally burst out. 'Who does she think she is? How dare she? How dare she? Taking the children, without my permission; going off herself like that, as though she was a free agent.'

'Val, she is.'

'She isn't. She's my wife.'

'You're her husband, but you behave like a free agent.'

'Spare me the feminist bibble-babble,' said Valdemar. 'The situation is entirely different. She has children, the castle to look after.' A calculating look came into his eye. 'Thomas. That's where I'll get her. She has no right to have Thomas with her. By God, I'll get my lawyers on to it, she's going to regret this.'

'Be very, very careful,' warned Virginia. 'I think you may be the one to end up with regrets.'

'Nobody gets the better of me,' said Valdemar rancorously. And then, more explosively, 'She can't do this to me. She can't.'

'Val, she can. And she has.'

10

Edmund heard the front door open and close. Funny, Dad wasn't usually at home during the day, although the way he'd been since Ma went . . . He hung his head over the banisters. 'Who's that?'

Thea flung her jacket on to the chair in the hall. 'It's me.'

'Not feeling well?' asked Edmund, coming briskly down the stairs. 'Bad head after last night?'

'I drank mineral water last night, as it happens. My head is fine.'

'So why are you home?'

'I've been fired.'

'What, by the singers?'

'The opera company library, yes.'

Edmund was not given to high emotion, but he had a kindly nature and could see that his sister was upset.

'Let's get you a stiff drink,' he said. 'No, I've got a better idea. Let's go to the pub and I'll buy you lunch. As well as a stiff drink.'

Thea hesitated, but Edmund draped her jacket across her shoulders, pressed her bag into her hand, and propelled her out of the door.

She said nothing more as they walked along to the pub in the corner of the square, nor while Edmund installed her on a plush settle and discussed sausages with the girl behind the bar.

'All fixed up,' he said, putting her drink down in front of her. 'Now, spit it out.'

'It's that Lucy,' said Thea. 'My assistant. Assistant! Ha, ha.'

'The hopeless one?'

'Yes. Can't read as far as I can make out, certainly doesn't know the first thing about music. Oh, I tell a lie, she once played the flute in her school's second orchestra.'

'Wow,' said Edmund. 'And?'

'And, what everybody else knew, but I didn't, she's been sleeping with Oliver.'

'Hence the job.'

'Hence the job. And while I was away, the sneaky horror clearly did all sorts of extras in bed with Oliver – and personally, I'd sooner sleep with a squid – and lo! my services are no longer required.'

'Have a nut,' said Edmund, watching Thea crunching her way through the bowl of crisps. 'Unfair dismissal, no problem.'

'Can't go that route,' said Thea.

'Why not?'

'Can't tell you, but it can't be done. I just have to take my pitiful pay-off and try to find work elsewhere.'

'Hang on,' said Edmund. 'You can't let them walk all over you like this.'

'Unfortunately, I have to,' said Thea. 'Things are a bit more complicated than they seem.'

'Who did you sleep with to get your job?' Edmund asked sarcastically.

'Lay off, Edmund. I don't do that, in fact I don't sleep with anyone these days, I'm totally off sex. Have been for ages.'

Edmund looked at her in surprise. 'You poor old thing. Clearly a change of scene is required. Or a new generation? Who's the guy who's rung you up about sixteen times? He sounds a bit out of your usual age group. Classy voice, deepish.'

'I haven't a clue. Oh, it's probably Valdemar.'

Edmund's eyebrows rose. 'Valdemar Mountjoy? Come on, Thea, you can't be serious.'

'If that's the man who rang, then that's who it is,' said Thea impatiently. 'No, I'm not going to bed with him, I told you, it's lonely nights for me at present. I'm just not interested.'

'So why the phone calls? I tell you what, he sounded pretty supercharged when he rang just now. He wanted to know where you worked; very insistent, I have to say.'

'You didn't tell him?'

'No, I did not.'

'Thanks. Not that it matters now, since I'm not there any more.' She flung a handful of peanuts into her mouth. 'I think perhaps I'd better keep out of his way for the time being.'

'Excellent idea,' said Edmund. 'Bad news, that man. You may not be going to bed with him, but half of the rest of the world is, from what one hears. Poor Magdalena, being married to a man like that. It puts Ma into a real frenzy whenever she hears of some new bint he's been stalking.'

'I'm not a bint.'

'Calm down, you know what I mean.'

'In any case, that particular worm has turned,' said Thea. 'Magdalena's buzzed off, taken her twins with her. Gone to Italy.'

Edmund looked at his sister, frowning. 'Italy? Thea, is Ma with her?'

'Might be,' said Thea.

'Pa's out of his mind with missing her, you do know that.'

'Tough,' said Thea. 'He shouldn't be carrying on the way he does, those stupid jewels, what a ridiculous fuss. Here comes lunch, Edmund, be a love and get me another drink. I'm feeling better.'

'Good,' said Edmund. 'I'm sure you'll just walk into another job, you know. With your qualifications . . .'

'I don't want to think about it,' said Thea firmly. 'And I'm not going to even try to find myself a job just at present.'

'So what are you going to do? You'll be bored stiff hanging about at home.'

'I'm going to Italy,' said Thea. 'To an island called Aeolus.'

Thomas walked carefully along the water's edge, carrying a tray laden with goodies from the tiny bar further up the beach. Magdalena watched him with great affection; he was such a mixture of young man and boy with his long, lanky legs and his serious expression.

'There,' he said triumphantly, as he left the sea and reached the place where she was stretched out on the sand. 'Shall I call Dido and the twins?'

Agatha opened an eye and her hand groped in the sand for

her sun-glasses. 'Here you are,' said Thomas helpfully. Then he loped down to the sea, where the twins, in a state of complete bliss, were romping and shouting with some little Italian children while Dido watched with a severe eye. They squealed with protest at the thought of coming out; Magdalena winced, and waited for louder screams to disturb the peaceful scene.

Nothing.

Magdalena frowned. What had Dido done to them? Had she threatened them? No, they were scampering up the beach wreathed in smiles. They arrived in a flurry of sand, shaking themselves like puppies.

'Not near here,' shrieked Agatha. 'Darling, your children!'

'Do you good, sea water,' said Magdalena. 'Dido, how did you do it?'

'What?' said Dido.

'Get them out. Without tantrums.'

'I don't hold with tantrums,' said Dido simply. She twisted a towel around her tiny waist and sat down, legs folded under her, in one swift and graceful movement.

Agatha sat up. 'You're a dancer,' she said accusingly to Dido.

'No way,' said Dido. 'I was, though.'

'Yes, you look like a dancer,' said Magdalena.

'Anybody can tell,' said Dido. 'Because of my horrible feet,' she went on in a matter of fact way.

'Dido,' said Thomas, shocked. 'How did they get like that?'

'Dancing,' said Dido. 'Like she said, I was a dancer. You want to dance, you destroy your feet.'

'What's that scar?' asked Thomas, simultaneously repelled and fascinated by Dido's ugly feet.

Dido's purple-nailed finger traced the long silver line which ran down her ankle.

'Operation. To remove a bit of broken bone. That's why I'm not a dancer any more.'

'Thomas, you shouldn't ask Dido such personal questions,' said Magdalena. A gentle enough reproof, but Thomas's face went a fiery red. 'Sorry,' he mumbled.

'Leave him alone,' said Dido. 'My feet aren't secret. If they were, I'd hide them. I'm not ashamed of them. Okay, they aren't pretty, so what? Plenty of uglier things in this world than my blooming toes. Come and sit here, Thomas, you can pour out that juice for Helena. Add some water, it'll be too strong otherwise.'

Hugh had been inspecting the rolls and little wedges of olive bread filled with cheese.

'Don't want that.'

Dido looked at him. She took a plate, selected half a roll and an apple, and handed it to the little boy. 'That's your lunch,' she said. 'You eat that up.'

'I won't.'

'When it's gone, I'll read you a story. After that, we'll play a game in the sand, and then we'll go in the sea again.'

'Won't eat it.'

'Then only Helena will get to go in the sea again. Unless Helena doesn't want her lunch, in which case nobody gets to go in the sea again, no skin off my nose.'

Magdalena watched, enthralled. The twins eyed her, wondering how quickly their mother would give way if they made a scene. They know that I don't have the patience or energy to stand up to them, thought Magdalena wearily. 'Nothing to do with me,' she said. 'Get on with it, do as Dido says.'

Hugh quite suddenly hurled himself at Dido. 'Love you, Dido,' he said, looking up at her from under his long, dark lashes.

'You still have to eat your lunch,' said Dido.

'Okay, you're the boss,' said Hugh sunnily, and plopped himself down with his plate.

How does she do it? wondered Magdalena, as Thomas handed her a glass of iced water. I can't manage any of the Mountjoys, not the ones who are four or those who are forty-five. I could just about manage Hugo, bless his heart, but he's dead. I wish he hadn't died, she thought. Then I wouldn't be in this state, we could be sitting here together, with the twins. He would have been so happy.

She rummaged in her bag for a tissue and resolutely blew her nose.

'Are you all right?' Thomas asked anxiously.

'Sand up my nose,' said Magdalena indistinctly.

Dido gave Magdalena a sharp look, and distracted Thomas's attention. 'Thomas, pass me that cloth, could you? Helena, don't slurp like that, what do you think this is? Friday night down the boozer?'

Marcus and the accompanying Quarles had shunned the hydrofoil from Sicily. They had come on a different route, driving from Rome to Naples to catch the overnight ferry. Quarles had been quite a lively companion on the road, not averse to stopping so that Marcus could breathe his fill of the noxious fumes from some bleak industrial centre, and ready to enter into interested debate on the virtues of items on the menu when they stopped for a meal.

Marcus wasn't keen to eat in any of the wastelands he was so enthusiastic about, Quarles noticed. Lunch was taken off the road, in an enchanting little town at a restaurant famed for its *porchetta*. Clearly, this was a man of contrasts; that would be a promising opening for his profile.

Quarles on board a boat was not, however, a conversable companion. No sooner aboard than green in the face, no sooner sick than in retreat to his cabin, where he locked himself away for the night. If you're prone to seasickness, he thought grimly as he fell into his berth, don't lunch on sucking pig stuffed with cheese and herbs and much else besides.

Marcus felt aggrieved; he had been looking forward to an interesting gossip about the current London musical scene over several glasses of something good. They shouldn't have sent a man who was prone to seasickness, he grumbled to himself. That was thoughtless, surely there were plenty of good writers about who could survive a short crossing without throwing up.

Peeved, he went up on deck, and soon forgot about the suffering Quarles as he watched the night's pyrotechnics while the boat steamed down the volcanic coast. Sparks and jets of flames dotted the hillsides, competing with the twinkling lights of towns and cities.

Like a scene from hell, thought Marcus appreciatively.

Thea heard the phone ringing as she packed. Summer things, heavenly.

Edmund came into the room. 'It's that man again. Valdemar. I must say, he is very keen, he's quite steamed up.'

'Edmund,' said Thea, wrenching at the zip on her bag, 'do me a favour and tell him I'm not in London. Say I'm not going back to work and I've left for the country.'

'I will,' said Edmund. 'But I don't think he'll believe me. He's very het up, I do wonder what you've been up to.'

'Best not to know, dear brother. Suffice it to say, the law was on my side, but Valdemar probably doesn't see it that way.'

Valdemar banged the phone down. He couldn't get hold of anyone. Well, his lawyer would have to see him, he'd made an appointment for three o'clock. He swung out of his office and walked at an alarming pace towards the pretty peace of King's Bench Walk.

The ancient hush and shabbiness of his solicitors was reassuring. Generations of Mountjoys had entrusted their affairs to Harknell, Whimple & Rowley. Their memories and files knew details of scandals which would have driven today's tabloids into a frenzy. Secrets were safe with H, W & R, who had never been known to tell a tale or spread a rumour.

Valdemar was seeing Rowley. He was a young man; pink-faced, sleek and ebullient. He darted forward with a 'My dear Val', and installed his client in a shiny old leather armchair before retreating behind his hideous oak desk.

Rowley didn't believe in beating about the bush. 'You said when you rang that you wished to talk about a personal matter concerning your wife. I trust Magdalena is well? And the twins?'

'I am not in any position to know how my wife is,' said Valdemar coldly, 'since she has seen fit to leave the country, and then to summon the twins to her side in the care of a perfect stranger. My main concern is that she has Thomas with her. Thomas is under my guardianship, she knows perfectly well that she should let me know where he is, so that he can come back at once and return to his school.'

'Appalling business,' said Rowley. He hated it when any of his clients' affairs reached the pages of the daily papers. Particularly when they reached the pages of the more lurid ones. 'I happened to bump into Austin Vaulx yesterday. We were at school together. He was Thomas's housemaster at Gryme, wasn't he?'

'Is,' said Valdemar shortly.

'Um,' said Rowley. 'I feel there may just possibly be a tiny problem there. Never mind. Let us return to the subject of young Thomas. Thirteen, is he now?'

'Fourteen,' said Valdemar. Rowley knew perfectly well how old Thomas was, the man had a memory like a computer, never forgot any detail. What was he up to?

'Now,' said the solicitor, drawing a file in front of him and flipping it open. 'Of course, while Hortense is alive, and is the natural mother of Thomas, she is responsible for him.'

'I know that. However, since Hortense never sets foot in this country, I'm Thomas's legal guardian. There's no question of that.'

'This is where we hit a little difficulty,' said Rowley, eyeing Valdemar with a touch of unease. Valdemar was a big man, while he, Rowley was more on the compact side. Big, tall men made him feel uncomfortable, especially when they tended towards the wrathful, and most especially when they were about to hear news they wouldn't like at all.

'Get on with it,' said Valdemar irritably. What was the matter with Rowley? He wanted him to get a message to Magdalena, threatening her with all kinds of penalties unless she sent Thomas home. If that didn't flush her out, nothing would.

'I had a call from Hortense,' said Rowley. 'Yesterday.' Might as well get it over with. 'She has altered her arrangements for Thomas. You are no longer his legal guardian. Instead, she has appointed your wife Magdalena to take on this responsibility. I am afraid that there is nothing we can do to make her bring Thomas back to England if she doesn't choose to. The boy's mother is, apparently quite happy for him to remain abroad with Magdalena for an indefinite period of time.'

He sniffed, a pained and fastidious sniff. 'I must say, she has a very inappropriate attitude towards English schooling. Her opinion of Gryme isn't high, in fact she had some very startling accusations to make about the school, which I shall enjoy passing on to Austin Vaulx next time I see him.' Rowley spread his plump little hands wide in a gesture of defeat. 'So you see, Val, there is very little I can do to help you.'

Valdemar remained perfectly still. He wasn't looking at

Rowley; his unseeing eyes were focused elsewhere. In the playground of a school in Eyotshire, where an eight-year-old boy would be waiting for his mother to pick him up from school. Tall for his age, probably. With dark, almost black hair, and startlingly blue eyes. Valdemar had a surprisingly accurate idea of what he would look like, this northern child, considering he had never set eyes on him.

Rowley fidgeted with some papers on his desk, arranging them into still neater piles. He fussily brushed a crumb from his mid-afternoon biscuit from the desk into his other hand and thence into the wastepaper basket.

Valdemar got up and went over to the window. Without turning round, he spoke.

'You know that Thomas is my son.'

Rowley made some throat-clearing noises. A touchy matter this; every nerve was alert, this was where family solicitors earned their large fees. 'I am aware of this, yes.'

Valdemar swung round. 'Then I, as his natural father, must also have some rights.'

'Do sit down, Val,' said Rowley, relaxing now that he knew where they were heading. 'That's a tricky one.'

'Why?'

'Hortense could deny your claim to paternity. Would almost certainly do so.'

'Aren't there tests now?'

How do I put this, thought Rowley. 'There are, and with recent scientific advances, these are proving very helpful.'

'And so?'

'Val, Hortense is your half-sister.'

'I know, I know,' said Valdemar. 'What has that to do with it?'

'You will share familial characteristics. It could be impossible to prove that Thomas's genetic inheritance comes from you and not from his mother.'

Valdemar looked at Rowley. It was a brooding look which gave nothing away. It alarmed Rowley, who would have felt on safer ground coping with his client's notoriously bad temper.

'So, in my opinion – and of course you're welcome to get another opinion – that road is closed to us.'

'It's not the kind of subject I choose to discuss with all and sundry,' said Valdemar. 'In fact, what you're saying is that the only way I can be recognized as Thomas's father, and therefore have some paternal rights, would be to make Hortense come out with the truth?'

'Paternal rights is a difficult area,' said Rowley cautiously. 'And at this stage in Thomas's life I think Hortense is unlikely to take such a course. Extremely unlikely. You are perhaps aware that a good deal of the trouble Thomas has been having at school relates to this particular matter?'

'I'm not aware he's been having any trouble at school,' said Valdemar coldly.

'He felt sufficiently, um, shall we say ill-at-ease, to run away?'

'He ran away because Magdalena, who is not related to him, has mollycoddled him. He's been over-protected, it was time he learned to stand on his own two feet.'

'Well, he's certainly found he can run away on his own two feet,' said Rowley incautiously.

Valdemar got up from his chair again. 'I don't need any advice from you or anyone else on how to deal with my son and ward.'

'Your ex-ward, Val,' Rowley reminded him gently. 'Your ex-ward.'

11

Thea stopped on the way to the airport to ring her mother.

'Darling, how lovely,' said Agatha. 'But what about your work?'

'Tell you about that when I see you,' said Thea quickly. 'How do I find you when I get to Aeolus?'

'Ring from Sicily to let me know which hydrofoil you're catching and I'll come down to meet you. I'm sure Carla can fit you in for a night or two, but we'll have to find somewhere to stay. We can take a house perhaps, although money's a problem.'

'I'm bringing some,' said Thea. 'Pips going, bye!'

Thea was travelling on a charter flight. Still early in the holiday season, the airport was comparatively uncrowded. The plane, however, was full, and seat space limited; an hour into the flight, Thea was wondering if she would ever recover the use of her numb legs.

A bright little woman in the next seat commiserated. 'Terrible for you tall ones. I'm all right, tuck me in an egg box, that's what my husband says.'

'Is your husband with you?' asked Thea, looking around.

'No,' said the woman with scorn. 'No way, his idea of a good holiday is sitting in front of the telly watching sport. I come by myself. Every year, two weeks with a friend in Sicily.' She held out a plump and beautifully manicured hand. 'Dora,' she said.

'I'm Thea. Sicily's a good place to have a friend.'

The little woman, eyes sharp and full of fun in her pretty round face, gave what sounded very like a dirty laugh. 'I've a friend in Sicily, he's twenty-four. Then there's my late-August friend, in

Spain. He's a bit older, twenty-six. Then I've got a new one from last year, in Morocco, only twenty. I like them young and firm, you see.'

Thea blinked. Was she hearing right?

'Oh, yes, when you get to my age, dearie, you've no use for a husband. Worn out, washed up, husbands are, you'll find that out for yourself one day. Just a quick bang now and again on a Saturday night, if they aren't too full of lager. No romance, no muscles, no finesse.'

'Whereas your friends abroad . . .'

'Plenty of everything,' said Dora with satisfaction. She gave Thea a sharp look. 'Is that why you're going? To try out the local talent?'

'No,' said Thea, thinking how unadventurous her trip was. 'My mother's there, and I'm joining her.'

'She with your dad?'

'No, my father's in England.'

'Ha, bet she's found herself something with a bit of shape in the pecs, not to mention elsewhere.'

Thea laughed. 'I don't think so. She's very fond of my father.'

'I'm very fond of my old man, don't get me wrong. But there's what you want and what you get, and I see nothing wrong to helping myself when the pudding comes round. You'll learn, dearie, just wait till you get to my age.' The woman rummaged in the woven straw bag she had at her feet and emerged triumphantly with a little paper bag. 'Have a liquorice allsort, I never travel without them.'

'Thank you,' said Thea.

'Sylvester, do you mind if I put Marcus in the guest house with you?'

Sylvester gave Carla a doubtful look. 'As long as I don't have to share a room with him . . .'

'Of course not, how could you think such a thing?'

'. . . Or a bathroom.'

'No, no, he will have his own shower.'

'I'll join you here for breakfast, though, if you don't mind. He and I get along more or less on a professional basis, but on a personal level, I find Marcus hard to take.'

'Carla finds him charming,' said Agatha. 'So she says.'

Carla laughed. 'Yes, and so I do, but only when he has dined well and had plenty to drink.'

'I have to say, I've never seen him mellow,' said Sylvester. 'If I've been working with him, my main aim is to get away from him as quickly as possible. I never met such a fellow for delighting in everything that's miserable and depressing.'

'He does have a bleak outlook,' agreed Carla.

'The artistic temperament,' suggested Agatha.

'Artistic nothing,' said Sylvester contemptuously. 'Indigestion, more like.'

Ferenc folded his paper and poured himself another cup of coffee. 'And here he is, if I'm not much mistaken.'

Marcus had been severely disappointed in his first view of the island as seen from the deck of the ferry. 'Soft,' he said disdainfully to Quarles, as he hustled him down to his car. 'Pretty, ugh!' he added, ladling him into the driver's seat. 'That volcano's not too bad, brooding, you know; but the rest!' He gave Quarles a forceful prod with his elbow. 'Come on, get moving.'

Quarles made a weak effort at protest.

'You'll have to drive the car off,' said Marcus brutally. 'We can't sit here all day on the car deck, the other drivers are already getting restless.'

'You drive,' said Quarles.

'Can't,' said Marcus. 'Don't know how. Come on, you'll feel better once we get going.'

That much was true. Quarles always felt better as soon as he was on dry land, and by the time he had followed Marcus's incoherent and misleading directions which had taken him through the town, back in again, up a dead end and to the fish market, he had almost rejoined the human race.

'Give me that map,' he said. 'Now, exactly where are we aiming for?'

'Villa Saraceno,' said Marcus, pointing to it on the map with a stubby finger.

'Then we're going in entirely the wrong direction,' Quarles said, pushing his car into reverse and roaring back down a narrow cobbled street. He swung the car round and headed up the hill. 'This is very picturesque,' he ventured, admiring the stepped houses with their gaily painted doors and the tumbling pink flowers which sang out against the white walls.

'Ghastly,' said Marcus. 'I hope the Villa Saraceno is a bit more interesting than this lot.'

And what a bundle of fun you are, thought Quarles, as he changed into a lower gear for the final ascent to the wrought iron gates of the Villa Saraceno. He stopped in front of them.

'What are you waiting for?' asked Marcus.

'For you to get out and open the gates.'

'Isn't there someone there who does it?'

'Doesn't look like it.'

'You do it, then.'

'No,' said Quarles, keeping his temper with difficulty. '*I* am driving. You are not. So you get out, open the gates, I drive through, you close the gates, get into the car again and we drive on.'

This was clearly a novel idea as far as Marcus was concerned, but he gave in with a bad grace, banging the gate shut after Quarles with a resounding clung. Then he stopped, opened the gate and banged it to again.

At the third bang, Quarles thrust his head out of the window. 'What are you doing?' he yelled.

Marcus took no notice, but opened and shut the gate several times more before giving it a final shove and returning to the car.

'What was all that about?' Quarles demanded.

'You wouldn't understand,' said Marcus.

'Good morning, Marcus,' said Ferenc, getting up and clasping his guest by the arm. 'Welcome to the Villa Saraceno. And? . . .' He gave Quarles an interrogatory look, which Marcus ignored; his attention was fixed on the coffee, rolls and bowls of fruit laid on the table.

Quarles extended a hand. 'I'm Quarles,' he said. 'I've driven Marcus from Rome. I'm doing a piece on him for the *Gazette*.'

'How do you do? This is Carla, and Agatha, who is staying with us.'

'Ah, you must be rottweiler Quarles,' she said with a delightful smile. 'The ruthless critic.'

Quarles blushed. 'Um, I suppose so.' His savagery with the pen didn't extend beyond the page, and he hated people to judge him harshly.

'Sit down,' said Carla. 'Have you had breakfast?'

Marcus had eaten on the boat, but was not averse to settling down to another large breakfast of rolls and fruit. Quarles, who was still unsure about the state of his stomach, sipped at a milky coffee and nibbled at a roll.

Dido was assembling the twins as Magdalena came into their room. 'Good,' said Dido. 'I need to get some things for these two. Can I have some cash, if you aren't short?'

'Of course,' said Magdalena, sitting on the bed the better to give Hugh a hug. Helena was there at once, chanting 'Me too, me too.'

'What kind of things?' she went on, when she had unwound her son's octopus arms from around her neck.

'Sun hats, the ones they've got are okay for England, but useless in this sun. More T-shirts, you can't let them be on the beach without tops on, they're far too young.'

'Seems a bit hard, to be covered up all the time,' said Magdalena.

'Soft skins they've got, won't do them any good to get that burned. You got to go easy on the sun when you're little.'

'Yes, you're right, of course,' said Magdalena. 'They've never been much in hot sun, just the odd few days in the summer.'

'Yeah, well, that's the north of England for you,' said Dido. 'Come over here, Hugh, and get your sandals on.'

Hugh extended a bare foot. 'You put them on.'

'Oh, no,' said Dido. 'You'll be going to school soon, you'll have to put your own shoes on there. Get on with it, we aren't going without you. Helena's already done hers, see?'

'Helena's a girl.'

'Yes, she's lucky, mate. You're the one who's got to work hard to learn things like that. Girls find it easy.'

'Easy if you do it,' said Hugh hopefully.

Magdalena couldn't help laughing. 'That's a family failing, get someone else to do the dirty work.'

'Little slob, you are,' said Dido. 'There might be ice-creams when we go to the shops, but only for people who've done their own shoes up.'

'I done it,' said Hugh, swiftly getting his shoes on.

'Did it,' said Dido. 'Got to get your grammar right, Hugh.'

Duly accoutred, the twins hurled themselves out of the room and along the gallery which ran round the upper floor of the courtyard. They stopped by each arched and pillared opening to peer down into the garden and whoop loudly before dashing on to the next one.

They reached the terrace in a hubbub of shouts and giggles, to receive a mixed welcome.

'Hi, kids,' said Ferenc warmly.

Carla opened her arms to give them a hug.

Agatha pushed her sunglasses on to her forehead and gave them a friendly wave.

Ettore greeted them with mock-solemn handshakes and a quick kiss.

Sylvester loomed over them, bidding them to hold their tongues or he'd beat them, a threat which they took in excellent part, with further delighted shrieks and giggles as he picked them up, one under each arm.

'Manners,' he said. 'Meet the new arrivals. This is Quarles, a writer. Of sorts,' he added.

Quarles looked wary, but managed a hello.

'And this is Marcus, a famous composer.'

Marcus stared at the twins with undisguised horror. 'Children!' he said, in the tone which other men might have used to say 'rats', or 'viruses'.

Helena looked Marcus in the eye. 'You're not a famous composer. Our friend Alban's a famous composer.'

Marcus closed his eyes in exaggerated horror. 'You aren't referring to Alban Praetorius, are you?' he said. 'Per-lease.'

'Do you know him?' said Magdalena. 'His wife is a cousin of mine by marriage.'

'I know of him,' said Marcus coldly. 'Which is quite enough. There's nothing to be said about his music, it's beyond listening to.'

'You like it, then?' said Sylvester, all innocence.

Marcus gave the shudder of a sensitive artist. 'It's quite simply unbearable, Sylvester. The man has no business calling himself a composer. Trite, hackneyed stuff, there's simply no place for that kind of garbage.'

'Talking of garbage,' said Ferenc, pushing back his chair, 'how about making a start right away, Marcus? Then we can take a break, go to the sulphur baths.'

'Sulphur baths?' said Marcus, keenly interested. 'Now, I like the sound of that.'

Dido came in on light feet to collect the twins. 'Hi, Quarles,' she said. 'Fancy meeting you here.'

Quarles had gone perfectly pale, as was his disconcerting way, and he stood wordless, gazing at Dido.

'You two know each other,' said Agatha, her quick eyes darting from one to the other.

'That's right,' said Dido. 'Old chums, eh, Quarles? Come on, you two, we got to get going or we won't get nothing done. See you, Quarles.'

'Have some more coffee, Quarles,' said Carla in a kindly voice. 'Do you feel you can manage anything more, yet? Would you like a powder for your stomach?'

'No, thank you very much, I'm fine now,' said Quarles.

'Do you have another name?' asked Agatha, who had been worried by this. 'I mean are you Quarles Smith, or is it your surname, are you Fred Quarles?'

'It's my surname,' said Quarles, his face returning to something like its normal colour as he bit into a roll spread with honey. 'My first name is Decimus, so I don't use it.'

'Yes, your parents would have done better to give you a more ordinary name. Given that you were stuck with Quarles. Are you a tenth child?'

'Sort of,' said Quarles, brushing the crumbs of his trousers. 'I'm the only one, but there were nine nearlys before I made it to the finishing post.'

'Nine miscarriages? Your poor mother.'

'Some of them were intentional,' said Quarles. 'She didn't want children, you see. She felt they would interfere with her life.'

'Did you?' said Agatha, fascinated.

'No,' said Quarles lightly. 'She left soon after I was born.'

'Oh, that's hard.'

'Not really. My aunt brought me up; she liked children, so it was okay. Now, where are they practising? I'd like to see Marcus at work.'

'Of course,' said Carla. 'But not today, I think. Let them settle down, get used to each other. This is very important for artists.'

'Oh,' said Quarles. 'Well, I suppose if you . . . I do have to book into my hotel.'

'Where are you staying?' asked Carla.

'Hotel Aeoli,' said Quarles.

'Not too far away,' said Carla. 'You have your car, don't you? Then go quickly, and you can give Magdalena and the others a lift to the harbour on your way.'

'Dido?' said Quarles, getting up quickly.

'Dido will be with the children, yes,' said Carla, a mischievous look in her eye.

'Thank you,' said Quarles.

Thea stood in delight as hot air wafted through the door of the aircraft. The view wasn't wonderful; airports are not, by and large, places of beauty. It was the heat, the light, the clarity of it.

Chiefly, it wasn't England on a grey and drizzling summer's day.

The plump little woman gave Thea an encouraging push from behind, and Thea went on down the steps, checking that she had her passport within reach, fishing for her sunglasses, sniffing the air with relish.

Thea might have been off men, but she was quick to take in the energetic masculinity surging around her. Even the passport officer, no Adonis, resonated with charm and a quickness which made her senses come alive in a way that hadn't happened for all too long. She understood why her companion from the plane liked Sicily; no fool her, thought Thea, watching her head for a bus with the ease of a familiar and experienced traveller.

Thea herself had travelled as the child of well-to-do parents does; holidays with the family when younger, and then basic student back-packing as she got older. This was different, this neat but solitary travel. This was independence of a new kind.

It appealed, she decided, as she made for the information desk to find out about getting to Aeolus. Armed with a phrase book and a hazy memory of a year's Italian at school, she was greeted in excellent English and in no time found herself outside the terminal on a Giunta bus which was about to set off for Milazzo.

Dora had given her some good advice as they sat eating their lunch out of plastic trays on the plane. 'Go by steamer, not by hydrofoil. Those islands are so beautiful, but you want to come at them slowly, out on deck, not in all that foam and looking through perspex.' Thea wondered how her friend had found time off from her other holiday activities to visit the islands, but she was always willing to take advice from people who knew.

Dora had been right. Thea was intoxicated by the dark blue, almost purplish sea and the green mountains rising above the water. She leant on the rail as the steamer chugged its way in a slow and dignified manner to the port of Aeolus, savouring the salty, warm air. One of the mountain peaks had fat cloud around it. Volcano, thought Thea, as she noticed the grey-black rocks visible through the thick green cover.

She hung over the side, looking for Agatha. There she was. She waved furiously, shouted out, 'Mum,' but her mother was talking to someone next to her. A man. Thea frowned. Surely Dora couldn't have been right; perhaps Sicily had a special and instant effect on women of a certain age. Of any age, she reminded herself, noticing once more the attractiveness of the men who lounged about on the waterfront or the livelier ones having energetic conversations with friends. But Mum couldn't have . . . Not that she'd blame her, not the way Pa had been carrying on.

'Darling,' said Agatha, giving her daughter two feathery kisses. 'This is Ettore, who is Carla's father.'

'Carla?' asked Thea as Ettore won the brief skirmish for control of her bag and led the way across to the car park.

'We're staying with Carla,' said Agatha, as Thea folded herself into the back of the tiny white Fiat. 'At the Villa Saraceno.' The car burst into life and tore along the road, stopping as Ettore braked abruptly to let a biddy in black cross the road, then phutting and roaring as he accelerated up the hill.

He stopped outside the villa gates with a screech and a jolt, Thea was extremely glad to lever herself out. She was as tall as Ettore, and he smiled deep into her eyes as he bowed over her hand. Agatha kissed him on both cheeks; very Italian, thought Thea crossly, and then waited as he pushed open the gate for them.

'I gather he doesn't live here,' said Thea.

'No, he has a house further up the hill. I met him when I was walking down to meet you, and he gave me a lift. Nice man.'

'Too much charm,' said Thea.

'Nonsense, darling, no man can have too much charm. No woman, either, if it comes to that. He saved us a steep walk, just as well, what have you got in this bag?'

'That's the light one,' said Thea, shifting the strap of her other one further on to her shoulder. 'Couldn't he have driven us up to the house?'

'No, I wouldn't have it,' said Agatha. 'He only went into the town to get paper. He's a writer, you know, in the middle of a book; he hasn't got time to hang about for us. Besides, it's the best way to approach the villa, on foot. Look.'

'Goodness,' said Thea, putting her bag down and surveying the creamy building with its medley of roofs, which ranged from steeply pantiled ones to fat little domes. 'It's very Moorish, isn't it?'

'Saracen origins,' said Agatha. 'There's a ruined Saracen castle nearby, we can go and see it one day.'

'Where are we going to stay?'

'I wanted to find a house, but Carla says she has more than enough room, she's opened up some rooms in another part of the house. Glorious views, and I must say, I like the company here.'

'Company?' said Thea suspiciously, heaving her bag up again.

'Magdalena and the twins, of course. And young Thomas.'

'He's been plastered over the papers. He can tell me what happened at that horrible school. It can't be as dreadful as the press make out.'

'Then there's Dido, of course.'

'She settled down okay?'

'Wonderfully,' said Agatha.

'Many messages coming through?'

'No, we haven't heard more than the odd remark.'

'Good,' said Thea. 'It doesn't bother one when you get to know her, you get used to them. But it can worry some people.'

'I can imagine,' said Agatha. 'Then there are the musicians.'

This was said in a more guarded tone, you never could tell how Thea felt about members of that profession.

'Like?'

'Ferenc Latterly, the pianist. He owns the villa, he lives with Carla.'

'Right. And?'

'Sylvester?'

Thea's wary look relaxed. 'Great. Gabriel, too?'

'He's coming later.'

'That's all right.'

'And a rather strange young composer.'

The composer's name was lost in a welcoming bustle as Sylvester swung Thea's bag from her in a large and easy gesture, and the twins, rosy from sand and sea, fastened themselves to her legs.

'Warm people, aren't they?' said Quarles to Marcus.

'If you like that kind of thing; personally, families give me the creeps. Full of incest and oppressed feelings, dangerous and troublesome.'

'And this is Marcus Mordaunt, the composer,' Carla was saying.

Thea's face went white.

'Hey,' said Marcus. 'Haven't I seen you before?'

Thea got herself under control. 'I don't think so,' she said. 'Except that I worked in a music archive. You might have seen me there.'

Marcus was frowning. 'Don't think so, why would I want to look at other people's futile outpourings? No, I'm sure . . .' He shook his head. 'It'll come to me, just give it time.'

'It had better not,' said Thea under her breath.

* * *

'This is your room, darling,' said Agatha.

Thea went across to the window and pulled the shutters open, letting out a sound of pure delight as she gazed out over the jumble of tiled roofs and white and pink and blue houses to a shining sea. 'What heaven, I'm so glad I came.'

'Close the shutters, Thea, because the room will be unbearably hot if the sun comes in. It was clever of you to find out where I was. I was going to write to you, to say I was here. I couldn't telephone of course, because the only time I tried, your father answered the phone.'

'What did you do?'

'Put the phone down, of course. I'm so cross with him, I won't speak to him.'

'Poor old Pa,' said Thea laughing. 'He's such an idiot. Still, Mum, it could be worse, admit!'

'How?' said Agatha coldly.

'He could have run off with a lady from the chorus.'

'What chorus? And she'd be welcome to him, he can run off with anyone he likes; if he could find anyone fool enough to put up with him for more than five minutes, I'd die of astonishment.'

Thea got up from the bed, pulled her suitcase towards her, flicked open the locks and started to put her clothes away.

She always was a tidy child, thought Agatha affectionately. 'I like that lemon shirt, Thea.'

'I got it in the Liberty sale,' said Thea. 'It cost a week's salary even then.'

'Why have you given up your job, darling? Or can't one ask?'

'I don't want to think about work while I'm here in this blissful place,' said Thea evasively.

I do worry about her, thought Agatha, as Thea hung a bikini and a one-piece costume on the back of the door. She used to be so open. 'You aren't in any trouble are you?'

'Oh, Mum, don't fuss. That was a dead-end job, with promotion only by patronage of the basest sort; I'll be much happier somewhere else. I haven't had a proper break for ages, so I'm entitled to a short lull.'

Agatha changed the subject to what she hoped was neutral

ground. 'Very good company here,' she said. 'You looked startled when you met Marcus, do you know him?'

'I've never seen him in my life before,' said Thea truthfully. 'He just reminded me of someone, that was all.' She tucked a hanger into her last dress and hooked it over the rail in the cupboard. 'That Quarles guy, is he the critic?'

'He is a critic, yes. And a writer.'

'Isn't it funny, I often read his pieces, and I pictured him quite differently. Much older and kind of dull.'

'And he isn't?'

'No, very elegant, don't you think? Rather *fin de siècle*, with that lock of fair hair falling over his eyes.'

'Do you think he's a homosexual?'

'Not the way he was looking at Dido, no,' said Thea. 'She'll end up drawing him, she likes men with lean faces and mobile mouths. I like the way he has a smile lurking in the corners; he looks as though he could be fun. It's surprising his articles are so savage, when he doesn't seem to be savage at all.'

'I hope not,' said Agatha, wishing she knew what was bothering Thea. 'Come along, darling, you must be hungry.'

'Always,' said Thea, pulling the shutters completely to, and following her mother from the room.

12

Valdemar manoeuvred his car into a parking space and sat for a moment, quite still, looking out in a rare moment of reflection at the pavements shiny with rain. Then he gathered himself together, got out of the car, locked it, and ran up the steps to the heavy front door of the stuccoed, double-froated house.

He pushed it open, and light and a babble of voices spilled out. Virginia was obviously entertaining in numbers this evening. Valdemar felt a flash of irritation, he wasn't in the mood for a crowd.

Once inside he could see that there weren't so many people. 'Only about twenty,' Virginia said. 'Ralph will get you a drink.' She paused. 'Any news of Magdalena?'

'No,' said Valdemar. 'Nor of Thomas. He could write, it wouldn't kill him.'

'He knows how angry you are.'

'Nonetheless . . .'

He took a large gulp of his drink, his eyes automatically glancing over the people nearby; that was an attractive-looking woman. A flash of the hunter instinct rose in him, then died. Not interested, he told himself, making his way through to the matching room across the hall.

A familiar figure appeared at his elbow. 'Hello, Val. I hoped you'd be here.'

'Gussie,' said Valdemar, bending to give her a kiss. 'Is Cleo here?'

'No, of course not, dreadfully dull going anywhere with your mother.'

'Not your kind of do, I wouldn't have thought,' said Valdemar, taking in the vivid clothes which few women of her age could have worn, but which became her so well.

'I get on fine with Virginia,' said Gussie. 'Even though she's a Mountjoy.'

Valdemar shrugged. 'She can't help that.'

'No, and being married to Ralph has made her more human than most of you.'

'You don't think being married to Magdalena has done the same for me?' said Valdemar acidly.

Gussie looked at him thoughtfully and popped a canapé from a nearby tray into her mouth.

'Well?'

'What can I say, Val, except that it looks as though you've managed to make her extremely unhappy. I thought for a while that you really cared for her.'

'I do care for her, if you want to know. Very much. I don't happen to care for her taking off into the sunset.'

'I thought she went to get Thomas.'

'If she has got him, then she isn't exactly rushing to bring him back. And I don't see why she needs the twins out there if she was planning a there-and-back visit.'

'Has she taken the twins?' said Gussie, surprised. 'That's more serious, then.'

'Oh, I'm glad you don't say, "How nice for Magdalena to have a week or so in the sun, enjoying the sights of Rome." And I don't think Rome at this time of year is any place to take young children. It's far too hot, probably very unhealthy.'

'Is she in Rome? The papers seemed to think Thomas was holed up in an Italian paradise. Is Rome that?'

'The papers get everything wrong.'

Gussie held out her glass for a refill as Ralph came past. 'Have you told Val your news, Gussie?'

'I'm just about to,' said Gussie.

'What news?' asked Valdemar, not greatly interested. 'A show? I assume you are still painting.'

'It's my profession, Val. No, it's nothing to do with work. It's Cleo. She's going to be married.'

'Oh, is she just? Who to? Do you want me to give her away?'

'You did that years ago, Val,' said Gussie gently.

Valdemar was silenced.

'Actually, they're having a register office wedding. Perry's been married before, and is divorced . . .'

Valdemar was frowning now. 'Perry who?'

'Perry Boston.'

'Used to be married to Angelina Carr?'

'That's the one,' said Gussie. 'I thought you'd know him.'

'Of course I bloody know him, we were at Cambridge together. Cleo can't possibly marry him, he's old enough to be . . .' He stopped in mid-sentence.

'Her father,' prompted Gussie. 'Yes, he is, which is probably why she's marrying him.'

'I won't have it,' said Valdemar, giving Gussie a very black look.

'Don't be silly, Val. Even if you had any legal rights over Cleo, which you don't and never have had, given the circumstances, she's old enough to marry who she wants. They all marry or live with whoever they like anyway.'

'I am her father.'

'Oh, goody,' said Gussie. 'Ring her up, then, and tell her you forbid it. See where that gets you.'

'Gussie, you can't be happy about this.'

'No, since you ask, I'm not. However, it's Cleo's life, and if it's a mistake, then she'll find out soon enough. Personally, I like Perry, but I'm not sure he and Cleo . . . Anyway, what I think has no bearing on it. I'll support Cleo whatever she does, that's what I'm here for.'

Valdemar flushed. 'Meaning I haven't been.'

'You could say that,' agreed Gussie.

'It's disgusting, he's twenty years older than she is.'

'Has that ever stopped you, Val?'

Valdemar plucked another drink from Ralph's hands.

'I hope you aren't driving,' said Ralph. 'Don't want any more tidbits for the papers, do we?'

'I'll walk back to the flat,' said Valdemar shortly. 'So, when is this happening, Gussie? This disastrous match which you say you can't stop?'

'In three weeks,' said Gussie. 'It'll be in the *Times* and *Telegraph* tomorrow; I wanted to tell you first.'

'Thanks,' he said laconically. 'One more bloody thing to worry about.'

Gussie was taken aback. 'You're hardly likely to worry about it, Val. You may be annoyed, but . . .'

'Much you know about it,' said Valdemar. 'Cleo's my daughter, of course it matters to me that she's happy. God knows, a rocky marriage is hell.'

'It rather depends who's doing the rocking, don't you think, Val?' said Gussie.

Magdalena and Agatha walked along the sandy path which wound along the side of the hill. It was a stroll, not a vigorous ramble; it was too hot in the still afternoon air for anyone to do anything vigorous.

Even a stroll was almost more than Agatha felt happy about. 'Was this such a good idea?' she asked.

'It'll be worth it,' said Magdalena, enjoying the heat of the sun on her shoulders, revelling in the contrast of colours; the greenness of the vines, the silvery grey-green of the occasional olive tree, the piercingly blue sky and the softer, darker blues of the sea, the exuberant colours of the flowers. Heavy scents hung on the air, and then, as they left the terraces, the smell of pine wafted out from the little grove of trees.

'Insects,' said Agatha, taking a swipe at something with too much buzz and wing which landed on her arm.

'There are bees here,' said Magdalena. 'Giulietta was telling me; her uncle keeps bees, marvellous honey apparently.'

'Even so,' said Agatha, with another quick slap, this time on her leg. She looked at Magdalena. 'You're feeling better, aren't you?' she said decisively. 'Happier. This island, the sea, the sun, the air, the warm nights, they're doing you a power of good.'

They are, thought Magdalena. And being at the Villa Saraceno, full of excellent company, and not seeing Valdemar. I've not been thinking about him at all, she realized with surprise.

'And Dido's a find,' said Magdalena.

'Much better than that depressing specimen you've got at Eyot.'

'Lottie's all right. Better for every day, probably. She's very highly qualified.'

'I think children enjoy someone with a bit of bounce, who isn't quite so everyday,' said Agatha.

'Routine,' said Magdalena.

'They have routine with Dido,' Agatha pointed out. 'It's just a different one.'

'Dido's very attractive.'

'All that sparkle, and those dancer's eyes.'

'Quarles is mad about her.'

'Clearly, but they wouldn't suit each other.'

'Oh, I don't know. People make the strangest matches, and they seem to work.'

'Sometimes.'

'Of course, Lottie isn't at all attractive,' said Agatha reflectively.

'No,' said Magdalena. 'Attractive nannies can be a problem.'

'Like that nanny you had for a while for Thomas, what was she called? Heather, that was it. She was knock-down lovely, like a golden Diana.'

'Yes, she was,' said Magdalena.

'But she didn't stay long.'

'No, she got pregnant. Married a man in Eyot. A mechanic.'

'Best thing for her, really. Not much brain to go with the stunning looks.'

Magdalena remembered how upset Thomas had been when his nanny left so abruptly. How angry Hugo had been, and Hugo was rarely angry. And how furious she had been with Valdemar for stalking Heather like a cockerel on a dung heap, and then taking no interest at all in her future or well-being.

'Is she?' he had said with complete lack of interest, when he had heard the news. 'She'd better get married to that tedious young man of hers in Eyot.'

'The child is yours.'

'She can pretend it isn't. Or tell him the truth, I really don't care. And don't ask me to worry about this unborn child, that's nothing but sentimental hoohah.'

Foisting his children off on other men, thought Magdalena, angry now all over again. I knew what he was like, why on earth did I ever agree to marry him? Because you found him so physically attractive; because he's such a good companion when he's in the right mood that he makes other people seem only half-alive.

Only I haven't seen much of that mood lately, she thought. He's been much darker, much more angry. If he were anyone else but Val, I'd think he was going through some kind of emotional trouble. But Val? Inner turmoil? Forget it.

'This is the plant,' she called out to Agatha, who was toiling resentfully up behind her.

'The things one does for one's friends,' grumbled Agatha.

'It's worth it, have you ever seen such a glorious colour?'

'It is a riot,' agreed Agatha. 'Got your eye on it for the castle?'

Magdalena had a knack of being able to get plants to grow and flourish in her northern fastness which experts swore would wither and die in no time at all.

'Wouldn't it look lovely in that corner by the small fountain?'

'Um,' said Agatha, sitting down and slipping off her sandal to give it a good shake.

'Such a hot pink, it will look wonderful against the walls.'

'You aren't supposed to go taking cuttings of wild flowers on Italian islands and carting them off to plant in England.'

'I shall do it just before I go back.'

'And when will that be?'

'Who knows?' said Magdalena.

Marcus had insisted on the mud baths, but he didn't take to the idea of going on his own.

'You'll come, too,' he told them blithely, as he went off to change, leaving a gloomy pair of musicians regretting their offer. They already felt that a little of Marcus was going to go a long way.

'Very smelly, all that sulphur,' said Sylvester. 'He could go on his own, and we could do some work on the Brahms.'

'Marcus will think we're plotting, working on his music without him.'

'He can't possibly imagine that anyone would spend a single minute more than they had to on anything he'd composed.'

'All composers are vain. You have to be, or you'd never write a note.'

'You could be right,' agreed Sylvester. 'It takes a lot of nerve to assume firstly, that someone's going to want to perform what you've written, and secondly, that anyone's going to want to listen to it.'

'Not much danger of that with Marcus's efforts.'

'The BBC and these people who give grants have a lot to answer for,' said Sylvester darkly. 'Ah, Marcus,' he went on as Marcus in leisure mode, clad in nasty tartan shorts and strange brown sandals, came forcefully into the room. 'Are we off, then?'

Thomas was burying Dido's feet in the sand. Dido wasn't paying much attention; she was keeping an eye on the twins, who were building a maze with much merriment but little expertise, while she painted away on a pad propped up on her knees.

'My feet that bad, then?' she said without looking up.

'No,' said Thomas. 'They have a strange beauty to them. In a gnarled way.'

'Ta very much,' said Dido.

'Warm sand will be good for them,' said Thomas, squatting on his haunches. He eased his way along the sand and peered over Dido's shoulder. 'Wow! Are you an artist? When you aren't looking after children, I mean.'

'Sort of,' said Dido. 'Got to get these colours down, never seen anything like it. Magic.'

'I wish I could paint or draw,' said Thomas wistfully.

'You can.'

'No, I'm hopeless at it. I have to do it at school, and the art master says he's never seen such rubbish.'

'Anybody can learn to paint,' said Dido. 'Fact. You just need to be shown the right way.'

Thomas's face lit up. 'Dido, would you teach me?'

'Course,' she said. ''Slong as I keep those kids under control, me time's me own.'

'I'd really like to be good at something,' said Thomas, relapsing into his more pensive frame of mind. 'I mean, I won't be good at drawing, but I'd just like to be good enough to enjoy it.'

'That's all right, then. What more do you want?'

Thomas sat down in the sand, his knees pulled up to his chin and his lanky arms clasped round them. 'I'd like to be good enough at something so that there was no question about it.'

'I thought you was good at music.'

'So-so,' said Thomas. 'I'm not ever going to be like Ferenc or Sylvester, not a professional, not even a lowly professional. A bit of talent, which is what I've got, isn't nearly enough for that.'

'Games?'

'I'm useless at games. I don't mind that, because I hate games.'

'That must go down well at your posh school.'

'It's not too bad, actually. When you're as hopeless as I am, they kind of don't bother with you. And lots of the other boys aren't too bad about it, because you aren't a threat. You're not trying for a place in the team.'

'That's what they call fostering the team spirit, is it? Being glad when someone's too awful to count as competition.'

'It doesn't seem so good when you put it like that. It must have been different for you, being a dancer. It must have been awful when you hurt your foot.'

'Best thing that ever happened to me,' said Dido. She shouted across to where the twins were playing. 'Hugh, your T-shirt isn't covering your back properly, pull it down.'

Thomas stared at her. 'Best thing?'

'Yeah. I danced because me mum wanted me to be a dancer. I had the right physique, see, and a good sense of rhythm, so I did all right. But there was all these crazy kids there, at ballet school, they was mad to dance. I wasn't. Not ever, take it or leave it. I was bored a lot of the time, but I couldn't let me mum down, could I? She had this dream of me pirouetting on to the stage at the Garden in a tutu, on points, Princess Aurora in Swan Lake.'

Dido swirled her brush in a little jar of water on the sand beside her, and applied some ochre in deft, dabbing strokes. 'It was her dream, not mine. I didn't give a tinker's, really. And if I hadn't done for that foot, I'd never have got out of the corps de ballet. My heart wasn't in it, and it showed. You can't be an artist because someone else wants you to. In the end you got to be driven from inside.'

'What about the drawing? Is that a hobby? Or is that being an artist?'

'That's proper work. Theatre and costume design, that's what I'm going to do as my profession, and that's a real art. Me mum's ever so upset, she still hasn't got over me not dancing any more, but I tell her, look, Mum, one of these days you'll be in the audience at the Garden, and all those costumes on stage will have been designed by me. Isn't that much better than seeing your daughter prancing round in someone else's tutu?'

'What does she think of that?'

'She thinks it's a rotten idea.'

'So why are you working as a nanny?'

'I did the nanny training to make me mum happy. When I done that ankle in. You got a qualification, you'll always be able to get a job. That's how her mind works.'

Thomas was fascinated. 'And all the time it's being a designer that matters. As far as you're concerned?'

'Yeah. I'm doing me Master's now. Then it's off into the big bad world, get myself some work.'

'It sounds really good,' said Thomas.

'What about you, then? What you going to do when you leave school?'

'I've already left one school,' said Thomas wryly. 'Don't know who'll have me now.'

'Local comp,' said Dido. 'They got to take you. Unless you've beaten up a master or something like that. You brainy? Do well in exams?'

'No, I told you, I don't shine in anything. I do okay. Mostly it's very boring, schoolwork. I can't get worked up about it.'

'You are in the doldrums, aren't you? I'll have to ask on the other side about you, mate, see what they've got to say. Now, you got any money?'

'Yes, I have, actually,' said Thomas.

'Right. There's a shop in that little square behind the harbour, you know, the one with the fountain in it.'

'Yes.'

'There's a kind of stationer's there. They've got sketch pads. You get one with paper like this, okay? And some charcoal pencils. And some watercolours if you've got enough cash. They're expensive, mind.'

'I've got enough,' said Thomas.

'And brushes. These numbers.' Dido scrawled on the corner of her pad cover and tore off the triangle of paper. 'That'll do you. Now, hop it; I got to take these two in for a swim.'

'A swim is what I'm going to have after this,' said Sylvester, wallowing in a shallow, stinking puddle of mud.

Marcus was in ecstasies. 'Died and gone to heaven,' said Ferenc, trying to lessen the smell by breathing through his mouth.

The sulphurous pools nestled among strange, twisted volcanic rocks and petrified lava flow. It was weird and eerie, and appealed greatly to Marcus. 'Hell must be like this,' he said happily, sitting up and slopping the dark, oozing mud over his shoulders. 'Sylvester, you look like a hippopotamus.'

'I do not,' said Sylvester. He was indeed a strange sight in his very large-sized swimming trunks which were plastered against his body by the mud, but he looked far too grand to be a hippo.

'Good thing Gabriel can't see you now,' said Ferenc mischievously.

'Not Gabriel's sort of place at all,' said Sylvester definitely. 'I think we should encourage Quarles to come here for a slimebath, though; it might soften his pen a little.'

'I hear the crater of the volcano's worth seeing,' said Marcus. 'Like the surface of the moon, only more desolate and unpleasant. How do we get there, Ferenc?'

'We don't,' said Ferenc firmly. 'It's years since I've been up there, and I'm not planning any visit in the near future. Get one of the locals to take you along.'

Marcus heaved himself up with a terrible slurp of mud. 'Can't wait,' he said. 'I'm told there's a wind which howls and whistles up there.'

'Yes, it's piercing and irritating,' said Ferenc.

'Sounds great,' said Marcus. 'Hey, you two had enough?'

'Yes,' said Sylvester. 'I'm going to have a shower, put on a more seemly garment or two, and then I'm going to go to the beach to meet Magdalena for lunch.'

'Okay by me,' said Ferenc. 'I'll bring Carla down.'

'Those children will be there,' said Marcus, disgruntled.

'Of course,' said Sylvester. 'Excellent; good company, those two.'

'We've got a lot of work to get through.'

'Plenty of time, plenty of time,' said Sylvester annoyingly. He flexed the fingers of his huge right hand. 'There's a little stiffness here, a bathe in salt water will be just the ticket.'

'I'll get myself some lunch then,' said Marcus, aggrieved.

'You do that,' said Ferenc. 'See you later.'

Quarles had no intention of taking a mud bath; he didn't think that was his kind of place at all, as he told Thea. She was lying on the terrace under a huge sunshade, reading a garish novel.

'Oh, are you pompous as well?' she said, peering at him over the top of her specs. 'My brother's very pompous; it can get extremely tiresome.'

'Of course I'm not pompous. And as well as what?'

'As well as being so venomous.'

'It's my job to be venomous,' said Quarles, dragging up a chair. He was more than happy to talk about himself; then, after that, he could steer the conversation round to Dido. Thea was Dido's friend, she could be useful.

Thea wasn't playing. She tilted the umbrella over to a new angle, pushed her glasses firmly on to her nose and returned to her book.

Snubbed, Quarles tried to pretend he hadn't intended to chat. He picked up a paper which was lying on the table beside him. 'Amazing how quickly the papers get here, isn't it?' he said, flicking the pages open.

Thea grunted.

Good legs, thought Quarles. Too tall, though, for his taste. He liked petite women, full of fire. Like Dido. His eyes idled over the page. Ho, what was this?

'Look,' he said, jabbing at a paragraph as he waved the paper in front of Thea. 'Is he any relation of Magdalena's?'

'I can't see a thing,' said Thea, reaching out for the paper and holding it up to her eyes. She peered at the words from under her sun specs.

'There,' said Quarles.

Thea read the short piece, and then read it again. 'It's

Magdalena's husband,' she said. 'Fluttering some doves in the cathedral dovecotes by the look of it.' She folded the paper and looked out to the horizon. 'He told me he was having a spot of bother with a Dean.'

'More than a spot of bother, I'd say,' commented Quarles, taking the paper back. 'The Dean seems to be accusing him of being responsible for a thumping great crack in the fabric.'

'Must be serious if they've had to close the Cathedral.'

'They couldn't take the risk if the tower's likely to collapse.'

'I must show that item to Thomas.'

'Why?'

'He was a chorister there. He'll be interested.'

'Man's obviously completely incompetent,' said Quarles.

'Who?'

'This Mountjoy guy.'

'Not at all,' said Thea coldly. 'The Dean's to blame. You shouldn't believe what you read in the papers, Quarles,' she added in a kindly way. 'Total rubbish, you know, nearly all of it.'

13

Valdemar tossed the newspaper into the waste paper bin, leant back in his chair and thought.

Virginia surged into Val's office. 'Val?'

'What now?'

'All hell's breaking out on the switchboard and I think there are a couple of press types hanging round the entrance.'

'Janus can tell them to bugger off.'

'What are you planning to do?'

'Nothing,' said Valdemar. 'There's nothing I can do, except publish our report. It's so technical they won't understand a word of it. It's much easier for them just to get a juicy heap of lies from our good friend the Dean.'

'I've had a word with the Archbishop.'

'Oh, good, everything's all right then.'

Virginia went on in her usual calm way. 'He says the Dean is a very tricky number.'

Valdemar's eyebrows rose. 'He said no such thing, Virginia, don't tamper with the text.'

'Not in so many words, but that was the gist of what he had to say.'

'Fine.'

'He said one has to be fairly subtle with this Dean, no good meeting him head on. Confrontation is the breath of life for him, apparently. He adores a good fight, preferably conducted in a blaze of publicity.'

'I had more or less gathered that.'

Virginia sat on the corner of Valdemar's desk.

'Any danger of that tower actually collapsing?'

'Difficult to say. Who's looking after it?'

'I don't know.'

'Let's get Ian on to it. Then I'll have a word with whoever it is. It's all so damned unprofessional. On paper we're still the structural engineers for the Cathedral. You can guess whose fault it will be if the whole lot does come toppling down.'

'It would be a tragedy.'

'Indeed it would,' said Valdemar grimly. 'And it wouldn't be the first time the church has been led into disaster by the stupidity, arrogance and pigheadedness of one of its senior clergy. Any organization which entrusts some of the most superb buildings in the world to idiots like this man deserves to fall apart at the seams.'

'You'd better use the basement entrance when you go out.'

'Skulking like a criminal on my own premises,' said Valdemar furiously. 'I won't have it. Throw me that address book, Virginia, I'd better see if I can get hold of the Bishop.'

'Jon?'

'Yes, not that he'll be much use. He's grown so emollient over the years that he's due to slide down a grating one dark night and never be seen again.' He picked up the phone. 'Get me a line, Pippa. Oh, for God's sake, just cut them off. Say it's Battersea Dog's Home when anyone rings in; what a nightmare this all is.'

Dido was instructing Hugh in the art of eating spaghetti. Yet again.

'He doesn't seem to pick things up very quickly,' said Magdalena in a worried mother's voice. 'Helena isn't finding it difficult.'

'There's nothing wrong with Hugh,' said Dido, patiently demonstrating once more. 'Except laziness.'

'You do it,' said Hugh encouragingly.

Sylvester roared with laughter and helped himself to another heap of salad. 'Good place this, Magdalena. Right on the beach, too. Handy. And the fish is first-class. I shall come here often.'

'You'll have trouble with Lily when you get back to England,' said Magdalena provokingly.

'No, no, I never put on weight in Mediterranean countries.

Mystery why not, but there you are. I must say, Dido, you pack away a lot for one built on small lines.'

'Yeah, I like food,' said Dido. 'Specially when it tastes like this.' She leant over and gave Helena's tomato-smeared mouth a skilful wipe with her napkin.

'Dido's teaching me to draw,' said Thomas, stuffing too many sardines into his mouth all at once.

'What a revolting sight,' said Sylvester amiably. 'Are you a trained artist?' he asked Dido.

'Getting there,' said Dido.

'So this kind of work is just to earn pocket money.'

'More'n that,' said Dido. 'My old man scarpered years ago, and Mum can't afford to keep me now I'm a big girl, let alone pay the fees.'

'Don't you get a grant?'

'Yeah, but it doesn't cover everything.'

'Does your mother work?' asked Ferenc. He liked Dido's easy spirit and strange appearance.

'Yeah, she's a dresser at the opera house.'

'Covent Garden?'

'That's it. Worked with all your top artistes, she has. Strewth, the stories she tells.'

'I can imagine,' said Sylvester. 'Opera singers can be very trying.'

'Not to mention dancers,' said Dido. 'And musicians.'

'Is that where you got your name?' asked Magdalena. 'It's unusual.'

'Yeah, it is, specially for someone like me, we run to Traceys and Kellys round where I come from. But Mum reckons she fell pregnant the night they was singing *Dido and Aeneas* in the opera house. Me dad was in the greengrocery line, you see. When the market was still there in Covent Garden. I was got on a heap of cabbages, that's what I reckon.'

'Novel,' said Sylvester, hugely amused.

'Are you making it up?' said Thomas, his eyes like saucers.

'No,' said Dido. 'I'm not much of a one for stories. Any fantasy I got goes into me costumes and sets, plenty of strange stories around without me having to make up any more.'

'And that's true enough,' said Agatha, enthralled. 'Why did your dad go off?'

'Got fed up with me mum being out all hours. With all them fancy folk, as he saw it. The men in tights got him particularly, he was too stupid to know they're nearly all bent. He just looked at the pictures of them with all their bulgy bits and he used to go berserk. Good riddance, Mum said, when he took off with Florrie from down the road. And her hubby was pleased to see her go. She was teetotal, and he liked nothing better than going down the boozer with his pals.'

'Wise man,' said Sylvester. 'Have some more fish, Dido. Have you got any of your work with you?'

'Bits and pieces.'

'Good, good, I'd enjoy having a look at what you're up to. If you don't mind.'

'Okay by me.'

The twins set up a clamour for ice-cream, and were quickly tamed by Dido, much to their mother's admiration. 'I don't know how you do it,' she said admiringly.

'They know I mean it,' said Dido. 'It's easier when you're not their ma, you just have to keep them on their toes. After lunch and a rest, I'm going to take them to the park, I think they've had long enough on the beach.'

'Dido, you must have some time off,' said Magdalena.

'Yeah, I will one evening when you're at the villa and not looking so blinking tired. I'll go down town with Thea, we can have a go at the local talent.'

'Thea?' said Agatha, alarmed.

'She'll be all right,' said Dido. 'Thea can look after herself.'

'What a surprising thought,' said Agatha. 'But I suppose she can.'

Ferenc and Sylvester went reluctantly back to tackle Marcus; Dido took the children off, and Magdalena, Agatha and Carla sat amid the ruins of the table, at ease, quite happy to sit and look idly at the sea. A waiter came and swept away the remains with charm and dexterity, and then came back with fresh coffee.

'Bliss,' said Magdalena.

'Now,' said Agatha. 'While you're feeling so peaceful, you can tell me something I've always wanted to know.'

Magdalena's face took on its wary look.

'No, don't look at me like that. I'm one of your oldest friends, but there are some things we never discussed. What I want to know is, why did you marry Ronnie?'

Magdalena laughed. 'Honestly, Agatha, why do you want to know that? It was all so long ago.'

'Even so . . .'

'Ronnie was your first husband?' said Carla. 'Were you very young?'

'Nineteen,' said Magdalena. 'It didn't last long, he wrote himself and his expensive sports car off one dark night on a lonely country road. Whether it was accident or suicide, we'll never know. He was drunk at the time, so I don't suppose he knew either.'

'Was he so young?'

'He was, oh, six, seven years older than I was,' said Magdalena, looking back to a time which seemed infinitely long ago. 'We got married after the war.'

'And he had been a soldier? A hero?' That was something Carla quite understood.

'He'd been in the RAF, yes. Very brave, very gallant. Fearless, and adored by his men. He was very handsome and funny and charming. A Catholic, and so when we met, my mother pounced on him.'

'Ah, so your mother was behind the marriage.'

'Oh, yes. She felt I was full of unruly passions, she'd wanted to get me safely married off ever since I was seventeen; she was terrified that I would get myself into trouble. And Ronnie was much grander than we were, and my mother was South American, she admired that sort of Englishman.'

'A romance,' said Agatha drily.

'In a way. I was desperately in love with him, the way you are at nineteen.'

'Nineteen,' said Carla. 'A dangerous age for a young woman with a fervent heart.'

'Pretty dangerous age for any woman,' said Agatha, thinking back.

'But you weren't happy?'

'He drank,' said Magdalena simply. 'I suppose he'd started drinking during the war, a lot did, you know. By the time we married, he was an alcoholic.'

Carla made a very Italian clicking sound, of sympathy and shock.

'So our marriage was a farce. He couldn't do anything in bed; of course not, with all that alcohol in his system, he was pickled. That made him angry, and naturally, he took it out on me.'

'Did your parents know?'

'They must have suspected, but as long as the marriage seemed all right, as long as the neighbours didn't know anything was amiss, then it was best to say and do nothing.'

'No way to treat a daughter.'

'Not uncommon,' said Agatha. 'Goodness, how terrible. And about the same time, I married George, whom I now loathe and detest; and we were so poor we nearly died of hypothermia in winter; and we were so happy. We spent hours and hours in bed, and then George went off and worked incredibly hard, and I went to an office and typed and typed, and then we'd meet on the bus and go home together and make love again. I'm quite sure we ate nothing at all for the first three years.'

'It was a long time until you married again,' commented Carla, lighting a cigarette and letting the smoke float restfully into the calm air.

'From what I'd seen of marriage, it was the next thing on earth to hell,' said Magdalena. 'No way was I going to get caught like that again. No, I went in for lovers. Of all kinds. Some married, some not, rich, poor, young and old. I stayed with them for a long time, or a very short time, as I felt inclined. I fell in love and out of love, and slept with men just because I wanted to. I had a very good time.'

Carla was laughing. 'So you were a rake, too.'

Magdalena had to smile. 'When you think about it, yes, I was. But those were my salad days. I'd already grown up and found I liked my own company by the time I met Hugo.'

'You met him at that exhibition,' said Agatha, signalling to the waiter for more coffee. 'Tapestries, when you were working at the V and A.'

'Yes, Hugo had lent some of the Mountjoy tapestries, from the castle. They were in very poor condition. I told him so, and he took me out to dinner. And that was that.'

'That must have been the only exhibition Hugo went to in his whole life,' remarked Agatha caustically. 'Hugo was more of a country type,' she explained to Carla. 'Guns, dogs, land.'

'I know this type. We have them, too, in Italy, although not quite like yours.'

'Almost certainly not like ours,' said Magdalena. 'But Hugo was very kind, very tolerant, very happy for me to do the things I liked. "Your arty things," he used to call them, but he took them very seriously.'

'Darling, Hugo was a real sweetie,' said Agatha with warmth, noticing the tears glistening in her friend's eyes. 'He was one of the nicest men I ever met, and you made him very happy.'

'In a way,' said Magdalena with a sigh. 'Agatha, can I have some more of that coffee?'

'So interesting, people's marriages,' said Carla.

'Not mine,' said Agatha. 'Mine isn't interesting, it's as dull as can be; chiefly because I'm married to the most tiresome man in England.'

Marcus was prowling about the Villa Saraceno, angered by its peaceful and ancient beauty. The place was deserted, and he was chewing over ideas in what was, for him, a burst of creativity. This had been inspired by a fit of temper. He had cherished hopes of finding here, on this fairly remote island, traces of *tabula rasa*. Of children who didn't sing tunes, were strangers to ditties.

What did he find? Children yodelling out popular tunes of the moment, men singing songs that were, he suspected, quite rude – which was interesting – but definitely tuneful – which was not. Just now, he'd come across a woman carolling away to her tiny baby in the pentatonic scale, and from inside her house, an older child was singing along to the *bel canto* pouring out of the radio.

He pounced on an unsuspecting Quarles. 'It has to start before conception,' he roared into Quarles's ear.

'What?' said Quarles, stunned.

'Pregnant women should be absolutely forbidden to listen to any music.'

'It's very good for them,' argued Quarles. 'Relaxation and so forth.'

'Never mind relaxation. This seeping pollution of sound has got to be stopped, and stopped at the very beginning.'

Quarles looked at Marcus, alarmed. There were excellent things about this assignment, viz, seeing Dido, staying in a comfortable hotel run by friendly people, the beauty of the island, time for his writing. There was one huge drawback, he realized, and it was standing here beside him, bellowing with rage, the muscles on its neck standing out with the tension of its fury.

'It is imperative,' Marcus ranted on, 'to isolate the next generation from traditional music.'

Composer autocraticus, thought Quarles, who had a habit of labelling people as though they were specimens in the zoo. *Musicianus obnoxiosus*. A red-necked *homo stupidissimus*, he was rapidly beginning to think.

Marcus was getting into his stride. 'Take that appalling nursery rhyme, "Twinkle, twinkle, little star". It has to be one of the most nauseating, primitive and destructive tunes going. It has to be banned.'

Pull yourself together, said Quarles the professional. His job could be on the line here. He wasn't paid to point out the weaknesses of the Marcuses of this world; that would be a seriously uncool thing to do. His deadly pen could aim with technical precision at flaws in Marcus's individual compositions, but he could never cross the line and condemn the man, let alone his oeuvre. Not if he wanted to retain an ounce of credibility.

'That's very interesting,' he said cautiously. 'Presumably you feel that even foetal exposure to the wrong kind of music can imprint the mind with unsuitable patterns.'

How can I be spouting this gobbledygook? he wondered.

Marcus's rage subsided as quickly as it had risen. Quarles was showing signs of intelligence; Marcus loved a sympathetic audience. 'Exactly. The mind must be as clear as nature intended when the infant is born.'

'No innate structures,' murmured Quarles.

'Nobody with half a mind can subscribe to the theory of innate structures,' said Marcus, his temper rising again.

'No, no, quite discredited as a theory,' said Quarles hastily.

Marcus gave a pleased harrumph. 'Then the next stage is to make sure that, for the first two years of the child's life, there is absolutely no exposure to tunes of any kind.'

'Ban all nursery rhymes and folk songs,' said Quarles flippantly. 'Away with the whole caboodle.'

Marcus gave him a suspicious look, but he was well launched on his favourite theme. 'This is the formative time when the real damage is done. The mind, which is, of course, essentially lazy, becomes so accustomed to tonal sounds that for the rest of its life it is unable to clear the clutter away.'

'Clutter, yes. Some minds are chock full of extraneous rubbish, I couldn't agree with you more.'

'So true music sounds strange, unnatural and uncomfortable.'

'True music being atonal?'

'Yes, that goes without saying.'

'Tell me,' said Quarles, propping himself on to a handy ledge and enjoying the warmth and scents from the garden below, 'how did you manage to eliminate these factors from your music? You must have been exposed to the wrong kind of music early on. And so must the people who listen to your music.'

Idiots all, he added to himself.

'It's an inborn gift,' said Marcus. 'Genius is overriding. I began training as a musician, so-called, very young, and I could have followed the traditional path of a classical musician. I was very good,' he went on, with no false modesty; Marcus wasn't strong on modesty.

'Being a genius, you would have been,' agreed Quarles.

'I reached a very advanced standard very young. But then my inner ear told me that this kind of music was wrong.'

'I'm sure all great composers have this kind of revelation,' said Quarles cunningly.

Marcus didn't look convinced on this point, he found it difficult to believe that any earlier composer's inner call could have been a true one.

All this was going down in Quarles's retentive memory. Marcus was far more of a character than he had expected. Good stuff, he thought. Excellent material, even if not for immediate use. He also wondered, with more interest, what was behind or under or beyond all this. The true Marcus, he suspected, was a very different person. Perhaps Ferenc or Sylvester could give him a lead; Marcus might reveal a different side of himself while working. He would sound them out.

'Ah, I hear the others,' said Marcus, breathing deeply after his refreshing bout with Quarles. He hung over the courtyard. 'Hi, Ferenc, Sylvester, get a move on there. We've wasted a lot of time today.'

Magdalena walked along the waterfront, delighting in the colours, the strong smell of fish, the elegant, curved lines of the fishing boats drawn up on a tiny stretch of sand. People were talking, laughing, gesticulating. Everyone is so full of life, thought Magdalena. She found the exuberance and zest with which people were going about their business invigorating and charming.

She crossed the road, skipping out of the way of a buzzing scooter ridden by a dashing young man. He flashed a brilliant smile at her and shouted a remark which she didn't catch.

Once, she thought, that would have been a suggestive remark, now it's the kind of thing he'd say to his aunt.

She was almost fifty, she mused, as she wandered along the little line of shops. Where had the years gone? Passing years don't bring wisdom, she thought with irritation. They bring tiredness and perhaps, at best, a certain resilience.

Worse, they mark your skin, your body, your hair, but leave you feeling very much the same inside as you did twenty years before. Where was this mythical serenity, self-confidence and all the other things that were supposed to compensate for your vanished youth?

Parrucchiere, she read, picked out in gold letters on a discreet window. *Istituto di bellezza*. She hesitated for a moment, and then, quickly, before she changed her mind, pushed open the door and went in.

A sleek woman in a white coat gave her a smile of welcome. Here goes, Magdalena said to herself.

It was more than two hours before she emerged, feeling guilty and even more unsure of herself. Curse her English upbringing. Why couldn't she enjoy all this, as her mother had done, as the people in there so clearly did? Why did she feel that she shouldn't pamper herself; that a basic hairdo once a month was quite enough?

A voice hailed her. 'Magdalena. Ah, you look very beautiful, you have been to the salon, how enchanting.'

'Ettore. Hello. I was just feeling guilty about it.'

'That is so Anglo-Saxon. I find the English so full of absolutes. When they take care of themselves, the results are so often horrible; blue curly hair, strange eye-shadow or, if you are very young, the whore-in-the-streets look. Or there is the horsy look, no nonsense, heh? No artifice? You shouldn't feel guilty, you aren't old, you have excellent bones. You must make the most of yourself. And now, to celebrate, and because I want to show off that I know such a lovely woman, I will take you to the best café here, for a little aperitif, or coffee, or ice, or whatever you wish.'

'Let's go,' said Magdalena.

14

Thomas and Thea were looking for Dido.

'Go for the noise,' advised Thomas. 'Where the twins are, there is racket and rumpus.'

'You were four once,' said Thea.

'A long time ago.'

'Nice being four,' said Thea. 'You can stand on your own two feet, no one's shoving you into a pushchair any more. So plenty of running about. You're too young for school, so no sitting still or having to be anywhere or do anything. And life is so uncomplicated.'

Thomas was very struck by this. 'It's true,' he said. 'Life does seem to get more complicated as you grow up. I think my life is very complicated, and I expect yours is, too.'

'You could say that.'

'And look at older people. Marcus seems all twisted up about things. Quarles jumps every time anyone speaks. Sylvester and Ferenc don't seem to have too many hang-ups, although I know that Sylvester has terrible rows with Gabriel sometimes.'

'Does he?'

'Did you know that Sylvester's gay?'

'It is generally known,' said Thea.

'Much better when you have secrets that aren't, if you see what I mean,' said Thomas with feeling. 'Secrets which don't really matter if they come out. That you don't mind people knowing about.'

'Secrets?'

'Family secrets, things to do with you or your life that you don't want other people to know about.'

'Yes,' agreed Thea. 'And things that you have to keep from your parents.'

'There's a lot I don't tell Magdalena,' said Thomas. 'I don't have parents in the usual way, you see, so Val and Magdalena are kind of there instead.'

'Do you get on well with Val?'

'Not at the moment,' said Thomas. 'He won't listen much. He thinks I'm like the twins, that he can just say something and that I'll have to do it. I don't think he was ever fourteen.'

'Do you think anyone else at the Villa Saraceno has a secret?' asked Thea, curious.

'Oh, yes. Your mum has, hasn't she? And Marcus and Quarles, like I said. And you, you've got a secret. I suppose Magdalena has a secret.' He kicked a piece of litter which lay in front of him on the dusty pathway. 'I hate it when Magdalena's unhappy.'

'I expect she hates it when you are, too.'

Thomas thought about that for a moment. 'Yes, and she hates not being able to stop Val being beastly.'

'He doesn't go for you or anything like that, does he?' said Thea, alarmed.

'No. He wouldn't, that's not his style. He won't argue, he just shouts and lays down the law, and he's kind of frightening. He frightens me, anyway. I used to, you know, wet the bed when I was little and he'd been shouting.'

'You'll soon grow,' said Thea encouragingly. 'My father can get very grumpy, although he's not too bad really, and he was always going on at my brother Edmund. Then Edmund grew, and he got much taller than Pa, and Pa laid off him then.'

'I doubt if I'll be taller than Val,' said Thomas. 'He's very tall, nearly as tall as Sylvester, and I'm not growing very fast.'

'People grow when they're happy,' said Thea. 'You're happy here, aren't you?'

'Oh, yes, it's brilliant.'

'Then you're probably growing.'

'Is that true? You didn't just make it up?'

'Scientific fact.'

They walked on, Thomas thinking about his inches and wondering if he was a bit taller already, while Thea, struck by Thomas's perception, wondered what secrets other people might have. Worse than hers? Unlikely.

'You didn't mention Dido,' she said. 'Has Dido got a secret?'

'Oh, no,' said Thomas eagerly. 'Isn't she great? She's so straight, she's the most unsecretive person I ever met.'

'Mmm,' said Thea.

'Of course, she gets all those messages, so I expect she knows all kinds of secrets about people. Do you believe in all that?'

'I wouldn't admit it in company,' said Thea, lowering her voice, 'but if Dido isn't in touch with something out there, then I can't imagine how she knows what she does. And she comes straight out with it, if that's what they've told her to do. It can get some people really worked up.'

'I bet,' said Thomas with relish. 'She hasn't come out with anything much so far, has she? Do you think she's saving it all up, or are the spirits or whoever they are just not interested in us lot?'

'Knowing Dido,' said Thea, 'I'd say it was only a matter of time.'

The café had a canopy. It was green and white, and cast a cool light beneath it, where Magdalena sat with Ettore, talking and flirting and enjoying herself very much indeed. All nonsense, of course, but it was such fun to push aside the serious matters of life and enjoy the company of an attractive man.

The tables and chairs were set out on the pavement, and people strolled by; a woman with a little dog, the young mother from the beach with her small children clustered round her, a relaxed holiday couple eating ices.

A peaceful scene, a peace which was shattered in an instant by a sharp voice.

'Why, it's Magdalena Mountjoy, fancy your being here. I thought you were in Rome, of course one was terribly shocked by all those vulgar stories in the tabloids, but here you are, in Italy, just as they said. Are you with Thomas? Surely not, you must be so cross with him, running away like that, disgraceful behaviour. Have you sent him back to England? Though of course, I hear that there's no way the school will ever have him back. Well, the scandal! Naturally, one doesn't believe what one reads in the papers, but there's always a grain of truth there somewhere, that's what I say.'

She stopped for breath, and took in Magdalena's dark, glossy hair, with not a single grey thread; her face, lightly but expertly made-up in a way that set off a honey-coloured tan. Then her lizard eyes flickered over Ettore, who had risen to his feet.

'Oh, I am sorry, I didn't mean to interrupt you, it's just that Magdalena and I are acquainted, through my brother, Nigel Norris, you know. We're neighbours, well, where we live, a few miles means nothing. And I was so surprised to see her here, the last person in the world I'd expect to see, Mr . . . ?'

'This is Ettore Graziate,' said Magdalena, giving in to the inevitable. 'Ettore, this is . . .'

Magdalena paused, thinking how like her brother this woman, whose name she could not remember, was. As far as she knew, she had met her exactly once, at some function in Eyotshire. At another time, in another life, she thought crossly. What was she doing here, raking her and Ettore up and down with her protuberant eyes, her pursed little mouth almost trembling with curiosity and excitement?

'Sandra, Sandra Moredon,' she said quickly, not in the least put out by Magdalena not remembering her name. Her attention was riveted on Ettore. 'Not *the* Ettore Graziate? The writer?'

'I am a writer, yes.'

'Well, how wonderful, I'm such an admirer of yours.'

'Do sit down,' said Magdalena.

'Well, I really shouldn't because I'm meeting a friend,' Sandra said, sitting down at once. 'I'm here for a week, sadly no more, just for a tiny break. With my son, and my nephew. They're on Little Leave from school.' She smiled graciously at Ettore. 'They're at Gryme, you know. The public school.'

'Ah, this is the terrible school which Thomas has told me about,' said Ettore. 'My commiserations to you, Signora; it must be a worry to you for him to be there.'

'It's a privilege for any boy to go there,' said Sandra indignantly. 'Of course, it's a very high-powered school,' and she cast a malevolent look at Magdalena, 'and only outstanding boys really cope with it well. My boy loves it, he's never been so happy in his life.'

'Some boys like to get away from home,' said Magdalena before she could stop herself.

'I couldn't agree with you more,' said Sandra. 'My boy is lucky, he fits in so well at school, and then he's just as happy when he comes home for the holidays.'

'Fortunate,' said Ettore.

Magdalena sipped her drink, determined to say nothing more. Ettore likewise remained silent, a pleasant, distant smile on his lips, a slight air of boredom about his eyes.

Sandra looked at her watch. 'What a shame, I have to dash, I'm meeting the others, and I'm late. Where are you staying, Magdalena? We've taken a villa, so comfortable, wonderful views. And a pool.'

'I'm staying with friends,' said Magdalena.

'In a rented villa? Now, let me see if I can guess . . .'

'Magdalena stays as a guest in my daughter's house,' said Ettore gravely. 'My daughter lives on the island, it is a private house.'

'I see, yes, I suppose it would be. Magdalena, it's lovely to see you, and looking so well, with all the problems you . . . Yes, you are looking well, I must say. I expect I'll see you around, we must have lunch. The boys might like to get together,' she added, a little doubtfully. 'That is, if Thomas is allowed out.'

'He isn't in quarantine,' said Magdalena. 'He's having a holiday. I'll tell him Giles is here.'

'You do that,' said Sandra. 'Bye, then.'

George and Edmund were enjoying a silent breakfast together. Edmund was reading a fascinating article on Microcosmic Absolutes; George was deep in the Sunday papers.

George grunted. 'Val isn't going to like this at all. Not at all.'

Edmund glanced up from his magazine. 'I don't know why you read that rag, Pa.'

'I read it because I like it. It livens up Sunday, lots of pretty girls and juicy scandals.'

'So what's in it that your chum Valdemar won't like?'

'This cathedral business. In Eyot. You probably haven't heard about it, not moving in the same world as the rest of us.'

'If you're asking, do I know that the central tower of Eyot

Cathedral is about to come crashing down, yes, I had heard a rumour to that effect.'

'Val's firm were the structural engineers. I gather from Val that they wrote a stiff report warning the Dean not to start pulling bits of the Cathedral out, such as he had in mind, but that the Dean's reaction was to sack Mountjoy Partners and carry right on.'

'End of story as far as Val's concerned, then.'

'Not a bit of it. The Dean started heaving the organ out, he's one of these tiresome clergymen who wants electronic sounds instead of the real thing, and a great crack appeared. So of course he's got to blame someone, so he's sitting on Val's report and blaming him. Now the papers have declared open season on Val, and they're raking up all kinds of personal matters which have nothing to do with the Cathedral or his professional standing.'

He tossed the paper over to Edmund. 'See for yourself.'

Edmund read. 'That affair of Val's ward running away from school can't have helped.'

'They mention that. Insinuating all kinds of things.'

'Is Thomas Val's son?'

'Yes, but officially Val is his uncle and guardian. For the boy's sake as much as anything.'

'If it's fairly generally known, I bet the other boys at Gryme made his life hell over it.'

'That may have been the trouble there; I hadn't thought of that.'

'This is nasty,' said Edmund, running his eyes down the columns. 'Libellous, one would suspect. Who's his solicitor?'

'Rowley.'

'Will he have seen this?'

'Rowley doesn't miss much. He won't like it, though; they're the kind of firm that hate having their clients splattered across the headlines.'

'Do you think there's anything about this in the other papers?' said Edmund, stretching and getting up from his chair. 'I think I'll just nip along to the newsagents and have a look.'

'Why the interest? Isn't all this a bit sordid for you?'

'Valdemar's wife is Ma's closest friend. If she's closeted in Italy with Magdalena, and the press are getting hot on this, she's going to wake up and find the reporters flying after them on a pedalo.'

George frowned. 'It's your mother's own fault entirely, going away like that.'

'If Ma's dragged into this, then we will be as well. Whichever way, Dad, you can't just ignore this. And Val may be a nasty piece of work, but he is a friend of yours. You'll have to rally round.'

'Val is not a nasty piece of work.'

'If half, a quarter, even, of this is true, then he's a very nasty piece of work indeed. Siring children in what seems to be a completely casual and careless way. It's disgraceful.'

'The morality of today's youth,' said George crossly as the door closed behind Edmund.

Magdalena was fuming by the time she got back to the Villa Saraceno.

'Who ruffled your feathers?' asked Sylvester, who was spread out lazily on the terrace. 'I like the hairdo.'

Thomas looked doubtfully at Magdalena, wary of any change in her, or any straying from the norm of his contemporaries' mothers. It did look rather nice, he decided after a long stare. And after all, he didn't have to conform to what those other boys approved or disapproved of any more, he'd never see any of them again if he had his way.

Magdalena sank into a chair. 'It's infuriating,' she said. 'Thomas, who would you most not want to see on this island? No, it isn't Val,' she added quickly, seeing a look of panic coming over Thomas's face. 'I know how you feel about him, but who else?'

'You're sure it isn't Val?'

'No, not Val, I promise.'

'No one would be as bad as Val.'

'Someone your age, from Eyotshire. At Gryme with you.'

'Not Giles?' Thomas looked at Magdalena with horror.

'I'm afraid so. Here for the week with his aunt, whom I've met, but don't remember. She's Nigel's sister, she lives near Eyot.'

'Ho hum,' said Sylvester. 'This is very sorry news.'

'It's infuriating. I was having a drink with Ettore in a café on the waterfront, when lo! up she pops out of the woodwork, oozing pleasantries, her foxy nose twitching with joy at the scent of intrigue.'

'I don't think being with Ettore is intrigue,' said Thomas, rising to her defence.

'No, of course it isn't,' said Sylvester. 'Pity you weren't with me, Magdalena, I'd have seen her off.'

'You can't see people like her off,' said Magdalena.

'She'll tell Nigel, won't she?' said Thomas acutely. 'As soon as she gets back to Eyot. That she's seen you here.'

'She may do,' said Magdalena.

'And if she does, then he'll find a way to tell Val.'

'Undoubtedly,' said Sylvester. 'In the most unpleasant way, you may be sure. Don't fret, Thomas,' he added in his kindly way. 'Val was bound to find out sooner or later where you were.'

'He'll come out and bully me,' said Thomas disconsolately.

'I don't think he will,' said Magdalena briskly. 'He's got a tremendous workload on at the moment, I think he may leave us alone for the time being.'

'Good,' said Thomas.

Sylvester had risen and pottered across to the table on which was a tray with a jug and glasses. 'Homemade lemonade,' he said, handing a glass to Magdalena. 'Delicious.'

'Are you still working?' Magdalena asked, looking at her watch.

'Oh, yes, got to press on, you know. But Marcus's sorting something out with Ferenc, so I escaped for a bit. The torture will resume shortly.'

'Is it truly awful?' asked Thomas.

'Quite bad enough, but don't you go making remarks about it,' said Sylvester. 'We don't want to offend Marcus.'

'He doesn't seem to mind offending people himself,' said Thomas.

'That's temperament,' said Sylvester gravely. 'The sensitivity of the creative soul.'

'Do you mean that?' asked Thomas doubtfully.

'I do not, you silly boy. You must learn to recognize irony, this will be of great benefit to you as you go through life.'

'Alban's creative, and he doesn't carry on like Marcus.'

'Different type,' said Sylvester. 'And Alban's quite difficult enough in his own way.'

'I think I'm going to be an accountant,' said Thomas. 'Or a solicitor, like Nigel. People like that have nice quiet lives.'

'Don't you believe it,' said Sylvester darkly.

Dido cast an expert eye over the twins, who were blissfully asleep in an abandoned heap after the exertions of the day. She went through into her room, spiked her silvery hair, applied some vivid purple and silver eyeshadow, blocked her eyelashes in dark blue, rouged bright pink contours on her cheeks and applied a bruised grape lipstick.

Ready for anything, she said to herself, closing the shutters and turning on her bedside light so that it would later cast a glow into the twins' room. Then she made her way with her dancer's walk to join the others on the terrace.

Quarles had been invited, and he was propped against a corner of the terrace, his light coloured suit and brown Italian sandals a picture of casual elegance.

'Got to hand it to you, Quarles,' said Dido. 'You know how to dress.'

'All right to wear those clothes when you've got Quarles's figure,' said Sylvester. 'I'd look like an ice-cream salesman if I tried it.'

'I like your gaudy shirts, Sylvester,' said Magdalena. 'Although they seem less astonishing here than they do in Midwinter.'

'Gabriel bought me some navy polo shirts for the summer,' said Sylvester. 'I think it's a hint.'

'Well, you wear those until he comes, and then you can turn sober.'

'I'm not sure navy's me,' said Sylvester.

'Doesn't matter,' said Dido. 'Your pal won't be here for a few days yet.'

'He's expected the day after tomorrow.'

'No, give it a week,' said Dido. 'I got a message.'

'By phone?' asked Carla.

'No,' said Dido. 'From the other side. They've been dead quiet since I got here, but now they've started bending my ear. They told me about that shit-stirrer you met today,' she said to Magdalena. 'Trouble coming, they warned me. Which will lead to unforeseen consequences.'

'If that woman gets on the phone to Nigel, which she will, I think the consequences are all too easily foreseen,' said Sylvester.

'Yeah, well, I'm only telling you what I got. Most of it doesn't mean much to me, it only makes sense to the person they're talking about.'

'Like what, Dido?' said Quarles, spearing one of the little cubes of seafood which were laid out on the table.

'Like someone's got to get in touch with someone they know, quick, about young love. I thought that might be you, Thomas, what you been up to?'

Thomas looked startled, and flushed. 'Not me,' he said, keeping his cool. 'Perhaps it means love that hasn't been going on very long.'

'Could be the name of a perfume,' said Sylvester.

'Or a piece of music,' said Ferenc. 'Sounds like a song.'

'I'm sure the message will get through to whoever it's meant for,' said Dido, flicking a quick glance from under her thick eyelashes in Quarles's direction.

Quarles said nothing, but chewed thoughtfully on a chunk of swordfish.

'Can you ask specific questions?' said Agatha, intrigued. 'Or do the messages just come?'

'I'm a channeller,' said Dido. 'It just comes through. I can't make it come, or stop it, and I don't ask questions.'

'Have you always been able to do this?' asked Ferenc.

'No. It started when I was struck by lightning, 'bout four years ago. You remember it, don't you, Thea? Just outside the underground, whoomph. I nearly ended up in a rubbish bin.'

'I thought you'd been killed,' said Thea, taking pleased sips of the fragrant white wine which was made from the grapes growing on the island.

'Naw, we dancers are used to being thrown around.'

'It's a pity you can't ask questions, though,' said Agatha, her thoughts on her own particular problems.

'You never know what they might come up with,' said Dido cheerfully. 'Keep hoping.'

15

Dark clouds descended as Valdemar drove across the Trent. They were in keeping with his black mood. Bright sunlight and sparkling air would have been very annoying.

'How long are you going to be away?' Virginia had asked before he left.

'God knows.'

'Are you seeing the Dean?'

'No. That's why I'm going now; he's away from Eyot for several days, attending some conference or other.'

'The Synod,' suggested Virginia.

'Not at all his style, he's into management, he'll be off learning personnel disposal or team tactics or some other faddy topic. He isn't, basically, a clever man, so he's sucker for any important-sounding humbug that comes his way. He reckons a Dean is a frontline decision-maker, so he's going to take decisions. In his simple way, he imagines that thinking in a series of capital letters is the key to getting things done and what he nauseatingly calls people management.'

Virginia laughed. 'He's obviously got up your nose.'

'I hate incompetent people rummaging around in a field where they don't really belong. I don't think this guy is any kind of a priest, all right, that's hardly a qualification for being a Dean, but he isn't anything else, either. He'd call himself an able administrator, which is balls.'

'Why did they appoint him?'

'Come on, Virginia, why do any of these types get appointed? He was in the right place at the right time, he knew someone, no one else wanted the job. If he had a flair for the kind of complex organization he's dealing with, you could forgive him, but he hasn't a clue. And he fancies that because he says something it's true. Or it will happen. No further action necessary.'

'He'll come a cropper in the end.'

'Unlikely,' said Valdemar cynically. 'Institutions are crammed full of people like Higgs-Boson, who thrive in a destructive way. Once they've screwed up in one place, they simply move onwards and upwards, leaving some other poor sod to pick up the pieces.'

'Literally, in this case.'

Valdemar found himself gripping the wheel at the thought of the ancient tower of Eyot Cathedral crumbling into dust. He was almost past caring whether he got blamed for it or not; his one aim was to stop it happening.

More damned rubbish in the papers this morning, and it had made his job immeasurably more difficult. Why should a chaotic private life – not that it was chaotic, of course, that was just what the half-witted reporters made it out to be – have any bearing on your professional judgement?

Nonetheless, there were some old friends and colleagues who'd taken a lot of persuading, particularly those involved with churches and cathedrals. As though looking after an ecclesiastical building somehow imparted an extra layer of godliness and a greater sense of morality.

I'll give them morals, thought Valdemar viciously, remembering what he knew about some of his keenest critics and doubters.

'It's not a moral issue,' Agatha was saying. 'It's a practical matter, only George has blown it up out of all proportion.'

'What kind of a practical matter?' said Sylvester, who had been longing to know why George and Agatha had parted brass rags.

He looked up to see Ferenc beckoning at him; he waved at him in an unhelpful way. Music could wait. 'You go and play some scales,' he said. 'I'll be along in a minute or two.'

'Sylvester, Marcus is champing and foaming in there.'

'Throw a bucket of water over him,' Sylvester advised. 'Go on, Agatha.'

Ferenc gave up and vanished; Agatha looked at Sylvester and shrugged.

'It's very trivial. Or I think it is. In, let me think, March, yes, March, I was in France.'

'Doesn't George's father live in France?'

'Did. He died. In March. That was what started it all. I was in Paris, staying with an old school chum. I'd had a slight cold when I left England, and by the time George rang me to say that his father was desperately ill and wouldn't last the night, I had a raging cold and a rising temperature. George was in Scotland, in some remote and inaccessible spot; he couldn't get to France until the next day. I was to get down to his father's house in Angers that very evening.'

'Hard on George, with his father so ill.'

'Hard, nothing. George and his father had scarcely been on speaking terms for years. His father had set up house with an old friend after his mother had died, and George never got on with her. I don't know why, she's perfectly charming.'

'Still, he would have felt better with you being there if his father was dying.'

'It wasn't that. It was his mother's jewels, which his father had refused to hand over. I was to get myself there, quickly, quickly; and the second he died, fly round to the bank and remove the safe-deposit box.'

'Huh?'

'The jewels were in it.'

'Why the speed?'

'Sharpen your wits, Sylvester. This is France we're talking about. No point in leaving property hanging about to pay tax on. They all do it, whisk the valuables away before the authorities can check up.'

'Ah, now I understand. So?'

'So, feeling extremely ill, I got on a train and struggled down there. He was unconscious by the time I arrived, well, he was eighty-four, and he hadn't exactly followed a healthy regime – ever. He duly died in the early hours, so Jacqueline and I nipped round to the bank manager's house – at three in the morning, please note – got the man out of bed and we all went round to the bank.'

'What, at three in the morning?'

'Do listen, Sylvester. It had to be then, because by the time the bank opened for business in the morning, the officials would be on to it, and we couldn't have got the damned thing out.'

'Tough on the bank manager.'

'Oh, no, apparently they're quite used to it over there.'

'Catch an English bank manager turning out at that time to help a customer.'

'Don't be fanciful, Sylvester.'

'Okay, so you got the box with the sparklers . . .'

'. . . Hardly sparklers; just some quite nice Victorian jewellery.'

'And?'

'And I stashed it away and got myself on the train back to Paris. I didn't feel like staying, because I knew George would arrive shortly and start quarrelling with Jacqueline – I wasn't in the mood for all the drama. Besides, I was feeling extremely ill, with a temperature way over a hundred. I wasn't what you'd call a welcome guest, not at a time like that.'

'But you got back to Paris all right.'

'I must have done, because I woke up in my friend's flat three days later.'

'Three days later? Three *days*!'

'Yup. With no recollection of getting there, or anything else from when I boarded the train in Angers. Nothing. Blank. Zilch.'

'Did you wander about for three days?'

'No, my friend said I'd turned up about six hours after my train must have got in, and just collapsed.'

'Were the jewels safe?'

'No,' said Agatha. 'That's the whole point. George had told me to put them into another bank, and he'd collect them later. I have a dim memory of doing that, but I have no idea which bank it was. There was no receipt in my handbag, nothing.'

'Ah. That could be difficult.'

'It was. George arrived much later, just in time for the funeral, and he wouldn't say a word to Jacqueline, the miserable old bugger.'

'Accidents do happen. I can see he might be put out, but it's hardly a divorcing matter, is it?'

Agatha took out a packet of cigarettes and held one up. 'Do you mind, Sylvester? I know you don't like it, but telling you this is making me nervous.'

'Carry on,' said Sylvester. 'Just this once I won't protest, or flap invisible smoke away from my face like Thomas does.'

'It wouldn't be a divorcing matter for anyone normal, no,' said Agatha, returning to her theme. 'But you know what George is like. He asked me where the jewels were, and I weakly said I didn't know, I had been too ill to deal with the matter. He at once jumped to the conclusion that I'd never got the blasted things, and therefore Jacqueline must have them. So he rang her up and started ranting and raging at her, and she said, very calmly, that all she had of his father's were things that she had been given.'

'Which he took to mean . . .'

'. . . that his father had given Jacqueline the jewellery.'

'What an unholy muddle,' said Sylvester delightedly.

'You may laugh, but I've never seen George in such a state.'

'Haven't you explained it all to him, now he's simmered down?'

'Nope. If he's going to be so unpleasant and leap to completely unwarranted conclusions, then he can suffer the consequences. He's been on and on about it, grumbling and fretting, and talking about getting his solicitors on to it.'

'Could be tricky, that.'

'Oh, he won't, he knows he hasn't got a leg to stand on. I'm being used as a punchbag for his rage against his father. And, let me tell you, he's full of rage.'

'A tricky situation.'

'No longer,' said Agatha, feeling much more cheerful now that she'd told someone the sad saga. 'Because I'm here, having a wonderful time; he doesn't know where I am, he can't get at me, and I'm not missing him at all. In fact,' she went on, 'just between you and me, I've got my eye on Ettore.'

'Really, Agatha, you can't do that to George.'

'Watch me,' said Agatha. 'Now, Sylvester, pour me out a glass of mineral water – with ice and lemon if you would, and you'd better be getting back to your plonks and tinkles. I'm going to lie here in the shade and have a gentle snooze.'

With which Agatha stubbed out her half-smoked cigarette, arranged her limbs in a more comfortable pose and closed her eyes.

Dismissed, Sylvester said to himself, much amused. Back to the grindstone with Marcus and Ferenc; who'd be a musician?

She knew that voice.

Thea surfaced from her pile of postcards and put her pen down. It was Quarles on the phone, he must be tucked away on the other side of the glass hotel doors, which had just been propped open by a maid.

What was he talking about? Was he dictating copy for a slashing exposé of Marcus? It didn't sound like it. It sounded like a trashy magazine piece, deeply embarrassing revelations of teenage love. What on earth was Quarles up to? Was this some kind of phone service, under-age sex over the wires? Quarles didn't strike her as that type.

Quarles's voice became louder and more businesslike. 'Got that?' he was saying. 'That should do it, and for God's sake don't let Gemma get her twitchy little hands on it again. This is all her fault. Yes, I'll turn the proofs round in forty-eight hours, but remember, that's forty-eight hours after I've got them, not forty-eight hours from the time they get franked in the post room.'

Thea ducked her head down and started scribbling furiously as Quarles came out of the little lobby where he'd been on the phone and lounged into the café in the front part of the hotel where Thea was sitting.

He stopped by her table. 'Hello,' he said. 'Let me join you.'

'Do,' said Thea.

'Not with Dido?'

'If you want to know where Dido is, why don't you just ask?'

Quarles acknowledged a hit, raising his hand in a gesture of defeat.

'Actually, there's no point in asking, I don't know where she is. She was taking the twins off on some expedition to look at flowers.'

Quarles frowned. 'It's scandalous; Dido, with all her talent, looking after a pair of brats.'

'She enjoys it. Makes a change.'

'And at everybody's beck and call.'

'Now, Quarles, that isn't true. Dido isn't at anybody's beck and call. Including yours, which is whose beck and call you want her to be at. Dido is one tough bunny; she'll do what she wants, when she wants.'

'All those boyfriends,' said Quarles in a disconsolate voice.

Thea ruffled her hair, which gave her the appearance of a slightly demented Raphael angel. 'What precisely do you mean by boyfriends? Do you mean the art school crowd she hangs round with? Or lovers who visit her garret with red roses?'

'Dido doesn't live in a garret,' said Quarles, surprised.

Thea just looked at him.

'It's those men who always seem to be at her flat. I'm sure she goes to bed with them. She can't like them all.'

'I'm sure Dido never goes to bed with anyone she doesn't like.'

'Well, she's never gone to bed with me. Does she dislike me?'

'You'll have to decide that for yourself. Or ask her, she won't be embarrassed. No beating about the bush with Dido.'

'That's what I'm afraid of,' said Quarles. He leant back in his chair and waved at a scurrying waiter. 'Thea?'

She shook her head.

'*Espresso, per favore.*'

'*Si, si,*' said the waiter, whisking away Thea's cup.

'Good,' said Thea. 'If you're going to be here having a coffee, I can stay a little longer and finish writing my postcards. Only don't go on about Dido, I need to concentrate.'

'I'm sorry,' said Quarles huffily.

'Sylvester!' said Agatha, pleased. 'Are you going out on a toot?'

Sylvester looked magnificent in a pair of vast and immaculate white twill shorts and an extra, extra large navy shirt. He had a flashy pair of sunglasses perched on his nose and a splendid panama on his head. The ensemble was completed by canvas shoes and white socks.

'You do look splendid,' said Magdalena, joining them. 'I've always admired your wild shirts, Sylvester, but I must say, this look does suit you.'

'You'll have to take a picture,' said Sylvester in his genial way. 'I'm not sure I'll be able to manage it again, but if there's a snapshot, then Gabriel will know I tried.'

'So where are you off to? Where's Marcus?'

'He's gone to the volcano,' said Magdalena. 'With Thomas.'

'Ferenc?'

'We voted ourselves a day off in Marcus's absence,' explained Sylvester. 'We felt we needed a time of recovery. Ferenc was up at the crack and went off with Carla; they were taking the hydrofoil across to Sicily to see some friends.'

'So what are your plans, Sylvester? You didn't fancy the volcano?'

'I don't think a mountain bike is my style,' said Sylvester. 'Besides which, I suspect that a Marcus in a holiday mood may be even more wearing than Marcus in the music room, if that's possible. Therefore I propose to potter about the town, take you two to lunch somewhere, together with any other friends who are about, have a swim this afternoon and then play Bach on the terrace before dinner.'

'You've already been playing Bach this morning,' said Magdalena, picking up a large straw hat. 'I heard you.'

'One can never have too much Bach,' pointed out Sylvester. 'Especially not when your ears are smarting from Marcus's little efforts. Are you ready?'

'I shouldn't,' said Magdalena. 'There are several letters I must write, and I'm not sure whether Dido and the twins will need . . .'

'What a clutch of modal verbs,' said Sylvester. 'Must, should, need; very dispiriting. Letters can wait. Dido is more than capable of seeing to the twins, so you have no excuses.'

'No,' said Magdalena. 'I suppose not.'

'The trouble with you is,' said Agatha, expertly placing a stripe of thick white sunblock on her nose, 'that you're feeling guilty about being here instead of rushing round in circles at home.'

'Yes, and you can stop worrying about Thomas for a few hours, too,' said Sylvester perceptively. 'Very educational, volcanoes, he'll learn more going up there than he will in a term's geography lessons.'

'All right, I'll just tell Giulietta that we'll be out for lunch, and I'll be with you.'

'Excellent,' said Sylvester, breathing in the scented air with gusto and giving a giant stretch. 'A day of delight awaits us.'

Thomas wasn't too sure that a day of delight awaited him as he toiled up ever steeper paths. The peak of the volcano didn't seem to be getting any nearer. Two, two and a half hours, the man at the bicycle hire place had said. 'If you are fit,' he added with a dazzling smile.

Thomas was fit, what with the games he'd been made to do at Gryme; hate, hate, plus all the swimming he'd done here. Even so, he was finding it a strain. So why wasn't Marcus huffing and puffing? He must be at least thirty, thought Thomas, and he doesn't look as though he spends any time in the gym.

Thomas was right, Marcus never went near a gym. He was just one of those people who are naturally muscular, and keep themselves fighting-fit by doing whatever they do with a hundred per cent energy. Marcus walked up a flight of stairs with as much spring as any athlete doing training, picked up a cup of coffee as though it were a twenty-kilo weight, and walked everywhere with great speed and ferocity.

This had been annoying Quarles, who didn't have an ounce of extra fat on his lean body, but who was a great one for not exerting himself unduly. In fact, Marcus had been annoying Quarles a good deal. All you got of Marcus, Quarles found, was the surface. He had his – to Quarles – cranky ideas about cleansing the world of nursery rhymes, and the natural and untarnished ear; he liked good food; he was aggressive with his fellow musicians; he looked on Magdalena with a lascivious eye . . . and that was about it.

Artistic impulses, youthful influences, family background; on these, Quarles had drawn a blank.

Thomas wasn't bothered by Marcus's deeper soul. Thomas was still at an age when he took people as he found them, and hadn't started to delve much into other people's motives or psyches. Likewise, Thomas took adults' often nosy questions more or less in his stride. One day, he vaguely supposed, they would lay off, just as the time must come when matron, masters or Magdalena would stop making remarks about when did he last have a bath, wasn't it time he had his hair cut, and did he have to wear those filthy old trainers all the time?

So he wasn't put out when, after a particularly gruelling stretch had caused even the indefatigable Marcus to falter and call a halt, his companion started asking about Valdemar.

'Does he treat you really badly?'

Thomas shrugged.

'Hey, kid, don't you mind?'

'He's my guardian, he doesn't have that much control. I mean, my mother is the one who has the final say.'

'Magdalena?'

'No, she isn't my mother. My mother lives in India.'

'But she's your stepmother. No, that can't be right.'

'It's all a bit complicated,' said Thomas awkwardly. 'Drop it, can you?'

Marcus was already off on another tack. 'So those foul twins, they're Magdalena's and this Valdemar's children, right?'

Here Thomas felt he was on firmer ground. 'They're Magdalena's. Their father was her husband before she married Val.' He pulled at a dry clump of grass, winding the tough leaves round his fingers. 'And they aren't foul.'

'She got divorced?'

'Why do you want to know?' said Thomas, now definitely growing suspicious.

'I like to know about people I'm with, get them sorted out. Divorce, then?'

'No, he died,' said Thomas shortly.

'So how long has she been married to this Valdemar?'

'About three years.'

'Not long after hubby popped it, then.'

Thomas stood up. 'I don't think I want to see this volcano after all,' he said in a dignified voice.

'Come on, kid,' said Marcus. 'If you want to play Hamlet, that's fine by me, but don't let it get in the way of a good outing. No one else is going to take you up there, they're all far too wound up in their own little lives.'

Thomas, his leg already over his bike, hesitated. It was true, he did want to see the crater . . .

'Okay, I'll come, but just shut up about my family.'

Marcus held up his hand. 'Truce,' he said. He mounted his bike and they set off side by side, Thomas resolutely focusing his attention on the rocky track, Marcus eyeing the boy thoughtfully.

'What about Thea?' he asked after another hard-won mile. 'She's very secretive, isn't she?'

'Is she?' said Thomas. 'I don't know her that well.'

'There's something up with her,' said Marcus. 'And I'm sure I've seen her before – or if not her, then a picture of her. Hey, is she a musician?'

'Not any more,' said Thomas. 'She trained, went to college to do music, played the clarinet, I think. But she got that muscle thing and couldn't play any more.'

'RSI?' said Marcus. 'Unusual for a clarinettist, I'd say. I wonder . . .'

Marcus wasn't the only stranger interested in Valdemar's private life, as was made very clear when he walked into the York offices of Grundling and Ruckforth. He gave his name to the girl at the desk, and could see the look of bright-eyed interest that immediately transformed her from a slouching typewriter zombie into a keen and alert person. A copy of that morning's *Gazette* lay on her desk; Valdemar knew perfectly well that there was a picture of him, together with further startling revelations, on page 5.

'Just tell Roger Ruckforth I'm here, will you?' he said, as her eyes signalled across to the other desks the message that here was something to enliven the day's routine. Roger came out of his office to greet him, and ushered him back into it, requesting coffee as he went, and Valdemar could hear the voices breaking out behind him.

'You're quite a celebrity,' said Roger cautiously. You never knew how Valdemar would take this kind of thing.

'Crass, the whole business,' said Valdemar. 'Now, Roger, bring me up to date.'

'This is strictly unofficial.'

'The whole bloody thing is unofficial. On paper, my firm is still responsible for the Cathedral; there's nothing in writing saying we aren't.'

Roger was startled. 'In that case, the Dean and Chapter can hardly appoint another firm . . .'

'Forget the Chapter,' said Valdemar caustically. 'This is all the Dean's doing. I expect the people in the offices there would have a fit if they knew half of what he'd been up to.'

'It does seem a very difficult situation there,' said Roger, picking his words carefully. 'I must say, the new Dean isn't universally liked or supported.'

'I bet he isn't,' said Valdemar. 'Not if he carries on like this all the time. Plus if the wretched building falls down, they'll all be out of a job.'

Roger blanched. 'It can't come to that.'

'It will from what I hear, if this pussy-footing around goes on. Get the damage fixed first, argue about it afterwards.'

'Mmm,' said Roger. 'I think they want to lay the blame fairly and squarely on someone's shoulders – and someone outside the Cathedral – and then they'll get round to doing something about it.'

'Incredible,' said Valdemar. 'Now, you've been there, seen this crack, I've only looked at a couple of not very good photos. What's your verdict?'

16

'No, Sylvester,' said Magdalena firmly. 'I do not want to sit and eat an ice from a little glass bowl. I want a big, double ice, chocolate and lemon, please, in a cone. And I shall eat it as we walk along.'

'You'll get ice-cream all down your shirt,' said Agatha.

'I won't,' said Magdalena. 'Sylvester might,' she added with a meaningful look at his bulk, 'but I can perfectly well manage to eat an ice without covering myself in it. When I can't, I shall be ready for a zimmer frame or a wheelchair. Now!'

Sylvester gave in, the ices were bought, and the three of them strolled contentedly along the edge of the harbour. Striped and blotchy island cats lazed in the sun, the canopy over a shop made a soft flapping sound, and out at sea gulls circled and mewed.

'Beats Brighton,' said Sylvester.

'I'll tell you one advantage Brighton has,' said Magdalena.

'What's that?' asked Agatha, surprised.

'That woman isn't there,' said Magdalena, as Sandra bounded out of the *farmacia* where she'd been lurking and into their path.

'It is Sylvester Tate, isn't it?' she crowed. 'What a coincidence, so many of us from Eyotshire here all at the same time.' She smiled her wide smile at Magdalena. 'You never mentioned that Sylvester Tate was here.'

'Didn't I?' said Magdalena.

Sylvester looked at Sandra in silence; nothing daunted, she turned her attention to Agatha. 'Agatha *Fimbul*, did I hear Magdalena say? Now, I know that name. Yes, of course, my cousin's daughter, a brilliant young musician, you know, I'm sure she was at college with a girl called Fimbul, it's a very unusual name, isn't it?'

'That would be my daughter, Thea,' said Agatha.

'Oh, really? Well, there's another coincidence. Faith said they were all so sorry when Thea had all that trouble; she was quite a favourite, one gathers. An unhappy love affair, wasn't it? Such a shame when a young person's education is destroyed by that kind of thing.'

'Thea had muscle strain,' said Agatha. 'That's all.'

'Oh, I don't think so . . .' Sandra looked at Agatha's polite but distinctly unfriendly face and beat a hasty retreat. 'Oh, well, you're her mother, of course you'd know. These rumours, I never listen to rumours myself, they can do such damage.'

'Can't they?' said Magdalena.

'A good gossip, passing on the news, well, we all enjoy that, but I never pass on anything that might be detrimental or hurtful to anyone. I think that's so wrong, don't you?'

Magdalena's ice-cream, so delicious a moment before, now tasted of sandpaper and pepper. Agatha didn't look as though she was enjoying hers very much, either. Only Sylvester licked imperturbably on; nothing ever ruffles Sylvester, thought Magdalena, with grateful affection.

Sylvester came to the rescue with all the force of his large personality. 'We must be on our way now, as we have friends waiting for us.'

She's going to ask where we're having lunch, I know she is, thought Magdalena. And she'll fix me with those fishy eyes, and I'll ask her to join us.

'On the other side of the island,' went on Sylvester. 'So we must get along. Goodbye.'

Before Sandra could open her mouth again, Sylvester had conveyed them as if by magic several yards down the street. As the gap between them widened, Magdalena let out a great sigh of relief. 'Thank you, Sylvester,' she said. 'I couldn't have stood her for another moment.'

'What a poisonous woman,' said Agatha, clearly shaken. 'What was she on about, all those remarks about Thea?'

'Forget it,' said Sylvester. 'You don't want to take any notice of what a woman like that says.'

'Sylvester's right,' said Magdalena.

'Just the same,' said Agatha slowly. 'I do wonder . . .'

'Dido's picked up an Adonis.'

Thea imparted this startling piece of news to Sylvester as they sat waiting for lunch. 'I am glad I bumped into you, I wouldn't have found this place by myself.'

'And why not, Thea?' asked Sylvester rhetorically. 'I'll tell you. It's because you wouldn't take the trouble to enquire about places to eat. I, on the other hand, just asked. A quiet restaurant, I said, with excellent food, a good atmosphere, and off the usual tourist track. All in perfect Italian, of course,' he added with great good humour.

'Stop showing off, Sylvester,' said Agatha. 'He did ask when we went into the *farmacia* to get some headache pills for Magdalena, but it was chiefly because he wanted somewhere that Sandra wasn't.'

'Sandra?'

'The dreadful woman from Eyot. Sylvester would have lunched on worms in order not to run into her again.'

'As it happens, we have both avoided her and found ourselves an excellent restaurant. And Thea, although I long to hear about Dido's Adonis, not in front of Magdalena, if you please. She has quite enough to worry her without thinking that Dido's going to neglect the twins.'

'Dido would never . . .' Thea began indignantly, and then shut up as a wan-looking Magdalena emerged from inside the restaurant. Her hair was slightly damp and she had obviously been washing her face.

'Feeling any better?' asked Agatha sympathetically.

'The headache's beginning to subside,' said Magdalena. 'Do you think wine on top of whatever it was, Sylvester?'

'Only aspirin,' said Sylvester, who knew you couldn't be too careful with strange medicines and could find his way round most labels in several languages. 'And the wine will relax you.'

'It's lovely here,' said Magdalena, taking in the shady, vine-covered little terrace with its handful of tables, each laid with a gleaming white cloth. 'Cool, and quiet.'

'And nobody else from Eyotshire,' said Agatha with feeling.

*   *   *

Thomas wasn't sure whether he liked his sandwiches eaten with a thin coating of grey dust on them. 'We should have stopped earlier for lunch,' he grumbled. 'Further down.'

'No, no,' said Marcus. 'This way we get to stop and soak up the atmosphere without wasting journey time. This is wonderful, wonderful!'

Thomas looked doubtfully around him at the barren, scarred and pock-marked landscape. Grey and black for ever and ever, he thought. Little puffs of smoke flared and subsided in a crater a little way away, and there was a strong smell of sulphur in the air.

'Fumaroles,' he said, trying unsuccessfully to rub his apple clean on his shirt.

'What?' said Marcus.

'Those little bursts. They're called fumaroles.'

'I didn't know that,' said Marcus, entirely uninterested. 'I think this is the most perfect landscape I have ever seen. I could live in such a place.'

'Oh no you couldn't,' muttered Thomas.

'This is real beauty, this is what the heart of all art should be like.'

You're nuts, thought Thomas, as he went on with his gritty apple.

'These are the landscapes I summon up in the human mind with my music,' said Marcus with increased enthusiasm.

Thomas looked around him. It was exciting coming up a volcano, he'd never done that before. It was terrific, looking into the great bowl of the central crater. It had been fun sliding down into a smaller crater and then scrabbling up the other side. He'd enjoyed picking his way along the petrified lava between the craters. He'd even got used to the smell. Sort of. But you could have too much of a good thing, and Thomas was rapidly coming to the conclusion that volcanoes were probably best at night, erupting in a spectacular way, and viewed from a great distance. Or on the cinema screen.

Still, good cred, climbing a volcano. It hadn't been a wasted day. But this Marcus, he was something else. Seriously out of his skull, Thomas told himself. Seriously better not to see too much of him.

Thomas gave a little shiver, and heaved his rucksack open. He pulled out a sweatshirt; it was much chillier up here, being so high, he supposed, and with the cloud that drifted round the summit. Marcus seemed impervious to the cold; wearing a thin T-shirt with great patches of sweat from his cycling exertions, he didn't seem to need anything more than his artistic fervour to keep himself warm.

'Here,' said Marcus, digging into his bag. 'Have a swig.'

'What is it?'

'Brandy.'

'No thanks.'

'Don't drink?'

'I don't like brandy.'

'Sensible boy,' said Marcus surprisingly; Thomas had feared a snub. 'Rots your brain cells, and you need to take care of 'em at your age; they're still growing, you know.' He took a hefty swig, and then stowed the bottle away. 'Okay for emergencies, and emergency is what it'll be if I try pedalling downhill with too much of that inside me. Do you ever drink?'

'Wine at home, although Val doesn't like me to. At school nearly everybody drinks.'

'Used to be beer in my day.'

'Some beer. Wine. The real topers drink a lot of vodka. Makes them feel good.'

'Does it?'

'I suppose so. Costs a lot, so it's a good show-off. Gets you in with the crowd if you turn up with a bottle.'

'Didn't you want that? To be one of the crowd?'

Thomas shrugged, keeping his head down. 'Not much.'

'Come on,' said Marcus, scrambling to his feet and brushing a mixture of crumbs and fruit peel off his legs. 'We'll go that way, there's a village down there that was destroyed in the last eruption, you can see the remains, they say.'

'Oh, great,' said Thomas, swinging his rucksack over his shoulder and following Marcus towards where they had left the bikes.

They picked their way down a lava stream; it does look like a river, thought Thomas, marvelling at the neatness of the lava with scrubby grass growing on either side of it. They passed trees stripped and burnt into strange, twisted shapes by the glowing torrent that had once passed by.

'Wonderful,' breathed Marcus. 'Incredible.'

Warped and depressing, thought Thomas.

They came to the ruined village, and gazed at the wide stream of lava which had cut through houses – and lives, Thomas said to himself – before it stopped abruptly, in a grey wall just beyond what must have been the centre of the village.

'Thirty years since this one,' said Marcus.

'Amazing,' said Thomas. 'All that red hot lava; it can travel at a tremendous speed. Like a horror film; boiling, liquid stone surging down after you. Ugh!'

'Think of the fireworks,' said Marcus with glee. 'A fountain of fire.'

'No,' said Thomas, pausing and bending over to pick up a lump of pumice. 'This is the wrong type.'

'What do you mean, the wrong type? How can there be a wrong type? Imagine the apocalyptic scene of devastation and destruction, the great iridescent tongues of fire sending their deathly sparks way, way up into the sky . . .'

'No,' said Thomas again. 'You're thinking of a fountain type of volcano. This is a Vesuvian volcano. No sparks, no fountains, no rumblings. Just kerboom! and the top of the mountain blows, red hot rocks and the lava pouring down. And terrible, choking dust.'

'I don't see it like that,' said Marcus after a moment's silence. 'I have a different picture.'

'It's not how you see it, it's how it is. Was. Will be if it blows again. Fact. You can't change the way things are.'

'No, it isn't like that, a volcano going off,' said Marcus frustratedly. 'Thomas, you're clouding my vision.'

'Erupting,' said Thomas helpfully. 'Volcanoes erupt. They don't go off.'

He wheeled his bike away from the lava rock. 'Some volcanoes rumble and bumble about nearly all the time. Stromboli's like that, never quiet. You know what it's up to, plenty of fireworks, but it doesn't tend to go bang much. Then you've got your dormant volcano. Like this one. You can tell it's not extinct, because of the amount of volcanic activity, hot springs, those fumaroles and so on. Could go on like that for years and years. Centuries. Then, suddenly, it blows. You see, the crust of the earth . . .'

'Spare me the lecture, kid,' said Marcus, thoroughly disgruntled. Then he cheered up as a surge of creativity hit him. 'I'm going to put this into my new piece. The greyness, the dust, the rock, the dead trees. This sterile landscape. And then the crescendo of despair into the fountain of fire.'

'But there isn't . . . oh, what the hell,' said Thomas, giving up. Some people just didn't want to know.

'It's amazing,' he said, much later on, when they had regained the path and were cycling downhill; a much easier task than the ascent had been. 'That people come back to live here.'

'You're so knowledgeable, you must know volcanic soil is rich. Look at the vines growing on the lower slopes. Look how lush it all is. That's fertility, born of that superb sterile hell up there. Contrast, Thomas, that's what it's all about. Grey Death against green Life.'

And I know which side you're on, thought Thomas as he took off the brakes and began free-wheeling down the final hill into the town, relishing the rush of speed and the breeze against his face.

Valdemar skulked by the magnolia tree in the park, full of wrath.

Cloak and dagger; quite ridiculous, he said to himself. Unable just to stride into the cathedral he'd known since he was a boy; where he'd sung, and been confirmed and married. He knew every blasted arch, every window, every stress and strain of the old building, and it had a place in his heart denied to all his tremendous modern award-winning schemes.

'Drop the Cathedral, Val,' colleagues had advised. 'It's a specialist area, right outside your field.'

But Valdemar would have none of it, and he was right. He understood how that huge northern building was built, why and how it stood, where its weaknesses were, what elements of design worked out by masons and master craftsmen centuries ago, without benefit of computer or calculator or slide rule, kept the towering edifice standing as it had stood for hundreds of years.

Valdemar loved that Cathedral as one loves a child.

And here he was, waiting until the Cathedral was closed, so that he could slip in a side door, unnoticed, allowed in by the courtesy of an old friend who knew one tenth what he knew about it.

Bugger it, he said in a fit of temper. Bugger, bugger and bugger. He looked at his watch. Five to eight.

Out of the park. Over the river on St Guillebert's Bridge. Past the just-closing central library, past the Mountjoy Arms, past the theatre and the Eyotshire Bank.

Into the cloisters via the small west door, open in summer until nine o'clock for the vergers' convenience. To the south door, there to be met by a lurking Roger, anxiously looking around to see that no one had spotted them.

What a performance.

What a farce.

All because of that mindless blockhead of a Dean. Infuriated, Valdemar followed Roger down the deserted choir aisle, their shoes echoing on the stone floors. A verger went past, bade Roger a good evening, nodded at Valdemar, went on her stately way.

'Here,' said Roger, squeezing between some scaffolding and the tomb of St Guillebert.

'Oh, my God,' said Valdemar.

'Appropriate comment in the circumstances,' said Roger drily.

'Roger,' said Valdemar. 'Have you the keys to the crypt?'

'I don't carry them about my person, no. I can get them from the duty verger.'

'We need to go down there,' said Valdemar. 'This is an old crack, Roger, don't you realize? And it's moving.'

'Ah, serious, then,' said Roger, subdued. 'You didn't know it was here.'

'It had that Victorian monument in front of it, which hid it. I suppose the Dean removed it when he started ripping the organ out. Then, with the bracing effect of the choir screen gone . . .'

'Bad,' said Roger sombrely.

'Down to the crypt,' said Valdemar. 'Got a notebook?'

'Of course.'

'Then I'll tell you what has to be done.'

'Is it urgent?'

Valdemar checked his striding walk. 'Could be all right for two years. Could go tomorrow. Tonight. It's urgent, Roger.'

Dido had left the twins tucked up in bed, rosy, sleepy and in a very good humour. Magdalena had read them a story, and they had long since sunk into the utter sleep of very young children.

Dido was out on the town, searching for that exquisite man she had chatted up earlier in the day. 'Meet you by the boats,' she had said.

And there he was. His English quite adequate for what Dido had in mind.

'I have a place near here,' he said.

'Great,' said Dido. 'I like that, more of that, more and more. God, do you know how long it is since I screwed with someone for sheer lust?' She sank her sharp teeth into the superbly muscled shoulder of Giuseppe, baker and the best baseball pitcher on the island. 'Love these pecs,' said Dido with a blissful sigh. 'And those thighs, and a hard, fantastic bottom, those gluteals, Giuseppe, unbelievable!'

Giuseppe was busying himself with other parts of Dido, less muscular, more inviting, softer. Warm and welcoming.

Dido wrapped her legs ecstatically round Giuseppe's taut and vigorous body, her dancer's suppleness driving him mad and finally out of control.

'Ayi,' he yelled in a great roar of final effort which sent Dido wild.

'Do you know,' she said, as he subsided on top of her, panting and drowning in sweat, 'I think sex is better when you don't do it for money.'

Valdemar strode towards the car park. Couldn't even park his car in its usual place at the Club, not with all this rubbish, having to slip into Eyot as though he were some kind of criminal. He scowled. A quick phone call to London, he thought, and then drive to London, he could be at Veronica's flat by one in the morning. He pushed his ticket into the machine at the car park, hating the grey evening skies. And now a nasty-looking mist was rolling in from the river; I want to get away from here, Valdemar said to himself.

'Why, Valdemar. I was only just talking about you.'

Valdemar jumped, his hand stretched out towards his car door. He turned round and glared at the man who had accosted him. 'Who are you?'

'Nigel. Nigel Norris. You know me.'

Nigel was a tall man himself. An important man, with a good solicitor's practice in the small town of Unthrang, active in local affairs, well-known and well-regarded as a pillar of the community. Yet when he was with Valdemar, he felt diminished, uneasy. There were no grounds for it, of course, just that the man had a knack for making him feel uncomfortable.

Ha, he was going to get his own back this time. See if his news didn't make Valdemar feel a bit uncomfortable.

'I was just speaking to my sister,' he said.

'Never met her,' said Valdemar indifferently.

'She's on holiday,' went on Nigel. 'And who do you think she's bumped in to?'

'Go on,' said Valdemar.

'Magdalena,' said Nigel triumphantly. 'And Thomas, what a shame about that disgraceful school business. Did I tell you how well Giles is getting on there?'

'Where?' said Valdemar, looking so threatening that Nigel felt almost alarmed.

'Where?' he repeated with a nervous laugh.

'Where did your sister see Magdalena and Thomas?'

'Oh, I see. On the island she's gone to for a week's holiday. With Giles, and her son. And from what Sandra – that's my sister – tells me, Magdalena's found herself some good company, eating *à deux* with a very dishy man was what she told me. You know the Italian type, silver hair, very smooth . . .'

Extraordinary, those blue eyes, thought Nigel, as Valdemar's dark brows snapped together and he took a step towards Nigel.

'Exactly which island is it,' he said, speaking very slowly and deliberately, 'where your sister is on holiday?'

'On Aeolus, off Sicily, you know,' burbled Nigel. 'It's becoming very smart, and . . .'

He spoke into the mist.

Valdemar was in his car, the engine roared into life, and he was gone.

'Damn nearly ran me over,' squeaked Nigel indignantly to a bollard. 'The nerve of the man.'

It was the slowest journey to London that Valdemar had ever made. The mist which had been a light, swirling affair in Eyot, gave way to thick fog on the motorway. What with hold-ups from minor accidents, speed restrictions and roadworks, not even Valdemar, who wasn't over-mindful of speed limits, especially at night, could manage more than a stately crawl.

He was full of rage by the time he drew up outside his London flat at five thirty in the morning. And of course now, after the rigours of such a dark and troublesome night, a clear sky gave promise of a fine day.

Valdemar had a rapid shower and changed his clothes. Then he took out the small overnight bag he used for short trips and tossed various garments in, heedlessly, and seemingly unaware that he was travelling to a warm spot. He opened his desk drawer, took out his passport, slammed the drawer shut, picked up his bag and was on his way out of the flat by ten to six.

By six he was in the office; first dictating a letter to his secretary and then sorting out a pile of folders and papers which he took into Virginia's office. He dumped them unceremoniously on her immaculate desk; Virginia always cleared her desk before leaving at night. Valdemar felt a vague satisfaction as he looked at the pile with a scrawled note on top. It would make Virginia shudder when she arrived later in the morning.

Back to his room. He thought for a moment, and then pulled his phone towards him. He dialled.

'What?' said a sleepy voice at the other end. 'Who's that?'

'Ralph?' said Valdemar. 'Put Virginia on, would you?'

There was a scuffling sound at the other end, and Virginia's cool tones came down the line. 'It's six in the morning, Val. What is it?'

'Wouldn't ring you unless it was urgent, Virginia. I'm going to Italy, to get hold of Magdalena, bring her and the children back.'

'Ah,' said Virginia.

'I'll be away two days; less if I can manage it. There are some bits and pieces you need to look through, I've left them on your desk.'

'Thank you,' said Virginia, not sounding at all grateful.

'I've left a letter about Eyot on tape. It must be done first thing this morning, then Pippa is to bring it to you. It's self-explanatory. When you've checked it, see that it goes by courier to Roger Ruckworth, would you? Straight away.'

'More trouble?'

'Couldn't be worse,' said Valdemar. 'Fortunately, it's so bad that the Dean won't be able to get away with any more of his stupidities for the time being. No doubt he'll start up again once we get on top of the immediate problem; we can worry about that when it happens. Roger can deal with things now, he's nominally in charge, and he knows how critical it is.'

'Val, there's something wrong with the line.'

'Can't you hear me?'

'There's a buzzing. On the line.'

'That isn't the phone. It's my electric razor.'

'Are you shaving?'

'Yes.'

'Haven't you been back to your flat?'

'Yes, but it's quicker to do it here, I can do something else at the same time.'

'Have you booked a flight?'

'No. I'm leaving now for Heathrow, I'll get on the first one available.'

'Where are you flying to?'

'Rome, Naples, Palermo, doesn't make much difference. Probably Rome, and I'll hire a car.'

'Take care, Val. It's dangerous to drive in a temper.'

'I'm not in a temper. I am, as it happens, completely calm.'

'Balls, Val. I've never heard you in such a fret. Just be

careful. I'll look after everything here, don't worry about it. And Val . . .'

'Yes?'

'Does Magdalena know of your imminent arrival?'

'I'm not sending her an announcement, no.'

'Why don't you have a few days there? A break would do you good.'

'I don't need a break, Virginia.'

Silence.

'One more thing, Val.'

'Yes, what? Is it important? I must go.'

'My love to Magdalena.'

Click.

The water in the coffee-maker came to the boil with a belch and furious hissing sounds.

'Blooming Henry,' muttered Dido, as she gingerly took it off the flame. 'What a way to make coffee. What's wrong with a good old percolator or filter machine?'

'It's the way Italians like it,' said Thea, hunting for cups.

'Kitchen's pretty basic,' said Dido. 'No fitted units, all a bit old-fashioned.'

'Doesn't matter,' said Thea. 'Giulietta makes terrific food in here.'

'Don't get me wrong,' said Dido. 'I like it in here. I'll take the cups, you bring that machine.'

They processed to the terrace, and Thea poured out two inky coffees. 'What time did you get in last night?' she asked curiously.

''Bout two,' said Dido.'

'Were you dancing?'

'I was not,' said Dido. 'I met up with that bloke, and went back to his place and had myself a ball.'

'Dido! Who is he?'

'A pick-up,' said Dido with satisfaction. 'And no, he didn't pay for it.'

'That's something,' said Thea. 'But really, Dido.'

'I know, I know, like some little slut from Bootle out for her fortnight of booze and sand and sex. It wasn't like that. You see,

I've been thinking. I got to give up doing it for money. And no more casuals, either.'

'Come on, Dido,' said Thea. 'Last night was a casual if anything is.'

'Yeah, okay, I don't have to give everything up right away, do I?'

'Are you going to become a nun or something?'

Dido nearly fell out of her chair for laughing. 'Me? A blooming nun? Can you see it?'

'No,' said Thea.

'I think what I've got to do is concentrate on my work, see? Earn money straight. Now, *I* think what I've been doing *is* straight. Bloke wants to sleep with me, and a lot do, so they have to pay, right? That's an honest transaction.'

'And a very old one.'

'Yeah. Okay, I don't walk the streets. I go with nice blokes, ones I get along with. Even ones I fancy a bit. I've never slept with some gross old slob just because he's waved money under my nose. No, I choose.'

'But it doesn't seem quite right any more.'

'No,' said Dido a trifle gloomily. 'That time is past, and I got to mend my ways. My whole life is going to change.'

'Change is always interesting.'

'Only you don't know if it's going to be a change for the better.'

'Can you earn enough without the extras?' asked Thea.

'Don't be so daft,' said Dido severely. 'It isn't extras, it's basic. No, I blinking well can't. So I'll have to get more nannying work. Actually, I don't mind, I really like kids. It's their parents I usually can't stand. Do you think Magdalena will give me a reference?'

'Of course she will,' said Thea. 'Everybody you've worked for praises you. Don't most of them want you to stay on?'

'Yeah, that's true.' Dido kicked off her shoes and waggled her toes. 'Tell you what, me feet don't look half so gross when they've got a bit of a tan. P'raps I should get a foot-tanning machine. From Peter Jones, bet they do one. They do everything else.'

'Your feet are fine,' said Thea. That wasn't true, but on the other hand, Thea knew that Dido was altogether such a live wire that nobody bothered about her feet.

'I wouldn't mind going on looking after the twins,' said Dido thoughtfully. 'If their own nanny felt like moving on, of course, I'm not doing anyone out of a job. But they don't live in London, do they, not even part of the time?'

'No, home is the grim old castle in the north. All year round.'

'No good for me, then,' said Dido. 'And what's her husband like? That's where the trouble starts. Either they're after you to take your pants down; or they treat you like you was something the cat brought in; or they're caring and full of stupid advice and suggestions.'

'I don't think Val's any of those things,' said Thea, considering. 'I don't know him very well, but I can tell you, wow, that is some man.'

'Magdalena deserves someone special,' said Dido firmly. 'Not many like her around, pity she's missing the one before this.'

'Hugo? Is she?' said Thea with interest. 'I hardly knew him, but I know Mum thought the world of him.'

'They tell me she didn't do her grieving properly. Well, with small children, you can't sit around howling all day, can you? But it's best if you do, get it over with. Then she feels guilty.'

'Guilty? Why?' said Thea.

'Oh, marrying again so soon, I expect,' said Dido vaguely.

'Where are the twins?'

'With Magdalena. She told me to take last night and this morning off. So when I've finished this coffee, I'm going down town to that perruci-whatsit to have me hair trimmed, and then I'm back on duty before lunch.' She stretched and yawned. 'Good life this, I can do with a bit of peace and quiet. Pity we're in for to-dos and upheavals.'

'What?' said Thea, alarmed. 'What are you talking about? Dido!'

But Dido had put her coffee cup down and gone, leaving Thea staring at a terracotta pot which was overflowing with red and purple geraniums. 'I don't like the sound of this at all,' she informed the geraniums. 'No, not at all.'

* * *

Marcus was out on a mid-morning prowl, hunting sounds. He was in a restive mood, and wanted to be soothed. The dustcart was making pleasing noises as it heaved the wheelie-bins into the air, depositing the contents with gratifying rattles and crashes. The engine whine, too, was different from the dustcarts he was familiar with.

There were some quite good clashings and hissings coming from a hotel kitchen, and he lingered for several appreciative minutes in the little yard at the back of the restaurant.

A squeaky bicycle went past; good one, thought Marcus, storing it away in his memory.

Fishing boat engines, each tuned slightly differently, were a delight to the Marcus ears, and so was a ferocious argument being conducted at full volume by two vituperative old women outside the bakers. Maybe there was just too much tune to that, though; you had to be wary of these Italian voices. Italian was altogether a dangerous language for a pure musician like himself.

Marcus pottered happily on, collecting a shrill whistle here, an unusual screech of brakes there. He bought himself an ice-cream; Marcus loved pistachio ice-cream. He sat in the sun with a cup of coffee, read the headlines of the English newspapers on a stand outside a shop and went into the bank to change some money.

Here all was orderliness, with queues lined up in every direction. He spotted Dido, who was waiting in a likely-looking queue, her nose in a book.

Marcus looked round suspiciously. Where were those ghastly twins? Dido raised her eyes from her book and looked straight at Marcus.

'They're with Magdalena on the beach, you're quite safe,' she said.

'What?' said Marcus, falling in beside her, to the evident distress of the couple behind her.

'That's queue-jumping,' said Dido.

'I don't mind about queues.'

'I bet you mind about it when someone pushes in front of you.'

'That's different. What's this queue for?'

'To get a form for changing money.'

'What do you do when you've got the form?'

'You take it to that window there, with your English money, traveller's cheques or whatever.'

'You have to queue again?'

'Yup.'

'So two lots of queuing to get your money?'

'Nope. Three. The second guy gives you a receipt. Then you go to that window over there, which is the cashier's window, to get the loot.'

'That really long queue?'

'That really, really long queue,' agreed Dido.

'I'm going to find another bank.'

'There are several in Palermo,' said Dido.

'You mean this is the only one on the island?'

'Yes, the only one.'

'I don't believe it,' grumbled Marcus. 'It's all so primitive.'

'They do things differently here,' said Dido. 'You should have brought a book, like I have.'

'What are you reading?' said Marcus nosily.

Dido turned the book over to show its cover.

'*Costumes of the Russian Ballet.* Oh,' said Marcus, taking it. He flipped through the pages.

'Don't suppose you do the ballet,' said Dido, retrieving her book.

'It's an absurd art,' said Marcus.

'All art is absurd,' said Dido, unruffled. She gave Marcus a friendly shove. 'Move up. If you leave a gap, someone else will squeeze in.'

'You were a dancer,' said Marcus.

'I was,' said Dido. 'That's no secret. I don't have secrets any more. None at all. Not like some others not so far from here.'

'I don't know what you mean,' said Marcus. 'I don't know what you're talking about.'

'Keep your blooming secrets,' said Dido cheerfully. 'They aren't that exciting.'

Marcus didn't like the turn the conversation had taken. He glared down at the marble floor and then across the hall at his own face, reflected in a speckled but once-grand ormolu mirror.

'Why are you changing money, anyway?' he demanded. 'I would have thought you had everything paid for.'

'Most things,' agreed Dido. 'But I need a new sketchpad and some paints.'

'Oh,' said Marcus. 'More absurd art, then.'

'Yeah,' said Dido. 'Ballet costumes, too, for *Swan Lake*.'

'*Swan Lake*,' said Marcus in a distracted way.

They had reached the head of the line, and Dido advanced to collect her money-changing form.

Marcus was struck by the small amount she was changing. He frowned. 'You shouldn't change small sums, you pay more commission that way.'

Dido collected her form and moved away from the window. 'It may be a small sum to you, Marcus, but it's all I've got to spend.'

Marcus looked sceptical. 'Doesn't Magdalena pay you?'

'Yeah, all into my bank account in London. I got fees and rent to pay; every penny's spoken for.'

Marcus collected his form and joined Dido at the rear of the next queue.

'You can't be that rich,' she said. 'Not so's you can throw money around. Composers don't make money.'

'I have commissions and grants,' said Marcus shortly. 'And I do some teaching in America.'

Lucky Americans, thought Dido.

The police car cut neatly in ahead of Valdemar, flashing for him to draw into the hard shoulder.

'Shit,' said Valdemar, as he came to a halt. He opened the door and got out; the police were just about the only people Valdemar was careful not to antagonize.

Even so, his 'Well?' came out as a bark.

'Morning, sir. Rear brake light not working. Driver's side. Can I see your licence, please, sir?'

Speechless with rage, Valdemar felt in his pocket and drew out his licence.

'Thank you, sir. All in order. But get that light fixed right away, please.'

Valdemar had, of course, no intention of doing anything about the light; he was leaving the car at the airport and to hell with the light.

'And be careful about the speed, sir. We could have pulled you in for that, you were a bit too far over the limit for our liking. Just a reminder, sir. I don't suppose it's the first time you've been stopped.'

The police car drew out into the flow of traffic and disappeared in search of further victims. Valdemar took several deep breaths. He looked at his watch. What a waste of time.

Ten minutes later he was at the tail of a motionless line of traffic, fuming. If those bloody police hadn't stopped him, he'd have been clear of here. What on earth was holding everything up? He pressed the radio 'on' button, got a burst of static, and then a smug voice came on air, announcing that news was just coming in of a hold-up on the approach to Heathrow from the London direction.

'A lorry has shed its load, and serious delays can be expected. Drivers heading for Heathrow are advised to take alternative routes.'

Valdemar jabbed at the radio and looked in the rear-view mirror. There was an endless line of traffic behind him. Three lanes, blocked solid for as far as he could see. 'What bloody alternative routes?' he shouted at the dashboard.

Valdemar was there for the duration.

Magdalena was basking on the beach, being buried in the sand by the twins. A shadow fell across her. 'Good morning,' said Ettore. 'May I join you?'

'I wouldn't recommend the mound of sand,' said Magdalena, sitting up, and brushing the beach off herself. 'But do, yes; please sit down, if you can bear the racket the twins are making.'

He's very trim for a man of his age, she thought, and then winced as she remembered that it wouldn't be so many years before she, too, was that age. Would she dare to show herself on a beach in a swimsuit then? She thought not, and then chided herself for being negative. Look at that woman there, with jolly rolls of well-browned fat squeezed into a bright blue costume. She must be well past sixty, and she obviously had no inhibitions.

Moreover, thought Magdalena, she looks a lot happier than I feel. Probably a widow who didn't marry again, she told herself viciously.

'You look very fierce,' said Ettore. 'May the twins come into the water with me?'

Hugh and Helena were at once frisking round him like a pair of puppies.

'Mummy always says, "Soon", when we ask to go into the sea,' explained Hugh. 'Only it's never soon enough.'

'Or she says, "In a minute",' said Helena, giving Ettore a flirtatious look from under her long lashes. 'Only her minutes are very long ones.'

'What an enchantress,' said Ettore, laughing. 'You are going to break hearts when you're grown up.'

'What about me?' demanded Hugh.

'You, too, perhaps.'

You, too, certainly, thought Magdalena, as she lay back and shut her eyes. Just like all the other Mountjoys.

She could hear the twins' cheerful chatter as Ettore escorted them to the water's edge. What a kind man he is, she thought. Does one only appreciate kindness in a man when one gets older? Is it a virtue worth nothing to the young, when only hot blood and the senses count? Does passion as a prerequisite go, and kindness take its place?

'No,' said Dido, dumping her bag on the sand. 'I'm young, and I like kindness in a man, unkind men are poisonous.'

'You startled me,' said Magdalena, sitting up and putting her sunglasses on. 'Have you had your hair done?'

'Yeah,' said Dido. 'Don't look too bad. Have the twins been behaving?'

'They've been quite good, for them,' said Magdalena. 'But they are exhausting. Ettore took them into the sea with him.'

'I'll watch them,' said Dido. 'In case they get to be a nuisance.'

'I don't think Italians find children a nuisance, isn't it strange?'

'You just lie down again and relax,' said Dido. 'Or read.' She picked up Magdalena's book to pass it to her. 'Cripes, *Unreal Images*, what's that about? Ghosts?'

'It's about symbolism,' said Magdalena. 'In tapestries and mediaeval paintings. Unicorns and so on.'

'You need a nice, fat, silly book to read on the beach,' said Dido in disapproving tones. 'Not this sort of stuff.'

'You could be right,' said Magdalena sleepily.

'You have a ziz, and then, when Ettore comes out, I'll take over the kids and you go for a nice drink and a chat with him at the bar there. I think he's a bit of all right, that bloke.'

'I think he is, too,' said Magdalena.

Sylvester was practising alone on the terrace. Ferenc was spending the afternoon working with Marcus on a particularly tricky piano section, and Sylvester had slipped away to indulge himself with music that, in his opinion, better fitted his surroundings.

'I like that,' said Thomas, slopping on to the terrace in his flip-flops. 'Isn't it from the *Magic Flute*?'

'It is. Some Beethoven variations.'

'You're singing along,' said Thomas accusingly.

'I'm singing the piano accompaniment, ignorant boy,' said Sylvester amiably. He took his bow off his strings.

'Sorry,' said Thomas at once, turning to slop away again. 'I interrupted you.'

'You could play,' suggested Sylvester. 'Borrow my cello.'

Thomas shook his head.

'Doing much music these days?'

Thomas looked at Sylvester warily. 'Not much, actually.'

'Gone off it?'

'It's difficult at school.'

'Supposed to encourage music there. That's what they tell me.' Sylvester played a resonant chord to make his point.

'They're keen on people who play the sax,' offered Thomas.

Sylvester looked at him. 'Oh yes?'

'The thing is,' said Thomas, plonking himself down on a striped canvas chair, 'they *say* they want you to do lots of music, but it's all talk. I mean, if you're a keen musician they let you drop divinity and so on, for practice time. You can't drop sport, of course, because that's the most important thing in the whole world as far as they're concerned.'

'So you did have time to practise?'

'The music school's a bit grim, when it's only you. And the cello doesn't ... well, they say it's cissy. A girl's instrument.'

'What?' Sylvester played a series of hideous Mordauntian

discords to express his disapproval. 'I never heard of such a thing. What can you play and keep your status?'

'Violin's almost all right, especially if you're foreign, Russian or something, and you look dramatic and you're some kind of youthful prodigy. Double bass is good, because it's big and beefy and it's a jazz instrument, too, which helps. Sax is best, like I said. Trumpet, trombone, they're really good.'

'How about the flute?'

'Don't even mention it,' said Thomas.

Sylvester puffed out his cheeks and blew out a long breath. 'Does Valdemar know about this?'

Thomas shrugged. 'Dunno. If he does, he doesn't care. While I'm there, I'm standing on my own two feet and not getting under his, so what does the music matter?'

'He was very proud of your music.'

'He's never been proud of anything I've done.'

'He was proud of your singing.'

'He said he was, but he hardly ever came to listen, did he? You came more than he ever did.'

Sylvester played a melancholy bar or two. 'Was that the problem? The cello business? Was that why you ran away?'

'Nope,' said Thomas. 'I just gave up playing the cello.'

'So what stirred you into action?'

Thomas shifted uncomfortably in his chair. 'Nothing, really. I just kind of got fed up.'

'See much of that boy who was in the choir in Eyot with you? Giles?'

'No more than I could help,' said Thomas. 'He's nauseating, and he'd sell his grandmother to get in with what he thinks is the right crowd.'

'Lots to tell about Eyotshire, is there?'

'Maybe,' said Thomas.

'You don't want to talk about it.'

'Not really,' said Thomas, looking so hunched and wretched that Sylvester was filled with unwonted fury. At the school; at Val; at all the callous and idiotic people who quietly and methodically set about wrecking other people's lives.

'Just sit and listen, then,' Sylvester said, taking up his bow again.

18

'It's this late afternoon light,' Dido said, head on one side. 'You got to get the light right, because it changes everything.'

Dido and Thea were in the courtyard of the villa. All was quiet; Hugh and Helena, who had woken at an all-too-early hour that morning, had spread themselves on a rug and promptly fallen asleep.

Dido was sketching, filling in the details of the ornate little fountain in the centre of the courtyard, with its backdrop of uneven walls and flamboyant, fragrant flowers. 'I never seen light like this before,' she said. 'Well, I never been to Italy before. Is it all like this?'

'In the south, yes. Different, though, when you go further north.'

'Not rain and fog and puddles, not like in the north of England, bet you.'

'Never as bad as that,' said Thea. She yawned; the whole household had been jerked into early wakefulness by the din the twins had made getting themselves up and starting their day in a particularly riotous mood.

Dido licked her paintbrush into a neat point. 'Lucky Italians, then. At least the ones who live in places like this.'

'Most don't,' said Thea sleepily.

'Good food, good place to kip, good company, good job to do, no tiresome blokes after you. It's great.'

'What about Quarles?' said Thea. 'He's keen on you.'

'No, he isn't tiresome, he's too much the gent to be that. And he's just after a bit of the old one-two; don't think it's personal.'

'Dido!'

'No, he's looking for someone special and it's not me, I can tell you that for nothing. Whatever he thinks.'

'He's quite well-off.'

'Yeah, wonder how he makes his dough?'

Thea stared at her. 'You know how he does. Crits, slashing bits in the papers. Articles. Books, even; I don't know.'

'Listen, you been to his house? No, course you haven't, you only just met him. I have, and places like that don't come cheap. He hasn't got lots of family money, nothing like that. So where does it come from?'

'How do you know it isn't from his parents?'

'His dad's dead. I met his mum, she's a nice old duck, used to teach. Lives in a pretty cottage down in Rye; she said Quarles bought it for her.'

'House in London, country cottage . . . I don't think criticism pays that well.'

'Course it doesn't. No, he must have other sources.'

'I heard him talking on the phone. It sounded very strange, he was reading something very slushy out to the person at the other end. That was after you'd tipped him the wink. You don't think he's into porn, do you? Kids, anything like that?'

'I do not,' said Dido with confidence.

'He must be making money somehow,' said Thea, intrigued. 'I shall do a bit of nosing.'

'He's all right, is Quarles. His heart's in the right place, although a lot of the people he writes about would say different. Clever, too,' she added.

'I shall talk to him,' said Thea.

'Yeah, he wants to pick your brains about Marcus.'

'What?' said Thea. 'I don't know Marcus. I never met him before I came here.'

'No, but there is the family connection, isn't there?'

'Dido, you haven't said anything to him.'

'No. Must've found out for himself.'

'Well, he can try, but he isn't getting anything out of me.'

'Might do you good, talking about it.'

'No way,' said Thea.

*　　*　　*

'What a pity,' the woman at the ticket desk said with professional brightness. 'You've just missed that flight. Let me see . . . no, that one's full. It's a bit tricky today, because several flights have been delayed or cancelled.' Her fingers clicked across the keyboard. 'No, that one's no good, either. It'll have to be this Rome flight. Alitalia. Boarding in two hours.'

'Two hours?' This was intolerable.

'That's if it's on time,' the woman said. She smiled her flashy smile at Valdemar. She had a name badge on, with 'Felicity' printed on it in gold letters. What an inappropriate name, thought Valdemar, waiting impatiently for his ticket to print out.

Valdemar liked to spend as little time as possible at airports; his aim when travelling was to go from A to B with maximum swiftness, and minimum delay or hanging about anywhere. Now he was stuck in this ghastly airport lounge, full of loathsome people.

He zipped irritably round the bookstall; there was nothing there he wanted to read. 'Pick up a Dostoevsky,' advised a promotional notice above a pile of shiny-covered classics. Just what I need, thought Valdemar, despair and desolation.

And no, he didn't want a detective story either; nor a major comic novel by a startling new talent; or a tale of horror; nor did he fancy a legal thriller; a book about financial scandals; a film star's scurrilous memoirs; advice on diseases for the traveller – or, indeed, any of the hundreds of books on offer.

He plucked a copy of the *Financial Times* from the rack. Serious reading, and it would have enough decorum not to be running stories about well-connected Valdemar Mountjoy's matrimonial hiccups.

He flung himself into a chair designed for the average traveller, who was clearly five inches shorter than him, flicked his way through the *FT* and tossed it on to the seat beside him. He crossed his arms, sat back; if nothing else, he could use the time profitably to think about some of his current projects and about other, future ones which would fill his time for the next year or so.

Hopeless.

It was impossible to concentrate in this place, with all these people coming and going. A woman went past with twins, just a bit older than Hugh and Helena, full of fun and excitement at the prospect of going on a plane.

Damn it, he missed the twins. How could Magdalena do this to him? She had no consideration for anyone except herself. Hugo had been a fool to marry her, he can't have known what she was really like, Valdemar told himself.

Then he'd made the same mistake, and all because of those twins. Children! Nothing but trouble and worry. What was he going to do about Thomas? Hopeless to pretend he could wash his hands of him, leave it to Hortense to sort out. Thomas would be past university age by the time Hortense got her thoughts clear and made any practical decisions.

Time idled past, moving on distinctly unwinged feet. Valdemar kept looking up at the board, watching the flights flash up, one by one. There it was, Alitalia, destination Rome; about bloody time, too.

Then, to his utter disbelief, the spaces for extra information about the flight flickered, and up came a single phrase. DELAYED INDEFINITELY.

Magdalena and Agatha were relishing the sights and sounds of the market. It was the main one on the island, and by half past nine in the morning was teeming with islanders and visitors buying meat and poultry, fish in extravagant abundance, piles of glowing fruit and vegetables, stalls with cheeses, others selling flowers, leather bags and purses, shoes, T-shirts in every conceivable colour and size. The little square and the surrounding streets were humming with conversations and transactions.

Agatha sighed. 'Sainsbury's just isn't the same,' she said.

It was Giulietta's day off. Carla, when pressed, had confessed that she did have quite a lot of work to do, and so Agatha and Magdalena had taken over the commissariat.

'Leave it to us,' said Agatha.

Sylvester, no mean cook, had offered to lend a hand, and had issued instructions and added many items to their list. Thomas said he'd come and chop and be kitchen maid, a kind thought which Magdalena and Agatha were a little hesitant about accepting.

'Please,' he said eagerly. 'I'm very handy in the kitchen, aren't I, Magdalena?'

Magdalena, remembering cut fingers, broken plates and the general chaos which went with Thomas's culinary efforts, wavered. Then she looked at his face, saw there the uneasy eyes of one fearful of rejection and snubs, and immediately co-opted him on to the staff.

'Poor Thomas,' she said now, as she piled lemons into a bag before handing them to the wizened man in charge of the stall. 'I wish he'd talk about school, it'd be better out in the open.'

'Doesn't he at all?' said Agatha, inspecting a cucumber.

'No, he simply says it was so dreadful he doesn't want to think about it.'

'Will Val send him back there? Surely not, if he's been so unhappy.'

'Val isn't very sympathetic about Thomas being unhappy. It's almost as though he wants him to suffer. Which isn't really like Val, he isn't a cruel man.'

'Hugo wouldn't have stood for Thomas being so unhappy. Does he miss him?'

Magdalena gnawed at her lip. 'I think he does, yes. They always got on well together, and Thomas felt very relaxed with Hugo, in a way he never is with Val. I think he feels Val is always weighing him up and finding him wanting.'

'Very strange,' commented Agatha, handing over a fistful of notes. 'It's so disconcerting, all these thousands of lire. How do they manage with their kidnappings? A million dollars in lire must be a lorry load, at least.'

Magdalena consulted her list and briskly ticked off the items they had bought. 'Where's Thomas?' she said, looking round. 'He said he'd meet us outside the little church.'

'Which church?' said Agatha, looking round.

'It must be that one there, with the crumbling steps. But I don't see Thomas. Perhaps he's inside.'

'Quick prayer for the good Lord to sweep Valdemar off to the nether regions in a puff of smoke,' said Agatha flippantly. Then she clapped her hand to her mouth. 'Oops. What a thing to say; my wretched tongue. I'm so sorry, Magdalena. I keep on forgetting he's your husband.'

'Don't worry about it; so does he.'

Thomas was inside the church, talking to Dido about the arrivals she had foreseen. He felt quite sure it meant Valdemar was on the way, and Dido agreed that it might.

'If he's close to you and Magdalena, then he's the one,' she said. 'But don't worry, because I'm getting strong feelings of protection here, I don't think it's going to turn out bad for you at all. You got to have courage, Thomas.' She sniffed, and looked disapprovingly around the interior of the church. 'Don't like it in here, gives me the creeps, all those weird statues with candles in front of them.'

'I'm meeting Magdalena here,' said Thomas. 'And Agatha. Well, outside here, actually, but I was early, so I thought I'd nip in and have a look round. Don't you like churches?' That struck him as odd. 'I mean, if you talk to spirits and so on . . .' His voice trailed off into silence as Dido gave him a shocked look.

'I'm not one of those spooky types,' she said firmly. 'Ectoplasm and all that; I don't hold with ghosts.'

'I don't go into churches much, now,' said Thomas. 'I used to spend a lot of time in the Cathedral when I sang, but I don't like them much any more, only to look at sometimes. I mean, what's the use of praying? Everything just goes on getting worse and worse.'

'What a cock-up,' Dido said, looking at Thomas's troubled face. 'What a real old heap of troubles. Your family's got a lot of sorting out to do, Thomas,' she announced briskly, getting up from her chair. 'I hate this sort,' she said, inspecting the back of her thighs, which were indented with a strange pattern from the stringing on the seat.

Thomas followed her to the door. 'Why did you come in here?' he asked. 'If you don't like churches, either?'

'Bit of cool,' said Dido. 'Thea's looking after the twins, while I buy a picnic for lunch. It's blooming hot out there, so I popped in here for a quick spot of chilliness; where could be better?'

'It is cool in there,' Thomas agreed as they emerged from the church into the blaze of late morning sunshine. 'Hello, Magdalena, here I am.'

Dido gave Magdalena a direct look. 'You need to stop worrying about your dead hubby, and do something about Thomas here,' she said. She didn't wait for an answer, but flicked a casual wave at them and disappeared into the network of streets.

'Bit much,' observed Agatha. 'She is the nanny, after all.'

'She's not like a nanny,' Thomas protested. 'She's quite different from Lottie.'

'You can say that again,' said Magdalena, recovering her equilibrium.

Dido suddenly reappeared, crunching a large red apple, and dangling some others in a plastic carrier from one finger. 'The twins like these, and they're good for their teeth,' she informed Magdalena. 'Now, why don't you go and have a nice, peaceful swim this afternoon? By yourself, away from the twins. I'm taking them fishing.'

'What, out in a boat?' said Magdalena, alarmed.

'Them two? In a boat? No way,' said Dido. 'Waist-deep with a net, don't you go worrying about them.' She gave Magdalena a particularly foxy look. 'It's yourself you got to worry about.'

'. . . Unfortunately, this means that our flight has been diverted. We will be landing at Cristoforo Colombo airport in Genoa, in approximately thirty-five minutes.'

The plane erupted into loud bursts of indignant Italian. Hands gesticulated, eyes were cast up to heaven, saints and the Mother of God were invoked.

To no avail. The plane was going to land in Genoa, and that was that. The hubbub subsided to a calmer level as coach, train and car-hire possibilities were discussed.

Valdemar, who had sat like a thundercloud during the announcement, looked at his watch. This journey, a simple, straightforward trip from one European capital to another, had so far taken more than twenty-four hours.

Strikes! Strikes in the air, and then, apparently, on the trains in Italy as well. All over some important issue, no doubt, but with the consequence that he had had to spend approximately eighteen hours in an airport lounge, waiting for a flight that flashed on and off the departure board like a light in Piccadilly Circus.

He wouldn't make it to the ferry tonight. He'd have to hire

a car, drive to Rome this evening, leave early in the morning. What a balls-up. He looked out of the window, unimpressed by the fluffy whiteness streaming by.

Limbo, he thought. Purgatory. A passing-place, a nowhere, a space between here and there.

Then he shook himself out of his fancy, and returned to the papers spread out in front of him.

Thea handed the twins over to Dido with great relief. Their antics were amusing to watch, but alarming when you were in charge of them. Especially when they were feeling lively. Which they mostly were, these days.

'Suits them here on the island,' said Dido. 'Helena had a nasty cough when we come, she's fine now. Reckon that castle they live in isn't good for their health. If it was mine, I'd rent it out to rich Americans or Germans, and live somewhere warm and comfy. Give me the creeps, that place did. Coming to the beach?'

'In about half an hour,' said Thea. 'I've got a bit of shopping to do.'

'Your mum's with Magdalena in the market.'

'Ta, I'll keep away from there, then.'

'They'll be on their way home now, I'd say. And you can't keep on avoiding your ma, Thea. She's getting worried about you.'

'I know, she wants to feel sure that I've got my mind fixed on getting a job as soon as I get back to London. She has a horror of me drifting, as she puts it.'

'You've done that already.'

'Yes, but she doesn't know about it. And I don't think drifting is the right word, that was a very exhausting time of my life,' Thea added with dignity.

'Exhausting? Okay, but you didn't achieve anything, did you? See you on the beach, usual place.'

The twins dragged Dido off, and Thea turned up a narrow side street, looking for an optician she had seen who could mend her glasses.

That was a bad move.

Marcus was in the optician's shop, and Thea noticed his square form lurking inside just too late for her to draw back.

'What did you do to them?' he asked as Thea handed over a pair of twisted frames.

'Sat on them,' said Thea briefly. 'Aren't you working today?'

'Had quite a good session earlier on,' said Marcus. 'But then they rather ran out of puff. They don't seem to be able to work for very long stretches, those two. Surprising, for professionals. So they called a break, and I whizzed down on my bike. My sunglasses needed adjusting.'

You need adjusting, thought Thea grumpily. And I hate your sunglasses.

They were large and formidable, just like Marcus.

At least he doesn't look like his brother, she thought, as she was swept along by the force of the Marcus personality to a bar to have a drink she didn't want.

'Okay, have an ice, then,' said Marcus, who was in one of his rare sociable moods. 'And tell me, what's bugging Thomas? I never saw a kid so screwed up, what's his problem? Just that school? Or is it more?'

'Uncertain parentage and being sent away to school,' said Thea, accepting a large ice from the man behind the bar. 'That's all, and it would probably be more than most of us could handle.'

'Sit,' said Marcus, steering her towards a little table on the pavement outside the bar.

'You have to pay more if you sit,' said Thea.

'I already did. This Thomas seems a nice kid. I don't like children . . .'

We'd noticed, thought Thea.

'. . . but he's almost human. I suppose English schools chew you up. Look at my brother.'

Thea winced.

Marcus laughed. 'You'd rather not, I suppose. How long did you hang out with him for?'

'Long enough,' said Thea.

'One night would be too long, from what I heard about his habits,' said Marcus surprisingly. 'He talk to you about music much?'

'Never,' said Thea firmly.

Marcus might be very different from his brother, both to

look at and in temperament, but he had an equally powerful personality. Deny everything, she thought, and then he'll leave you alone.

Marcus's attention wandered as the television, which had been quietly muttering to itself on its perch above the bar, suddenly launched into a crescendo of crackles and hisses.

Marcus's face lit up. 'Hey, I like that,' he said, getting up from the table with such energy that he nearly sent his glass flying. He advanced towards the television; snapped at the astonished barman for trying to adjust the sound; and listened hard.

'Is terrible,' the bartender said, a pained expression on his face.

'It's beautiful,' contradicted Marcus.

'You nuts?' the man asked agreeably.

Marcus took no notice; meanwhile, Mrs hoisted herself on to a chair and gave the set a hearty thump, which restored normal reception.

'Pity,' said Marcus. He headed back to his table, enlivened by the pleasing noises and ready to interrogate Thea further about her relationship with his brother.

'Hey,' he said, looking like a bewildered bull. 'She's gone.'

'Take the afternoon off,' said Sylvester, relieving Agatha and Magdalena of their shopping. 'I and Agatha will cope, with Thomas's expert help. Carla's offered to lend you her car; drive yourself to a remote spot and laze.'

'Go to the grotto at Solforóso,' advised Thomas. 'I went there with Ettore, it's super. Hardly anyone there, and the water's amazing, it's really clear. And it's peaceful; you can have a snooze, if you want.'

As if I were an old dink, she thought indignantly. But she couldn't be cross with Thomas. He always treated her in a slightly protective way, and he had been fussing about how much rest she was getting. No doubt he had noticed the dark rings under her eyes; despite the relaxing air of the island and the tranquil pace of life at the moment, she wasn't sleeping well.

Problems escaped from aren't problems resolved, she reminded herself as she rolled up a beach towel and tucked it into a bag. Once you get away, you can see things more clearly, but you still have to take some decisions, make changes in your life. Otherwise you go back home, away from your island, and everything there is exactly the same.

The silence in the grotto was intense and complete, and patterns of light danced in front of Magdalena's eyes as she floated in a dreamlike state.

The tranquillity was broken by some lively bursts of German, as other bathers arrived, exclaiming at the beauty of the rocks, the greens and blues of the deep sea water, the fantastic colours of the reflections.

Magdalena turned on to her front and swam to the rocky ledge at one side. She smiled and returned the newcomers' friendly greetings, and then hauled herself up out of the water. She made her way out of the grotto and across some rocks; she would dry off on the sandy beach which lay on the other side. A few families sat in clusters, a couple lay motionless, arms entwined.

And one man sitting by himself, on a folding chair, reading a paper.

He lowered the paper as Magdalena went by. 'Good afternoon, Magdalena.'

'Ettore,' said Magdalena, pleased.

'Join me, here,' said Ettore, rising. 'Please, sit down.'

'Thank you,' said Magdalena, spreading her towel. 'I'd rather lie down, I've just come out of the water.'

'As you wish,' said Ettore.

Magdalena fished in her bag for the book she'd brought with her. She liked Ettore, and enjoyed talking to him, but she wasn't feeling in a chatty mood. Ettore took the hint, returned to his paper, and Magdalena propped the book open in front of her. It was a fat and juicy read, borrowed from the villa bookshelves on Dido's recommendation. Exciting, but not exciting enough to counteract the warmth of the sun and the feeling of well-being from her swim.

The words dissolved before her eyes, and they closed.

19

'If you're dry now,' said Ettore, his pleasant voice breaking into Magdalena's troubled and uneasy doze on the sand, 'then may I suggest a walk?'

Magdalena stirred reluctantly. Images of doom and gloom might be chasing themselves round and round in her dreams, but nonetheless, she was feeling comfortable and lazy, and very reluctant to do anything energetic.

'If we go up that path which you can see,' Ettore was saying, gesturing towards a footpath which wandered up between vineyards and towards a tree-covered hill, 'we find some very fine views. Also, there is a place there which I visit, and I would like to show you.'

'Yes,' said Magdalena, standing up. She stepped into her cotton skirt, fixed her sunhat on her head, and rolled up her towel. 'I'm ready,' she said.

'*Con permésso*?' Ettore held out a hand for her bag, and after a moment's hesitation, Magdalena gave it to him. Naturally, she was more than capable of carrying her bag, but how churlish to reject the politesse. Especially since Italians didn't usually spoil their beautiful summer outfits by carrying a straw bag over one shoulder.

The path was dry and dusty, the air hot and Magdalena's mood languid. The path narrowed, and Ettore led the way, throwing remarks back to Magdalena, very knowledgeable remarks about the flowers, the geology of the rocks on either side of the path, the weather, the nature of volcanic islands, the temperament of islanders as opposed to those who lived on the mainland, and the timing of a very complicated element of the plot in his latest book.

Magdalena wasn't concentrating; 'Yes,' she said, and 'I never knew that,' and 'Goodness.' I must sound quite inane, she thought. Doesn't he notice I'm not really listening?

'I think your mind is elsewhere,' Ettore said gently as he led her away from the path and on to a stretch of wider track; a little road, really.

'I'm sorry,' said Magdalena. And then, surprised, 'Do many people want to drive up here?'

'They come to the church,' said Ettore.

And there, indeed was the church. Very old, by the look of it, with a small rounded apse. A single bell hung in the tiny bell tower above the baroque façade.

Magdalena and Ettore walked round to the front of the church through the little graveyard, with higgledy piggledy stone monuments and marble slabs set at odd angles on the hillside. 'My wife is buried here,' said Ettore, pointing. 'There is a monument inside to her. All her family lie here.'

Ettore didn't seem distressed, more matter-of-fact, thought Magdalena. How long was it since she had visited Hugo's grave? He lay in the family vault in the church at Mountjoy, the most recent of a long line of dark and often wicked men who had been tucked away there over the centuries.

Though Hugo was the least wicked of men, thought Magdalena. She would go there, to the church, the minute she got back home. She would take the twins, they loved it there, especially the early crusader tomb, with its knightly legs crossed in their sculpted chain-mail and the little dog supporting his feet.

The church inside was dark after the brilliant light outside. White walls, the wide curve of an ancient arch, some saints, little groups of candles . . .

Magdalena shivered.

'It is chilly here,' said Ettore.

'It's not that,' said Magdalena. 'It just takes me back to my childhood.'

'You are a Catholic?' Ettore sounded surprised.

'Was,' said Magdalena. 'Nothing much, these days.'

On an impulse, she took out some coins and slipped them into the little coin box by the candles. She went over to the painted figure of the Virgin Mary, lit the candle from one already there, and stuck it firmly on one of the metal pins.

'For your mother?' asked Ettore.

'For my husband,' said Magdalena. 'My second husband. Hugo.' Who wouldn't appreciate it at all, she thought with a silent laugh. How he had hated anything that smacked of idolatry. Such things were unEnglish, and not to be trusted.

Like his wife.

She felt confined and uneasy in here, and began to walk towards the door. Ettore followed her out on to the top of the wide steps which led down to the rough road. Magdalena took a deep breath, full of sea air and flowers and trees. The shimmering blue of the sea stretched to a distant horizon, with other islands visible to the north, and a strip of land beyond them.

'What a view,' said Magdalena, her eyes prickling from the sun. 'You can see for ever.'

'Yes, very calm, very serene, very beautiful.' Ettore made his way gracefully down the steps ahead of Magdalena. 'But you know, this can also be quite different, this peaceful sea. This area is famous for its winds, and when there is a storm, the sea becomes very dark and rough, and it is dangerous to sail them.'

'Of course,' said Magdalena, joining him on the road. 'Aeolus and the bag of winds. This is an exciting place to live, with a volcano up there, and storm-ridden seas all around.'

Ettore laughed. 'Mostly, though, it is just beautiful and sunny and it makes you feel good to be alive. Unlike my wife,' he added. 'She loved it here.'

'Do you often come to the church here?'

'Yes, to reflect. I made her unhappy, you know. Because I had other women.'

'Ah,' said Magdalena. 'You touch a nerve there,' she said lightly.

'I'm sorry?'

'I meant that I know how wives feel when their husbands have other women.'

'Not Hugo, I remember him as very English, very faithful.'

'You make him sound like a dog,' said Magdalena. 'Yes, Hugo was faithful.'

I was the one who was unfaithful, she thought.

'But your husband now, he is a philanderer? This is why you come here with the children, alone? This is traditional, for wronged wives, to take the children and leave.'

'I suppose it is,' said Magdalena. 'It wasn't really why I came, though. I came to find Thomas.'

'Of course. And having found him, you decided to stay for a while. Away from your husband. Do you love this husband?'

'I thought so,' said Magdalena. 'Now I'm not so sure.'

'You can't tolerate some indiscretions?'

'The odd lapse; well, I'm hardly in a position to throw stones,' she said. 'But with him, it's long-lasting affairs too. A mistress here, another one there. He takes the situation and them and me for granted.'

'He has no children.'

A pause.

'Not really,' said Magdalena at last. 'He is like a father to the twins, though.'

'I see,' said Ettore. 'How old is he? Perhaps as he gets older, he discovers that a wife is worth taking trouble over.'

'Did you?' said Magdalena directly.

'My wife died very suddenly, an infection of the blood. We had no time to talk anything over, to make our peace. Marriage is difficult in a Catholic country, particularly for my generation. One married young, and it was for life. So either you become very much the family man, devoting yourself to your wife, your children, with perhaps just a very discreet flirtation here and there . . .'

'Or?' prompted Magdalena.

'Or, if you are like me, if you have a need for women, to draw energy from, which I do, for my writing, and perhaps, like me, you have only one daughter, no sons . . . Then you maybe live a separate life. More outside the home than in it.'

'And your wife minded.'

'When she finally found out, yes, she did, unfortunately. She was faithful to me, because she believed in marriage, as an institution. And she was a good Catholic; she went to church, took confession, listened to what the priest said.'

'The priest, yes,' said Magdalena, remembering the appalling advice of her confessor when her first husband was venting his spleen on her. 'Priests can take a very moral line about a completely immoral situation. To support the status quo, you understand. To uphold the sacrament of marriage, particularly.'

'Exactly,' said Ettore, a little sadly. Then he smiled, a charming and slightly wicked smile. 'And so now I am alone, with only a daughter to keep her eyes on me. But I still like women, very much, especially women who have the – how did you put it? – the odd lapse. If you feel like a lapse . . .'

'Thank you,' said Magdalena, laughing. 'I tell you, Ettore, a lapse with you would be delightful,' and it would, she realized with surprise, as bits of her felt as though they were unfreezing for the first time in months. 'But my life is too complicated already.'

'It is an offer,' said Ettore gravely. 'Now, be careful here, because this plant is very bad-tempered, and will hurt you if you come near it.'

'Just like Val,' thought Magdalena.

It was impossible. Unbelievable.

No cars available? Not one? Valdemar looked as thunderous as he felt, but it was no use.

The uninterested-looking Italian in a wilting white shirt spread his hands. '*Signore*, everybody wants a car. Many, many others before you. I am sorry. Tomorrow, perhaps.'

Of course there were many others before him. Others had just sailed through passport and customs. He was the only one to be stopped, questioned, his passport subjected to minute scrutiny, his bag searched. Do I look like a terrorist? A drug runner? Valdemar asked himself, fretting at the delay.

So by the time he had snatched his bag back and retrieved his passport, the queues at the car rental desks had vanished; happy travellers, keys in hand, were heading for their Fiats and Fords; and the staff had returned to idle chatting and filing their nails.

His was not the only diverted plane, that was the problem. Irritated, and beginning to wonder why he had ever come to this benighted country, Valdemar made his way outside. Look at the queue for taxis, what was the matter with everyone?

No doubt the hotels would all be full as well, thought Valdemar, and he dived back inside. At least he could make sure of a room where he could change, snatch an hour or so of sleep. Maybe the hotel would be able to fix him up with a car for the morning. What a waste of time, he said to himself, his fingers drumming on the desk as the admittedly very charming-looking girl found him a room.

In a hotel he'd never heard of, in some distant suburb by the look of it. Couldn't she do any better than this?

No, there were conventions, conferences, fashion showings, every hotel was full to the attics. This was a modest hotel, it was true, but clean and comfortable. And not expensive, she pointed out with a wonderful smile.

Valdemar feared the worst.

Quarles wondered if he could take a few unobtrusive notes, or even switch his little portable recorder on. He tipped his panama a little further forward on his head, shading his eyes so that he could see Thea's face.

She's finding this very hard to talk about, he realized. I thought she didn't know Marcus.

'It's seeing Marcus here on this island that's brought it all back again,' said Thea. 'I wish I'd never come. Or, rather, I wish he'd never come.'

Who or what was 'it'? Quarles wondered. He could just ask, it often worked.

It did.

Thea turned her head and looked straight at him, although her eyes weren't seeing him at all, Quarles felt. 'I knew Marcus's brother. In London,' Thea said flatly.

Quarles's interest grew. He knew nothing about Marcus's family. His editor had warned him that Marcus was a secretive guy, and no article or entry in any work of reference gave details of any family. 'Probably sprang fully tuned out of a heap of barbed-wire,' his editor had commented gloomily. 'It would be a coup if you can discover any more.'

'His brother?'

'Yes. You'll have heard of him. Dauntsey, the singer.'

'Dauntsey?' Quarles stared open-mouthed at Thea. 'The pop

icon? The original squeaky-clean, million-album superstar? Marcus's *brother*?'

'Yes,' said Thea. 'Not many people know that. They both like to keep quiet about it. For different reasons.'

Quarles went over and nudged Thea to move along. She was sitting on a ruined wall in the crusader castle; her sandalled feet rested among the thistles growing between the huge stone slabs laid as the floor of the great hall.

'Funny to think of all those knights and their servants, and local people all coming and going here,' she said dreamily. 'Centuries ago. And now here we are, and in a hundred years' time, there won't be the slightest trace to show that any of us were ever at this castle.'

'No trace of us here in a hundred minutes,' said Quarles more prosaically. 'And who knows, if Dido's right, you could be completely wrong.'

'I suppose so,' said Thea with a sigh.

'Dauntsey,' said Quarles. 'Did you know him well?'

'As well as anyone could know him. I slept with him, if you can call it that,' she said bitterly. 'I existed at his beck and call for many unhappy months.'

'How did you meet?' asked Quarles cautiously, not wanting to scare her off. He wasn't that interested in Dauntsey, although one had to admire anyone who had made so much money so quickly and had so many fans of all ages, races and classes.

'I was training as a clarinettist,' said Thea. 'Second year at college, getting together with friends to play a lot of modern music; we were planning to work as a wind ensemble when we graduated. I was into jazz, too, lots of things. As music students are. Then, one day, a guy came up to me in the cafeteria, he was a trumpeter, I think. Said he had a friend looking for a good clarinettist, able to do crossover work, was I interested in a gig, Friday night? The money was okay, and I was ready for anything, so I went. The person running the show was Dauntsey.'

'Is that his first name?'

Thea shook her head. 'It's a made-up name. Mordaunt, drop the M-O-R, add 'sey'. It's a good name for the music business.'

'He was a musician, too, then? Like his brother?'

'Yes. Piano. Classically trained; well, they both were. Their father's as a professor of music.'

'You're kidding.'

'I'm not. He teaches at some American university. He split up from his wife, who was English, and went off to live an Ivy League existence. He took Marcus; his wife stayed in England with the younger boy. Sent him to Winchester.'

'Winchester?' That surprised Quarles, although there was no reason why Dauntsey wouldn't have been there. 'Only Winchester doesn't seem a very pop music kind of place.'

'It isn't,' said Thea. 'Dauntsey hated it there. "Piano and maths," he told me. That's all his schooling was about. Then he went through conservatoire, more piano, although he'd got away from maths by then. And so, out into the world, heading for jazz, synthesis, crossover and then mainstream pop. He made it with his first number, do you remember?'

'Yes,' said Quarles. '"Walking on my Dreams". Catchy tune.'

'Yes,' said Thea, taking a deep breath and shuffling her feet. 'Great tune.'

'So did you join his group, or what?'

'On my humble clarinet? And me only second year? Oh, no, I wasn't a good enough musician for him to want me for that for very long. No, Dauntsey had other plans for me.'

'Where you in love with him?'

'Does one love a python?' asked Thea. 'I was fascinated, intoxicated, you name it. He had a very powerful personality. A bit like Marcus, only he's dark and wiry; quite different physically.'

'So you found him oppressive,' said Quarles.

'What perception,' said Thea sarcastically. 'You could say that. I found his friends oppressive, too. He shared me round, you see.'

'What?' said Quarles, startled.

'Yup. He was a communist, that was what he said. So what was his was also his friends'. Including me. He'd saunter out and push me towards one of his greasy mob of hangers-on, saying, "Fuck her, Joe, or Sid, or Malcolm," or whoever it was.'

'And you let them?'

Quarles was quite sophisticated, and he'd come across a fair amount of unpleasantness in his life, but he was definitely shocked. You read about this kind of thing, but it didn't happen to people you knew. Especially not to people like Thea, sitting there looking so attractive and lively and in control of herself.

'How could you let him?'

'You wouldn't understand,' said Thea. 'He had a power to subjugate, let's put it like that. And I was mad about him, so I'd do anything to please him. If that meant his friends, well, so be it. He was into SM himself,' she added as a throwaway extra. 'And I wasn't the only one in his thrall, if you want to know.'

'I don't think I want to hear any more of this,' said Quarles, getting up and taking his hat off. He flung it to the ground, roused to temper. 'Damn it, he has such a clean, mummy's boy image. How has none of this ever come out?'

'He's clever. That's the advantage of a first-class education at a top school, you become masterly at covering things up. Do you suppose Thomas knows what he's giving up if he doesn't go back? Don't do that, you'll ruin your hat, and it's a nice one.'

Quarles bent and picked up his hat. 'You put it on,' he said, adjusting it on her hair. He tucked a stray tendril behind her ear, and then, very gently, he kissed her on the mouth.

Thea looked at him, her grey eyes giving nothing away. 'Why did you do that? Because you feel sorry for me?'

Quarles held out a hand to help her up. 'Because I like you,' he said.

Valdemar recoiled from the blast of heat which reached him as he opened the door to his hotel room. The temperature must be in the nineties, and this was a hotel without air conditioning. A rest seemed unlikely; undesirable, even.

Valdemar was well able to cope with physical adversity, as long as he didn't have to. He threw his bag irritably on the bed and tugged at his tie. At least he could put on cooler clothes. Then he opened his bag and pulled out the contents.

A tweed suit.

Long johns from skiing trips.

Two brushed-cotton country shirts.

A pair of silk pyjamas.

And what were these? He held up a pair of black trousers, astonished. These were the bottom half of a dress suit.

He stared in disbelief at the clothes heaped on the bed. What on earth had he been thinking of? He'd intended to bring the casual clothes he took with him as a matter of course on his visits to Hong Kong, Singapore, America in the summer.

So how had he managed to put in this motley collection, suitable for nowhere at all? He didn't even know he had that tweed suit in London; it belonged to the northern half of his life. He never wore it outside Eyotshire.

Valdemar ran his hand through his thick, dark hair. Good Lord, no socks, one pair of shorts, a pair of heavy black Oxfords. This was too much. He stuffed everything impatiently back in the bag, and then turned it out again to hunt for his shaving things.

They weren't there. Valdemar rubbed his chin, now with a dark shadow on it. Damn it, he needed a shave. And this wasn't the kind of hotel which had shops in the lobby. He looked at his watch. Getting late; he just hoped there would be shops open where he could buy some clothes.

Few Italians could match Valdemar's height, and when he said what size shoes he was looking for, the assistants burst out laughing. Ruffled, Valdemar finally managed to acquire the basics, although not in the style nor of the quality he was used to.

Today was not turning out to be a good day.

20

'Bugger,' said Valdemar.

He grappled impatiently with the gear lever as the clutch slipped yet again. What kind of a car was this? How could any reputable company hire out such a heap of old metal and have the nerve to call it a car?

The truth was, as Valdemar well knew, that he wasn't renting from any kind of reputable company. Genoa was struck by an acute shortage of rental cars, and in desperation Valdemar had accepted an offer from his hotel porter.

'Is a very good car, will take you many, many miles. To Naples, in fact. There you take the car to this garage; here, I write it down, and leave it. My cousin will arrange another hire, so that the car comes back up here, to Genoa.'

This car, thought Valdemar wrathfully, is never going to make it to Naples, let alone back to Genoa. This ramshackle vehicle should have been confined to a scrapyard long ago. His teeth rattled as the car jolted and heaved its way along the motorway. Valdemar hated being passed by anything, and to be crawling along the inside lane while fat little Fiats and family cars full of grannies and *bambini* flew past him made him wild.

He was going to dump this car at the next big town, where there would surely be a proper car available to hire. One to suit his long legs, one with windows that went up and down, one with a radio, and air conditioning. A normal, functioning car, in fact.

The juddering was getting worse, and a strange burning smell was building up inside the car.

'Shit,' said Valdemar.

There was a slip road just a little way ahead, and he eased the faltering car off the *autostrada*. He freewheeled down the wide curve which led him under the motorway. The car coughed, then rumbled into life again, as Valdemar drove slowly and uneasily along a road which was centuries away from the six-lane carriageway with its stream of cars and lorries flashing past only a hundred metres behind him.

Ahead was a hill, picturesque with dark cypresses, and, at the top, the massive walls of an old hill town. The road was deserted; siesta time, Valdemar supposed. No garage, no hamlet lay within easy reach; no, it was the hill town or nothing.

He nursed the car up the ever steeper road, past a sign which said 'Umbroglio', and drove through the arched gateway of a mediaeval town. He made it into a little square, which was occupied by a cat, several dozy pigeons and a tourist with a camera. What he needed now was a garage, before the wretched thing gave up the ghost completely.

It was too late. The car gave a final mighty fart, followed by a bang which echoed round the square, and rolled gently to a halt outside a tiny bar.

The tourist came up alongside the driver's window. 'Say, I think you've got real problems with this vehicle. Did you know there's black smoke pouring out of the exhaust?'

Valdemar extricated himself with difficulty from behind the wheel and got out. He stood beside the American tourist, surveying the evil-smelling smoke which was coming out in revolting gusts from the rear of the car.

'Fuck,' said Valdemar.

Agatha sprinkled almonds on the pan-baked fish with gay abandon. 'A work of art,' she said.

'Hmm,' said Sylvester, inspecting it.

'I've finished the salad,' announced Thomas, emerging happily from behind a giant mound of greenery. 'Lots of garlic in the dressing, I love garlic.'

Magdalena put her head round the door of the kitchen. Her skin was faintly flushed with the afternoon's sun, and she looked more relaxed than Agatha had seen her for several days.

'What have you been up to?' asked Agatha, with a knowing look.

'Nothing,' said Magdalena. 'And certainly not what you have in mind. Although I might have; the offer was made.'

'You must tell,' said Agatha, intrigued. 'Once I've finished in here, that is. Sylvester, can I squeeze past?'

'You look like the three bears,' said Magdalena.

Thomas gave a guffaw of laughter. 'Am I the baby bear, or is that Agatha?' he asked cheekily. 'No prizes for guessing who daddy bear is.'

'Enough of that,' said Sylvester. 'Out of the way, young Thomas, I want to see how my lamb is coming along.'

'Smells wonderful,' said Magdalena, sniffing the aromas which were drifting out of the oven.

'Cooked with capers,' said Sylvester. 'They grow them all over the island; funny, that, I always used to wonder where capers came from.'

Agatha was busy untying the strings of her apron. 'I've finished for the time being, darling,' she said to Magdalena. 'Time for a glass of chilled wine and a flop on the terrace. I'm parched and exhausted.'

She tripped after Magdalena to the terrace and slid on to a reclining seat. 'Heaven,' she said, shutting her eyes. Then she opened one again. 'Spit it out,' she demanded. 'Who have you been with this afternoon?'

'It isn't hard to guess,' said Magdalena calmly, pouring a glass of wine for Agatha and taking it over to her.

'Darling, you save my life,' said Agatha. 'Marcus?'

Magdalena was so surprised that she burst out laughing. 'Marcus? Agatha, come on.'

'He's got his eye on you.'

'He's half my age.'

'He's the sort who'd go for older women. And no wilting adoration, either, not with that sort. Plenty of energy and vigour, everything stiff about him.'

'That,' said Magdalena crossly, 'is very crude.'

'That's as may be, but it's a compliment to put ideas into the head of a young man like that, especially here with all those astonishing Italian beauties in exiguous costumes. Cheers!'

'Agatha, you're outrageous,' said Magdalena. 'Now I shall get the giggles every time I look at Marcus.'

'Sylvester and Ferenc get the giggles every time they listen to his music, what's the difference?'

'He's a perfectly nice young man under that rather brusque and difficult exterior. And not interested in me.'

'Oh yes, he is. You can tell the way he eyes you. Kind of calculating and devouring. So, if it wasn't our resident genius, who was it?'

'I went to the Grotto for a delicious bathe,' said Magdalena. 'And Ettore was there on the beach, so we went for a walk together. Up to a pretty church, San Falario Solforóso. His wife is buried there.'

Agatha wrinkled her little bump of a nose. 'That's not very romantic. Ghoulish, rather. But of course, he'd love to get his hands on you, you can see that quite clearly. Carla thinks so, too.'

'Agatha!'

'You know what a gossip I am, darling, no harm done. Carla is very level-headed about her pa.'

'I do wish you wouldn't.'

'I'm madly jealous,' said Agatha contentedly. 'Ettore is a treat. And imagine rolling up with him in London, wouldn't George go wild?'

'I don't suppose Ettore ever goes anywhere near London,' said Magdalena.

'He does. He's going there later this year, for some literary do; he was telling me all about it. I shall ask him to stay, if I'm still living with George, which I very much doubt.'

The night was heavy and soft with heat. There was a clear sky with a brilliant moon, which exaggerated the dark, purple softness of a Mediterranean night. The island was full of noises, the sounds of the night. And of Sylvester, finishing the Bach suites which had been interrupted earlier in the day. It had been worth stopping for, thought Sylvester, musing over his culinary efforts and the splendid meal they had cooked.

Dido came with her dancer's walk on to the terrace. She sat

down silently in a pool of moonlight, legs crossed at the ankles, hands wrapped neatly round her knees.

'I know you're there,' said Sylvester as he began a Sarabande. 'You could dance; these are dances I'm playing.'

'Yeah, I can tell,' said Dido, getting up. She began to dance with the lack of self-consciousness only possessed by the professional and the very young. 'You better play this to the twins, do them good.'

'Wasted,' said Sylvester. 'They won't listen to Bach.'

'You'd be surprised,' said Dido. 'They like music.'

Sylvester brought the linked chain of notes to an end, and rested his bow. 'Why are you awake and prowling around at three in the morning? Indigestion? Not at your age, surely.'

'No, I was woken by the moonlight.'

Sylvester slackened his bow and reached out for his cello case. 'I'm not surprised,' he said.

'Tell me about Valdemar,' said Dido. 'Is he a very thundery man?'

'You could say that, yes.'

'Then he's on his way. Getting nearer and nearer.'

'He's taking his time about it, considering all he has to do is hop on a plane.'

'Maybe he's not having an easy journey,' said Dido.

'Valdemar's a very old friend,' said Sylvester. 'But I really don't want him here, driving Magdalena mad; distressing Thomas, as he's sure to; stirring everything up.'

Dido laughed. 'It may not happen,' she said. 'And I can see air being cleared, so perhaps it'll be all to the good.'

'Time he got himself sorted out,' said Sylvester severely. 'He can't just think of himself all the time. For the rest of his life. He has to join the human race at some point.'

'I expect he can go on thinking only of himself,' said Dido. 'Lots do. On the other hand, he might have to pay a very high price, higher than he wants.'

'Mmm,' said Sylvester. 'I'm not entirely convinced. Not where Val is concerned. Now, what about Thea? I don't care to see her looking so tense. And did you notice her with Quarles? Very offhand, hardly said a word to him this evening, did you see?'

'No, but she looked at him a lot,' said Dido. 'Subtly.'

'Is this a party?' asked a voice from the shadows. 'If so, is it invitation only, or can anyone come?'

'Thea,' said Sylvester, pleased. 'Another insomniac?'

'I heard music, so I came to see who it was.'

'No prizes for guessing,' said Dido caustically. 'Hardly going to be that Marcus out here playing Bach.'

'He may approve of Bach,' said Sylvester fairly. 'Many composers of Marcus's ilk do.'

'Nah,' said Dido. 'Not his cup of tea at all, judging by the squeals and squonks coming out of the studio when you lot are in there rehearsing. When's the concert, then, Sylvester? Just so's we know to keep away.'

Sylvester shook his head at her. 'You're a representative of modern youth, Marcus's music should speak to you.'

'His music doesn't speak to anyone,' said Dido firmly.

'Marcus would be ashamed if it did,' said Thea. 'He'd die if his music was accessible.'

'Ah, accessible, the ultimate insult,' said Sylvester.

Thea drifted to the edge of the terrace, breathing in the rich scents of the night air. 'It's so quiet; utterly still. Look at the sea down there, hardly a ripple, just a gentle surge and plash.'

She swung round. 'I'm going to go for a swim,' she announced.

Dido rose gracefully to her feet in one swift movement without uncrossing her legs, much to Sylvester's admiration. 'Me too,' she said.

'Towels?' said Sylvester. 'Costumes?'

Dido and Thea looked at each other. 'No need,' said Dido.

'Ah, youth,' said Sylvester, gathering up his cello.

'Going back to bed?' asked Thea.

'Of course not. But I must put my cello away, I can't leave it out here. Then I shall accompany you, partly because I love bathing at night, and partly because who knows what strange creatures may lurk on the island?'

'None stranger than Marcus,' said Thea. 'And he's tucked up and asleep.'

'I heard from Valdemar last night,' said Virginia, coming into the bathroom where Ralph was shaving.

Ralph didn't like to be interrupted during his morning shave, but this was interesting news. 'He's found Magdalena, has he? And the boy?'

'Not at all,' said Virginia happily. 'He's had the most terrible journey; he hasn't got even to Rome yet.'

Ralph was so surprised that he gave himself a nasty nick with his razor. 'Damn,' he said, mopping his chin with the nearest towel.

'Don't use that, it's mine,' said Virginia, taking it away from him. 'His plane was delayed; there wasn't a decent hotel in Genoa; no cars available to rent, and he was ringing me from a remote spot called Umbroglio.'

'Good God,' said Ralph. 'My uncle was there in the war. I don't think that's Val's kind of place at all. How did he end up there?'

'Apparently, he did finally manage to get hold of a car, but he only made it as far as this hill town or village, or whatever it is. And no help at hand. The car he was driving will take days to repair, and none of the car hire people can send a car out for him.'

'What's he doing, walking?'

'No, he told me he'd found a room. By the sound of it, not at all a desirable kind of room. And he was going to catch a bus to the nearest big town in the morning.'

'A bus,' said Ralph, filled with unholy glee. 'Val, on a bus? An Italian village bus? Oh, I wish I could see it.'

Virginia was laughing so much she could hardly speak. 'I wish Magdalena could see him.' She grew more serious. 'I expect he'll hire a car in wherever it is and drive straight down, to the ferry. Or he may drive to Rome and fly from there. However he gets there, he's going to be in one lousy mood when he does catch up with Magdalena and Thomas. You know how Val hates to be thwarted.'

'I'm sorry for Magdalena,' agreed Ralph, 'but I think it's time Val experienced a bit of discomfort.'

'Poor Val,' said Virginia. 'His career in tatters here, his personal life in a very parlous state, and now this.'

'Career in tatters?' said Ralph. 'Because of this cathedral business? Surely not.'

'I fear so,' said Virginia. 'He could be in big trouble.'

Valdemar had just spent what he thought was the most uncomfortable night of his life. Even worse than the noise and heat of his Genoa bedroom had been the dusty stuffiness of the extremely small inn room in Umbroglio. He had passed a grim night on a lumpy mattress set on a bed which was too short for him; on a mattress, moreover, which had the dual malice of being slippery and saggy.

Valdemar was not in a good mood. He descended to the little bar to be greeted by his ecstatic host, who was thrilled by the excitement of the broken-down car and the tall dark Englishman.

'Such a terrible temper,' he had told his cronies in the bar the night before. 'So many dreadful words, I had to close my ears.'

'You don't understand English, how do you know the words were terrible?'

He cast his eyes up to heaven. 'Anybody could tell that these were oaths and curses. He is like someone out of the opera, this one.'

Valdemar downed a rapid coffee, paid his bill and headed for the square like an avenging angel.

Only just in time. An ancient and decrepit bus wheezed its way to a halt. Immediately the square, which until then had seemed deserted, was full of people. A wave of women clutching bags and baskets swept past Valdemar and on to the bus. Two or three creaky men followed at a more reasonable pace.

Stunned, Valdemar picked up his things and swung himself on to the bus. He stood by the driver, looking in horror at an interior bulging with good-humoured humanity. A fat woman in black with gleaming teeth and sharp black eyes beckoned him, gathering up a squirming toddler from the seat beside her to make a place for Valdemar. He installed himself gingerly, with a brief nod of thanks, to be rewarded by a beaming smile and the infant deposited on his lap.

The bus gave a rousing honk, everybody except Valdemar crossed themselves, and they were on their way.

*   *   *

'Only Marcus wasn't tucked up in bed,' said Thea, her mouth full of peach. She licked the juice off her chin.

'Where was he?' asked Agatha, who was being regaled over breakfast with the tale of the midnight swim.

'In the sea. We arrived on the beach, hurled off our clothes, and flung ourselves naked into the sea. Two sea nymphs. And a whale, that was Sylvester. So imagine the shock when Marcus suddenly rose out of the waves. Sylvester nearly drowned, didn't you, Sylvester?'

Sylvester downed his cup of very black coffee and vigorously denied it all. 'I was in perfect command of myself,' he said. 'Only I slipped on a stone.'

'Got a good body, Marcus,' said Dido judiciously. 'Keeps himself fit, you can see, wonder how he works out.'

'I won't ask which portion of the Marcus anatomy you're referring to,' said Sylvester.

'Interested?' said Dido.

'Not my type at all,' said Sylvester cheerfully.

'Bit of all right in all departments, I'd say.' Dido turned her attention back to Helena, who was fighting a melon and losing. 'I said you should let me cut it up, you're having a bath there,' she said, mopping up as she spoke.

'He spoiled our swim,' said Thea.

'No, he didn't,' said Dido. 'Nothing could spoil it.'

Thea relented. 'It was beautiful, Mum. You should try it. The sea sparkles at night, did you know that?'

'It's phosphorescence,' said Agatha, her thoughts on a moonlit sea some thirty years before, remembering how she and George had swum naked in a tropical ocean. 'Little plankton glowing in the dark. Magical.'

'Giulietta says there's going to be a storm,' observed Ferenc, who appeared with more coffee. 'The sea will be too rough for bathing then.'

'For long?' asked Dido.

'No, just while the wind blows. We call it the wind of Odysseus, because it blew him on to these islands on his journey home.'

'Odysserss,' said Hugh carefully. 'Oddyserus.'

'Odysseus,' said Dido. 'Be a good boy and eat up your breakfast, and then I'll tell you and Helena all about Odysseus.'

'Homer, too,' said Sylvester, raising his eyebrows.

'Yeah,' said Dido. 'A learned pig, what a surprise.'

'Dido!' said Thea, laughing.

'Dancers don't usually know much about anything except their feet and how many calories they ate yesterday and who the principal's going with,' said Dido. 'But you want to design costumes and work with the ballet, you need to know about myths and legends. So I do.'

Valdemar came off the bus at Pesto a shaken man. Every bone in his body hurt, and that bloody child with the eyes of a cherub and the soul of an infant Satan had not only pulled the buttons off his shirt, and demolished his jacket collar, but had then puked all over him.

The bus had deposited him in the main square. And there, across the road, was a sight to gladden Valdemar's sore eyes. A hotel. A proper hotel.

That was all very well, but the hotel was inclined to consider Valdemar a far from proper guest. Valdemar didn't have much sense of humour left, but the sight of himself in the mirror in the reception lobby did bring a wry smile to his lips as he argued with the receptionist.

The sight of a wallet full of more-than-acceptable credit cards brought a gleam of interest to the receptionist's eyes, although she clearly thought that Valdemar might have stolen them. '*Passaporte* please,' she snapped. She looked long and hard at the passport photo and back at the dishevelled man in front of her, and finally, grudgingly, pushed a form towards him.

'I only want a room for a few hours,' said Valdemar. 'To have a bath and change.'

'Is not possible,' said the girl gleefully.

'Oh yes, it is,' said Valdemar. 'I'll pay for the night, so don't fuss. Now, I'll want to hire a car. And where is there a shop selling men's clothes?'

21

Valdemar stretched out his legs, opened his eyes to take a quick look at the Italian countryside flashing past, and closed them again.

At the beginning of the week, he would have been appalled at the prospect of travelling across Italy in a train – any train. Now, he was simply thankful that it was a fast train, that he was in a first-class compartment, of which he was presently the only occupant, and that the train was air-conditioned.

And so far, the train was on time. There had been no sudden strikes, nor signal failures, nor obstacles on the line; not a single bomb threat or hijacking attempt. This was, so far, a perfectly normal train journey.

Even a pleasant one, thought Valdemar. His usually limitless energy had been markedly diminished by two bad nights with little sleep, and however much he preferred to drive, there could be no doubt that this was a comfortable way to travel.

I shall have to ring England to get Pippa to arrange a replacement driving licence, he reminded himself. How stupid, to lose it. He knew where it was, too. In the passenger glove compartment of the broken-down car abandoned in Umbroglio, where he had thrust it in his haste to leave Genoa and get to his destination.

More haste, less speed.

He had been pleased when he had quickly and easily found a car to rent from an international company. A BMW, modern, well-maintained, almost new. Everything had been fine until the clerk had asked for his driving licence and he realized with horror that he didn't have it.

There was nothing to be done. No licence, no car, and that was that. Which is why he had made his bad-tempered way to the station, had queued interminably to get a ticket to Rome, and had caught the only fast train for six hours with a whisker to spare.

Valdemar yawned again, and arranged his long frame more comfortably. He'd be in Rome by this evening. With luck, there would be a plane from Rome to Palermo; if not tonight, then first thing tomorrow. Then the quickest way across to the island, and he would be face to face with Magdalena. By tomorrow evening at the latest. Not to mention Thomas, he thought grimly; the cause of this whole farcical business.

Quarles emerged from his hotel looking very lanky and dapper in his habitual panama and shades. Under his arm was a fat parcel.

'Is it your birthday?' asked Agatha, who was scanning the carousel of postcards at the entrance to the bar. She wanted to find one, not of the island, but elsewhere, so that she could send a mystifying and annoying message to George.

'Birthday?' said Quarles, puzzled.

'The parcel.'

Quarles started. 'Oh, this,' he said, holding up the parcel as though it might bite him. 'This. Um, no, just work, I'm afraid. Proofs.'

'Pity to work in such a place as this,' said Agatha.

'You don't work, then?' Quarles fell into step beside Agatha as no suitable postcard was to be found, and she stepped back into the street again.

'Not these days, no,' said Agatha.

'How do you pass the time?'

'Good question. I look after the house, or did before I walked out. I feed the children, who show no inclination to leave home. I do some work for Save the Children. I watch a lot of videos. I read books. I go to language classes. I see friends. I go out to the theatre, the opera, the cinema. I entertain with my husband.'

'Ah,' said Quarles.

'You may well "Ah", darling,' said Agatha. 'You're thinking, what a tedious way to spend one's life.'

'Perhaps,' said Quarles.

'You're right,' said Agatha. 'It is very tedious. I think I was a lot happier when George and I were very hard up, and I had to work all the hours I could. But, do you know, one becomes accustomed to not doing so very much. It's not good for one; that's why I'm so anxious to see Thea establish herself in a proper career. Something she can do now, and go on doing, even after she's married and got a family.'

'Is Thea planning to get married and have a family?'

'People do,' said Agatha. 'I don't understand her. She went to college, has a degree or whatever you get when you study music. She doesn't want to be a musician, although she's always loved music. I know she injured her arm, but I would have thought . . . Anyway, that's beside the point. Being a musician is a risky business, but there's plenty of other work, behind the scenes, administration, that kind of thing. Of course, she's very secretive, one's children are, I suppose. I never liked my mother to know what my plans were.'

She doesn't know about Thea and that appalling Dauntsey, thought Quarles. 'How nice to have Thea living at home, though. Has she always lived there?'

'No, when she first went to college she was wild to be independent, she found a room for herself, and after that she shared a house with Dido and some others. Then, quite suddenly, she came home. Said it took too much of her time being away from home and she needed to study. She didn't seem to study much when she came home; brood, rather, I would say. But that's what you're like when you're a student.'

'Perhaps she'll get a flat or something when she finds herself a new job,' suggested Quarles. 'Has she got a boyfriend?'

'No, she doesn't seem very man-minded just at the moment. It surprises me, because when I was that age . . .'

She touched Quarles on the arm to halt his progress along the harbour front. 'A bar, hold on, I'm dying for a smoke, I'll just pop in and get myself a packet. Then you can come with me and help me choose a sun hat.'

'For you?'

'No, for Thea; she left hers on the beach yesterday, and it vanished. She has that pale skin which goes with red-brown hair, and she must protect her complexion. Once lost, gone for ever, as I'm sure you know.'

Dido was drawing dancers. 'Got to get the body right before you can put the costume on,' she said. 'Then, you got to know your dancers individually. See, some of the boys, they want it cut very smooth across the torso. That's tricky, because they got to breathe, and they've got a lot of muscle there as well.'

Thea squinted at her sketches. 'Looks like something out of an anatomy textbook.'

'That's what it is,' said Dido seriously. She flipped over the sheet of her pad. 'That's what you start with. Then you got to turn that lump of muscles and sinews – and I'm talking about the girls, here – into a swan or a fairy princess or what-have-you.'

Dido made some lightning squiggles with her charcoal pencil, and the tough athletic physique she'd drawn turned into a weightless and fragile nymph floating in the air.

'May I see?' Marcus had surged in, unseen. He leant over Dido's shoulder and took the pad. He flicked through, looking at her drawings. *'Les Sylphides,'* he said. *'Swan Lake, Giselle*, all the classics. What's this, *Romeo and Juliet*?'

'The knights,' said Dido. 'Thea, where are you off to?'

'Things to do,' said Thea, eyeing Marcus and sliding out of the room.

'Scared of me,' said Marcus brusquely, noticing Thea's stealthy departure. 'Don't know why, I'm not interested in her.'

'You remind her of your brother,' said Dido.

Marcus was affronted. 'I do not. I'm not in the least like my brother.'

'Same big ego,' said Dido. 'Perhaps that's it.'

'I like this,' said Marcus, who wasn't listening. 'I don't recognize it, what's the ballet?'

'It's not been performed,' said Dido, taking back her pad. 'It's Odysseus. Make a good ballet, I was thinking when I was telling the twins about the Odyssey. Big stuff, though, it'd have to be, and that's expensive. Unless it was just two, him and Penelope. She could dance Calypso, too, and . . .'

'Big role for a good dancer,' said Marcus. 'It would suit someone like Yuri Karamazov.'

'Yeah,' said Dido. 'Yuri's good.' She looked at Marcus, eyes narrowing. 'How come you know about a dancer like him? Ballet isn't your scene at all, not from the way you go bad-mouthing any music that isn't mathematical and screechy.'

'I know something about it, that's all,' said Marcus. 'Doesn't mean I have to like it. It's a load of crap, actually.'

Dido was furious. 'Crap, huh? Crap! Listen, Mr Mordaunt, what's crap is that junk you compose. If you can call it composing. You write music with the wrong side of your brain, that's what's the matter with your music. All think and no heart, and it stinks. And it doesn't please anyone, unlike this crap ballet stuff, which has pulled in millions and millions of punters. And most of them leave feeling a lot better for being there.'

'My music isn't about feeling better,' said Marcus. 'You wouldn't understand it. If you did understand it, I'd have failed.'

Dido looked at him and laughed. It was a genuine laugh, intensely annoying to a ruffled Marcus.

'Listen, I'm an artist, yes? A trained dancer. Raised on the boards, I've spent more hours in the opera house than you've spent at school. I know music. I've lived and breathed music for years. And danced it. Professional, okay?'

'Dancers,' said Marcus contemptuously. 'What do dancers know about music?'

'Dancers have music in their bones. So if I don't understand your music, then you got no hope, because no one else will. If no one understands it, and no one likes it, and it doesn't make an audience feel anything, only bored out of their skulls, then you're on a fast train to nowhere as an artist.'

'Art has nothing to do with pleasing people.'

'Teach your granny to suck eggs,' said Dido rudely. 'I know what art is, a lot better than you.'

'You know what art is? You! Oh, that's very funny.' Marcus's neck was getting redder and redder; always a bad sign.

'Your stuff isn't art; it isn't anything except a heap of pretentious noise. It's ghastly to listen to, and it's got no feeling. You don't feel anything, and the poor mugs listening to it don't feel anything either. What a great night out.'

'I'd like to point out that experts don't share your views. Do you read the critics? And if it's so boring, why do I go on getting commissions?'

'Big deal,' said Dido. 'A string of world premières, great. And do any of the audience come back for a second helping? No way.'

'You just talk to Quarles about it. Quarles is a words man, maybe he can get into your little brain exactly what my music is all about.'

'Don't kid yourself,' said Dido. 'Quarles would save his breath. He doesn't like your compositions any more than anyone else. Do you think he's there with his feet up listening to recordings of your *Evolution IX* or that horrible piece, what was it, *Matter*?'

'That's one of my most successful pieces,' said Marcus, stung.

Dido took no notice. 'No, he is not. He writes nice things about you because he wants to keep his cred with the small group of weirdos who hype your kind of music.'

'There's no point in talking to anyone like you,' said Marcus, who was now an alarming shade of red.

'No, but you should bleeding well listen, because the wind's changing, and you're going to get stuck if you aren't careful. Lot of musicians reckon your kind of music is dead, out of touch.'

'College-trained, imagining that neo-classicism is interesting and modern, I know the sort,' said Marcus with scorn. 'They're afraid of real modernity.'

'You're up a dead end, Marcus Mordaunt,' said Dido fiercely. 'And I find you as boring as your music, so why don't you just piss off and leave me to enjoy the dance.'

Defeated, Marcus retired.

And moreover, he thought angrily as he roamed on to the terrace, she's made me feel incredibly randy. He looked hungrily out at the landscape, as though a willing nymph might waft out of the vines and into his arms.

Another hunger rose in him. Not for food; Marcus ate well and regularly, as was necessary to keep his huge energy going. No, this was a secret and abstract hunger.

Marcus was on the move.

He propped himself against a gleaming stainless steel bar, a much-needed glass of whisky in front of him. The rest of the day stretched out ahead of him, solitary and empty.

Valdemar was perfectly happy to spend the odd evening alone in his flat, pottering around, reading, eating something he'd brought home from Harrods Food Hall or from the excellent delicatessen round the corner.

That was different. That was from choice.

A meal in a restaurant would be good; Valdemar appreciated Italian food. On the other hand, it would be lonely, Italy was a country for shared meals. Who did he know who lived in Rome?

Professional, business acquaintances? He had only to ring them, and they would sweep him off with genuine enthusiasm and pleasure in his company. No, he wasn't in the mood for that.

Cinema?

No.

This was Italy. He would go to the opera.

Agatha was on the move as well.

'What are you doing?' exclaimed Magdalena, as she put her head round the door of Agatha's room. 'Packing, why?'

'Darling, so exciting,' said Agatha. 'Dido is a wonder, you have to keep her, you do realize, at all costs? Pension off that Lottie creature, find her another job, pop her down the castle oubliette – anything, but you must keep Dido.'

'Calm down,' said Magdalena, rescuing a silk slip which had been cast on to the floor. 'What has Dido to do with this?'

'Darling, she came in here this morning, with, I may say, a cup of delicious coffee, what a treasure. Would Edmund marry her, do you think?'

'Agatha, get to the point.'

'Dido,' said Agatha, pausing dramatically with her cosmetic bag held aloft, 'had a message for me.'

'Oh, Dido and her imaginary messages,' said Magdalena, unmoved by this information.

Agatha looked at her crossly. 'Darling, this is It. The big news. Dido knows the street in Paris where I went on that fateful day. It's the Rue de la Paix. She doesn't know the name of the bank, but she assures me that there is only one, with a black and gold sign hanging outside it, or near it.'

'So?'

'So, I'm off. To Paris.'

'Agatha, you can't be serious.' Magdelena started laughing, it was so preposterous. 'Look, this is nonsense.'

'It is not,' said Agatha, affronted. 'It isn't nonsense, I am completely serious, and I'm off.'

'You haven't any money, how are you going to get to Paris? And why? You can't go chasing off on a wild goose chase like this.'

'Dido knows.'

'Agatha, you know perfectly well that Dido says all these things to make herself seem interesting. It's an affectation, something she'll grow out of in due course.'

'That's all you know,' said Agatha.

A large figure filled the doorway

'Voices raised? Is this a private argument, or may I join you? Good morning, Magdalena, Agatha. Another beautiful morning it is, too, so much for the woeful prophecies of storm and tempest. Magdalena, you look amused, what's up?'

'Good morning, Sylvester,' said Magdalena, standing on tiptoe to give her large friend an affectionate kiss. 'I'm so glad you've appeared. Listen, Agatha's planning to rush off to Paris, you must tell her how ridiculous it is.'

Sylvester looked at Agatha in surprise. 'Why are you going to Paris? Don't you like it here?'

Agatha gave an impatient shrug, looking at Magdalena with a distinctly peeved expression.

'It's Dido,' explained Magdalena. 'She's told Agatha that she knows where she stowed George's father's jewels. And Agatha believes her.'

'Quite right,' said Sylvester, sitting down on the bed, which creaked alarmingly. 'Want a hand with the packing, Agatha? You won't need much; you won't be away long, straight there, collect the goods, and back again.'

'Sylvester! Why are you encouraging Agatha like this?'

'Who needs encouraging?' said Agatha defiantly. 'Now, I must go and find Thea and borrow her credit card.'

'Agatha, you can't do that.'

'Magdalena, darling, you're becoming very negative in your old age; when you were younger, you were always game for anything. What's happened to your spirit of adventure?'

The door closed behind her, and Magdalena sat down abruptly on the bed beside Sylvester. He put a large and strong arm round her. 'She's right, got to keep up with the unexpected, otherwise life gets very dull.' He gave Magdalena a squeeze and released her to stand up with a great yawn. 'Good for Dido.'

'Sylvester, you can't believe in all this.'

'Of course I can,' said Sylvester.

Valdemar felt that life was improving. He had obtained, admittedly for a very large sum of money, a ticket for a Mozart opera. *The Marriage of Figaro*, one of his favourites. With a fine cast, world-class singers. Just the kind of music to drive away any dark clouds. Eighteenth-century style, wit and elegance. Perfect music; what an excellent way to pass an evening.

Valdemar stirred in his seat. It had seemed comfortable enough, but perhaps there really wasn't enough leg room. He moved his shoulders slightly, to ease a feeling of discomfort.

'*Il destino me la fa,*' sang the Count.

I must have heard and seen this opera dozens of times, thought Valdemar. Why does it seem more intense than usual tonight? Why do I feel sorry for the Countess, why don't I feel sympathy for the Count; after all, what man could resist such a pretty Susanna? Why don't I feel that Figaro is well able to cope with all this, as I always have?

Usually, Valdemar lost himself in the music, the story was an amusing fribble, a vehicle for fine voices and some of Mozart's most inspired writing. Never before had the plot come across so clearly, or so uncomfortably. This was an opera to entertain a sophisticated audience, Valdemar reminded himself. It was intended to amuse and delight, not to preach morality.

The Count was tricked and confounded; the orchestra played its final chords, and the curtains swept together to a storm of applause, cries, a few hisses and the other joyful sounds Italians make at the end of an opera.

Black-browed and not now feeling at all like dinner, Valdemar made his way out through the crush of cheerful, talking, lively opera-goers.

Good God, what an idiot the Count was, to allow himself to be made a fool of like that. What a stupid, threadbare plot, why had he never noticed it before? This was the last time he was going to go to a performance of *Figaro*, he could promise himself that.

Valdemar hailed a taxi, and flung himself gloomily against the back seat.

This wasn't at all the evening out he'd had in mind.

22

Sylvester couldn't believe his luck when he reluctantly arrived in Ferenc's studio to begin the day's work, and found Marcus gone.

Ferenc was smiling with satisfaction. 'Great, isn't it? The guy's just skipped. He'll be back, he told Giulietta, only gone across to Sicily for a night, but only think of the hours of peace which lie ahead of us.'

'What a pity Gabriel's been delayed,' said Sylvester, sitting down and pulling out the spike of his cello. 'We could have had a really good session or two without Mordaunt's powerful presence.'

'We still have plenty to do, just the two of us.' Ferenc pulled his stool up to the piano. 'I wish I knew what drives that guy. I have this feeling that under all this garbage there's some real music struggling to get out.'

'Real as in what?'

'I don't know,' said Ferenc. 'Popular, maybe. Or classical but playable and interesting to listen to; who can say? But there's something there, I'm sure of it.'

'Triumph of hope over experience,' said Sylvester. 'He's the most intense and the most exasperating young man I've ever worked with. Never again; the recording company can sue until they're blue in the face. No more Discordant Mordaunt for me.'

'That's the spirit,' said Ferenc, playing a few exultant chords on the piano. 'Now, off we go.'

Magdalena, put out by Agatha's defection, set her sun hat on her head, borrowed Carla's binoculars and set out for a walk. Without intending to, she took the path which led up to Ettore's house. She could see him in his garden, a typewriter on a teak table, shaded by an umbrella, a cat lying stretched out in the shade by his feet. She half hoped he would see her and perhaps join her, she would have appreciated some company.

No luck. He did look up, and he saw her, but he merely paused in his typing to wave, and then went straight back to his writing.

Magdalena had left Carla deep in a thick manuscript, pencil in hand, dictionary beside her. Ferenc and Sylvester had been practising furiously and happily in the studio, Dido was doing her job and minding the children on the beach, with Thomas for company. Thea had gone into the town with letters to post and some chores to do for Carla. Quarles, as far as Magdalena knew, was holed up in his hotel, wrestling to put Marcus on paper.

And now here was Ettore, hard at work.

All of them had some purpose to their days. Even Agatha, off on her pointless mission to Paris, had some zest in her. While she, Magdalena, wandered about, not needed, not useful . . .

Pull yourself together, she told herself. Enjoy the beauty of all this. You can't stay here for ever; time is passing, and like it or not, you'll soon be back at that bloody castle. Cold as sin, and about as bleak, Magdalena thought resentfully. Never, not in the wildest dreams of youth, had she ever imagined herself spending her days in a northern castle.

'It's damp, cold, grey and has nothing but a certain shabby and historic charm to recommend it,' she told a smelly goat who had paused to peer inquisitively at the solitary walker. The goat trotted off, its bell tinkling; Magdalena walked on.

What had she to show for her life?

Two dead husbands.

One a disaster, who had bruised her literally and in her spirit.

The other who had loved her, and whom she had betrayed. Even if he hadn't known it, that was what she had done.

A third husband who was all too alive and kicking, and busy hurting her, in his way, as much as Ronnie had done. Perhaps it was all her fault; perhaps she was a born victim, destined to attract the wrong kind of men. Men who would bully and despise her.

Hugo hadn't.

Of course he hadn't. But then she had destroyed her happiness in that marriage through a single rash impulse of lust, a fling which had lasting consequences. And Hugo was dead, and she couldn't ever put that right.

The twins.

They were the only good to have come out of the mess which her life seemed to have been. Yet they wouldn't have been there if she hadn't had that fling with Valdemar. Did Hugo really die believing she was pregnant with his child? He'd known that he had a sperm count so low that the doctors had told him years before that he could never father children. Had he believed in a miracle, a thousand-to-one chance? Or had he suspected the truth, and had that made him unhappy; caused his heart to stop one day while he walked alone on the fells?

They had brought him down from the hills on a stretcher. Jack carrying his gun, Hugo's beloved dog whimpering at his feet. Hugo had looked so calm and composed when she saw him then, thought Magdalena, finding a rock and sitting on it in melancholy fashion.

If she hadn't slept with Val while on that rare visit to London, there would have been no twins. Val would have inherited the castle from his uncle, might have married, had children in any case . . . Would that be better?

It would have left me free, thought Magdalena for one tantalizing moment; then she thought of the twins with their endless mischief and huge enjoyment of life. What a futile thought; she'd rather have them than freedom. Even if the price she had to pay was another unhappy marriage and that castle hanging round her neck.

It was funny, really, how eager Val had been to marry her. Funny how Val, who had never wanted children and who always despised other people's, had been so possessive about his own. How he hadn't been able to bear the thought that Magdalena might marry someone else, so that he would be written out of the twins' life.

Not that he has much to do with them now, Magdalena

reminded herself; she didn't want her heart to soften as far as Valdemar was concerned. She was going to fight him for Thomas's sake, if not for her own. And if the price of that was separation, well, theirs was already a semi-detached marriage.

There's always Ettore, she thought with a quick smile. Such a nice man, and his courtesy and ease and charm would be such a relief after the squalls of being married to a man like Val.

The path began to wind its way downwards.

If I follow it, thought Magdalena, it will bring me out near the little beach where Dido has taken the twins. I shall surprise them, and we can have lunch together. Her spirits rose at the thought. It was impossible to feel gloomy for long on Aeolus; there would be time for that when she went home. For the moment, at least, she could push her memories and concerns to the back of her mind. Out of reach of Val, she could just take each day as it came.

'Stormy weather coming,' said Dido cheerfully, as she pulled a clean T-shirt over Helena's head.

'How do you know?' said Hugh argumentatively. 'You don't know, because there isn't a television to see the weather on.'

'I use me eyes, which is better than any telly weatherman,' said Dido. 'And my nose. Smell the air, it smells different. And look out to sea, at the colour of the sea where it meets the horizon there, look.'

'There's a black line across the sea where the sky starts,' remarked Helena, looking up from inspecting her sandy toes.

'Yes,' said Dido. 'We'll have to find some good games to play inside at the Villa Saraceno. There'll be no beach for a day or two.'

Hugh pouted, and then his face lit up as he saw Magdalena sliding and jumping down the last part of the path on to the beach. He and Helena hurled themselves towards her, their voices getting louder and higher as they bellowed the morning's news about giant sandcastles, wet T-shirts and an encounter with a sea-shell.

Life, thought Magdalena, does have a way of going on.

Dido calmed the twins down, and agreed that it would be a good idea for them all to have lunch at the restaurant.

'Agatha's gone to Paris,' said Magdalena, as they sat themselves down at a table.

'Yeah, to find them jewels,' said Dido.

'Will she?'

Dido's lively face lit up with laughter. 'You wait and see, she'll come back with her little package, ever so happy.'

'I would be very pleased if that were the case, and naturally, since she took them there in the first place, she must know where they are.'

'If she'd known where they were, she'd have got them long before this. It's all been a nasty shock, so Thea says, her husband carrying on like nothing on earth, and her walking out. At least once she gets her hands on them, she'll have some bargaining power.'

I shouldn't be discussing Agatha's affairs with Dido like this, Magdalena told herself. She tried again. 'Look, I know it's all good fun, saying you know about things from the other side, but don't you think it's rather a silly pose?'

Dido looked at Magdalena with her head on one side, considering. 'I got a feeling that you're fussing about your husband. The previous one, not this guy who's about to arrive.'

'I hardly think . . .' said Magdalena, taken aback, but Dido took no notice.

'Like, you're guilty, because you slept with the one you're married to now before the last one died. And these two are the result.'

Magdalena looked with horror at the children, but they were bickering happily and paying no attention to the conversation of their elders.

She was angry now. 'Dido, I don't know where you've been getting this gossip from, but I have to tell you . . .'

'No,' said Dido. 'You don't have to tell me anything; there's no point. I'm not interested in your life. I do me job, look after these two for you, and you pay me. I'm not blackmailing you, and I'm not out to make trouble. I'm just trying to help. Your Hugo's dead, and that's that. You can't undo what you done, so don't waste your energy thinking about what you might or might not have done, and how it would be better if or if not.'

Dido broke off to rescue Hugh from a particularly dangerous

onslaught from Helena, and defused the tension by telling them they could go inside to choose the ices they were going to have for pudding.

'You carry that load of guilt around and it'll get heavier and heavier, and it'll work off on the twins. It isn't their fault, whoever else is to blame. And it's souring your marriage now, and that's no good. You're on your third husband, that's enough for anyone, better make it stick this time.'

'Dido!'

'Hello,' said Thea, standing by the table with a carrier bag in each hand. 'Can I join you? I've been doing some shopping for Carla.'

Magdalena was too angry to say anything.

'What's up?' said Thea, pulling out a chair and sitting down. She looked from Magdalena's furious face to Dido's calm one. 'I know what, Dido's being saying something you don't like; I know that look. You don't believe any of it, do you, Magdalena?'

'I do not,' said Magdalena.

'Dido saved me from a really disastrous mess,' said Thea matter-of-factly. 'I had a nasty affair going, that nobody knew about, and Dido suddenly popped into my room one morning and put me straight. Don't ask what it is, Magdalena; just trust it. You don't think Mum will have any luck in Paris, but I bet you she does. Then you'll have to believe her, won't she, Dido?'

Dido rose to collect the twins, who were about to start a fight at the entrance to the restaurant. 'My own mum doesn't believe it,' she said cheerfully. 'No skin off my nose. I pass the news along, and if people don't take no notice, then that's their lookout. 'S long as it doesn't affect anyone else,' she added, her glance flickering from the children to Magdalena's face.

The waiter came for their order, apologizing for the delay and for the clattering noises going on inside the restaurant. 'We put up shutters, against the storm,' he explained.

'Is it going to be very bad?' asked Thea with interest.

'I think so. At this time of year, it come very quickly, and blow very hard, and then it go, and everything is okay again.'

'Oh, good,' said Thea.

'For your own comfort and safety, please fasten your seat belts.'

The seat belt sign flashed on; the plane lurched violently and then bounced up and down as though on a spring. Several passengers were looking pale; one or two were clutching sick bags; a child was crying.

Valdemar looked out of the window at the storm which was providing such a spectacular display. Rivulets of rain streamed across the window as the plane dropped and then rose again.

'It is turbulence, nothing to worry about,' said the stewardess soothingly to an alarmed woman sitting across from Valdemar. Then the plane gave another violent wiggle and she hastily sat herself down in a vacant seat and fastened herself in.

'Look, even she thinks we're going to crash,' wailed the man in the seat next to Valdemar.

'Nonsense!' said Valdemar. 'This is a thunderstorm, it just means a slightly bumpy landing. Really, there's nothing to get yourself into a state about. We'll be coming down in a minute.'

'Coming down *where*?' said the man.

As he spoke, the engine sound changed, and they could feel the plane banking as it started a steep descent. There was a bump and a jolt and the scream of brakes as the plane, safely down, hurtled down the runway before turning off to taxi to its place.

Valdemar looked at his watch. Good, he should be in plenty of time. Then a thought struck him. He stopped a bustling stewardess. Was the storm a local affair, how would it affect sea crossings to the islands?

'Oh, *Signore*,' she said, shocked at his ignorance. 'The Tyrrhenian Sea? On a night like this? Of course not. You will have to find a hotel, they will help you at the airport. Maybe it will be better in the morning, but the winds can blow across the islands for days at a time.'

'Thank you,' said Valdemar with a sigh.

For God's sake, a journey which should have taken a day! An evening in a rainswept Palermo; just what he needed. It never rained in Sicily at this time of year. Why did there have to be a freak storm now; this year, this week?

'This storm!' said Sylvester. 'What a beauty!'

Dinner was being eaten indoors at the Villa Saraceno. Oil lamps and candles were dotted round the dining-room and in the bedrooms. 'The electricity usually goes if there's a bad storm,' explained Carla.

With the thunder breaking overhead and flashes and streaks of lightning illuminating the sky, it had been felt that the twins would be unable to sleep, and so they were at table, too, sleepy but excited by the tumult outside.

'That's the wind,' said Helena. 'Listen to it whooshing.'

'Howling like wolves,' said Hugh. 'I'm glad I'm not outside. What a storm.'

'Do you realize we're cut off from the mainland?' said Sylvester, reaching for the wine. 'No ferries or hydrofoils are going to be out in this weather. Lucky that Marcus and Agatha got away this morning, otherwise we'd have them muttering up and down like caged beasts.'

'Why did Marcus go?' asked Magdalena. A shower and a pleasant chat with Sylvester, who was in a very good mood after a Marcusless day, had restored much of her equilibrium. At the back of her mind was a lurking thought that Dido's advice, although not accepted as coming from any other side, might still be sound; but this wasn't something she was going to think about for the moment.

There was a particularly loud crack of thunder, and the lights dimmed, flickered and then went out.

'Bed for you,' said Dido to her charges. 'I'm coming with you, and I'll stay with you until you're asleep. No arguing. Say good night to everyone.'

'Thank you, Dido,' said Magdalena.

Sylvester pottered back to his seat after taking a look out of the window. 'You can hear the sea,' he said. 'Thrashing about down there, quite violent. Lot of rain, too. Almost as bad as Eyotshire, eh, Magdalena?'

'Nothing is as bad as Eyotshire,' said Magdalena with feeling.

And I hope the weather's terrible there, too, she found herself thinking, and that Val is there, in a cold room, by himself, hating every minute. Then she laughed at her fantasy; much more likely that Valdemar would be in London, in the company of friends.

More likely still that he'd be alone with Veronica or that tiresome Belle . . .

Damn the man for being the way he was, she thought, and damn myself for minding so much.

They were playing a variant of Cluedo invented by Quarles. This consisted of declaring notables dead, and then working out how they had died, and which other notable, hanger on, worn-out spouse or disgruntled lover might have committed the murder. Victims ranged from politicians through film stars, distinguished actors and singers, conductors – Sylvester's special field – critics, journalists, writers and television personalities, taking in a few well-known lawyers and athletes on the way.

It was a noisy and absurd game, with these worthy citizens meeting ever more astonishing deaths, and the players providing increasingly libellous explanations as to who had done them in and why and how.

Carla acted as controller, and as Sylvester said to Ferenc, she had missed her vocation. 'Could have earned a fortune in the law,' he said admiringly, as Carla ruthlessly cross-examined a supposed witness as to the unseemly death of a famous theatrical director.

The candles grew low, and the assembled company grew quieter and more mellow.

'It's kind of peaceful without Marcus,' said Ferenc, yawning widely.

'Yes, but it's good when he's here,' said Carla. 'He crackles.'

'Crackles?' said Sylvester, raising himself from his semi-incumbent position. 'You make him sound like a bag of crisps.'

'No, he crackles with life, like the thunder and lightning out there. It's tiring and sometimes difficult, but then you feel more alive because of him.'

The others thought about this.

'Pity that nothing comes of all that energy, then,' said Dido. 'I had a spat with him, told him his music was useless.'

'I bet you were popular,' said Sylvester.

'He did get a bit worked up,' said Dido.

'He's got ego inflation,' said Thea.

'Too big for his boots, you mean,' said Magdalena. 'I know

what Carla means about the energy, though. No one who met him would easily forget him.'

'Would that one could,' said Ferenc. 'Seeing that his energy is mostly used to beat everyone else into submission.'

'Wonder what he's doing in Palermo,' said Sylvester. 'Nipped off very smartly, didn't he? Say anything to you, Carla?'

'No. Not a word.'

'George!' said Valdemar. 'What the hell are you doing here?'

'Don't shout like that,' said George. 'You made me jump. And don't loom over me, Val. If you're staying, then sit down.'

Valdemar flung himself down in the seat across from George. 'You're the last person I would expect to see in Sicily. You don't like abroad.'

'Nor do you, unless you're pounding after some fat contract,' said George sniffily. 'I dare say I'm here for exactly the same reason as you are. Well, no, not exactly,' he added after a moment's reflection. 'I mean, I've come to find Agatha, and I suppose you're here for Magdalena. But we're both trying to catch up with straying wives. God, it is undignified.'

Valdemar sat back in his chair and gave George a cold look. He didn't like the way George had put that.

'I've come to join Magdalena, yes.'

'You haven't,' said George. 'You've come to have a huge row with her and bring her back to heel.'

'I do not have rows with Magdalena.'

'You do. You have rows with everybody. We all know it, and I'll tell you something else, we all feel bloody sorry for Magdalena, Val. She doesn't deserve a husband like you, that's what. If she's got any sense, she'll have found herself some charming man here, who won't treat her as the resident doormat.'

'George, are you drunk?'

'I am not,' said George with dignity. 'Not one drop have I had all day, although I'm proposing to have plenty this evening, I can tell you. I had the most ghastly flight from London, hurtling all over the sky, and my nerves are on edge.'

'I do not treat Magdalena as a doormat,' said Valdemar.

'You do. Dumping her in that gloomy hole up north, and

then swanning about London with all your bits on the side. It's humiliating for her, and I can tell you, Val, it isn't a very edifying spectacle for the rest of us.'

'Mind your own business, George.'

'No, why should I? We aren't in the club, no one's listening, why shouldn't I tell you a few home truths for once? That flight's given me a nasty shock. I thought "This is it," and while I was holding on to my safety belt and the plane was diving about all over the place, I spent a bit of time pondering on my life. Chiefly Agatha, of course, but also about how seldom I say what I'd like to. Out of politeness, you know, and not rocking the boat; not wanting to offend. No more!'

George shifted in his chair, and leant towards Valdemar. 'Did you know that nearly all divorce proceedings are started by women?'

'What are you talking about? You aren't planning to divorce Agatha, are you? Don't be ridiculous.'

'No, but she may want to divorce me. That's what worries me so much. And have you thought about Magdalena? How do you know she hasn't already been on to her lawyer?'

'Of course she hasn't,' said Valdemar. 'She's got more sense than to think of divorcing me. What would she do on her own?'

'She is on her own most of the time,' George pointed out. 'That's how it starts. They get fed up, and next thing you know is, "The petition will be heard . . ."'

'Stop it, George. Agatha knows which side her bread is buttered, and as for Magdalena . . . well, she wouldn't dream of such a thing. Besides,' he added, 'her family's Catholic.'

'Fat lot of difference that makes these days,' said George.

'Just shut up about it, George, will you?'

George looked at his friend reflectively. Then he rattled the coins in his pocket. 'Come on, Val. Get your coat if you've got one. The chap here has given me the name of a good restaurant not far away. We'll brave the tempest, and I'll stand you dinner.'

'Oh, bugger you, George,' said Val, getting up. He touched George on the shoulder. 'I'll be down in a minute.'

* * *

Thea was last out of the room. Yawning, she snuffed out the few guttering candles, and picked up the remaining oil lamp to light her way. As she held it up, she saw a carrier bag on the table. She peered inside, and drew out the fat parcel that Agatha had seen Quarles carrying.

Quarles's proofs, she said to herself. I'll give them to him in the morning. If I leave them here, Giulietta might carry them off to the bin; what a way to carry papers around, in a tacky bag like this.

23

Magdalena came out on to the terrace to a world washed clean by the storm. The air was fresh, and cooler than it had been, though Carla assured her that by midday it would be as hot as ever. The sea hadn't settled down to its normal tranquillity, but the wildness of the waves had gone. Everything sparkled, the colour of the flowers seemed more vivid, the sky a brighter blue.

Dido and the twins arrived in their normal cocoon of noise. 'We,' announced Helena, 'are going to the beach, to see the waves.'

'Crash!' said Hugh, happily. 'Whoosh!'

'And then we're going to go to the market, to see about those wooden animals. Because we can't go into the sea yet; it's still too rough.'

'Tell you what,' said a tousled Thomas, clad in a long and dilapidated T-shirt over a pair of old shorts, 'it'll be fun to watch the ferries and the hydrofoil come in. Gosh, I bet all the passengers will be green.'

Helena fixed her dark eyes on him. 'Why will they be green?' she demanded.

'Seasick,' said Thomas with relish. Sylvester gave him a friendly clout, telling him that he shouldn't revel in the misfortunes of others, but it was obvious that Thomas was unconvinced. 'About midday the first one's arriving, that's what Giulietta says.' He sat himself down and heaped several rolls on to his plate. 'Pass the jam, kiddos, I'm starving.'

Thea yawned, stretched, padded over to the window and pulled back the shutters. If she leant out of her window, she could see the volcano, and she looked up at its purple grey shape, clearly outlined in the rain-washed air.

We're all living in the shadow of a volcano, she thought, as the slight remaining breeze blew across her face. Carla and Ferenc literally, but the rest of us, too, never knowing when something dramatic and explosive is going to blow our life to pieces.

Like Dauntsey, she thought, going into the bathroom and starting the shower.

She sang under the spray, something she hadn't done for a long time. Wish I had a clarinet here, she thought, as she wrapped herself in a big white towel. She remembered her mother asking about her clarinet.

'Where is it, darling? I never see it, and you never play it any more.'

'Don't nag, Mum. I keep it at college, it's easier. And I do all my practice there, that's what music college is for, you know. Proper practice rooms with the right acoustics.'

Anything not to tell her the truth. Which was that she had sold her clarinet because Dauntsey had needed money. This was before he had made the recording which would bring him fame and fortune.

'You'll never need it,' he told her. 'You'll never make a professional, take it from me. You aren't good enough.'

She'd believed him.

'Your clarinet's a good one, quite valuable, and I'm skint.'

'My parents gave it to me.'

'Still hooked on bourgeois family values, sweetie? Time for another lesson on what life's really about. Give me the bloody thing, I'll sell it.'

And she had.

Thea did up the belt on her shorts. Breakfast, she thought, suddenly hungry. Then, as she was opening the door, she spotted Quarles's carrier bag on the table where she'd dumped it the night before. Better take it now.

She picked it up, hesitated, and then, overcome by wicked curiosity, opened the end of the parcel and pulled the proofs out. It was long, must be a book, she thought respectfully; and all about modern music, no doubt. No wonder he worked so hard down there in his hotel.

She turned to the opening chapter, and began to read.

The ferry terminal was seething with people who had been unable to catch a ferry the day before, others who had hoped to catch early morning vessels which hadn't sailed, and the normal complement of travellers on their way to the islands for business or pleasure.

'What a scrum,' said Valdemar. 'Let's see what we can do.'

'Not a hope,' said George gloomily.

Valdemar wasn't having any of that. Sheer size carried him to the front of the throng milling about the ticket desks; his height got him attention, and his air of authority, not to say power, got him what he wanted.

'As bloody usual,' muttered George, who was not gifted with Valdemar's height, looks or commanding presence.

'Shut up, George,' said Valdemar. 'You're always complaining. I thought you wanted to see Agatha as soon as possible; well, we're on the first hydrofoil.'

'You don't understand,' said George, still a little maudlin after an intoxicating tasting the night before of all the best of the Sicilian wines. 'I miss Agatha. I love her, I want her back. I can't do without her. You don't need anybody, but I do, and what I need is Agatha.'

'Oh, go to sleep,' said Valdemar. 'I'll wake you up when we're boarding.'

'Is anyone sitting here?'

Valdemar found himself accosted by a big young man with crinkly red hair, who was built like a pugilist. Valdemar had noticed him at the ticket desk, because he also had the knack of getting what he wanted.

Like looked at like, Valdemar's startlingly blue eyes meeting the young man's light brown ones as they frowned at each other.

Valdemar moved his bag from the seat beside him. 'Help yourself,' he said.

'I could tell you weren't Italian,' said the man. 'Although you could be, have you noticed that a lot of these Sicilians have blue eyes and dark hair? Norman, I suppose.'

Valdemar returned to his book, but the young man was disposed to chat. 'Are you on holiday? You don't look as though you're on holiday.'

'I'm going to meet up with my wife and family,' said Valdemar repressively.

The young man laughed. 'I'm staying on Aeolus,' he said. 'Don't know where you're going, but plenty of husbandless wives there. Two of them where I'm staying. And a chap waiting for his boyfriend to turn up, funny old world, isn't it?'

'Is it?' said Valdemar, icily.

'Nice women, too. *Their* husbands won't turn up. At least, they hope they won't. They've both done a flit; couldn't stand it any longer back home. It sounds as though they're married to fairly unsatisfactory types. And one of them, well, she's a stunner. Amazing. Very beautiful, you know, but remote, and rather sad. Her husband must be a bastard to make her look like that.'

'Oh?'

'Beyond me how he could treat her so badly.'

'Perhaps she was the one in the wrong.'

'Her? No way.'

'You don't know.'

The man's thoughts were elsewhere. 'I find her incredibly attractive, but I'll have to bide my time. You can tell she's a bit sensitive about men. The only one she's at ease with is her gay pal, they're old friends. Magdalena needs friends, I can tell you.'

Carla greeted her father warmly, and at once abandoned him. 'I have some work which must be finished and sent off very urgently,' she explained, giving her father a quick peck on the cheek. '*Ciao!*'

Ettore strolled across the terrace to where Sylvester and Magdalena were finishing breakfast and arguing amicably about the day ahead.

Sylvester stood, and gave a gigantic stretch. 'Sit here, Ettore. I'm going to have a swim.'

'This is not a good time,' protested Ettore. 'The sea is rough, and it may not be so warm.'

'I like a rough sea,' said Sylvester genially. 'Invigorating. Then I shall come back to spend some time working with Ferenc; let's hope Marcus isn't on the midday boat that Thomas keeps on about.'

'Everybody working,' said Ettore, settling down for some serious flirting with Magdalena.

'Not me,' said Magdalena.

'*Cara*, there are some women who exist simply to be. You have your house, very beautiful, one hears, your children . . . that's work enough.'

'No,' said Magdalena. She wasn't feeling at all flirtatious; rather, she was on edge, nervy, waiting for something to happen. 'I think I drank too much coffee,' she said.

Ettore changed gear. 'Okay, I flatter you. Women like to hear that it is enough to exist as ornaments. Some women like to hear this. But it isn't true. My wife lived like this; she was unhappy, I was unhappy. And my mistresses were women who worked, they had busy lives, careers. This made them interesting to me, very attractive.'

'There you are, then,' said Magdalena.

'Can you work where you live? Is the castle very remote, no city nearby?'

'Eyot,' said Magdalena.

'A university town. Much business. A big festival. Surely there is something for you there?'

'Perhaps,' said Magdalena.

'Are you trained, a professional?'

'Textiles. Old ones. Conservation techniques. I was offered a job by one of the big auction houses. Part time.'

'Then, you must do it!'

'It's in London.'

'So, you need to live in London.'

'It's not so easy,' said Magdalena. 'The country is better for the children, the village school is so good. And someone has to look after the castle.'

'This belongs to you? From your husband? Or to your present husband?'

'Neither, it belongs to Hugh.'

'Then there is no problem. He is too young to argue with you,

you find tenants for the castle, some historically minded persons who put up with some inconveniences, no heating, maybe, and some damp. Poof! It will be nothing to them.'

Magdalena was laughing at his enthusiasm. 'It would be nice,' she said. 'I don't like living there. I don't have strong ties to it, except that my late husband was born and bred there, and he loved it very much. I feel I owe it to him to stay and look after it.'

'Not so,' said Ettore, becoming very intense. 'We owe nothing to the dead. You go to London, live your life. Hugo would have wanted to see you happy, not walled up in his castle.'

'You make it sound very mediaeval.'

'How you live your life now is, I think, very mediaeval. And,' as Thea came bounding on to the terrace, eyes sparkling, 'here comes a young lady who is not mediaeval at all.'

'Good morning, Magdalena, good morning, darling Ettore,' said Thea. 'I'm so hungry, is there anything left?'

'You're in very high spirits, Thea,' said Magdalena.

'Oh yes, such a beautiful morning, and Mum will be back today, with Pa's horrid jewels, I feel it in my bones. And I learnt something about someone which is very good news, and I feel extremely good about life in general.' And Quarles in particular, she said to herself.

She bit fiercely into an apple. 'Who's mediaeval?'

'You aren't at all,' said Ettore. 'Perhaps Magdalena is, in her castle, sometimes.'

'In thrall,' said Thea, taking another bite of her red apple and chewing it thoughtfully. 'Oh, I've been that. No more, though.' She stretched violently, spied a chunk of the crusty white island bread and pounced. 'Pass me that honey, please, Magdalena. Where are the twins? With Dido?'

'Yes; they've gone to look at the waves. And Sylvester's gone to the beach, too. To swim. I hope he'll be safe.'

'Good gracious, it would take a mighty sea to get the better of Sylvester,' said Thea disrespectfully. 'All that bulk, and he's just like a porpoise when he gets into the sea. Born under a watery sign, our Sylvester, you may be sure.'

'Here it comes,' said Thomas. He was sitting on the beach, his feet at the water's edge, enjoying the waves breaking over his legs and feet. Sylvester was a little way along the beach, towelling himself vigorously.

Thomas had his binoculars trained on the hydrofoil. 'Of course you can't really see the green on their faces until they disembark,' he said. 'They must have had a pretty bumpy ride, look at the way it's thumping up and down.'

'It can't be too bad, otherwise they'd have cancelled,' said Sylvester, heaving himself into an ultra colourful shirt.

'I'm going to go along to the hydrofoil station and watch,' said Thomas.

'Off you go, then,' said Sylvester. 'I'm going back to the villa.'

Thomas ran along the road to the port, waving at his friends among the fishermen as he went, jumping over the fishing nets and anchors laid across the pavement to the peril of unwary passers-by. He sat himself down on a capstan, waiting for the travellers to emerge. Perhaps Marcus will be on board, he thought. No one knows when he's coming back.

Yes, there was Marcus. He started to wave, and then stopped, stiffened. He knew that person walking along behind Marcus. That was George Fimbul. What was George doing here? Particularly when Agatha was in Paris. Did anyone know he was coming? He thought not, he'd heard nothing and Thea would have mentioned it. Hey ho, this could be fun, he thought.

Then he heard a voice, ringing out across the harbour. 'George! Is this yours? It was on your seat.'

It was Valdemar.

Tall and terrifying.

Here.

Thomas fled.

George thought that Valdemar was being more than usually rude. 'What on earth's got into you, Val?'

'Drop it, George, will you.'

George wouldn't. 'A perfect stranger, a man you've met for the first time on the crossing, he's staying at the Villa Saraceno, and you won't say another word to him. What is he, a psychopath or something? Did he pinch your bottom?'

'We need a taxi,' said Valdemar, ignoring George's comments.

'Yes, and I'm going ask that young man if he wants a lift.'

'He doesn't,' said Valdemar.

'How do you know?'

'Just take it from me, he doesn't. "Very beautiful. Sad. Remote",' he added under his breath. 'What an absolute bloody nerve.'

'We can't take a taxi and not share it.' George could be very terrier-like when he felt in the right. 'It would be very rude.'

'I don't care,' said Valdemar. 'He doesn't know we're going to the villa and I'm not going to tell him.'

Marcus solved the problem by swooping past on his bike and giving what Valdemar felt was an offensive wave.

'There,' said Valdemar. 'He's got transport. Now shut up, George, there's a good fellow.'

'That's all right, then. A fit young man, obviously,' said George approvingly.

George thought fitness was a very desirable quality for other people. He himself tended to the rotund, and for years his only exercise had been cheering from the touchline during rugger matches at Edmund's school. Edmund hated rugger, but his father cherished the belief that such games made a man of you.

'No way,' Edmund had pointed out with his usual delight in contradiction. 'Hallikin, JL there, see him?'

'That's a fine lad,' said George. 'Six foot four? And he must weigh, what? Fifteen, sixteen stone?' He beamed at such a wholesome specimen of young and muscular masculinity.

'Rams the fourth formers whenever he gets the chance,' said Edmund laconically. 'Bent as they come.'

'Come *on*, George,' said Valdemar, pushing his friend into the taxi. 'This journey has taken an extraordinary amount of time and trouble. I want to get to that villa as quickly as possible; then we can catch a plane back to London from Palermo this evening.'

'What?' said George. 'You're mad. Good heavens, did you ever see such a beautiful island? You can't leave a place like this as soon as you get here.'

'I can,' said Valdemar. 'I've already been away from the office far longer than I'd intended; the sooner I get back the better.'

'What if they won't go with you?' said George, clinging to the strap by his seat as the taxi driver entered into the spirit of Valdemar's haste and belted along the bumpy roads at a reckless speed.

'They will,' said Valdemar, sure of his powers of persuasion.

'I wouldn't, if I were them,' said George, gazing out with delight at the view as they climbed towards the Villa Saraceno. 'Good gracious, I can see why Agatha's always nipping off abroad to see friends. It's so warm. And the sea, the colours. And there's a volcano up there, look!'

His voice rose with excitement, but Valdemar sat back, arms folded, quite uninterested in his surroundings.

'This is tremendous,' said George. 'I'm not going back tonight, no, nor tomorrow. In fact, I'm going to stay as long as I can. I wonder if it's easy to buy property here?'

'Oh, come off it, George. You couldn't exist for a week without the club and all your London schemes.'

'I could. I could spend weeks here. And if it would make Agatha happy, then I shall do just that.'

The taxi skidded to a halt outside the gates. 'Villa Saraceno,' the driver announced with a flourish.

'Fine,' said Valdemar. 'Open the gates and drive on.'

The taxi driver wasn't having any of that. While he was out of the car, his passengers would undoubtedly leap into the front seat and drive his car away. He had known this to happen, many, many times. No, one of the *signori* must open the gates.

'What's he saying?' asked George. 'Have we come to the wrong place?'

'God save us from fools,' said Valdemar, getting out of the car and slamming the door so hard that the ashtray inside lost its lid. He stalked to the gates and dragged them open.

'What a performance,' he said, as he got back in. 'What would we do with his bloody car if we stole it? Joy ride round the island? Or drive it on to the ferry to sell it in Sicily, I dare say.'

'Oh,' said Thea, peering down from a rooftop where she was

having a pleasant sunbathe, clad in nothing at all. 'Here comes trouble,' she added, as Valdemar leapt out of the car. 'And I don't believe it. Pa!' she shouted, holding an arm across her breasts in a pointless attempt at seemliness. 'Pa, what on earth are you doing here?'

Valdemar looked up. 'Your daughter's up there, prancing about with nothing on,' he said severely to George. 'Can't you control your children?'

24

'Hark,' said Sylvester, stopping in mid-phrase.

'What is it?' said Ferenc, swinging round on his piano stool in surprise. Usually nothing interrupted Sylvester when he was playing.

Sylvester was rapidly putting his bow and cello in the case. 'I hear trouble,' he said. 'Oh, my word. Come on, Ferenc, no more work today, I think.'

Intrigued, Ferenc followed Sylvester out of the room and towards the distant sound which had had this glavanizing effect on his friend.

Raised voices. Men's voices.

Visitors? wondered Ferenc.

'Ah,' said Sylvester, letting out a long sigh as he saw who it was. 'I thought so.' He sailed into the big room which served as entrance hall and sitting-room and led out on to the terrace. 'Hello, George. Admiring the view? Go and see it from out there, it's much better. Val! Well, well, I suppose you were bound to turn up sooner or later.'

'Hello, Sylvester,' said Val, not greeting him with any real warmth. 'I'm surprised to see you here.'

'I come every year,' said Sylvester, knowing that wasn't what Valdemar meant. What he meant was, if you knew where Thomas and Magdalena were, why didn't you let me know?

'Can't interfere, you know,' he said. 'Magdalena's a grown-up, you have to respect her wishes.'

'Her wishes! What about my wishes?'

'Calm down, Val. Now, what you want is a cool drink, a

shower, and I'll tell Giulietta there'll be two extra for lunch. And say hello to Ferenc.'

Valdemar gave Ferenc a cool nod. This was the man who had been harbouring his wife and family, and hadn't even had the decency to let him know they were all right.

'I'm not staying,' said Valdemar shortly. 'Not even for lunch. Where's Magdalena?'

Carla, alerted by Giulietta that two Englishmen, one small and happy, the other very big and angry, had arrived, hurried to greet the new arrivals.

'Carla,' said Sylvester, 'this is Valdemar, Magdalena's husband, and one of my oldest friends. And out there on the terrace is George Fimbul.'

Carla cast a quick glance towards the terrace. 'And no Agatha?'

Sylvester shook his head. 'Not back yet.'

'Oh dear.' Carla put out her hand to Valdemar. 'Welcome to the Villa Saraceno. It has been so nice for us to have Magdalena and the children here with us.'

'How do you do?' said Valdemar formally.

Merciful saints, no wonder Magdalena had trouble with her husband, thought Carla, feeling rather as though a large and dangerous member of the cat family had stalked in from the jungle. What an attractive man, but not easy to handle, not at all, you could see that at a glance. And no wonder Thomas was so alarmed by him.

'I think Magdalena has gone to the beach, with Dido and the twins,' said Carla.

Valdemar's face grew darker. 'She has no business,' he began, and then he stopped as he realized that there was no reason why Magdalena should have been there waiting for him.

'You should have let us know you were on your way,' pointed out Sylvester.

'Yes, so that they could all have moved on before I arrived,' said Valdemar. 'Very clever. And who's Dido?'

'She's looking after the twins,' said Ferenc. 'A very capable girl.'

'Kidnapper,' said Valdemar furiously.

'Who's a kidnapper?' Marcus advanced bouncily into the room, and stopped short, an amazed look on his face as he saw Valdemar. 'You're the guy I met en route. What are you doing here?'

'None of your business.'

'Hey, join the human race,' said Marcus. Sylvester came to his rescue. 'Magdalena's husband, Valdemar,' he whispered.

'Oh, Jesus,' said Marcus. 'And the little fat guy?'

'Agatha's husband.'

Marcus started to laugh.

'What's so funny?' said Valdemar, towering over him.

'You,' said Marcus, unalarmed. 'The whole set-up. Oh, what the hell. Sylvester, Ferenc, are we going to get down to some work? I've had some ideas while I've been away.'

'No,' said Ferenc and Sylvester, simultaneously and firmly. 'Not today, Marcus.'

'In that case, I'll use your studio, Ferenc.'

'No banging on the piano,' said Ferenc warningly. 'No plucking the strings, no tinkering with the hammers, and no playing it with objects inside. I mean it, Marcus.'

Marcus frowned. 'You ought to get rid of this sentimental attachment to out-of-date instruments, Ferenc.'

'You bust up your own piano, right? Leave mine alone.'

'Okay, okay. See you later.'

Sylvester was trying to explain to Valdemar that they really didn't know where Magdalena was. She could have gone to any one of half a dozen places; in fact, Carla felt fairly sure that she had been planning to spend the day at a particularly pleasant spot on the other side of the island. Or maybe not. One thing was sure, she wasn't intending to be back for lunch.

Baulked of one prey, Valdemar turned his mind to another. 'Fine,' he said. 'I can see it's going to be extremely late before we can get away. Meanwhile, where's Thomas?'

Ferenc looked at Carla, Carla looked at Sylvester. Sylvester gave a massive shrug. 'I suspect he saw you arriving, Val. I think it's just possible that he's decided to absent himself a while.'

'You mean he isn't here, either?'

'That's it, Val.'

'And you have no idea where he is?'

'No, none at all.'

*   *   *

275 •

Thomas wasn't, in fact, far away. He had taken refuge with Ettore, who had given the trembling boy a stiff slug of brandy, thus startling him into sense and loquacity.

'Sit down, here in the garden,' said Ettore. 'It is shady, there are trees, you can be calm.'

Thomas looked anxiously towards the path which wound round the edge of Ettore's land.

'If anybody comes, we will know about it before they see us,' said Ettore. 'And there is no reason why this person of whom you are so nervous would come up here to find you.'

'You don't know Valdemar,' said Thomas.

'If he has the powers of Satan, I will still hear him coming,' said Ettore. 'Now, what will he do to you, this man? He's your uncle?'

'Actually,' said Thomas unhappily, 'he's my father.'

'Ah,' said Ettore, sitting back and clicking his fingers to call his cat, who was stalking butterflies beneath the trees. 'But Magdalena isn't your mother?'

'No, she didn't know Val when I was born. She hadn't even met Hugo, that was her second husband. He was my great-uncle. Val's uncle.'

'Complicated,' was all Ettore said. 'So you are illegitimate?'

'A bastard.'

'I thought everybody in England was illegitimate these days. Is there any stigma? Do people care?'

'Not as much as they used to, I don't suppose,' said Thomas. 'But it's worse in my case.'

'Why?'

'My mother is Val's half-sister.'

At this, even Ettore, who had heard and seen most things, was taken aback.

'You see,' said Thomas miserably. 'You're shocked.'

'Nothing shocks me, but I find it surprising,' said Ettore. 'The English are more adventurous than I realized.'

'He and Hortense, that's my mother, didn't grow up together,' said Thomas. 'They didn't know each other at all until they were grown up.'

'It isn't necessary to talk about this,' said Ettore. 'This is the past, and can't be undone. So this makes being Val's son more difficult, I can see that it does.'

'Do you know what they called me at school?' said Thomas bitterly. 'Oedipus.'

'Oedipus?' said Ettore, puzzled. 'Why?'

'Incest,' said Thomas gloomily. 'That's what he's famous for. So . . .'

'I see, I see. Not very good at classical literature, then, at this school.'

'No, I suppose not,' said Thomas with a reluctant smile.

'Your mother is still alive?'

'Yes. She lives in India.'

'In India?' Ettore's faults were many, and he hadn't been a model husband and father, but he had a strong sense of family. 'Why is she in India?'

'She went out soon after I was born,' said Thomas. 'She comes back, from time to time. She's keen on gurus and yoga and helps in medical clinics and things.'

'I see,' said Ettore. He got up from his chair, and tucked the papers on the table in front of him into a file. 'In a minute we shall have some lunch, cheese, a salad, fruit, very pleasant. So you can relax.'

'I'm being a nuisance,' said Thomas awkwardly. 'You want to work.'

'As it happens, today I'm taking a holiday,' said Ettore. 'I've been writing letters, nothing important. And also, my garden needs some attention, I have been very busy, writing, and the weeds take this opportunity to go everywhere.'

'I'm stopping you weeding, then.'

'No, no. After lunch, you can help me, and we will do it in half the time, the two of us.'

'Are you sure?'

'Of course. Now, I will phone the Villa Saraceno.' He raised his hand to quell the dismay in Thomas's face. 'I shall do so very discreetly, to tell Carla and Magdalena that you are safe. Otherwise, maybe they think you have run away again.'

'I suppose so,' said Thomas.

'And you will spend the afternoon pleasantly here, and then this evening, we shall go together to the villa, and then everything will be sorted out.'

'It's very kind of you,' said Thomas doubtfully.

'You came to us for sanctuary,' said Ettore simply. 'It is a matter of honour.'

George was stunned. 'Not here?' he said. 'But where is she?'

'Bear up, Pa,' said Thea kindly. 'She'll be back any time, honest.'

'And there's Val ranting and raging because Magdalena isn't here, and Thomas seems to have vanished again. It's that boy,' George went on. 'He's the cause of all this trouble. You should never have sent him away to that school, Val. Then none of this would have happened.'

'What?' said Valdemar.

'If Thomas hadn't run away, then Magdalena wouldn't have followed him here, and Agatha wouldn't have joined her, nor Thea, and we wouldn't be here, either.'

'But Pa,' said Thea. 'You were saying how beautiful it is here. You have to thank Thomas, not moan about him.'

'We could all have been at home, comfortably, just as we were,' said George unreasonably.

'Oh no, we couldn't,' said Thea. 'You forget, you were the one who drove Mum away, by being so horrid to her.'

'I don't mind about the jewels,' said George. 'They can be at the bottom of the sea for all I care. I just want Agatha back.'

'Well, hang on, and you'll get a lovely surprise,' said Thea. 'Now, stop it, Pa. And you too, Valdemar, coming here and making scenes. What must Carla think? She's asked you to stay, and all you do, Pa, is whinge, and as for you, Valdemar, you go on and on about catching a plane back to London.'

Valdemar was not used to being addressed like this by young women half his age, and his face showed it.

'And you needn't glare at me like that, either,' said Thea with spirit. 'I'm not your daughter or your wife, nor one of your mistresses, thank goodness. So I can say what I like.'

Valdemar was, for once, silenced.

'I'll ask Carla where's she's putting you,' said Thea, 'and you can go and freshen up before lunch.'

What a very bossy girl that is, Valdemar said to himself as he

thumped his bag down on the bed. A single bed, he noticed with
rising ire. An unoccupied room. Good God, not even allowed into
Magdalena's room; well, we'll see about that. Ah, a telephone.
Good. He needed to phone London, he could settle with Ferenc
later. He picked up the phone and dialled.

Thea watched and waited. A ferry came in, and she scanned
the crowd of disembarking passengers; no Agatha. Never mind.
She could wait. There would be a hydrofoil in half an hour;
maybe Mum would be on that. Meanwhile, she would potter
idly in the sun, happy to be away from all those complaining
and domineering men up at the villa.

I'll go and leave a note for Quarles, she thought. Tell him to
come up for dinner again, he mustn't miss the fun. She wandered
over to a shop selling postcards, and chose one which reproduced
a scene from an ancient Greek vase painting. It was startling in its
frankness, and on a theme which she felt was sure to appeal to
Quarles. She scribbled a few words on it and left it at the hotel
to await his return.

The crowd at the port began to thicken, and then the distant
white dot of the hydrofoil appeared. Thea sauntered forward as
it came in; yes, she could see Agatha's hat. Goodness, she looks
pleased with herself, thought Thea.

'Mum, here!'

'Darling, how sweet of you to come and meet me.'

'Mum, did you get them?'

'Clever, clever Dido; darling, we must make a sacrificial
offering or burn incense, or whatever's appropriate. I went
straight to where she'd said, in a taxi, and I remembered
it as soon as I got to the street. Of course, there was some
hassle at the bank, but it was all sorted out, and I have them
with me.'

'Is that safe?'

'Strapped to me,' said Agatha in dramatic whisper. 'Very
uncomfortable. I'd hoped to be back yesterday, but there was
trouble with the planes, bad weather or something. All lies and
excuses, of course, look how lovely it is. Not a cloud to be seen!'

'No, it's true, there was a bad storm, Mum, but it's all blown
over now. But listen. Pa is here.'

Agatha, who had been walking briskly along the waterfront, stopped in her tracks.

'George? Darling, has the sun affected you? George never, ever goes abroad. It's one of the most maddening things about him, because I do love anywhere that isn't England.'

'He's here, at the Villa Saraceno. Very contrite, Mum, he has missed you dreadfully. He says he doesn't care about the jewels.'

'Darling, you didn't tell him.'

'No, of course not.'

'I think I'll keep the news and the jewels to myself, darling. They are valuable, and after this little episode, one never knows when one may need a little nest egg.'

'Mum, that's disgraceful.'

'No, practical, darling.'

'You aren't going to be nasty to him?'

'I wouldn't dream of it, fancy him coming all this way. We did go abroad about a thousand years ago, when we were younger, and he liked it then, but since he became middle-aged, I've never been able to budge him.'

'I tell you what,' said Thea. 'He's fallen in love with this island.'

'Has he now?' said Agatha thoughtfully. 'I wonder . . .' She went into a reverie, only broken by Thea's next piece of information.

'Valdemar's here, too.'

'No!' said Agatha. 'Has he seen Magdalena? Has he strangled her? Has he murdered Thomas?'

'Mum, really,' said Thea, laughing. 'He isn't that bad.'

'Worse!'

'Anyway, Magdalena wasn't at the villa when he got there, and she hadn't come by the time I left to come down here. So she won't be dead yet.'

'Taxi!' cried Agatha.

'Mum, we can walk.'

'Not in these shoes, I can't. Besides, every minute counts, we must be on hand to give Magdalena our support. I tell you, Thea, that man's a fiend.'

* * *

The fiend was talking to Virginia.

'A press conference?' he said incredulously. 'To denounce my and Roger's plans for shoring up the tower while the foundations are dealt with? Is the man mad?'

'Very zealous in his cause, one could say.'

'Bugger his cause. Virginia, he can't do this.'

'He's got the architect in his pocket, as you know. He claims that the architect has had a look at the crack and down in the crypt, and that there is no immediate problem. Roger's gone to see the Bishop, and Ian's with someone from the Church Heritage people right now.'

'God, what a balls-up. And I'm stuck here on this damned island, I won't be able to get back before tomorrow at the earliest.'

'How's Magdalena?' asked Virginia after a short pause.

'I haven't seen her yet; she's swanned off somewhere, typical.'

'Ah. Well, Val, I think it may be best for you not to be out of the country. I'm afraid the press are having a field day.'

'Rubbish,' said Valdemar. 'Let me know what that lunatic has to say, press conference indeed! You can get me at this number . . .'

It was late afternoon before Magdalena got back to the villa. She and Dido were laden with the twins' loot from the beach, including a dead starfish. 'Which will go straight in the bin as soon as they're asleep,' Dido promised. 'Coo, what a pong!'

The beach party had come in through the back of the villa, and Magdalena headed for the kitchen with her picnic leftovers. She thus evaded the combined guard of Sylvester, Agatha and Thea who were lurking to warn her that trouble, in the shape of Valdemar, was waiting in the sitting-room.

Vexed, and irritated by having no one to shout at, Valdemar sat with his legs outstretched and his fingers drumming on the arm of his chair. Then the twins, roaming in search of a lost toy, found him and loud screams of 'Daddy, it's Daddy,' rang through the villa.

In the kitchen, Magdalena felt suddenly very cold.

It couldn't be.

Of course, in time, he had to find out where they were, he would get in touch, remonstrate with her, make demands. But on the phone, which she could put down when the going got tough.

Not in person.

Now she could hear his voice. Her heart lurched and was thumping very uncomfortably. Had he been here long? Had he spoken to Thomas? And here she was, wild-looking from the beach. She wondered if she could slip away to her room, at least face him with brushed hair and some lipstick on.

The twins' shrieks died away. A respite, he was taking them on to the terrace, perhaps.

Footsteps approached and the door opened.

25

They looked at each other for a full minute, neither saying a word.

Then Magdalena edged round to the other side of the table. 'Hello, Val,' she said finally, in what she hoped was a normal voice.

'Magdalena,' said Valdemar, coming into the kitchen and shutting the door behind him.

'I didn't know you were coming,' said Magdalena weakly. 'I wasn't expecting you.'

'Why didn't you ring again? Or write?'

Magdalena looked down with detachment at her clenched hands. She was wound up like a spring, too tense to think clearly. But she could hear the hurt in Valdemar's voice, and she chose her words carefully.

'I wanted the air to clear. I knew that if we spoke, we would argue.'

'Is that how it seems to you? Arguments involve two people, you know.'

'No,' said Magdalena. 'I say something, or have an idea, or want to do something that you don't like. So you try to browbeat me into agreeing with you. If I don't, you get more and more offensive. You're a bully, Val.'

Stung, he looked frowningly at Magdalena. 'I think not,' he said quietly.

'Val, I can't stand the way you behave.'

'What in particular?'

'Where shall I begin? The castle, where you ride roughshod over any ideas I may have. My having to be so much at the castle, when I don't want to be there twelve months of the year.'

Valdemar raised his eyebrows. 'Where do you want to be?'

'London. Going abroad. Visiting friends.'

'A round of your ex-lovers, I suppose. That would take some time.'

'Not as long as yours, Val. And, since you've raised the subject, I object to your mistresses. Not ex-mistresses, please note. We're talking in the present tense here.'

'Mistresses?'

'Oh, come on, Val. We're too old to play silly games. Belle. The various odds and ends you go home with after dinner parties or evenings out with friends. While your wife, that's me, sits in a cold sitting-room in Eyotshire watching television. And most of all, I object to Veronica.'

'Veronica's an old friend.'

'Philip is an old friend of yours as well. Do you go to bed with him? Or is it enough for your old friend to be made a fool of because the whole of London knows you're still sleeping with Veronica?'

'As you said, we're too old for games. I like women.'

'Great, but not this one, Val. From now on, you count me out.'

The chill, the frozen tension had gone, and what Magdalena felt now was pure anger. To Valdemar's great surprise, she didn't stay for what was turning into a promising wrangle, in which he would, as always, come out on top. No, instead she swept round the table to the door with such force that she was gone before he could stop her.

He gazed at the strange and evil-smelling object on the table. What on earth had Magdalena left there? He went closer.

It was a very dead starfish.

Agatha gave the little bag to Thea to hide. 'You never know, if I put it in my room, your father may come across it while he's looking for a sock, I can't risk it. You take it, darling, and keep it safe. Now, where is George?'

'On the terrace, Mum, look.'

'Agatha.'

'Hello, George.'

George held out his arms. 'Agatha, I'm sorry.'

That's that, then, thought Thea with satisfaction. Now, where's Dido?

Giulietta was beside herself in the kitchen, creating a special feast for the large gathering. 'We'll be fifteen including the twins,' Carla had told her. 'You'd better ask your niece to come and help.'

Giulietta flew from pan to oven, chopping, straining, arranging, all the while keeping up a flow of gossip with her niece, a solid girl, who installed herself at the sink and awaited commands.

Ferenc had ejected Marcus from his studio some time earlier, ostentatiously locking the door behind him and pocketing the key. 'That's enough, Marcus,' he said. 'More than enough, judging by what I could hear.'

'Philistine,' said Marcus, as he went along to his room to shower and change. 'Big party tonight, huh?' he said, to Quarles, who was sitting on one of the broad ledges overlooking the courtyard.

'Is there?' said Quarles. 'If you aren't working, Marcus, it would be a good time to have a session with you before dinner. I haven't got nearly enough for this article.'

'Concentrate on the music,' said Marcus.

'It won't do,' said Quarles. 'This is a personality profile. Marcus the man. I've got a few questions I want to ask you.'

Marcus looked uneasy. 'Personal questions, huh?'

'About where you get your inspiration, who's influenced you, where you feel your music is going. Why you write music at all. We need to get at the essential Marcus.'

'No way,' said Marcus, departing rapidly.

It was a watchful and a wary group of people who gathered before dinner. Valdemar walked moodily about the room, looking at the frescoes, examining a marble table, his mind clearly elsewhere.

Agatha and George squabbled amiably on the terrace; Sylvester was keeping the twins away from Valdemar while Dido put on her sparkle, as he put it. 'Never know how she'll look next,' he said admiringly. 'Purple tips to her hair yesterday, did you notice?'

Carla came into the sitting-room. 'Valdemar, a moment if you please.'

Annoyed, he followed her out of the room; he was waiting for Magdalena and didn't want to be taken off.

'In here,' she said. 'This is my father, Ettore. And here is Thomas.'

She whisked herself away. Ettore remained, sitting himself down in a stately throne of a chair in a corner of the room, watching from the shadows as father and son stood face to face. How alike they are, was Ettore's immediate thought. Not just looks, but personality. Thomas was still young and callow, but he would grow into himself, probably in his twenties, and then he would be just like Valdemar.

'What have you got to say for yourself, Thomas?' said Valdemar, his face giving nothing away.

Ettore raised his eyes heavenwards. This boy had fled from his school, alone, halfway across Europe. His father hadn't known where he was, now he found him, safe, but troubled, and there was no greeting, no word of affection. I should have liked a son, thought Ettore. But I would never have treated him like this. I would have hugged him and shaken him, and laughed and shouted. This terrible chill, this formality, this was frightening.

'I'm not going back to that school, Val,' said Thomas.

'I don't suppose they'll have you back. I hope you realize that it's going to be difficult to find a place anywhere for you. Nobody wants a boy with a bad record.'

'It's the school that should have a bad record, not me,' said Thomas hotly. 'They're the ones who employ funny masters.'

'Funny masters? Thomas, don't be childish.'

'All right, then. Masters who creep in when you're having a shower, or you're in your room, and try to feel you up.'

'What? You're making this up.'

'I'm not,' said Thomas. 'It's the truth. You won't believe me, because you never do. You never take any notice of what I say.'

'Don't be silly.'

'I'm not being silly. I told you I didn't want to go there, and it didn't make any difference, you never took five minutes to try and find out why I didn't want to go there. It isn't my kind of school.'

'It's a very good school.'

'Good school!' Thomas mimicked his father with rare accuracy. 'Good for what? Turning out perverts and social misfits? It's not good at the things I like, so what's the point of my being there?'

'Your mother wants you there.'

'Oh no, she doesn't,' said Thomas, growing bolder. 'She thinks it's a terrible place. She's heard things about it from friends of hers.'

'Idle gossip,' said Valdemar.

'You could have asked other parents about it. But you couldn't be bothered.'

'So what more do you want to do at school? Academically, Gryme is outstanding, it can't be bettered.'

'Yes, if you want to be crammed for exams and jumped on every time you have a thought of your own. And it's rotten at music.'

'Music! There's no future in music.'

'I'm not worried about a future in anything,' said Thomas. 'I like music, and I want to go to a school where they take it seriously.'

'Magdalena's put you up to this,' said Valdemar, his temper barely under control.

'Stop going on about Magdalena,' shouted Thomas. 'As least she cares about me, which is more than you do. And she isn't even my mother. I don't know why she ever married you, she must have been mad. All you do is shout at her and steamroller over her, like you do me. I hate you, Val.'

Ettore rose to his feet. 'Thomas,' he said soothingly. 'Quiet, now. You must not say such things to your father.'

'Father?' said Valdemar, looking at Ettore in a very unfriendly way. 'What has Thomas being saying to you? What are you doing here, anyway? This is a private matter.'

'Don't you speak to Ettore like that,' said Thomas. 'He's been really kind to me, and so have Ferenc and Carla. And he's been nice to Magdalena, too, she's been much happier since she came to this island. Not surprising, since she's away from you!'

Thomas gave a hiccuping sob and dashed out of the room. Ettore gave Valdemar a quizzical look. 'The young are always difficult,' he said temperately. 'And he is a good boy, one to be proud of. He is very like you, I think. Now, I expect my daughter and her guests are waiting for us.'

The others sat or stood on the terrace, having drinks before dinner, eating some tiny, spicy, fishy morsels sent out by Giulietta. The evening was warm, the smells drifting in from the kitchen more than promising, but the ease of the past few days had gone. Everyone felt the tension of Valdemar's presence, and the tension grew as he followed Ettore and Thomas to join the group on the terrace. His expression was forbidding and he looked coiled, ready for a fight.

'Hell,' said Magdalena under her breath, after one brief glance. Then she collected herself, and tried to look interested by what Marcus, who was standing too close to her, was saying.

Valdemar looked at Magdalena with disapproval. What was she up to? Had she no sense of decorum at all? She had obviously dressed to please, but she wasn't dressing for him, oh no. Look at the way Marcus's eyes kept wandering to her cleavage. Look at the appreciative smile on Ettore's face as he laughed and joked with her, his very voice a caress, thought Valdemar wrathfully.

A chance remark of Ferenc's diverted Marcus's attention from Magdalena's shapely breasts, and he began to address the company on the subject of music, by which he meant his music. He was well away on his favourite hobby-horse, enumerating the iniquities of songs, rhymes, tunes, folk music and all his other *bêtes noires*.

'Oh, shut up,' said Quarles. 'I've had enough of you, Marcus.'

Sylvester leapt into the fray. 'Now, Quarles, it's types like you who keep the Marcuses of this world in business. You know this whole cacophonous charade is just one big scam. You've heard the strings strumming "Twinkle Twinkle Little Star" throughout the whole of one of Marcus's pieces without anyone in the audience noticing – and without you or the conductor noticing, either, Marcus. But you never mention that in your write-ups, do you, Quarles?'

'What?' said Marcus. 'Where was this? When?'

George had been sitting in a pleasurable daze, happy to be reunited with Agatha, to be drinking a glass of good wine out here in the warm air, looking out over such a charming landscape. But as Marcus shouted, he looked up, frowning. 'Ah,' he said. 'I've got a programme of yours,' he said. 'You left it on the seat in the hydrofoil, and I thought you wouldn't want to lose it. I enjoyed reading it, I must say. I'm very fond of the ballet. I'm pleased to see someone with such modern ideas liking the ballet as well.'

Marcus looked like a large bull who had just been given a nasty thrust by the matador. He eyed George with suspicion. 'I don't know what you're talking about. I never go to the ballet. Archaic, out-dated music, a dead art-form, why should I waste my time on that?'

'I don't know,' said George simply. 'But this is yours, whatever you say.'

'That's why you went to Sicily!' said Ferenc in a voice of revelation. 'To go to the ballet. Hey, what do you know about that? We thought you'd gone on a toot, to find a girl, maybe.'

Sylvester nodded. 'You were right, Ferenc,' he said. 'There's more to Marcus than meets the ear.'

Thea, who was feeling very buoyant, flashed a huge smile at Marcus. 'Tell them, Marcus, about "Walking on My Dreams".'

Silence.

'What?' said George. 'What are you talking about?'

'It's the name of a song,' hissed Agatha, her eyes fixed on Marcus's face. 'A very successful song.'

'Marcus is Dauntsey's brother,' said Thea. 'And he wrote the music for that song.'

'Well, I'll be blowed,' said Sylvester. 'Thea, you're making this up.'

'I am not,' said Thea. 'Dauntsey's real name is Mordaunt, same as Marcus. And I lived with Dauntsey for six horrible months, and he found that tune which Marcus had left in the flat, and he pinched it. And Marcus couldn't say anything about it, because he wasn't supposed to write that kind of music. Tunes! Same as you don't like ballet, Marcus! Huh.'

Dido had been entertaining the twins in a corner of the terrace while this interchange had been going on, but she had been listening hard. 'Well, stone me,' she said, her cheerful voice breaking through the hubbub. 'Good for you, Marcus. Blooming heck, got any more tunes like that under your belt? What you doing, mate, wasting your time on all that dross? And you like the ballet! Well,' she went on, raising her glass to him. 'Good for you.'

With skilful management, Sylvester had arranged the seating for dinner so that Magdalena sat with Ettore on one side and Marcus on the other. Valdemar was down at the other end, where he could see Magdalena, but not easily speak to her. He sat between Thea and Carla, minding his manners for the moment, but fretting. Thomas, too, was out of reach; it was too bad.

Ferenc had chosen excellent wines, and those and the delectable food soothed jagged nerves and rough edges. Thomas defiantly accepted a glass of wine; Valdemar didn't like him to drink. Magdalena smiled encouragingly at him, earning a furious look from the other end of the table.

Look at her flirting with those men, thought Valdemar. Shameless.

That composer's young enough to be her son, and Ettore's probably a grandfather. Easy thoughts, but Valdemar knew rivals when he saw them.

Thea was much amused. Her attempts to catch Valdemar's attention were more or less in vain, as he kept his eyes fixed on the other end of the table. She turned and smiled in a conspiratorial fashion at Sylvester, her other neighbour. 'What fun,' she whispered.

'And there'll be more fun before the evening's out,' predicted Sylvester.

Quarles was ecstatic. 'Aha,' he crowed. 'This news about you, Marcus, is going to make headlines.'

Thea gave him a very direct look. 'I've got something of yours, Quarles,' she said.

'More surprises?' said Sylvester. 'What an evening of wonders.'

'I've got your proofs.'

Quarles went quite pale, and subsided into an uneasy silence. 'What proofs?' he asked.

'Book proofs,' said Thea wickedly. 'The proofs of *Jessica's Love*, Denise Tempest's latest title for the Teen Dreams series.'

'You had no right,' began Quarles. Then he shrugged. 'Okay, so I do a bit of editing on the side. Writing for the newspapers doesn't pay the bills, you know.'

'Come off it, Quarles,' said Thea. 'You aren't editing those books. You're writing them. You're Denise Tempest. Confess.'

Quarles looked round the assembled company like a baited bear. Then he put down his napkin, leant back in his chair and started to laugh.

'Better and better,' said Sylvester. 'Unless there are any more secrets, let's have some more wine, Ferenc.'

'Telephone for you, Val,' said Carla. 'Take it in the hall, you can be quiet there.'

'Hello?'

Virginia's voice crackled in his ear. 'What?' he exclaimed. 'The Dean? In the organ loft with the organ scholar? That weedy young man with big feet? With practically no clothes on, and in an ardent embrace? No!'

He listened for a few moments more, laughing out loud as Virginia filled him in on the effects of such a scandal. 'Taken off for counselling to a Church safe house?' he said. 'How preposterous, he should be kicked out of the Church, defrocked or whatever is it . . . he'd defrocked himself, yes, I suppose he had. So no more trouble with him, then. Have you spoken to whoever's taken charge? Canon Vobster? Well, he's as meek as can be, unusual for one of them. He'll be no trouble . . . He's already confirmed our appointment as their structural engineers? Excellent. Well, Ian can handle it at our end . . . Yes, I may need to stay on here a little longer than I had planned, I'll keep in touch. Good night, Virginia.'

'I've rarely had a better meal,' said Sylvester, sipping his coffee on the terrace. Magdalena had carried the twins off to bed, Ferenc and Carla were in the kitchen, congratulating Giulietta; Marcus had vanished into the darkness with Dido. Thomas was nowhere to be seen, gone to ground, thought Sylvester. He looked across to where George and Agatha were sitting talking to Thea, good thing they were functioning as a family again. And why was Quarles watching them so intently?

Thea was being vague about her ideas for job-hunting, which was worrying her parents. She made an impatient and dismissive gesture, and at that, Quarles advanced on the small family group, looking elegant and ripe for mischief.

'Your turn, Thea,' he said. 'Now you've got a confession to make. To your parents, who are wondering why you're so cagey about getting a job, and are dying to ask you about that time you spent with Dauntsey.'

'Quarles!' said Thea.

'It's time to come clean about those qualifications you haven't got.'

'You beast,' said Thea, completely taken aback.

'Darling,' said Agatha. 'What is all this?'

'Well, then,' said Thea, with a baleful look at Quarles, who merely looked fixedly up at the stars. 'I dropped out of college. In my second year. I sold my clarinet, for various reasons which I won't go into, and I never took my finals.'

'Hang on,' said George, puzzled. 'I gave you the money for your fees. You said it was treating you like a child for me to pay them direct, and you had to learn to handle money.'

Thea had the grace to blush, and then she stuck her chin in the air. 'I'm sorry Daddy, it was wrong. I didn't spend that money on fees. And I'm going to ask you for more money, because when I get back to England, I'm not going to find a job or only a temporary one. I'm going to re-apply to university, and this time, I'll get a degree. I'll live at home, so it'll be very economical.'

'We aren't going to be at home so much,' said George surprisingly. 'I'm thinking of buying a place abroad. Somewhere warm. Like here. But you're welcome to stay.'

'Of course you are, darling.'

Quarles looked at Thea with considerable affection. 'Good

for you,' he said. 'And there's room for you in my house at any time.'

'Is that a firm offer?' said Thea.

'Bed and board, anything you like,' he said. 'Any time.'

Magdalena came on to the terrace, a worried look on her face. 'Sylvester, did Thomas come this way?'

Thea took her eyes off Quarles for a moment. 'He went towards the vineyard,' she said. 'I think he's heading for that place where he sits and looks out to sea.'

'The cliff?'

'Yes.'

'Magdalena, I'm sure . . .' began Sylvester.

Magdalena touched him on the arm. 'I don't think Thomas would do anything stupid, Sylvester. But I'm going to go and find him.'

Magdalena went through the archway in the wall which marked the boundary of the villa grounds, and disappeared into the velvety darkness.

'You've just missed her, Val,' said Sylvester, coming slowly down the shallow steps from the terrace to where Valdemar was standing by a bougainvillaea. Its flowers hung heavy in the night air, providing a backdrop which made Valdemar look like a character in an Italian opera, about to launch into an aria.

It would be an aria of rage and revenge, thought Sylvester.

'Gone looking for that bloody boy, I suppose,' said Valdemar bitterly. 'She cares more for him than she does for me.'

'I think she feels that he needs her at the moment more than you do.'

'Damn it, Sylvester, she's my wife. I love her. And she's behaving like . . . well, you saw her in there.'

'Val, if you care about Magdalena, if you love her, then why do you carry on the way you do? What's the matter with you? You can't spend all your time with the Veronicas of this world and expect Magdalena to live as though nothing was the matter.'

'Other women cope,' said Valdemar sulkily.

'Then you should have married one of these other women, not Magdalena. She's different. She's special. You can't treat her like this, Val, she simply won't put up with it. She's had a lot of unhappiness in her life, and you've got no business adding to it. You continue like this, and you're going to lose her and the children. All three of them.'

Valdemar returned to his original moan. 'But Thomas! What can you do about a boy like that? What does he expect?'

'He expects his father to be on his side. He'd quite like a father who took him and his concerns and interests seriously. No, don't get ready to go off pop! again Val. You just listen to me. I've gradually wormed out of that boy some of the horrors he's had to put up with. Apart from the starting point of everyone knowing that his parents committed incest. What possessed you, Val, to send him away to that kind of school with a millstone like that hanging around his neck? No, shut up, I haven't finished.'

Sylvester was known for his amiability and good nature. Valdemar, who had known him for years, couldn't remember ever seeing him like this. It was as though a teddy bear had turned round and revealed itself to be a full-size grizzly.

'They first of all locked Thomas in a wardrobe and pushed it over. Just to warn him what would happen if he didn't toe the line. He then had to sit on top of the wardrobe, surrounded by much older boys and tell them filthy stories. About you and his mother, among other happy topics.'

Even in the uncertain light from the terrace and the rising moon, Sylvester could see that Valdemar had gone pale.

'Next, two of the masters have had a go at him. Not to mention some of the older boys. Good-looking lad, Thomas. Oh, and the housemaster's au pair has been at him, too.'

'Why should he complain about that?' said Valdemar.

'That's what he said your reaction would be.'

'Why didn't he tell me about this?'

'Because he thinks that your sense of sexual morality is such that you would tell him he was making a lot of fuss about nothing.'

'Oh, shit,' said Valdemar. 'Christ, what a mess. Sylvester, you aren't making this up? All right, no, you wouldn't.'

'Now look here, Val. One of the great no-nos in life is telling other people what to do with their children. But I am going to tell you what to do about Thomas. First, he needs to know that you love him, and that you do mind about what he's been through. Second, you've got to let him choose which school to go to. Third, you must encourage his music. It's a very good balm for bruised psyches. Fourth, which is probably the most important, you've got to get things sorted out one way or another with Magdalena.'

'There's nothing to sort out.'

Sylvester shrugged his huge shoulders. 'And so no doubt you'll go your own way, as you always have done. Well, all this is very bad for my blood pressure; I'm going to have a pleasant glass of brandy, and then I shall play my cello for a while before I go to bed. Good night, Val.'

Thomas, his eyes bright with excitement, was talking to Magdalena. 'Are you sure it's going to be all right?' he asked anxiously. 'About Valdemar? I was very rude to him.'

Valdemar's tall figure emerged from the shadows, where he had been standing, watching his wife and son bathed in moonlight. 'You were,' he said, putting his arm round Thomas's shoulders. 'Look, I hear there's a Saracen castle in these parts. We'll go up there tomorrow, and have an explore.'

'Just you and me?'

'Yes. Just you and me.'

'Great,' said Thomas. He looked from Valdemar to Magdalena, and gave a wide and very boyish grin. 'Everything's all right, then?' he said hopefully.

'You go back to the villa,' said Valdemar. 'We'll be along in a moment. Go carefully. And tell Sylvester I said you could have a glass of wine.'

'Oh, great,' Thomas said again.

'A small glass of wine,' Valdemar called out after him.

Thomas turned and waved, and then was lost amid the vines.

Magdalena looked down the steep slope to the small beach below. Beyond the tiny strand was the sea, shifting and mysterious under the moon.

'I'm sorry,' said Valdemar after a while.

'Are you, Val?'

'Yes. Sylvester's been having a go at me, about Thomas. I've managed all that very badly.'

'We both did,' said Magdalena.

'You're very generous. I'm to blame.'

'Val, are you feeling all right? The sun hasn't affected you, has it?'

Valdemar frowned. 'Why do you ask?'

'In all the years I've known you, you've never once said sorry. Not for anything.'

'I'm not saying sorry now.'

'You just did.'

'Make the most of it, then. It won't happen again.'

'Because you won't be able to bring yourself to say the words, or because you'll have done nothing to be sorry for?'

'Don't go on about it,' said Valdemar irritably. He tried again. 'Look, I want to put things right between us. I honestly don't understand why you're so upset . . .'

'In that case, there's nothing to discuss.'

'Oh, very well, I do understand why you're upset. I don't want you to be unhappy. I want you to go on being my wife. I don't want you going off with some man much older or younger than you, who'd make your life a misery.'

'Thank you for having my best interests at heart,' said Magdalena. 'But it's sauce for the gander, Val.'

'Don't be trite, it doesn't suit you.'

'You are a bastard, Val.' Magdalena's voice rang out, clear and cold. 'You aren't prepared to change your ways at all, are you? You think a few days in the sun will calm me down, this will all blow over and we can go on as we were before. Well, we can't. If you carry on as you have been, then I'm divorcing you and taking the twins away. You have no rights over them whatsoever; you do realize that, don't you? No access, no say in their upbringing. And the same goes for Thomas. Hortense agrees with me about that.'

'I don't like threats.'

'Tough. Threats are what you use to bring me to heel, the threat of losing you. Let me tell you, I'd rather lose you than go on with this kind of half-life.'

'You sound as though you hate me.'

'I do,' said Magdalena, throwing caution to the winds. 'At this precise moment I do. I hate what you did to other people, before you married me. I hate the careless way you've ignored Cleo and Thomas, and goodness knows who else. And I hate the way you can't leave other women alone. But if that's what you want, fine. Go ahead. Alienate your children, lose your family, be a laughing-stock among your friends . . .'

'What?'

'Oh, Val, do you think they admire you because you keep mistresses? They do not. If you want to know, I think the way you carry on is pretty vulgar, and so do plenty of other people.'

'Vulgar?'

That hurt.

Valdemar turned away, looked out over the hillside, his senses stirred by Magdalena's presence, by the heavy, scented night air, by the beauty of the landscape. He put out his hand and reached out towards her.

Magdalena moved away, her hands firmly behind her back. 'We're too grown-up for kiss-kiss and everything's solved, Val.'

'Do you want a divorce?'

'Do you?'

'No,' said Valdemar. 'No, I don't.' It was inconceivable, no twins, no Magdalena. No castle, even. 'Is your mind made up? Divorce?'

'Not necessarily. Not finally and absolutely. Not if you'll agree to one or two things.'

'Okay, okay, you've made your point. No more Veronica or Belle.'

'Or anyone else.'

'Right.'

'And I'll tell you something else I hate about you,' said Magdalena with new spirit. 'The way you pee with the door open.'

'What?'

'Yes.'

Valdemar looked at her suspiciously, but her face was in shadow. 'Are you making fun of me?' he said suspiciously.

'No, it's just another one of your habits which I won't put up with any more.'

'Is that what this is all about? Habits?'

'No. This is actually about loyalty and commitment, Val. And family. And living with another person, and changing your ways a little so that you can get along together.'

'I've always had a strong sense of family.'

'Yes, that's true, Val, for all your dead forbears. What's much more difficult is looking after your own, living family. The future, not the past.'

'I can't do my work from Mountjoy.'

'I know. I'd like to spend much more time in London. Can we afford a bigger flat? With plenty of room for all of us.'

'I expect so.'

'There are perfectly good schools for the twins, I'm sure. And I want to work.'

'Work?'

'Part-time, I should think. Hudnotts are looking for someone.'

'The auctioneers.'

'Yes. And I'll see if Dido can stay on.'

'That strange girl?'

'She may be strange, but she's wonderful with Helena and Hugh.'

'She looks to me as though she knows too much.'

'Oh, she does, Valdemar, she does.'

'It sounds a very stressful household,' he complained.

'Those are my terms.'

Valdemar looked at her, and this time drew her to him. 'Very well,' he said. 'Now, back to the villa.'

'Oh yes?'

'And so to bed,' said Valdemar.